Asking for Trouble

I thought about Ilya constantly. Since my debut as his whore we'd got into a thing of just phoning each other or calling round if we were in the mood for some steamy action. Whenever I heard his voice my pussy would tingle. Sod feminine wiles and dignity; I was infatuated; I was horny; I wasn't going to pass up any chance to be with him. But it was getting to annoy me, being kept in the dark. He knew what I did for a living. Why wasn't I allowed in on his secret?

Asking for Trouble
Kristina Lloyd

BLACK LACE

Black Lace books contain sexual fantasies.
In real life, always practise safe sex.

This edition published in 2006 by
Black Lace
Thames Wharf Studios
Rainville Road
London W6 9HA

Originally published 1999

www.blacklace-books.co.uk

Typeset by SetSystems Ltd, Saffron Walden, Essex
Printed in Great Britain by CPI Bookmarque, Croydon, CR0 4TD

ISBN 0 352 33362 6
ISBN 978 0 352 33362 9

The Random House Group Limited supports The Forest Stewardship
Council (FSC), the leading international forest certification
organisation. All our titles that are printed on Greenpeace approved
FSC certified paper carry the FSC logo. Our paper procurement policy
can be found at: www.rbooks.co.uk/environment

Chapter One

The room is small, hot and crowded. Coloured lights glide over the punters; the music thumps incessantly. But no one's dancing. They're transfixed by the woman on stage, who's bumping and grinding, strutting her stuff.

At first, you think she's dressed in a catsuit, skin-tight. But she's not: she's naked and her catsuit is body paint – pale metallic blue, silver and cream. Clever that, because, whether you want to or not, you end up stripping her mentally, removing clothes that aren't clothes in search of nipples and a hint of skin.

She prowls on spike heels, wears gloves to her elbows and has a chainmail G-string slung round her hips. A metal disc covering her mons bears a NO ENTRY sign.

From the corner of my eye, I spot Ilya looking over at me. I'm sitting on the floor in the space of Luke's open legs, leaning against his chair. My arm is propped on Luke's thigh.

Ilya is sitting at a dinky little table with one of the best views in the club. And he didn't even need to get here early for the privilege: I had to reserve him a place, and I don't do reservations. If you want a seat, you get here before everyone else, or it's tough shit and you have to stand.

Seeking Luke's attention – more for Ilya's benefit than mine – I stroke his knee and tilt my head back. His cock is pushing a bulge in his combats and he responds as I want him to, absently tracing his fingers down the curve of my throat. Questing further, Luke's fingertips slip within the edge of my scoop-neck T-shirt. Gently, he strokes back and forth, tickling along the upper swell of one breast. Ilya returns his gaze to the stage show.

As usual, I wonder if he's jealous – and, as usual, I tell myself of course he isn't.

Everyone watches as a black guy, naked but for black leather shorts, falls to his knees before the body-paint bitch. His wrists are cuffed at his crotch. For so long now, he's been kicked and spurned. He bows at her feet, his muscular torso gleaming with oil. She touches the toe of one stiletto to his shoulder. Theatrically, he twists away on to his back.

The strobes start to pulse and the silver-blue woman stands astride the guy's shaven head. Knees open wide, she lowers herself into a half-squat and he stretches up, his tongue poking eagerly in search of that no-entry pussy. The frenzied violet lights make their bodies jerk robotically. They hover, shuddering, tongue and sex inches apart; then the guy drops away, feigning exhaustion.

Luke's fingers steal under my bra. He teases my nipple, brushing lightly until it crinkles to a peak. Suddenly I'm so hot for him. In a room full of people, his sly caress excites me fiercely. My heart races with the panicky strobes; the hard fast music pumps my blood. Adrenaline and lust hammer in my veins.

I want more. I want hands all over me, fingers in my knickers. I want Luke to join me on the floor, open my jeans and feel just how wet and swollen I am.

But I can't have him do that. It's a gig, not an orgy. If

you want to see some action you watch the stage. You don't watch me – the woman who supposedly runs the club. At least, not yet you don't.

So I ease Luke's hand from my bra and, me leading, we nudge our way through the crush. It's so damn hot it feels tropical. My office is cooler. Office? That's a laugh. It's a small, dingy boxroom the owners don't use much so they let me have it as a work base.

I don't bother with the light switch. We can see well enough because a street lamp glows through the small bamboo blind, and the room's all orangey.

Luke's quick to kiss me, and his hands, just as quick, slide up my T-shirt. Together we stumble towards the wall where he presses me against the dented old filing cabinet. He pushes my bra over my breasts, massaging my bared flesh with broad, eager hands, while his tongue in my mouth circles and thrusts. My back is damp with sweat and the metal chills where it touches.

The bass from the club room is a muffled thud. Every now and then the roar of a passing car surges up from the road; giggles and shouts move in and out of the pub below; and somewhere in the distance is the faint shrill ring of a burglar alarm.

I raise my arms and Luke drags my top over my head, snagging out an ear-ring. I deal with the bra. Then he whips off his own shirt and casts it to the ground.

His combats sit low on his hips, baring his flat belly and the streak of dark hair that runs up to his navel. His chest is smooth and tanned, beach-boy athletic.

'Oh, Beth,' he enthuses, heeling off his trainers. 'Oh, you make me so fucking horny.'

And it occurs to me for the first time that Luke is not merely beautiful – he's *appropriately* beautiful. Appropriate because he is just so much surface. His hair, peroxide blond, is dark at the roots. He wears a thin silver sleeper in one eyebrow and a leather thong round his neck.

Three beads nestle just under the hollow of his throat. His features are clean and perfect.

If he didn't have such great externals, Luke really wouldn't have much going for him.

But I'm not complaining. Right now, a dumb blond is just what I need – a kind of antidote to the head-fuck I've got caught up in with Ilya.

And I'm probably being cruel. I liked Luke well enough the other day. But tonight, the mood I'm in, there aren't many people who I like.

I reach for Luke's crotch and mould his trousers to the solid jut of his prick. My groin flushes with heat, and my vulva is fat with sensation. Luke moans throatily; he's squeezing my breasts together, mashing them urgently. With one hand I unzip him, while unbuttoning my soft, worn Levi's with the other. The jeans drop to my ankles and suddenly we're both frantic, tugging down underwear, kicking off trousers. Luke rubbers up.

He clutches me below my arse and lifts me. I'm suspended, my thighs either side of his waist, my back hard against the filing cabinet. Luke's stout glans nudges at my labia and I'm so wet and ready for him.

'Yesss,' I hiss. 'Fuck me hard, Luke. Make me sore tomorrow.'

Sharply he penetrates, his cock slamming high into my cunt. I groan deep pleasure and, for a moment, he stays there, lodged. Then he starts fucking into me, faster and faster.

The cabinet bangs against the wall and I flail, grappling to hold onto something. There's nothing so I cling on to Luke, wrapping my legs round him, digging my nails into his shoulders.

'Oh yeah,' he says through clenched teeth. His face contorts with near-ecstasy, and with the strain of driving upward while bearing my weight. But he's strong and he does it well. A thin film of sweat makes his chest glisten. I try to picture his arse, pumping away in the gap of my

4

spread thighs, but, in truth, I can imagine only Ilya's. I push the image away.

Luke's breath comes in ragged grunts. I grip his hammering shaft with my inner muscles and he says 'Oh yeah' again. 'Oh fuck. Come, Beth. I can't hold on. Fucking come.'

His mouth stretches in a grimace and he screws his eyes shut, thrusting violently. The first hint of my orgasm, infuriatingly weak, shivers within my thighs then disappears. I try to recall it but it evades me. A metal handle on one of the cabinet drawers grates against my spine. Then Luke releases a sudden gasp, like he's been holding his breath, and climaxes with a gravelly, 'Ahh, wow.'

'Shit, Beth, sorry,' he pants, slipping out of me and setting me down.

He presses his body against mine, sticks his hand between my legs and finds my clit.

'Come for me, girl,' he whispers, frigging me briskly.

I'm struck with a sudden, intense dislike for him.

Outside, a car – stereo on full volume – thumps up the road. Its booming bass hits a crescendo as it passes beneath the window.

I'm not going to come. The moment's gone.

Gently, I push Luke away.

'You owe me an orgasm,' I say, wrinkling off his condom and knotting it.

He gives a sheepish grin and ruffles his fingers through his softly spiked hair. 'Sorry,' he says. Then he adds, 'It's your fault. This place is so horny. I never knew it was like this.'

'It's not usually,' I reply coldly.

Luke flings himself sideways into the shabby armchair, legs crooked over the edge, and stretches to rummage in his heap of discarded clothes.

'There's a crowd of us going on to The Escape later,'

he says, leaning back and flicking open his Zippo. 'Fancy it? Or do you have to hang out here?'

'Something like that,' I say.

Luke sucks on a Marlboro Light. I place an ashtray on the floor by the chair and when casually he flicks ash, he misses. It's a crappy old carpet. Dozens of people have flicked ash on it and spilt stuff. But I get a clutch of fierce irritation. I want to scream at him to get out of my office but I don't. I tell myself Luke doesn't deserve my venom. It's not his fault I'm using him.

I dress hurriedly, knowing that one of us has to leave before I get nasty. And it doesn't look as if it's going to be Luke, lying there, smiling inanely, smoke drifting up from his nostrils.

'I need to see what's happening,' I say, tossing the keys in his direction. 'Lock up when you're done.'

I head back to the club room, get myself a Becks and stand at the bar, scanning the crowd for Ilya. I can't see him. He's not where he was.

I swig from the bottle, going through the various options. Maybe he's gone for a piss; or maybe it's all been sorted and I don't have to go through with it any more.

Tears sting my eyes. I'm suddenly scared: scared for Ilya; scared for me.

I turn to the stage, my vision blurring. A woman with chemical-red hair sits spread-legged on a chair, dressed in purple latex. She's plunging the haft of a multi-tailed whip into her vagina. Leather thongs spew from her open thighs like entrails.

I blink back my tears and look away.

I cannot believe this is Body Language.

I cannot believe I'm doing all this for Ilya.

Oh Christ, how the hell did I ever get caught up in this mess? It was only meant to be a game.

* * *

6

Months ago, I took up a tenancy on a new flat – half the first floor of late-Victorian grandeur. I'd got tired of sharing with other people; Body Language was doing pretty well; and I thought, since I'd just turned thirty, it was time I grew up and got a place of my own.

I'd been there over a fortnight and had finally got round to sewing up some muslin – my attempt at making halfway-decent curtains. People round here don't go a bundle on curtains.

Brighton's population is a transient, raggle-taggle affair, drifting in and out like the tide. It lives in flats and bedsits: tall, stucco-fronted town houses, all chopped up for squashed, modern living. And that means massive bay windows that would cost a fortune to drape properly.

Almost everywhere you look, there are broken blinds and crap curtains: too short, too narrow, too cheap, too ugly. And those rows of once-elegant houses, with their peeling paint and mish-mash windows, all seem to declare: 'Whoever's inside me, they're not staying long; they've got places to see, dreams to move on to.'

Although there are plenty of people who, like me, never actually get round to moving on. They didn't mean to stay in Brighton. It just happened: 'Sorry, forgot to leave. I was having too much fun.'

Anyway, who needs curtains? Brighton doesn't stay at home. Brighton goes out to play.

But I was playing house. I was inordinately happy. I'd cobbled together some second-hand furniture from Portland Road and the Sunday market and I was delighting in the froth of 'Where shall I put this, where shall I put that?'

But I wanted curtains. Before my muslin I'd had, for privacy's sake, a motley arrangement of bedsheets, throws and sarongs nailed across the bottom half of my sash windows. During the day, I'd loop them up with

7

knots and scarves. They looked a mess and kept falling off the nails. So I bought my muslin.

It was night, past eleven, when I started to hang them. I had to stand on a chest of drawers to reach the rails, clamber off it when I'd done a section, shove it further along, then clamber back on. My bedroom's at the front of the house and I did those windows first. Then I started on the living room, at the side of the house.

I remember I was doing the big central window of the bay and I was aware of my reflection in the dark glass. I was barefoot, wearing my beige combats and my navy T-shirt with the white stripes on the sleeves. I was vaguely thinking that I always look a little bit chaotic, a little bit off-beam.

Back then, my hair was a streaky mix of brass-gold – a sun-tarnished dye I was growing out – and natural light brown. It's somewhere between wavy and straggly. That evening, it was more straggly, and I had it tied back in a loose, messy ponytail. My eyes are brown, almond-shaped, and my lips are full. To me, it doesn't seem right to have sloping cat-eyes plus big fleshy lips. My nose is good: it's small and straight. I like it so much that I had it pierced a few years back. A tiny diamanté stud glints there now.

I've got a small, heart-shaped face. I suppose I'm pretty enough in my own sweet way, but I'm not balanced. So I was idly pondering whether, given the choice, I would choose narrower lips or wider eyes, when I noticed someone in the house opposite; corner building like mine, first floor like me, just standing in his side window – a simple oblong window, not a bay like mine.

I stole a glance. The orange glow of a street lamp shone into his room and behind him was a paper lantern, a big ball of hazy yellow light. I could see him clearly – as clearly, I thought, as he could see me. He seemed to be looking my way and suddenly I grew self-conscious about my belly button. Could he see it when I was stretching up? Was he interested in it?

I carried on with my task. It was fiddly because I was trying to do a fancy overlap thing and I had these miniature bulldog clips to attach to my muslin. I had to keep unclipping and reclipping when I spaced the fabric badly. Not enough curtain hooks, that was the problem. The guy across the street carried on watching.

I was convinced, at that point, that he *was* watching. My building's on the corner of a small, quietish T-junction; to the right there's not much to see except the other road and he certainly wasn't looking left. Yes, he was definitely watching.

I completed a curtain and a half, then climbed down to heave the chest of drawers into a new position. Inelegantly – there was no other way – I clambered back, a swathe of muslin over one shoulder, a couple of clips between my lips. He was still there, unnerving me a little, but, more than that, annoying me. I made it to two whole curtains, aware that I was turning awkwardly, trying to use the muslin hanging from my shoulder to shield myself, to hide the stripe of flesh that peeped between my T-shirt and trousers.

This isn't on, I thought. This really isn't on. Why should I let him get away with it? Why should I let some nosy twat upset me?

So, in a swell of bravado, I stood rigid and met his stare for five or six seconds, challenging him to look away. He was tall and slender, olive-skinned, his head dark with close-cropped hair. He didn't look away, and five or six seconds is a long time to confront a stranger with your eyes. I broke the contact, my annoyance simmering, and continued messing with hooks and clips.

I glanced across regularly. He didn't move and I began to get pretty pissed off. Who the fuck did he think he was, invading my privacy this way? Entering my flat, *my* personal space, with his rude, brazen eyes? Anger tightened my jaw, made my breath deep and heavy. I dropped a clip – not concentrating enough – and swore violently. It was too much. I couldn't take any more.

I swished the curtain away from me, determined, this time, to stare him out. Thrusting a hip to one side, I put my hand there and glared.

He mirrored me; he actually mirrored me! He shifted his weight and camply placed his hand on his hip. I thought I saw him smile. Feeling a touch uneasy, I straightened my body. He did the same. I paused, then folded my arms in front of me. So did he.

I didn't know what to do. For an eternity we stood there, strangers across a darkened street, one floor up and framed in boxes of light. If he moves next, I thought, I'll mirror him. But he didn't; he was stock-still. Maybe I should call it a day, was my next line of defence. I'll finish the curtains tomorrow. But then, no, why the hell should I? I wanted the damn things up. Anyway, tomorrow looked busy.

Even now, I can hardly believe I did this, but I did. I checked quickly over the other houses, satisfied myself that no one was watching and yanked my top over my head. Beneath was just my purple bra.

I stood there on my chest-of-drawers stage, T-shirt in hand, my heart drumming wildly. Defiantly, I put back my shoulders. It was my way of saying with my body: 'So you want entertainment? Well, here it is, mister. You don't scare me. Now fuck off and leave me alone.'

It hadn't occurred to me that he might copy me. But he did.

After several long, long seconds of looking, he swiftly removed his rollneck. The lines of his naked torso were lean and strong and his skin was nut brown – Mediterranean depth rather than summertime gilding. He held his sweater in his left hand the way I was holding my top in my right. I swallowed hard. My tongue felt thick and heavy. My knees felt watery.

10

What was he thinking? Had he done this before? Was this how he got his kicks? And more urgently: it's my move now. What do I do? Is this dangerous?

I dropped my T-shirt. He dropped his sweater.

For some reason, this was worse than all that had gone before, more sinister. A moment's acute terror crushed a hundred heartbeats into one. I rode the wave – act now, think later – and let my stubbornness surge again. Nervously, I cast my eyes over the high terraces beyond my glass show-case. Just above the rooftops, the sky was pale tangerine, a street-lamp sky. The trees were dark and the windows around me were calm. I had, as far as I could tell, just the one spectator.

I wasn't going to be cowed. I was going to outwit him. With trembling hands, I reached behind, unhooked my bra and let it fall. My breasts are firm and high, nicely rounded on the underswell. When I remove my bra, they don't drop heavily or anything. So I stood proud, my back arched slightly to give them that extra lift.

He can't mirror that, I thought, triumphant yet afraid.

I saw his shoulders heave with a deep-drawn breath and I felt a rush of elation. I was a glorious, bare-breasted Amazon and he, my foolish foe, was awestruck, staring defeat in the face.

Then, deftly, the guy unbuckled, unzipped, pushed everything down and stood upright to meet my challenge. His cock was erect, angling high from a dark bush of curls.

I was no Amazon.

A taxi sped past the bottom of the road.

I was Beth Bradshaw – stupid Beth Bradshaw with her tits out.

And I was suddenly very, very frightened.

I whipped the curtains in front of me and scrambled down from my pedestal. Show over. Clutching my T-shirt to my breasts, I looked frantically around the room – searching for what, or who, I don't know. Blood

11

pounded in my ears. My skin was on fire, hot with terror and shock. My legs were weak. I rested my arse against the chest of drawers then sank to the floor.

I didn't dare move. Half my windows were still uncurtained. The lights were on. He would still be there, watching, waiting. Images of what had just passed churned in my brain. What on earth had possessed me? What the hell had I done?

For far too long I just sat there, hugging my knees to my naked upper body. Sweat prickled on my burning skin before plunging me into iciness.

I had to live here, opposite a pervert, a flasher, a voyeur, and I'd just egged him on. Would he be able to see me during the day? Would the muslin be too thin at night? Would he break in when I was sleeping?

I wished I was back in my old place, safe with Jenny and Clare. I tried to focus on them, probably in the big messy living room right now. They'd be doing ordinary things, perhaps watching TV, or maybe they'd been to the pub and had other people round. I began to feel slightly calmer. Jenny, plump and gorgeous on the sofa, would be skinning up – 'one last spliff then I've really got to crash'.

Someone moved heavily in the flat above me. It made my ceiling bump, my pulses lurch, my panic rush. Get a grip, I urged myself, it's only the couple who live there. Stop being foolish.

Shivering a little, I pulled on my T-shirt and crawled across the floor, switching off the table lamp and the angle-poise. Street lighting added an amber tint to my darkened room. I would be, I hoped, invisible to him now.

On my knees, I craned my neck, peering out to where he had stood. I sighed with relief to see that his window was a restful square of black. Like mine.

He'd got bored. It was over. Tomorrow would come and I'd reflect on it as just a weird bit of nonsense. Maybe

12

I'd feel nervy about the prospect of bumping into him, but nothing monstrous was going to happen. I'd just ignore him; no big deal.

I was about to draw the half-fixed curtains when a horrible thought occurred to me: A square of black – *like mine*. Was his unlit window more copy-cat stuff? Were we still playing our strange game?

Or could it be worse than that? Was it a sign that he'd left, not merely his window but his flat? Perhaps, right now, he was crossing the street, standing at the communal front door of my house, persuading someone else to buzz him in.

In the madness of a mind after midnight, in a dark silent room, the latter seemed all the more likely. I scuttled from the living room to my tiny hall. In my imagination I could hear him: 'Really sorry to wake you ... key seems to be stuck ... can you buzz me in ... cheers, mate.'

I checked the main door of my flat. Already locked. I double locked it and pressed my ear to the wood, straining to listen. I could hear nothing except, faintly, the noise of someone else's television. No footsteps. No creaking stairs. No knife-wielding psycho coming to get me.

I drew steadying breaths, rationality filtering drip by drip into my brain. I was OK, safe. I'd been a bit stupid but there was nothing I could do about it. And I wouldn't do it again.

In the kitchen, I poured myself a huge vodka and tonic, then breezed through my living room into the adjoining bedroom.

My flat's pretty compact: one room leads more or less to another. In its former life it was probably one massive space – the Drawing Room or the Library, la-di-da. Then someone came along and stuck in lots of walls to divide it all up. They did a sturdy, seamless job, so you can't tell an old wall from a new one. They've all got deep skirtingboards, dado rails and cornices. It's a good flat. I like it.

Anyway, I was tight as a coil and nowhere near sleepiness. My bedroom overlooks the other road and it had curtains.

I sat on my brand-new solid pine bed, resting against the wall, swirling and sipping my vodka.

Beth Bradshaw: everyone thinks she's tough and sassy, an independent kind of girl who knows how to handle herself. And sometimes she is. And at other times she's just a vulnerable nobody in a big, bad world who does some really stupid things.

The vodka softened my body and began to chill away my fears. Though I was no longer afraid and over-wrought, I wasn't quite relaxed. I was shot through with an undercurrent of energy, a strange animation – something like the feeling you have as a kid just before an exam, in a subject you know you're good at: excited, nervous; you want it and you don't.

I drained my glass and lay, hands behind my head, gazing up to the high ceiling with its blue globe lamp-shade. Over and over, I replayed the scene: two people swapping secrets in the public arena, stripping off – *for* each other? *At* each other? I didn't know. Had we shared a naughty game, a bit of harmless fun? Or was it more aggressive, territorial, a drawing of swords? Or was it seriously sexy?

Christ, but he had a nice body. And, I thought smugly, he'd had a hard-on – for me, for whatever it was that had passed between us. With a slight shock, I realised I was aroused, had been for some time. A thrill born of terror was tingling in my cunt. Smiling gently, I nudged up my T-shirt and trailed idle fingertips over my tautly stretched belly.

I wondered who he was, what would happen when we saw each other again – at our night-time windows or maybe in the street, in a daylight, fully clothed, workaday world. No, I didn't want that to happen. I didn't want workaday. It didn't make sense. This was madness-after-midnight stuff; it didn't make sense either, but then that didn't matter.

My hand slid up and I caressed my breasts with firm self-indulgence. What had he done with his boner? I mused. Had he wanked while thinking of me, of that woman across the street with messy hair, good tits and a face that wasn't quite balanced?

But no, we'd been too far away for details, although I was sure I'd recognise him, somehow, if I saw him close up.

My nipples were tight. I scuffed and tweaked them. Somewhere I had a vibrator, a sleek gold-coated thing that I kept in an empty Glenmorangie tin. But I wasn't sure where it was. Probably lurking in a taped-up box labelled NOT VERY IMPORTANT BOOKS or OLD PHOTOS AND BAD CROCKERY. It hadn't exactly seen much action in its time. Shared house, bedroom next door to Jenny's. Buzz buzz. No thank you.

I ought to have rooted it out when I first moved in, a present to myself. But then, I thought, the batteries have probably leaked. No matter.

Unzipping my trousers, I eased a hand into my knickers. I was silky wet; my clit was hard. I made it harder, circling then rocking until it was fully pumped up and dense with sensation. Hastily, I wriggled my clothes to my ankles so my knees could flop wide, then I drove two fingers into my sweet, slippery pussy.

In my head, a man with no face fucked me. Violently. He bent me over and took me from behind. We were in a non-place. Windows surrounded us, squares of light and dark flicking on and off like some whizz-bang arcade game. And in those windows were men watching us, men with no faces, all wanking themselves off because I was being fucked senseless. They loved to see me, dirty little bitch on her hands and knees, taking cock from a faceless man.

I thrust and frigged, arching up from the bed, gasping quick breaths. When I masturbate I think of cheap things and seediness: squalid rooms, Soho neon and crude, lewd adverts. I picture myself as one of those wet and willing porn-mag sluts.

I made my faceless-man fantasy more concrete. I brought the spectators down from their windows, made them jeer and laugh. They were foul-mouthed and boorish, hungry for a piece of the action, for a piece of me. They were ready to take over once the faceless man had finished. And though I might be wet and willing, there were too many of them for me.

But they wouldn't care about that. However exhausted I was, they'd still fuck me in their turn, telling each other, 'She loves it, she loves it,' as their arses humped away.

I came. My orgasm crashed, squeezing spasms around juice-hot fingers. Ah God, was there anything better than coming? The flutters died and, with a sigh, I dropped on to my duvet.

My populated mind thinned and a tranquil glow crept over me, soothing my body to languor. My mind stayed awake – not alert, more meandering pleasantly. I was dreamy, drifting in and out of fantasy, recalling the night's events.

Untouched by anxiety, I mulled over the window game, seeing it in soft focus as if it were a thing I hadn't quite been involved in. I mused on its consequences.

We couldn't end it there; something else had to happen. Should I be passive, I wondered, and simply keep a sharp eye on my view? Or should I take action, go across the road and say – what? – 'How about it, big boy?'

I smiled lazily. He could be pig ugly, I thought. But surely not. God didn't give people great bodies and rotten faces. But then, I told myself, He damn well did. What was he called, the guy Jenny was seeing for a short time? Ages ago. 'Bag Over' we called him. Seeing 'Bag Over' tonight, Jen? As in 'Put a bag over his head and you might consider fucking him.' I thought of bag-faces, the Ku Klux Klan, Marlboro cigarettes, cowboys. My mind grew woolly, slipping in and out of surreal nonsense. I was sleepy, very sleepy.

I was just trying to cling to the thought that I should get out of my clothes and crawl under the duvet when, in the living room, the phone rang. My heart leapt. After a split-second's confusion, recognition and memory slammed into my brain. Fear quickly followed. I struggled to reason with it, to calm my fast-beating pulse.

Let it ring, I said to myself. Phones don't hurt. Phones don't expose themselves from across the street.

I lay there, trying to breathe slowly as I waited for the answerphone to click into gear. Probably Jenny or my mother. They were the only people I knew who called at ridiculous hours.

'Hi, this is Beth,' said my machine voice, chirpy and stilted. 'You seem to have caught me out. But you know how the technology works. Beep, message, then I get back to you, ASAP.'

It beeped. A male voice spoke: 'What are you doing, Beth? Are you wanking?'

Long pause. The voice was soft and husky. I didn't recognise it. It was him, had to be. He knew my name! He had my fucking number!

A cold dread flooded my limbs. For the second time that night, I held my breath, listening. But this time, I did not have the safety net of 'just imagination' to fall into. This was reality: stark, scary, pitiless.

'Sorry if you are. Didn't mean to disturb you. What do you think about when you touch yourself, Beth? How do you touch yourself?' Another pause, then: 'You should call me sometime. We can have a chat.'

A click, and the tape started to rewind.

I jumped from my bed and raced to the phone thinking,

Please, Mother, please, Jenny, please, wrong-number-person, do not phone me now.

Snatching up the receiver, I viciously one-four-seven-oned him. I clawed for a newspaper and jotted down the number on the top corner. My hands shook. I tore around my writing and, after a moment's thought, I labelled it: 'Him'.

I sat there for a while, my mind spinning. How, how, how? How did he know who I was? Why did he know who I was? How long had he known? Did I have a stalker?

Then I one-four-seven-oned again, just to check. On the scrap of paper I wrote the time I was called. I thought: that'll help the police when someone finds me dead.

Then I played back his message. Again and again and again.

Chapter Two

*B*ody Language.

It's Body for the performance art stuff: the dancers, cabaret, weird theatre and so on; and it's Language for the spoken word: the poets, the writers, the wags and raconteurs. Or at least it was, originally.

And it was – still is – only part of what I do. I don't have a career, just a career direction, which is working in the arts for something more lucrative than love. My life's a patchwork quilt made up of running the club night, writing for a couple of local rags, sporadic voice-over work and, when I'm skint, I can usually find some bar work. Sew it all up and you've got something that covers rent, bills, food and leaves me enough to enjoy myself with.

Anyone with half an eye on the local arts scene knows who I am. I'm a fairly big fish in one of Brighton's many little ponds. My name's always in the listings: 'For more information, call Beth on . . .'; my photo pops up occasionally, alongside interviews or little news items; I'm forever dishing out publicity flyers; and anyone who's been to a gig will have seen me on stage, introducing the acts, doing my mistress of ceremonies routine.

That, I reckoned, was how he knew who I was.

He'd been watching me for longer than I thought.

After that, I didn't see him for three or four days. He wasn't there. His window was dark at night, his blind was permanently down and there was absolutely no movement. He'd gone away, I concluded.

But even so, every ring of the phone made my heart shoot. I would stare at the phone, fingering the slip of paper with his number on, and my pulse would accelerate. Several times I went so far as pressing in the first five digits, daring myself to tap in that final sixth. Maybe he really was at home. Maybe he'd be walking into his flat as I was letting it ring. Maybe he'd have an answerphone and I'd leave a message. Saying what? Who are you? How dare you? Leave me alone! Kiss me! Fuck me!

I couldn't put him from my mind.

I couldn't press that final number. I knew he would one-four-seven-one me; he would listen, faceless man, to that staccato nasal voice telling him: 'The caller – withheld – their number – but the caller – is mildly – obsessed – by you. The caller – is no longer – sane.'

On the outside, I was fine. I was Beth Bradshaw going about her normal hectic business. On the inside, I was fanciful and pathetic. Our exchange at the window lingered in my mind, vivid and yet nebulous, like a crazy dream.

But I couldn't file it in the dream bit of my brain; nor could I file it in the reality bit. It belonged to neither category. So instead it roamed around, restless and haunting, infecting me with its strangeness. If it weren't for the tape of his voice – that soft, gentle 'What are you doing, Beth? Are you wanking?' – I might have forced it into the dream file: subsection 'tired to the point of delirium; not to be reopened'. But I had the tape; I knew it off by heart. I had reality on record.

I bought a plant – not because I particularly liked it,

but because it needed lots of sunlight and water, love and attention. I moved a small table into one side of the bay window, put my new plant there and smothered it with love.

Nothing moved in the flat across the road.

One afternoon, when I was working from home, the entry phone buzzed. I jumped – it's such an aggressive sound and I was used to a doorbell with a melodic 'ping-pong'. And in my teenage-fantasy head, my first thought was: It's him.

I picked up the receiver, a touch nervous: 'Hello?'

'Hi, Beth!' comes a fuzzy intercom voice. 'Only Martin.'

Only Martin – so sweetly self-effacing.

'Honey-pie!' I trilled merrily and buzzed him in.

I stood in the doorway of my flat, smiling and listening to him clomp up the steps.

'This way,' I called. Moments later, Martin rounded the corner: mop of black hair, broad cheeky grin, tatty little rucksack hanging from one shoulder; that's Martin, only Martin.

As soon as he reached me, he hooked an arm round my back and dramatically pulled me close like we were a couple of cheesy tango dancers. He pressed his lips to mine and we kissed – a long smacker of a kiss ending in a mutual 'mmwah!' – a kiss loaded with history.

'Not bad for a shoebox,' he said, making for the living room, his head turning this way and that.

He set his bag down and began wandering about, inspecting the rooms and chatting away. I followed him, telling him how great my flat was and pointing out all the good bits he'd miss: look at all this storage space; did you see the marble fireplace in my living room?; this shower, now *this* is truly state of the art; I made these curtains, Martin. I actually made them. Pay homage.

'Lot of big old windows,' he said, and clucked ironically. 'Be a bastard to heat in winter.'

21

'Fuck off,' I said in a light-hearted riposte. 'Summer's here.'

In the living room, Martin plonked himself on the sofa, put his rucksack between his feet and began loosening the drawstring.

'Didn't get my invite to your flat-warming party,' he said, rummaging in the bag.

'I'm having a serial flat-warming,' I replied. 'No more than three guests at a time. Tea or coffee?'

'Neither,' he said, pulling out a bottle. 'We're drinking wine.'

I was just heading for the kitchen and his words pulled me up short. I turned to him, uncertain, awkward. It must have shown on my face.

'It's just wine,' he said with a hint of exasperation. 'No candles. Don't worry. No shag.'

I smiled an apology.

'Unless you're offering,' he added with an impish grin.

I lunged to poke him in the ribs, and for a few seconds, we squealed and grappled, trying to be like we once were: old friends, uncomplicated, our bodies and desires our own individual business. The charade worked for a while, then there was a moment's eye contact that was just too long; and, on Martin's part, too longing.

With a final playful punch I drew back and went to fetch glasses.

Oh, Martin. A decade of friendship blasted apart by sex.

For ages, I clattered around in the kitchen, washing glasses that didn't need washing, hunting for a corkscrew that didn't need hunting for.

Only Martin. He's one of the rare people I still know from when I first arrived in Brighton, a happy little undergraduate, full of ideals and party spirit. Over the years, we've grown together – tears, laughter, the lot. He became, to me, a guy who could hold my hair back when I was drunk and throwing up and I wouldn't feel disgusting; we could snuggle up in front of the telly, eating crisps, watching scary films; we'd fall out – anything from 'I can't stand that man/woman you're so in love with' to 'you've bought me the wrong sort of peanuts' – and then we'd patch things up just as quickly.

We were as comfortable together as on old pair of jeans, and we loved each other massively. But somewhere along the line it all went a bit pear-shaped and we ended up sleeping together.

I put it down to a combination of Martin being miserable because Emma had just dumped him; and a tacit frustration of 'my love for you is so much bigger than this cuddle'. It's so difficult, so confusing when you have limits on bodies and none on love.

So we found ourselves in bed – a mistake that lasted four months. I finished it; it was so wrong, like sleeping with your brother or something.

Martin didn't quite see it that way. He still wanted me. 'It's just a phase,' I told him. 'In a few weeks' time, you'll wake up one morning and think, I must've been mad. I fancied Beth.' But he disagreed, said he must have been repressing his true feeling for years, or he'd just been blind to how goddamn sexy I was.

I went back to the living room. Martin had put a CD on, something poppy and unthreatening, and we drank a toast to 'Beth in her new pad'.

'Oh, I forgot,' said Martin, delving in his bag once again. 'Clare asked me to give you this. The woman who's moved into your room found it.'

His lips were pursed with the effort of not laughing and, with a flourish, he produced my vibrator, gold and gleaming in brash June sunlight.

I blushed. I don't often blush, but I did then.

'Shit,' I said softly, closing my eyes and repressing laughter of a fool unmasked. Then I snatched it from him. 'Thanks,' I snapped with mock vitriol. 'I didn't know you cared.'

Martin laughed in good-natured delight, trying to turn the moment into mere mischief. But it was more than that for me.

As lovers we'd always been tentative and shy, inhibited by our years of friendship. Sex hadn't been experimental or exploratory; that would've been like saying, 'Hey, we're doing the right thing, us, naked like this. Let's push it further.'

But we both knew it was wrong; affection rather than lust fuelled our sex – at least it did on my part – and so we stuck pretty much to the basics. My vibrator was a totem to that gap between us, a very personal and embarrassing totem.

Much as I wanted to bury it in my deepest, darkest drawer, I decided that laying it on the table would be wiser. Feigning indifference and making a quip about batteries and 'a woman's best friend', I crossed the room. My eyes flicked automatically to the faceless man's window.

Ever since our weird night, I'd been unable to pass my own window without checking on his. This time I was rewarded: his blind was up. I saw movement in the shadows. He was back.

Oh, notice me, I thought. See me here, glass of wine in hand, entertaining a friend. See me as a person who has a rich, vibrant life, not as someone you've frightened and excited, not as someone stupidly infatuated.

I set down my vibrator and loitered in the bay, pretending to check on the health of my new plant. Martin, sprawled on the sofa, began to chat. I perched my arse on the radiator beneath the window, told Martin how lovely the sun was, how deliciously it warmed my back through the glass, and soon we were bantering and gossiping – friends once more.

Except I was Janus. I was a nasty, deceitful, self-centred bitch, prostituting our friendship for the sake of another man's attention.

24

It didn't seem like that at the time, though. And I didn't turn round; I didn't invite Faceless to look at me. I showed him the back of my strappy vest top and all that went with it – the naked upper third of my back, my bare shoulders, arms, the nape of my neck. I showed him skin, newly gold after the year's first sunshine. I showed him my sandy-brown, not-quite-curly hair, the ends caught back in a band. When I turned, ever so slightly, to the side, I showed him a couple of straggles falling, oh so artlessly, over my cheek. Perhaps the light would sparkle on the stud fixed in my nice, neat nose. No, too far away for details.

If Martin hadn't been sitting opposite me, I might have twisted on my perch and propped a foot on the radiator. In my knee-length denim skirt, I might have offered him a hint of leg – unwittingly, of course – and he would wonder who else was in my flat. Who was she laughing with and chatting to? Who was it that joined her in afternoon wine?

But you can't flirt for one person when there are two watching. And I knew he was watching. I could feel his eyes, as tangible as the sun's heat, caressing my flesh.

'I've missed you,' said Martin, destroying a comfortable lull in our conversation. His cute, comical face was drained of its bright energy.

'I see you all the bloody time,' I scoffed, trying to deflect the intensity. 'I saw you two days ago and before that it was –'

'Yeah, but we're always with people,' he replied, his tone wistful and soft. 'We never used to be.' His brows drew together in an upward slant and he looked at me steadily, his expression so painfully sad. 'We've got scared of each other, Beth. I hate it.'

For a moment, our silence was awkward and tense. I wished he wasn't so nice. If he had a touch of the bastard about him, maybe I could fancy him. Or maybe we could have a God Almighty row, hurt each other to bits and then call it a day. But he was Martin: good and kind and unbearably generous.

Decisively, I set down my wine glass and stood, holding my arms open as if he were a big tearful child.

'C'mere,' I said with a gentle smile.

He came to me and we hugged – a big squeezy bear hug – and we rocked each other from side to side. For a long time we stayed that way, saying nothing except for weary mumbles of 'Oh, Beth', 'Oh, Martin'.

Apologies and regrets, as we knew only too well, were useless. The past is the past and 'if only's make rotten Band-Aids. So when the time came for one of us to speak, it was me, ruffling his hair and reassuring him that things would be all right. In time, we'd be back to what we once were. In time. We can't force it, sweetheart. Be patient.

And though I longed for that future with my heart and soul, I could not, for the whole of our embrace, shut out thoughts of the faceless man spying on us.

Martin didn't know he was there, but I did. My eyes were attuned and I'd seen him, standing deeper in his room than the last time and slightly to one side – but, nonetheless, most definitely watching.

I was immeasurably thrilled to think he might assume Martin and I were lovers, about to get down to some hot, hard action. I should have been concentrating on Martin more. I should have noticed that he was pushing our sexless bear hug in a different direction. I should have picked up on the changed tone in his voice, should have listened when his playful rap of 'I love you – I love you – I love you' melted into a soft 'Oh God, I want you'.

His hand, eager and insistent, was scrunching at my skirt, wrinkling the denim up my thigh. Then it darted beneath the hem and he was squeezing and caressing me just above the knee.

'Martin,' I said in a faint breathy protest. I stroked down my leg, pushing weakly at his hand and trying to straighten the rucked-up fabric. My half-hearted attempt

26

to deter him merely strengthened his ardour – as I'd hoped it would. His grip grew firmer and he was sliding higher, lifting one side of my skirt – the side facing the window. I made a show of lame resistance, allowing him to slide up my thigh until his thumb brushed the edge of my knickers. Then I stopped his hand with mine.

'We mustn't,' I whispered. And my words, like those of someone on the brink of adultery, said: 'But, God, I want it. Just let me play the part of someone struggling with their conscience, then I'll yield.'

And I did want it. I was aroused; my groin was gently tingling. I bore a passive lust for Martin, a legacy of our time spent as lovers. While I didn't actively long for him or seek his touch, his questing hand had the power to turn me on. That's why platonic hugs were so dangerous: our bodies held too much promise for each other; we knew them too well.

In a stronger frame of mind, I might have looked to the future and stepped back. 'No,' I should have said. 'For the sake of this friendship we want to rescue, no.'

But in the haze of afternoon wine and sunlight, sex didn't seem like such a bad idea. It was no big deal, really. And wouldn't it be the perfect complement to this languid decadence, this drinking together when the rest of the world is in its office?

And of course, I had my audience to consider. That probably tipped the balance for me.

So I allowed Martin's hand to slide up my thigh again. I feigned a dilemma, batting feebly at his hand, uttering gentle moans and mixing quiet 'no's with throaty 'ahs'. His touches were restless.

'Oh, Beth,' he whispered plaintively. 'Please.'

Beneath my skirt, he hooked a thumb in the top of my knickers, pulling them down a little and tickling briefly through my pubes. He cupped my sex through the silky cotton, massaging me firmly through the gusset. His hungry fingers pushed into my folds and my seeping moisture made the fabric damp.

'No,' I murmured huskily. 'No.' I pressed my body to his.

'Yes,' he breathed. 'You're wet for me, Beth. Let go. Don't deny yourself.'

Then his hands were pushing under my vest top, reaching for my breasts. I was bra-less and he groaned to feel my soft, naked tits. He sowed kisses, light as raindrops, over my neck and face, then drew back and fixed me with an agonised gaze.

For a long time we looked at each other, in tension, in tenderness. Our eyes were full of quick lust, and a resigned acceptance of the regret that would follow.

'Come to bed, Beth,' he said, stroking my cheek.

I shook my head. 'Here,' I said. 'I want you here.' I sought his lips with my own and offered up a passionate, lingering kiss. A Judas kiss.

'The curtains,' urged Martin, casting a nervous sideways glance.

'Yes, yes,' I replied. 'The curtains.' And swiftly I drew them, snatching a peek at the opposite window as I did so.

He was still there, half in shadow, watching me. I smiled inwardly, triumphant and smug. I knew how sexy my closed curtains were – far sexier than any undressing and caressing. It was a tease to feed his imagination. And besides, there were other windows to take into account. I was a whore: I didn't do peep-shows for free.

Martin and I stripped hastily, silently agreeing to do it before we came to our senses. I saw his nudity with remembered unease.

Our first, fatal undressing had shocked me, though I'd concealed it well. There's nothing unusual about Martin's body – it's pale and slender, not particularly muscular, and his cock's a pretty ordinary cock – but the revealing of it all had thrown me into confusion. I couldn't quite believe that Martin – my best mate, Martin – had a nice neat arse, black hair at his crotch and a prick that was rearing high.

There was something faintly obscene about his erection, especially his glans, so red and so raw. Because we weren't abandoning ourselves; there was no surge of passion. We were wary, shy, apologetic almost; and in that context his blood-pumped cock had seemed so lewd and out of place.

I felt as if I'd corrupted an innocent, sexualised him, and his exposed body had unsettled me deeply. It continued to do so.

'God, you're beautiful,' he said, sharing none of my disquiet.

He ran his hands over my naked flesh, pulling me close then stepping away, not knowing if he'd rather look or touch. He rolled the weight of one breast in a widespread hand and cupped my buttock with his other, drawing our groins together. His hard-on pressed against my belly, then he dipped his head to take a nipple between his lips. His tongue lashed wetly. I moaned in true delight, sensation filtering into my cunt, filling out my sex-lips.

'I ache for you constantly, Beth,' he murmured, his lips smudging over my neck. 'I don't care that you don't want me. But let me have you sometimes, like this. Just a fuck here and there. It won't mean anything. No lovemaking. I won't get hung up about it, I swear.'

Guilt forced me to my knees.

I told him to hush, enjoy the moment, then I took his prick far into my mouth. I caressed his tight little arse while sucking him in great gulping swallows. My saliva trickled freely and I sloshed it around his stiff, warm shaft, my tongue moving ceaselessly.

His grip on my shoulders and his moans of enjoyment troubled the part of my soul where some principles remained. This meant so much more to him than it did to me. I was merely giving him pleasure, foolishly trying to compensate for everything else I refused him.

And, in turn, I wanted pleasure back. My motivation was ugly – nothing grander than temporary lust. And it was treacherous – I was trading on Martin's heartfelt desire, using it so I could close my curtains on the faceless man and gloat over him wondering about me.

'Enough,' said Martin, stilling me with a hand on my brow.

He slipped his cock from my mouth and pushed at my shoulders, urging me to lie down. On my arse, I shuffled backward across the carpet, Martin following me on hands and knees. Hoisting myself on to the sofa, I sat back and clasped Martin's head, drawing his lips into my sex as I spread my legs wide. Greedy. Ruthless. I knew he would give me oral until I died of pleasure – trying to make me want him, not just as a friend but as a lover.

I was horny. I was happy for him to try.

His mouth met with my vulva, juices mingling. His tongue squirmed into every crevice, probed at my entrance. He nibbled, sucked and lapped at my clit. He took it all so slowly, indulging me in luxury rather than striving to make me come. And at any moment, he could so easily have made me come. Technique, in the absence of much, was one thing we'd worked on. He knew how I liked it; he knew how to push me over the edge.

But that afternoon he chose not to. Every time my orgasm began to gather Martin would shift his focus and his pressure. He would kiss my inner thigh or skim his tongue over my labia, just when I needed him else-where. My nearness would subside then he'd lunge in again, drenching me in heat and teasing me back to the brink.

Sprawled on the sofa, I clutched at his hair, smothering his face in hot cunt. I massaged my breasts. I beat and squeezed at cushions.

I begged him: 'Make me come, Martin. Oh Christ, make me come.'

But he refused me, over and over, until I could barely speak. I could only wail incoherently and snatch gasps of 'oh fuck' 'oh please' 'Jesus fuck' 'please'.

Then, finally, Martin released me from the torture, not by making me come, but by stopping. He knelt back and looked at me, slack-jawed and hungry. His lips and the skin around them glistened damply. It was my cue.

I lurched forward, urging him to lie back on the floor. He obliged, his pelvis lifting, his cock upright, searching for my lush, irresistible hole.

'Just a sec,' I said, and scurried to get a condom from my desk drawer. That had been a real treat for me when I'd first moved in: hiding little condom stashes here and there, making every room in the flat a potential fuck-zone. No more having to worry about other people. The whole place was mine.

Returning to Martin, I knelt astride him, rolled the sheath down his shaft, then, so slow and so deep, I sank myself to his root. I groaned loudly as the bliss of penetration filled me and spread through my veins. For a long moment I didn't move. I simply sat there, stuffed with his flesh, gasping with delight.

Then I started to ride him. My tits swayed as I rose and fell. I sucked my muscles round his cock, pacing myself so I wouldn't peak too soon or too often – I didn't want him to think I was having a whale of a time. When I sensed Martin was close, I rested my hands on his pubic bone, knuckled into my clit and surrendered to my need. I bucked hard and fast, letting the joints of my thumbs chafe me to ecstasy.

My orgasm was prolonged – cartwheels of bliss on the edge of collapse. Martin followed, his body curving like a bow, his prick pushing into my convulsions. Then we slumped together, heaving for breath.

Regret, as always, was slow to catch up.

In our post-coital stupor, we basked happily. We lay side by side, easy with each other's body, sipping wine and murmuring bits of nothing. I brought in cheeses and crackers, and we ate, still naked, and talked – about some book Martin was reading, a thing I'd heard on the radio, getting out of Brighton for a day, perhaps Sunday, to remind ourselves what cows looked like.

We didn't discuss the biggie: Us. We weren't awkwardly skirting around the issue; it just wasn't relevant. We'd slipped into lovers' familiarity and it was nice. To hell with 'us'; to hell with analysis.

But when the glow wore off and the bottle was empty, something had to change.

'So,' began Martin, toying with my hair, 'is this a one-off, then? Or is it the restart of something beautiful?' He smiled, faint and hopeful.

'It's a one-off,' I replied, hoping my voice wasn't too firm or too kind. 'A very pleasant and very stupid one-off.'

Martin gave a resigned 'I see' nod and fell silent.

I watched him staring at his finger as it swirled patterns in the pale-grey carpet. I felt thoroughly miserable, leaden inside. But I didn't want to talk about it. I was in no mood for getting heavy, for discussing what couldn't be resolved. It was pointless, just scribbling with words.

'Don't be pissed off,' I said, stopping his trailing hand with my own. 'You'll spoil the afternoon.'

His head bobbed up in a snort of ironic laughter. 'Yeah, right,' he said, snatching his hand back like he'd been stung by a viper. 'The afternoon. Lost my sense of proportion there for a while.'

I cursed under my breath and rolled on to my back, away from him. I closed my eyes.

A bitter silence stretched between us. There was nothing to say: he knew my position; I knew his. But I hate sourness and I thought maybe an apology was in order. So I tried it: 'Sorry.'

I heard coins clink as Martin reached for his trousers. Glancing up at him, I watched him wrench the strap of his belt and stuff it in the buckle.

'What for?' he sniped, his face darkened with anger and hurt. 'For being so free with your fucks?'

'Yes,' I said through gritted teeth. 'You said you could handle it and you can't. So, sorry. Sorry for being an insensitive, selfish, frivolous little bitch.'

Martin drew on his hooded top and sat on the armchair, lacing up his trainers. 'You forgot stubborn,' he said matter-of-factly. 'And callous and unscrupulous and thoughtlessly hedonis–'

'All right, all right,' I cut in, relieved to see a vague grin flickering on his lips. 'I want forgiveness, not a demolition job.' I reached for my clothes, feeling violently naked before his fully dressed state.

'Forgiven,' he said flatly. 'It wasn't all your fault anyway. More like six of one and two dozen of the other.'

We exchanged half-smiles, accepting blame and offering forgiveness. I smoothed down my vest top.

We were both dressed, no longer touching. We'd entered that awkward no-man's land of ours: not lovers and not 'just friends'. We were forced to tread gingerly.

'D'you fancy an afternoon pint or something?' I suggested uncertainly.

Martin shook his head. 'Best if I was off,' he said.

'You sure?' I asked, hoping he was.

He was. I showed him to the flat door, where we stood, not knowing how to broach the subject – in a casual, non-lovers way – of 'When shall we see each other again?'

'You going to The Geese on Friday?' ventured Martin.

'Dunno,' I said. 'Not my end of town any more. You?'

'Dunno.' He shrugged, toeing the carpet. 'I might go . . . Beth?'

He looked at me. I looked at him.

'Beth,' he went on. 'I think we should cool it a bit. Maybe, you know, not see each other for a while.'

I was taken aback. Martin and I have never, ever not seen each other for a while. Oh, we've been apart, for months on end, but that's always been because we've had other things going on in our lives. We've never actually decided to be apart. Even in the messy end stage of our affair we still managed to be sociable. Anyway, in Brighton, it was impossible not to see each other.

'Tricky,' I said, 'when we go out with the same bunch of people. Or different bunches of people in the same places.'

'Yeah,' he answered quietly. 'But maybe we should avoid each other. I might . . . go and stay at my brother's for a couple of weeks or something.'

'Oh,' I said. Martin never went to stay at his brother's. This was serious.

'It's just . . .' He stared at me, his face all twisted with pain. 'It fucking hurts, Beth. It fucking hurts when I see you. Especially when . . . like today . . . you suggest . . . You gave me hope, Beth. *Hope*. I'd rather have despair. At least you know where you are with despair.'

I nodded, deeply ashamed. 'Sorry,' I whispered, my eyes stinging.

He hitched his rucksack higher on his shoulder. 'I'll give you a ring when I get back,' he said, and turned on his heels.

'Don't I get a goodbye peck?' I asked, my voice cracking.

At the top of the stairs, Martin looked over his shoulder, holding my gaze for a second or two.

'No,' he said firmly, then he jogged down the steps and turned the corner, out of sight. A moment later, the heavy front door creaked on its springs and banged shut.

For the next hour or so, I did nothing much except hate myself.

All this heartache because of me: stupid me who'd thought horniness was reason enough to fuck; stupid me with stupid fantasies about some guy across the street who happened to have got his dick out the other evening; who happened to know my name and number; who happened to have asked me what I thought about when I masturbated; who happened to have returned home recently after several days away.

Shit. Though my mind was spinning the needle kept getting stuck. Faceless man. Faceless man. I wanted to be in the mood to open my curtains again and see what, if anything, was happening in his window. But I had no game-playing spirit. I was too sad, too drained.

I pottered round my flat, flicked the TV on and off, thumbed a book, lay on the floor and stared at the ceiling. I wished I didn't like sex so much; wished you could get it without the strings that tangle everything up. A relationship where sex and friendship are separate – was it really as impossible as it seemed? Maybe I could pay somebody to fuck me. Or maybe I could be a whore, a special whore who worked according to 'Beth's Prerogative': I get to choose the punters.

I debated whether to phone Martin. I could suggest meeting up to try to talk things through. But then, I reasoned, my motivation was purely selfish. I wanted to stop him from going to his brother's because I'd miss him. Me, me, me. I decided not phoning was more generous, more loving.

I had a shower and thought of Lady Macbeth trying to wash away her crime then going bonkers because her brain was still stained. But I felt better for my little water – cleansed of sweat if not cleared of my deed. I got dressed, changed my top and put the radio on. Bit by bit, I distanced myself from the afternoon.

And, bit by bit, my fingers grew twitchy about the curtains. It was early evening – softly light – when I opened them. I was nervous. If he were still standing there, wouldn't that mean he was dangerous and deranged? Normal people didn't stare at drawn curtains. And yet I wanted him to be there. I wanted him to be dangerous and deranged.

I was disappointed. His window was lifeless.

I was cross with myself for being so foolish and desperate. But I rose above it. I stood there, willing him, challenging him to step into view. He'd started this intrusive exchange; he'd watched me getting off with Martin. I was damned if it wasn't my turn now; damned if I was going to wait to be summoned.

Whether he could see me from somewhere, or whether it was mere coincidence, I don't know. But within a shortish while he moved into the frame of his window and took up his staring post.

My heart pounded. Excitement. Terror. We just stayed there, looking over at each other; rabbits and headlights stuff. And, just like the last time, I didn't know what to do.

So I stood perfectly still. After all, the last time I'd made the first move, hadn't I? I'd stripped off my top and he'd simply copied me. Well, this time, he'd have to take the initiative. I was out of ideas.

I psyched myself up to mirror him. Whatever he did, I would follow. Would I have the nerve, though? Everywhere I looked there were uncurtained windows. But if he was bold enough, maybe I could be bold too.

As it happened, I wasn't given the chance. His only move was to walk away from his window: 'away' as in I could no longer see him; 'away' as in he was no longer interested.

'Bastard!' I spat. He'd beaten me again. I wished I'd done it first. I wished I'd walked away: cool, casual, indifferent, bored. Bastard.

I turned, resolving to forget it, to get on with the book I was supposed to be reviewing.

The phone rang.

I flew to it, then paused, hand hovering above the receiver. It had to be him – anyone else was too much of a coincidence. Had to be. What would I say? Should I encourage him? Be offended? Insult him?

Three and a half rings and the answerphone was about to kick in. I lifted the receiver, my throat dry, my heart going thud, thud, thud.

'Hello?' I sounded worried, like an old woman on the end of a 2 a.m. wrong number.

'Beth. At last.'

Gentle, husky, deep; as real as the voice on the tape. Except, this time, I didn't know what came next; and I had to respond.

I suppressed a 'Who are you?/What do you want?' because it was too Hollywood. But no other words came to mind and I was silent.

He spoke: 'Did you come? This afternoon, did you come?'

My blood rushed. What was I getting into? I felt the buzz of fear, like watching *The Exorcist* or surging along the biggest big-dipper: seeking the pleasure of being scared stupid. Except with films and fairgrounds, you know you're safe. You can see the borders, the end. I couldn't.

'Well?' he urged. 'Did you?'

We'd made contact. It was sexual. This was the point where I backed down and told him to mind his own business, or I took the plunge.

My voice was slightly hoarse when I spoke.

'Yes, thanks,' I said. Then, to make myself seem sexier and full of appetite, I added a lie: 'Twice.'

Chapter Three

'**W**hy didn't you call me?' he asked.
    'Call you? How?' I answered. I couldn't help
but feel nervous, though I was determined not to show
it. I really wanted to hold my own with this guy. 'I don't
know who you are,' I said. 'I don't have your number.
And anyway, why should –'

'Liar,' he cut in. There was a smile in his voice. 'You've
got my number. You one-four-seven-oned me, Beth.
Don't tell me you didn't.'

'How do you know I did?' I heard my question,
mistrustful and wary, as if I suspected him of magic.

'Because you're not stupid,' he said. His voice was
deep and slow, so very sexy. 'Well? Why didn't you call
me?'

'But you haven't been home for –' Shit. Fool. Think
before you speak, Beth.

'Ahh,' he replied, knowing and smug.

So now he knew I'd been keeping an eye on his movements. I tried to rescue myself: 'Anyway, I don't know
you. Why would I call you? You could be anybody. Some
headcase who gets off on flashing. Or . . . or a curtain
fetishist. Or . . . Who are you? What do you want?'

Damn. I'd done the Hollywood cliché. Keep a cool head, Beth. Don't let him frighten you.

'Ilya,' he replied. 'Ilya Travis, if you think surnames matter.'

I felt compelled to repeat his name. I liked it. So I cupped my hand over the mouthpiece and moved the receiver away. 'Ilya,' I said, very quietly. 'Ilya.' I liked the way my tongue undulated and pressed, then withdrew on the final 'ya', like I was licking his name into my mouth.

'Is that foreign?' I asked. Of course it is, shouted a voice inside my head.

'Travis?' he said. 'No, it's an ordinary Eng–'

'You know what I mean,' I replied, a little put out at his sarcasm.

'Yeah, I do.' There was a pause. I moved on to the sofa and lay back. The phone wire snaked across the floor. He obviously wasn't keen to answer. His silence, his refusal to expand, unnerved me.

'How do you know who I am?' I asked.

'Body Language,' he said, his voice smiling again.

Did he say that with capitals? Did he mean he knew me from my club? Or was he referring to me, to my body language? Perhaps I'd met him once, flirted a little but never got around to asking his name. Was he some kind of body-reading expert? Had he seen into my soul because I'd angled my head a certain way, crossed my legs just so? Jesus. Is that the kind of 'knowing' he was referring to – deep stuff rather than passport stuff?

'There aren't many B Bradshaws in the phone book,' he said, breaking my troubled silence.

'But I'm not listed yet,' I replied.

'I rang your old place. Someone gave me your new number.'

'Oh, I see,' I said, making a mental note to tell my friends not to be so free with my details.

'So what about Beth?' he asked. 'You're obviously not an Elizabeth. Is that Beth in its own right? Or are you –'

'Bethany,' I said, glad we were back on safer ground. I shifted a cushion and wriggled to lie full length on the sofa. 'But I prefer it shortened. I'm not a Bethany. I'm a Beth. My father chose Bethany because –'

'No histories,' he said firmly. 'I don't want to know about your parents or your pet rabbit. I don't want to know your birthplace or your star sign. I like purity. Take people as you find them. Much more interesting.'

'Maybe,' I replied, settling into the conversation, though I'd no idea where it was leading. 'But background can be interesting too. Or helpful.'

'Yeah?' he challenged. 'So tell me something about your background that I might find interesting. Or helpful even.'

I did my CV in my head: literature at university; bumming around; hotch-potch jobs in arts admin and bookshops; falling in and out of love far too often; voice-over work; set up Body Language. Was any of that interesting?

'I once had sex in the grounds of Kenilworth Castle,' I said.

He gave a short, quiet laugh. 'Who with?'

'That's history,' I replied, pleased he wanted to know more. 'It's neither interesting nor useful.'

'It might be,' he said. 'Tell me another.'

'I once had sex in St Ann's Well Gardens.' This revealing of my titillating little secrets thrilled me. I hoped he would find it intriguing, arousing even.

He laughed again. 'That's in Hove. Congratulations. Who with?'

'History.'

'Tell me about it.'

'It was pitch black. We could hardly see each other. We were near some bushes. We fucked.'

'Do you like fucking outdoors?'

'I've only done it three times. But, yeah, I like it.'

'Why?'

'I like the sun. It makes me feel horny.'

'Why?'

'Because you don't wear many clothes. Your skin's out in the open, getting all warm and slightly sticky. It feels good. And it's easy for your lover to touch you. Take off two items of clothes and you're virtually naked. And knowing that, when you're just walking in the sun, is so horny. It makes you want to fuck. But usually it's imposs-ible. People. So you've got to go home.'

'What was the third?'

'What?'

'The third. You said you'd only done it three times. What was the third?

'Ford train station.'

'Who with?'

'History.'

'When?'

'In the past.'

'Pitch black?'

'No, broad daylight.

'Sunshine?'

'Yes. Brilliant sunshine.'

'Tell me about it. Tell me everything.'

I paused, made helpless by the ending of his quickfire questions. I couldn't just launch into a story. Did he want to lie back and listen while I regaled him with smutty anecdotes? Did he see me as a telephone sex worker? Cheaper than an 0898 version?

'What were you wearing?' he prompted.

Should I? Dare I? I'd never met this guy; couldn't picture his face. But in a way that made it easier. If I'd known him properly, I might have felt embarrassed. But he was disembodied, just a voice on the phone. And I liked his voice; I liked the things he said.

'I was wearing a denim skirt,' I began. 'I'm wearing it

now, actually. It's one of my favourite things. It's A-line, comes down to about my knees. It's cute.'

'Mm-hm. Is that what you were wearing earlier?'

'Yes.' I hated the reminder of Martin, of how I'd let him seduce me in the window for the benefit of this Ilya guy.

'Very cute,' he said. 'Especially when it's halfway up your thigh because some bloke's trying to get into your knickers. Is it the same man? The Ford one and this afternoon's?'

'No. Very different. And I'd rather not talk about this afternoon.'

'Fine. Just trying to get a picture. What else were you wearing?'

'On top? Erm ... some little strappy vest, white I think.'

'Bra?'

'No. I hate vest tops with bras. It looks ugly. Though I can understand the need. But my tits – they're not big, they're not little, they're just ... they're good. They can support themselves, in small doses.'

'Do you shave under your arms?'

'No.' I smiled. 'I do my legs and bikini line. But not under my arms. I like the hair there. It's soft and wispy. Just a hint of shading and texture, really.'

I was doing well. I liked his questioning: it relaxed me. His voice was clipped and practical, as if he were a bureaucrat writing down my answers. There was no heavy breathing, no husky eagerness.

'What did you have on your feet?' he asked.

'Er ... I can't remember. Trainers, probably. Or maybe sandals. I have these sandals – I call them my geisha-girl sandals. They've got thick wooden soles and the top bit is just two broad criss-cross straps. I might have been wearing those. Although, I think it was probably trainers because we'd planned on walking a bit and my geisha-girl sandals aren't that comfy.'

42

'Did you walk? Is that what made you horny?'

'Yeah, I suppose so. We'd been to Arundel. I was with a guy called Ben. He's a kind of on-off lover, travels a lot. But when he gets back to Brighton he usually looks me up. Sometimes we just meet, catch up on news and stuff. Sometimes we go places. Sometimes we go to bed. Depends on what else is happening in our lives. Sorry, is this history? Am I boring you?'

'Yes, it is. And, no, you're not. Go on.'

'Well, he – Ben – he'd just got back from months in Mexico. He said he had this desperate ache to see something green and something posh. So I took him to Arundel. It's got a castle that's posh. And it's in the middle of lots of green.'

'Another castle,' he said. 'First Kenilworth and now this one. Do you have a thing about castles?'

'No,' I said with a gentle laugh. 'Not that I know of. Coincidence, I swear. Anyway, we didn't go inside the castle. We just had a great day. There's a trout farm and we fed trout. We're good together, me and Ben. Easy. Our skin was hot. Yeah, that's another thing about sunny days. The heat makes you feel all languid and floppy. So I was feeling a bit like that, relaxed and carefree, and –'

'Cut to the chase, Beth.'

'Hmm. Well, do you know Ford station?'

'Never been, no. What's it like?'

'It's like any other arse-of-beyond train station, just a . . . a hiccup in a track that cuts through the countryside. It's got one of those level-crossing things that clunks down to stop the cars. Just two platforms opposite each other. Pretty basic – some buildings under canopies, a few blue tubs with flowers in. You'd probably struggle to buy tickets there. But that's where you have to change trains to get the Brighton connection and we'd walked from Arundel to Ford. We ended up missing the Brighton train by minutes, so we had time to kill and there weren't many people about. Can't remember why, but we went

43

over to the opposite platform, not the Brighton side of the track. I think we just fancied it. There was only one building there. Maybe we were playing explorers. Anyway, this building was like a red brick box with windows in. It was a waiting room, but a dead one – benches and a broken chair inside, a fireguard covering a heater. And that's where it happened, where we had sex.'

'What? Inside?'

'No, no. The door was locked. Leaning against it. Well, I was. We were just taking a breather, wondering what to do until the next train came. We were standing by this building, at the side of it, and I was pressing my shoulder-blades to the wall and swigging water from a plastic bottle. Ben was next to me, leaning as well and sharing the water. There was a clock on the wall above us, clicking the seconds away. It was quite loud. The back of my neck was really damp and hot. I complained, and Ben was going to cup some water in his palm and wet my neck with it. But I said, no, I liked the heat really. And then Ben, in a cheeky kind of way, bent to taste me there. He kissed and licked my neck and said I was salty. His touch, his nearness, just made all my horniness flare up. It'd been bubbling under all day – because of the heat and the not many clothes. And we'd had a smoochy kiss earlier, by the river, and his hand had slid up my vest, stroked over my back. We knew at some point we were going to end up in bed. Neither of us was seeing anybody else at the time and, like I say, that's just what me and Ben do.'

'So you felt aroused. Then what happened?'

'Well, we kind of pressed close, then Ben sandwiched me between his body and the building. His feet were astride mine. And we kissed for ages, groping a bit. Then we moved round to the back. It was less exposed, more private, and we fucked.'

'Slower, slower, Beth. Take me through it.'

I stalled.

44

'Why?' I said, my wariness returning. 'Do you ... Are you going to wank or something? Do you want me to do lots of detail? You know, he rammed his huge throbbing meat in my ... my dripping-wet snatch, that kind of stuff?'

'No, tell it your way. Whatever you're comfortable with. And I'm only going to wank if you are.'

'Jesus,' I said, more to myself than to him.

'Does it make you feel horny, remembering sex at Ford?'

'A bit,' I confessed, full of shyness. My mouth was getting dry. I ran my tongue around my gums and the inside of my cheeks. 'Why? Do you ... Does it make you feel horny?'

'Yes,' he replied, much bolder than me. 'Listening to your voice makes me feel horny. Imagining some guy squashing you up against a wall makes me feel horny. Thinking about you feeling horny makes me feel horny.'

We were silent for a moment.

'Are you erect?' I asked quietly. My voice was nervous, scared.

'Yes,' he said. He paused. Then he asked: 'Are you wet?'

I took two long breaths, trying to steady myself, make my voice clearer. 'I'm tingling,' I replied. I could hear the tremor in my words. 'I'm tingling quite a lot.'

If it were possible to hear smiles, then I heard one.

'Go back to your story,' he said, coaxing me with a gentle tone. 'You and this guy, this Ben, you're kissing against the wall. You're feeling horny. What next?'

I didn't feel capable of running through the story, not explicitly. So I said: 'Ask me some questions.'

'This Ben, was he hard? Could you feel his erection when you were kissing?'

'Yes,' I breathed. 'Yes. He was wearing these long, baggy khaki shorts, so his cock had space to ... to push. I could feel the angle of him and he pressed his groin

45

into mine. We were so horny, just kissing, and we were nervous and giggly. Someone might've been watching us from somewhere and there were cars going along the road and over the track just a bit further down. We kept breaking off and checking around. Then we'd grin like naughty schoolkids and carry on.'

'Did he touch your breasts?'

(Oh! He spoke so softly and so slowly. I don't know why, but those words, that simple 'Did he touch your breasts?' sent a current of lust into my sex. I could feel my pussy really pulse and start to salivate.)

'Yeah,' I replied. 'But only a bit. He kind of held my waist, his hands just under my top, and his thumbs nudged up. He skimmed my tits underneath, very lightly, and he kept his body close to mine – just in case anyone was watching. I really wanted more – more of his hands. I was so horny, so hot. He pushed at my breasts with the tips of his thumbs and his touch made dents in my flesh, lifted me a little.'

'Did you touch his cock?'

'Not properly. Not at that point, anyway. I just slipped my hand between our bodies and felt him through his shorts. He made a little groaning noise.'

'Then what? Did he touch you properly? Did he reach up your skirt?'

'No. He couldn't really get at me like that because we were still on view. There was no one around, at least, not as far as we could tell. But if there had been, if anyone could have seen us, they'd have just thought we were snogging. We didn't do anything too ... too risky. Not when we were at the side of the building.'

'So you went around the back. Who suggested it? You or him?'

'Him, I think. But I was ready for it. We'd been edging in that direction anyway.'

'What's round the back?'

'A bit more of the platform. It drops down into a load

of bushes and trees. You can see fields where the bushes aren't so tall. Oh, and you could see the top of a tall shed and you could hear chickens there, clucking and making weird whining noises. We didn't fuck straight away. We weren't brave enough. We had to settle in. And we were enjoying all the teasing and the danger. The heat. The sticky skin. But Ben unzipped my skirt. I was still pressed against a wall, and he unzipped me.'

'Where was the zip? At the back?'

'No, front. It's got a fly, a bit like jeans.'

'This is the skirt you're wearing now?'

'Yes.'

'Unzip it.'

'What?'

'Unzip it. Put the receiver there then I can listen. And unzip it the way Ben did.'

'No, I don't want ... Why? Why do you want me to do that?' Anxiety mingled with my excited desire and chipped away at my courage.

'Sound effects,' he replied. 'You're creating such a nice picture, it's a shame not to have some sound effects as well.'

I gave a nervous half-laugh. 'Do you want me to do chicken noises? Or shall I do the train approaching after we've had sex?'

'Only if it turns you on,' he replied. (That smiley voice again.)

'Cluck cluck,' I said dully. I was playing for time, trying to get myself back to that pitch of daring.

'Go on, Beth,' he challenged gently. 'Just unzip. That's all. You're on the platform at Ford, pressed up against a wall, at the back of this waiting room. You're so horny, so hot. The sun's beating down, probably making the concrete white, hurting your eyes. Behind Ben – his body's up close to yours – you can see trees and bits of fields. The sky's blue, blue, blue. No one's around, so Ben unzips you. How did he do it, Beth? Was it slow and teasing? Or was he hungry for you? Was he desperate to slide his fingers inside your knickers?'

I swallowed hard. 'No,' I said. 'It was like this. Listen.'

I moved the receiver into position, holding it across my belly. Making sure the mouthpiece was close enough, I fumbled for the zip-tag with my left hand. The metal gave a light, tinny clink. Then I unzipped. As my fingers eased downward, the teeth unlocked with a low, steady purr.

Congratulating myself, I released a gentle sigh. Then I cradled the receiver into my neck, hunching one shoulder to keep it wedged there.

Eager for his response, I let my fingers stroke mindlessly along the grinning lips of my fly.

'That was nice,' he said. 'Not too fast; not too slow. What happened next? Did he slip his hand into the gap? Did his fingers slide into your knickers? Did he touch you?'

'Yes,' I whispered.

There was silence. Then he said: 'How? What sort of knickers were you wearing?'

'I . . . I don't know. Can't remember. I just remember – oh God, I was so horny – I remember his fingers running along the leg of my knickers, just a fraction inside. Then he kind of moved the gusset and he began . . . he began touching me, fingering me. "God, you're wet," he said. His voice was all whispery and groggy, and his body was still close to mine, shielding me. I had to hold on to his shoulders. I felt weak. I was about to come.'

'Did you come then? Did you come with his fingers? Or was it later, when you fucked? Or both? Twice?'

'No, when we fucked,' I said. 'I came when we fucked. I really, really came. I was so –'

'So horny.'

'Yes.'

'And now? Are you horny now?'

48

'Yes.' I could scarcely hear my own words. My voice was like a breath catching in my throat.

'Where are your hands?'

'One's kind of here, readjusting the phone every now and then. And the other . . . It's near my fly.'

'Are you masturbating?'

Oh, his voice. It was hypnotist-soft.

'No,' I said throatily. As I spoke one of my fingers stole past my open zip and into my knickers. I skimmed across my swollen vulva then withdrew. I felt as if he were watching me.

'Do you want to?' he asked. 'Are you ready to?'

'I don't know,' I said weakly. 'But I need to –'

'Touch yourself, Beth.'

It was what I craved. I ached to caress myself, and I don't know why but I wanted his permission. Feeling freer, I edged into my knickers once again, via the zip of my skirt. With my index finger, I sawed along my cleft – it was so slippery and open – and my moist flesh pulsed in gratitude.

'Is it good?' he asked.

I dipped my fingertip into my entrance and stirred a lingering circle there, resisting the urge to penetrate myself fully. 'Yes,' I murmured. 'It's very good.'

'Keep doing whatever you're doing, Beth,' he said, 'and tell me about you and Ben. The train station, behind the red brick thing, and his hand is in your skirt, past your knickers. His fingers are all over you, inside you. Is that right?'

'Yes, yes. His fingers were so good. I was . . . my cunt . . . it was just melting into his fingers. I could hardly stand. He kept me pushed against the wall, holding me upright with his body. And his fingers worked. There was no one around. I was ready to come. I was groaning, trying to be quiet, just in case.'

'Did you tell him you were ready to come?'

'Yes.'

49

'What did Ben do?

'He unzipped. He checked over his shoulders and he unzipped.'

'Sound effects?

'What?'

'Listen.'

I held my breath, my fingers teasing. My clit was fat and tender, like a fruit about to burst with ripeness. I heard the sound of flies being unzipped. His flies. I could picture a crotch, bulging, and the zip unteething over it, gaping to expose underwear. I imagined an erect cock springing out: the erect cock of my faceless man whose name was Ilya. Ilya Travis.

'What are you doing?' I asked thickly. 'Are you sitting? Lying?'

'I'm on the sofa,' he said. He sounded so languid and husky, so comfortably aroused and ready for indulgence. 'I'm lying back.'

'Me too,' I replied faintly. 'Are you touching yourself? Holding your cock?'

'Yes,' he said. 'Yes, I am.' His voice had deepened. It resonated with the strain of lust.

'What's your cock like?' I whispered.

'Very, very hard,' he said, emphasising each word. 'Full of blood.'

'Oh.'

'What did Ben do?'

'He fucked me. I lifted my skirt at the front and he got up close, keeping my knickers to one side with his fingers. And he pushed his prick, high and hard, right up me. And then he was just fucking me, fucking me up against the wall.'

'At Ford train station.'

'Yes.'

'Is your skirt lifted up now? Is that how you're touching yourself?'

'No. I'm . . . My hand's in the zip opening. Oh, Jesus God.'

'Lift your skirt up and touch yourself from that angle, from underneath.'

'Yes,' I said, hurriedly tugging the denim from under my arse. I bunched the fabric round my waist, let my legs flop wide and pushed past my knickers into my heated cunt. 'Ah, God, yes.'

'Where are your fingers?'

'Where are yours?' I asked softly.

'Wrapped around my cock, moving slowly up and down. I can feel the pressure in my balls. Where are your fingers?'

'Inside me. My vagina's so hot. I can feel myself, all wet and . . . and squishy.'

'What do you think about? Usually, I mean. What do you get off on? What images, what fantasies do you wank to?'

'Stuff,' I said, suddenly inhibited. 'I don't know. It varies. Nothing special. Men.' I couldn't tell him the kind of things I thought about. It was too crude, too sleazy. I didn't look good in my fantasies. I was an object, a thing abused and humiliated. I couldn't reveal that. I tried to deflect him. 'What do *you* think about?' I asked. 'No, what are you thinking about now?'

'You,' he said. 'You being fucked at the station. You now, on your sofa, your hands between your thighs. And you and me, and the things I'd like to do to you.'

'Oh,' I said breathily. 'What things?'

'I like picturing you at Ford station. I'd like to fuck you there, but not hiding behind some building. And not with your clothes on. I'd make you strip. I'd have you naked, out in the open. Maybe I'd tie you up. Yeah, I'd tie you to a pole by the level-crossing. I'd make you face away from me. Your arse cheeks would curve out, pale because they hadn't seen sunlight. And I'd take you from behind. I'd really ram it up you, fast and hard.'

51

'Impossible,' I murmured, my fingers rubbing gently on my clit. 'Someone would see.'

'This is fantasy,' he replied. 'It doesn't matter. I can do anything. A thousand people could watch me fucking you.'

'Oh.'

'But then maybe just the two of us would be good. What about somewhere dark and dingy, somewhere I know, somewhere we both know, because I've never been to Ford. What about Brighton station? Yeah, Brighton.'

'Too many people if we're to be alone,' I breathed.

'Nearby then, under the low bridge that goes over the top of that road, what's it called . . .?'

'Trafalgar Street,' I replied. 'It's really grim there.'

'Yeah,' he said. 'Just picture it. The forecourt in front of the station, going across to the taxi place, and diving underneath is Trafalgar Street. It's dark and gloomy. Above is the . . . the ceiling of the bridge, iron girders. There are pigeons up there and water drips down, even when there's been no rain for ages. As you walk down the slope, there's a doorway on the left. Can you picture it?'

'Yes, I know it. There's usually a beggar or a smack-head slumped there.'

'That's the one. And when there's no one there, it's just litter on the step. Say, an empty binbag plastered into the corner, newspapers that've been slept in or on or whatever they do with newspapers. There's a couple of crushed beer cans, maybe a –'

'It's horrible,' I protested. 'It's squalid and dirty and –'

'I know,' he replied. 'But that's where I'd fuck you. I'd push you up into the doorway, force your face into the corner. I'd stand behind you and scrabble at your skirt. You struggle but I manage to lift it up and I tug and pull at your knickers, drag them down to your knees so I can see your pale little arse. I penetrate you hard and I warn you to shut up. I give you one thrust, then another and another, pausing in between so you feel every slam of my cock.

'People might walk by,' he went on, 'but they'd ignore us. Oh, they might glance over, but they'd know that you were a worthless bit of trash. "She loves it," they'd think. "Loves every minute of it." Or they'd think: "She's asking for it, the cheap little tart. She deserves a good fucking." And you keep on struggling, trying to escape, get out of that doorway, but it just makes me fuck you harder and faster. You feel my dick banging high into your cunt and you beg for mercy. And I snarl in your ear: "Shut up, whore. You dirty little slut. You want it. You know you do."'

'Jesus Christ,' I gasped, partly in shock, but more because my lust had soared violently and my sex was really throbbing. No one had ever spoken to me that way. 'What else?' I urged. 'God, what else? Please.'

'Take your knickers off.'

'Yes, yes.' I shoved them down my legs and whipped them from my ankles. 'Off.'

'How are your feet placed?'

'One's on the sofa. My knee's flopping against the back, against the cushions. My other foot's on the floor. My legs are wide open. My skirt's round my waist. And now I'm pushing – Oh, Christ. My pussy's so wet, so hot inside.'

'Are you wanking?'

'Yes. Yes, of course I am. I had to stop to take my knickers off, but now I am again.'

I could hear his breath, light and fast. 'Where are your fingers, your hands?' he asked.

'Two are inside me; my left hand – it's thrusting. My other hand . . . I'm rocking my clit. My clit is so fleshy and hard. Are you?'

'Wanking?'

'Yes. Are you wanking?'

'Yes. Jesus, Beth. The times we're going to have together.'

'In fantasy?' I moaned.

'Yes. And reality.'

'When?'

'Soon.'

'Oh God,' I gasped. 'I'm going to come. Any moment.'

'Have you ever been fucked up the arse, Beth?'

I couldn't suppress a tiny gasp of excitement. 'No,' I groaned. 'No.'

'Imagine I'm there,' he said. 'I make you kneel on the floor. I make you bend over, your arms and tits resting on the sofa. Your knees are wide apart and I'm raising your skirt, your cute denim skirt, and folding it over your back. I'm being slow and you're so hungry and urgent. Your arse is bared and you're jerking it towards me, begging me to fuck you. I slide my fingers into your hot, wet slit. I'm collecting juices to lubricate your arse-hole, to open you up so I can bugger you hard, really hard.'

I made a noise of protest. 'Why don't you fuck me?' I moaned. 'Tell me how your cock feels inside me, in my cunt, not in –'

'This is *my* fantasy,' he whispered, his breath quickening.

'OK. Yes. Go on,' I urged. My fingers were flying over my clit and I was driving into myself, struggling to slow down because I didn't want to come yet, not when he was mid-flow.

'So you're kneeling, bending over the sofa,' he said. 'My fingers are just easing out of your pussy and smear-ing upward, over that ridge that runs from your cunt to your arse. And now they're rubbing at your arsehole, relaxing you, making you damp and easy there. You're scared. You think it'll hurt. It's too intimate, too private. So you make a move to escape, but I catch you, twist an arm behind your back, press you hard into the sofa cushions, curse you. You can feel my knob against your anus. And now I'm breaking through. My dick's forcing you open and I'm penetrating you. My cock's sliding right up there, right into your virgin little arse. All your tightness is yielding, and I'm driving deeper into your dark, dark hole until –'

'Oh Christ.'

'Until I'm lodged. I'm right up you. The whole length of me is stuffed in your backside. I'm rock hard. It's the deepest thing you've ever felt. As I pull back –'

'Oh, God. I'm coming. So close.'

'Yes. Think of it. Of my prick –'

'Yes, it's fucking into me. Oh.'

'Into your arse, Beth. Over and over, pumping to the hilt. Your arse is so smooth. It's slipping along my prick, really squeezing me as I thrust. You're so hot, so snug, and you're screaming and howling. I shove high and hard, faster and faster. You're so stretched. God, you're so fucking stretched, Beth. Really tight. Oh fuck.'

'Yes, oh God, yes. Now. I'm ... I'm ... now ... Ah. Ah. Oh, Je–' My orgasm lashed out, full force. I panted, gasped, moaned and cried.

'Oh Christ,' he rasped. 'You sound so fucking beautiful. Oh, fuh – aaah.' He made a long, low groan that twisted to a noise of near-pain. Then it sank into a rumbling sigh. 'Ah, yes,' he said softly, his breathing shallow and faint. 'Ah, yes.'

I couldn't speak.

Sometimes when I come I feel so shocked afterwards. I feel dazed and numb, like I've just been assaulted, like I've been picked up and hurled down. I felt like that then: shocked and stunned. The fact that I'd just mutually orgasmed with a stranger down a phone line probably had something to do with it. But it was ecstasy and its aftermath that left me truly reeling.

'You OK?' he enquired in a murmur. 'Nice?'

I still couldn't speak.

'Beth? You still there?'

I managed to say, 'Mm.'

'You OK?'

'Mmm.'

'You sure?'

I took a deep breath and told him: 'Words fail me.'

He gave an appreciative half-laugh, half-snort. Then he fell silent.

We were like that for a while, quietly recovering, ignoring phone etiquette, which demands someone make a noise.

Eventually I said: 'OK. I'm OK now. I've got my words back.'

'So,' he began, 'you've never had anal sex?'

'No, never.'

'Why not?'

'Dunno. Just haven't. I'm quite happy with the orifice I've always used, thanks.'

'Do you like the idea of it?'

'I . . . I don't . . . You tell it very nicely. But –'

'I can do it very nicely as well.'

'Oh.'

'Let me. What I just did in fantasy, Beth, let me do it in reality. Let me fuck –'

'You're moving too fast,' I cautioned. 'Slow down.'

'Is that no, then?'

'Slow down means slow down,' I replied. 'Call me old-fashioned but I generally like to meet a guy before I agree to drop my knickers, let alone offer up my arse to him. My virgin little arse.'

'How very principled,' he said. 'We should meet.'

'I might not like you in the flesh.'

'Hmm,' he said, as if he were thinking it over. 'Maybe not. Perhaps we should leave it here then. We met on an abstract plane, fantasised, and it was perfect. Finito. Nothing after that to taint the memory.'

Was he serious? Was he trying to call my bluff? I

desperately, desperately wanted to meet him, and I knew I'd like him in the flesh. I'd only said I might not just to tease him. I was simply playing, ever so slightly, hard to get. I didn't expect him to take my words at face value and back down. I'd expected him to banter, to persuade me that he was stunningly beautiful and well worth meeting.

'Maybe you're right,' I said, praying that I wasn't taking too big a risk. 'End on a high note. Finito.'

He paused. Then he said, 'Yeah, it's probably best. And it's probably best not to discuss it too much. It'll only bring the high note down.'

Silence. In my head, I screamed and cursed.

'Well then,' he began, in a signing-off tone. 'I enjoyed our little chat.'

'Yeah, me too,' I said, feigning casual brightness. I struggled to think how I could rescue the situation, how I could ask for more of him without losing face. I didn't want to appear too keen, especially when he was so infuriatingly cool. An idea came to me and I blurted it out: 'You should send me a photo.'

'A photo,' he echoed. I heard that smile in his voice.

'Yeah,' I said hurriedly, trying to make amends for my eagerness. 'I mean, it's not fair if we end it here, not fair on me. You know what I look like – at least, I assume you do. I've only ever seen you from across the street. I can't ... I think of you as a faceless man. It's not fair. That's how I'll have to remember everything – this, the fantasy, the things you –'

'Is that how it was for you?' he asked, still smiling. 'In your imagination, were you buggered by a faceless man?'

'Yes,' I said.

'You're right,' he replied. 'It's not fair. So you want a photo to imagine it all anew?'

'I'm just curious. I'd like to know –'

'OK, I'll send you one. And if you like the look of me, we can meet. Is that a deal?'

'Sure,' I said, trying to be offhand.

'There's one condition,' he said. 'You've got to send me a photo of you.'

'I haven't got any. Not recent ones. They're all –'

'Have you got a camera?'

'Yes. No. I mean, I have, but it's fucked. The wind-on thing got jammed. It won't –'

'I'll get one to you. A camera, I mean.'

'What? Don't be ridiculous. If you want a photo, I can just go to a booth. I'll send you four and –

'No, I don't want passport nonsense. I want a photo you wouldn't put on your mantelpiece. I'll send you a Polaroid.'

'Of you?'

'No. I mean I'll send you a Polaroid camera. Then you can take the picture and get it to me quickly. Deal?'

'What . . . What sort of picture will you send me?'

'One I wouldn't put on my mantelpiece. Deal?'

I hesitated before making my wary reply: 'OK. Deal. But really, you don't need to get me a cam–'

'Bye, Beth,' he said. 'See you soon.'

'Oh, OK,' I breathed, shocked by his abruptness. 'Bye.'

Chapter Four

*F*our days later I got my camera. The postman brought it – and just seeing my address in Ilya's handwriting was a thrill.

When I find somebody interesting, for whatever reason, and I don't know much about them, then the tiniest snippet of information becomes valuable. It was the same at school. I adored a guy in the year above me. I was nothing to him and we never spoke except once, when I seized a chance to say, 'Oi, you – you've dropped your pen.'

But I knew a hell of a lot about him: shoe size, phone number, date of birth, number of goals scored for the school team and – best of all – his timetable, off by heart. I would live for those changing-classroom moments when we'd pass in the chaos of the blue-blazered corridor.

I had a shoebox for storing souvenirs of my fantasy-boy. On the lid I wrote his name (beautifully felt-tipped, of course) and inside I kept my diary ('Saw him today after double Physics. He had white socks on again. He looked well gorgeous,' etc.). I had a couple of chocolate wrappers, that I, lovesick in his wake, had scrabbled to retrieve when he'd chucked them away; I had bus tickets that added up to 21; I had a cigarette butt, although I was never really sure if his lips had touched it; and – oh – I could have had his pen if I hadn't, in a spasm of hope, shouted after him.

I'm supposed to be older and wiser now, but that teenage neurosis returned when I clasped my package, all wrapped in brown paper. Ilya's handwriting was a delight – something tangible, more proof that he existed – and it added to the little I knew about him.

I'm no graphologist and I didn't look for clues in his writing. I was simply satisfied to see it: thin and angular, enigmatically scruffy.

If I'd had a shoebox, I might have kept the wrapping. But, instead, I hurried upstairs to my flat and tore open the parcel. My new bulky camera came with a note. It read:

Tease me. Make sure your photo lands on my door-mat this Friday. I'll make sure you receive mine, same time. No waiting to see what the other one sends. Synchronicity or nothing. If you change your mind, don't want to send anything, then we'll just forget everything, past and future. I won't contact you again. Won't watch you. Promise. And the cam-era's still yours. Enjoy.

Ilya.

Friday. That meant Thursday post, first-class. Morning post to be safe. Unless I posted it by hand. No. Supposing I met him at the door? It would ruin things, make it all awkward. I read his note again. 'Tease me.'

And I remembered what he'd said on the phone: 'A photo you wouldn't put on your mantelpiece.'

I lay naked on my bed, chin cupped in my palms, pondering the lewd photos scattered across the duvet.

They were all of bits of my body: close-ups of an erect nipple; my cleavage in a push-up bra; lots of open-leg shots, some off-centre, some OK. It's tricky when you can't use a viewfinder.

I wondered what would land on my doormat Friday morning. He was bound to send me a photo of his erect cock. What else did a bloke have that could be classed as non-mantelpiece fare? What would his prick be like? And would he take the picture from above? Or hold the camera in front?

And what should I send him?

I reckoned my pouting-vulva shots were probably the best. Before my photo session, I'd given myself a vicious bikini line and snipped at my pubes, leaving just a sparse triangle of light-brown hair. I'd also masturbated. So in the snaps my sex lips stood out proud and plump, flushed and glossy.

Yes, I thought, I'll send him one of those. They were brazen and fearlessly explicit. And he probably thought I wouldn't dare. He'd taken the lead so far: spying on me, phoning me, encouraging me to talk dirty.

I wasn't going to carry on playing catch-up. If he wanted to swap intimate photos then I was damned if mine was going to be subtle and coy.

So that's what I did. I chose my favourite snatch-shot and posted it.

Oh, silly me.

He was bare from the arse upward, his naked back facing me. His olive skin was overlaid with a sheen of dark bronze, and he was perfectly muscled: sinewy, work-strong contours rather than vulgar brawn. His black hair was cut in a grade-two crop and the suggestion of skull beneath was menacingly beautiful. His head was slightly turned, eyes downcast, mouth set in a firm line. You could see an ear, jawline, a high cheekbone, and part of a big hawkish nose.

His left arm was angled at the elbow; his hand was in front of his body. It looked like he was wanking, oblivious to anyone else.

It was, quite simply, the horniest photo of a bloke I'd ever seen. It was so intimate and erotic, so utterly free of any macho 'get an eyeful of this' nonsense. And gazing at it made me feel like a voyeur, peeping at a private, blissful moment.

I felt a sudden stab of jealousy. This was not a photo he'd taken himself, not unless he had one of those self-timer things and the patience for a lot of trial and error. Who had taken it? Who else had seen it?

It wasn't fair. I wanted something that was for my eyes only, something to equal the Polaroid I'd sent him.

The more I looked at Ilya's picture, the more I began to regret my own gynaecological effort. Right at that moment he'd probably be smirking into my glistening pink crack. How unimaginative of me, how stupidly dull and tasteless. I'd revealed far too much and had given him nothing – just a bog-standard, two-a-penny beaver shot; the kind of thing any old wank mag could provide him with.

Once again he'd outmanoeuvred me, this time with subtlety.

'Nice photo.'

I smiled ruefully into the receiver. 'Thanks,' I said. 'I'm better in the flesh.'

'Likewise,' he replied. 'So now what?'

'What do you mean?'

'You agreed to meet up if my photo appealed. Did it?'

'Yeah, sure. Though I think you cheated a bit. Compared to me, to my photo. You kept yourself well hidden whereas I was very –'

'Open.'

'Ha, ha,' I said. 'How amusing. I was going to say honest and upfront. So I think you cheated. I mean, you might have a great arse and everything but, for all I know, you could have a tiny little prick.'

I wasn't going to reveal how delicious I found his photo, nor how dismal I found my own. I'd psyched myself up for his phone call and I wanted to appear sassy, so very proud of my gaping-wet-pussy shot.

'Is that all you're interested in, Beth? he asked. 'My prick?' There was a faintly challenging note to his smiley voice.

'Yeah,' I lied. 'We haven't really bothered with small talk, have we? It's been sexual from the word go. Why change a winning formula?'

'Hmm,' he said, as if mulling the idea over while not quite believing me. 'Is that what you want then? For us to be just sex?'

'Yes,' I replied. 'Just sex. Pure, unadulterated, meaningless sex.'

I hadn't really given it much thought up until that point. While I'd thought about him a lot, too much, I hadn't really thought about 'us'.

Oh, there'd been a thousand fantastical moments of 'us', but they were just isolated incidents. I was constantly playing 'what if . . .': What if that's him at the door? What if I phoned him and said come round and fuck? What if he's seriously kinky and wants to chain me up and whip me?

But all those 'what if's didn't add up to a greater whole. I hadn't envisaged anything so concrete as an 'us', as a relationship with, for God's sake, a future. And when Ilya said 'us', I felt a pang of disappointment. It sounded so mundane and couplish. I was enjoying our tantalising phone calls and risqué photos. I wanted more of the same.

'I'm not looking for a relationship,' I continued. 'I don't want anything serious or heavy or messy.'

I thought of Martin and of all the pain involved in caring for someone. Could I be detached enough to have a relationship that was pure sex? Could I shut my brain off from my body? It sounded iffy because already I was fascinated to the point of lunacy by this Ilya guy and we hadn't even met. But hey, I reassured myself, wasn't that fascination fuelled by lust? And by Ilya setting himself up as Mr Dark Man of Mystery? Once we got it together, that would all fade. So yes, I decided, an angst-free, no-commitment, sexy good time could be had by all.

How naive I was back then.

'I just ... I'm in the mood for a fling,' I said. 'A summertime fling.'

'So autumn's our cut-off point then?' he replied matter-of-factly.

Christ, he was talking about finishing and we hadn't even begun. I could picture him writing 'the end' in his diary.

'Maybe,' I said, trying to be light. 'We'll see how it goes. We might not last that long.'

'We will,' he said. 'I reckon we'll be good together, Beth. Suggest something. Tell me a fantasy I can help fulfil.'

I fell silent for a while, unusually shy. I'd never bared my sleazy soul to long-term lovers, let alone to someone I'd yet to meet.

'It doesn't have to be major league,' he prompted. 'Start off small. We can build up if things work out.'

'OK,' I said quietly. 'Then it's really simple ... but it's something I've thought quite a lot about in recent days. It's not really fantasy; it's more ... I just want us to fuck. Nothing wild. I mean, I don't even know what you look like, not properly. A fuck would be a good starting point, don't you think? No small talk, no big talk. Just a fuck.'

He didn't reply. Immediately, I feared I'd disappointed him by being far too pedestrian. Was a simple fuck not part of his game-plan? Had I put him off? Did he expect more from me? Was my request like the photo I'd sent him: dull and unimaginative?

I could hear his disapproval in the lengthening silence.

'You asked me to suggest something,' I said, defending myself with aggression. 'And that's what I suggest. I'm not saying it's my ultimate fantasy or anything. What's wrong? Do you only get off on weird stuff? Are you –'

'Nothing's wrong,' he said levelly. 'I was just waiting for you to elaborate. You know, a time and a place, that kind of thing.'

'Oh,' I said, severely humbled. 'Oh, OK. Well, what about my place? Say, tomorrow evening? If you're free, that is.'

'Sorry,' he said, a little too chirpily for my liking. 'No can do. Tuesday night, maybe?'

I curbed a rising anger. Tuesday night was Body Language night. He must have known that. He was fucking me about, playing games.

'I'm busy,' I replied curtly.

There was a pause, then he said, 'Tell you what, let's forget about arranging a time. I'll just call on you. If you're there, you're there. If you're not, you're not.'

My instinctive reaction was 'no way'. We weren't talking about a social call here. We were talking about fucking. I didn't want a surprise attack. I wanted to be armed and dangerous, sweet-smelling and sexy. I couldn't just fuck at the drop of a zip. Supposing he called at a really unsexy moment, when I'd just staggered up the hill from the supermarket? Or when I had a face pack on? Or people round?

His suggestion would condemn me to living in a continuum of 'what if's. What if he buzzed me in the next second? Or the next? Or the next?

But I was pretty much living like that already; and besides, I probably *could* just fuck at the drop of a zip. My lust was set on long, slow simmer. It wouldn't take much to bring it up to boil.

So perhaps I should exploit that and turn those foolish fancy 'what if's into reality.

Go for it, Beth, I told myself. Live dangerously. Anyway, if his timing's bad, you don't have to answer the door.

'I'll keep an eye on your window,' he said. 'If it looks like you've got company or –'

'OK,' I said as casually as I could. 'The ball's in your court. Call on me sometime.'

'Great. I will,' he replied. 'It'll be within the next fortnight.'

I wanted to shout: 'Within the next four minutes!' But I just said, 'OK, fine. See you when I see you.'

When he'd gone, I masturbated to 'what if's.

A girl can only take so much anticipation. And six days is a long time to anticipate sex, especially when you don't know that it's going to be six days and you have to think it could be any moment now.

But six days it was: six days of nervous, horny tension; six days of wondering whether I should risk a shaving rash and do my legs yet again; six days of being on stand-by, completely at the mercy of Ilya Travis's whim.

My time was his, not my own.

Every morning I dithered before my wardrobe, choosing clothes with great deliberation: this is sexy; this is easy access; this colour's good on me. And my underwear was top-notch; not once did I slacken and think, So what if knickers and bra don't match?

The wait was unbearable. I hated being indoors. I couldn't settle to any work. I had to question every sandwich I made in case it was now – buzzzz – with a mouthful of cheese and pickle. And my evening meals got seriously sexy.

But I hated being outdoors as well, in case it was then – buzzzz – while I was holed up in a recording studio, or trundling around town with an armful of posters, or simply having a fine old time at the pub.

I kept watching his window. Sometimes I saw movement; sometimes nothing. Movement got me all fired up, but stillness didn't calm me. It didn't mean he wasn't at home. I wished I had a view of his front path then I could have monitored his ins and outs. But his house is in a low-walled garden – more gravel than greenery – and there are some big messy shrubs at the side. I couldn't see a thing.

Martin called on me once, back from his brother's. Buzzzz. I was furious.

'Why the hell can't you phone before coming round?' I yelled as he sauntered into my flat.

'Since when have you been appointments only?' he replied, eyebrows all surprised.

'Since now,' I fumed. 'Since I started living here and . . . and valuing my privacy.'

'I was just passing,' said Martin, clearly shocked at my outburst.

He wasn't. I don't live in the part of town where people are just passing. It's residential.

I told him he'd called at a bad time.

'I brought you a present back from my hols,' he said, slinging a paper-bagged box onto the sofa. 'Fudge. Same as what you get on the Palace Pier 'cept the box says Devon.'

I love fudge. This was emotional blackmail.

'Just passing?' I enquired sarcastically. 'With fudge?'

He spat out a sigh of exasperation.

I told him I was in no mood for talking and, besides, I was just about to go out for the evening.

'Who with?' he wanted to know.

'Tom and Clare,' I said viciously. 'We're going down the Arts Club to hob-nob, and no you can't come.'

'Tom 'n' Clare! Tom 'n' Clare!' he mimicked, sour and truculent. 'Can't anybody say one fucking name without the other?'

'They're in love,' I snapped. 'You got a problem with that?'

'Pah,' he spat. 'In fucking love.'

'I see the break's done you good,' I snarled, and he gave me a killer look before saying he might book an appointment with me one day, if I could possibly deign to squeeze him in. Then he left in a huff.

My most noble emotion was relief.

Ilya called on a hot, hot day. I should've known he would, after everything I'd said about the heat making me horny.

I'd spent the afternoon down the beach with Jenny, Mike and some mate of Mike's by the name of Luke, who we'd met en route. This was my first encounter with Luke – Luke who I was later to seduce into being my very casual, far-too-young-for-me lover.

I hadn't intended going to the beach, but the three of us, me, Jen and Mike, had been in the office, sorting out some Body Language publicity. I employ Jen and Mike – art-school drop-outs – on an ad-hoc, cash-in-hand basis. Things just weren't working out that day and so we'd agreed: 'Sod this. It's too hot. Let's hit the beach.'

And we did. We locked up and ambled down Queens Road, which was thronging with a freshly disgorged trainload who were, like us, beach-bound. They were all babbling away, towels and mats poking from their bags, eager to reach that brilliant blue sea under that brilliant blue sky which lies, so enticingly, at the foot of the road.

To us hardened Brightonians, Queens Road is an everyday road; we walk past its shops and offices when it's miserable and pissing down, when the sky is grey, the sea is sludge and the horizon's completely lost.

But to visitors on hot sunny days that road must scream out: 'Go directly to the beach, do not pass go, do not stop to collect £200.' It's got those street lamps that you only ever see in holiday towns – the tallest street lamps in the world, with white glass balls on ornate black brackets. The road, full of traffic, slopes down to the sea in a series of slumps and bumps, like a gentle big-dipper; and, at the bottom, squashed between buildings, is a slice of the English Channel, shimmering blue and hazy with heat: Mum! I can see the sea!

In the midst of the excitement, we trundled down to West Street, past higgledy-piggledy buildings in any style of architecture you care to mention.

At the bottom, the amusement arcades were all pulsing and glittering, whooping and beeping – trying to out-shine the sunshine and saying 'yah boo sucks' to the concrete monsters opposite. But that's Brighton: for all the flowing white grace of its posh squares and crescents, harmony is not something that the town, as a whole, is big on.

Shunning the subway, we crossed far too many lanes of traffic and reached Kings Road. At last the seafront, with its dead fairy lights strung between lampposts and its piers east and west – one bright and brash, its big wheel spinning; the other elegant and derelict, its win-dows all glassless. The sky was flawlessly blue and the sun was high.

We strolled along the esplanade, glancing beyond the mint-green railings and out to sea, encouraging each other to take deep breaths of the salt-and-vinegar, exhaust-fumed air.

We paused for a while to lean on the railings and wonder exactly where, in that mass of flesh, umbrellas and deckchairs, we might find space to park ourselves.

We were just complaining about the tourists packing out our beach and hogging the tables at our bars down below, when this blond thing in long red shorts roared up on a skateboard. He did a bit of a snaking and turning, then clattered to a halt. He knew Mike, but not, as it later transpired, quite as well as he made out.

When we moved on, he sort of scootered along beside us. When we made our way down the stone steps and joined the milling crowds of the lower esplanade, he followed, chattering away to Mike. And when we drifted past the gaudy stalls with their carousels of postcards, jelly shoes, windmills and special-offer seven sticks of rock for a pound, so did he.

Eventually, we squashed ourselves into a patch on the pebbles. Jen and I continued our meeting in a half-arsed fashion, then we just lazed. Luke hung around for most of the afternoon, bouncing off once or twice when he spotted someone he knew. He went for a swim as well – very brave, I thought, considering all the shit that's supposed to be swilling around in there – and he emerged vibrant and dripping, combing his fingers through tangled wet hair, a beaded thong round his neck, thin red shorts clinging to his thighs.

I didn't really pay much attention to him, except to think: nice face, nice body, could be a model in an Australian-soap or a kids'-TV-presenter kind of way; shame he's such a prat.

It was lethargically hot, with only the merest of breezes coming in from the sea. I lay there, arm across my eyes, top rolled up to bare my midriff, skirt raised high to bare my legs. The heat pressed on my sweat-damp skin. We drifted in and out of conversations.

In the distance, one of the bars played sunny salsa rhythms. Eager kids scrunched across the shingle, chasing and screaming. Gulls wheeled and squawked or strutted near the squatting camps of people, fearless and huge, shaking at litter. Luke brought beer over in plastic glasses. It was almost too much of an effort to drink the stuff.

I was itching to get back home.

I kept thinking, Ah, his hand here, trailing across my belly; his head here, nuzzling into my thighs; his cock here, sliding into my cunt.

Would he be slow and seductive? I wondered. Or rough and hungry? I was greedy for him. I wanted red-hot passion and gallons of testosterone.

I tried to imagine his face, to build up a picture of him from the glimpse he'd offered in his photo. I couldn't do it. I still thought of him as my faceless man.

Perhaps he'd called while I was out. I hoped so, because, while I was at the mercy of him deciding when, I liked to think of him being at my mercy too. He might decide, 'Yes, now's the moment,' and I would be out somewhere, innocently thwarting his anticipation, just as mine had been thwarted by the ending of every day.

I forced myself to stay at the beach until the crowds thinned, the shadows lengthened and the dipping sun cast a burnt-gold sheen on the water. We sat for a while, clasping our knees and gazing at the ghostly West Pier – connected to the shore these days by a makeshift jetty because one day soon, so they say, the pier's going to be restored to its dance-hall glory and we're all going to have one rip-roaring, hootin'-tootin' helluva knees-up there.

The evening ahead looked like being a warm one and the others made lazy plans to move on to a bar. I declined and went home to shower.

As I was passing through my living room, towel turbaned around my head, I glanced across to Ilya's flat – a habit I'd quickly formed. I saw movement. He was watching me. I stood for a brief while, unwrapped my hair and rubbed at it, then went on into my bedroom.

The bay window there looks across to two shabbily grand houses, spaced apart by a small row of garages. Behind the garages are the juggled backsides of more houses, with zig-zag fire escapes and black satellite dishes. I closed my curtains. You never know who's looking.

I didn't rush to dress, nor did I linger over staying naked beneath my robe. I tried, best I could, to do the post-shower thing at a natural pace. My skin glowed pleasantly after the day's sun, especially on my shoulders, which were feeling slightly tight – not sore, just tight. I tan pretty easily but my shoulders had just caught. They were a bright ruddy-gold and I slapped moisturiser everywhere before lying on my bed to let the stuff sink in.

It was a hot, muggy evening and the raised windows made no difference.

I waited for the entryphone to buzz. I felt sure he would call soon. He must have seen from his window that now would be a good time, me half-naked and obviously not busy.

But no. So I dried my hair to its usual wavy straggles and swished at clothes in my wardrobe.

After some thought, I stepped into my flimsy, flippy black skirt and buttoned up my pale-blue crochet top. Being kind to my shoulders, I decided against a bra. Slipping on my geisha-girl sandals, I twisted in front of the slightly mottled wardrobe-door mirror. My legs were caramel and my shins gleamed. I was glad I'd put in the hours down the beach.

I looked good, although I wasn't exactly to my taste. Normally I wouldn't be seen dead in such a glut of girly high-street fashion. While I like things that are pretty or flirty or cute, I like them in small doses.

But, tonight, I wanted to be a little girl for Ilya, a sweet submissive miss who would coo inwardly at his swaggering dominance.

My breasts were too evident though. You could see their paler flesh and the dusky pink of my nipples. I reached beneath the crochet web and teased my thumbs over the tips. I smiled to myself, feeling lust tingle as they wrinkled to cones. When I took my hands away, my hardened peaks strained against the blue mesh, threatening to push through the holes.

I quite liked the effect, but I was keen not to look as if I was gagging for it. So I began to rummage in my drawer for a suitable bra.

72

Buzzzzzz.

Oh hell. My heart slammed. My sex flared.

In a mad panic I wrenched on a plain black bra, buttoning up my top as I went to get the entryphone. Deep breath.

'Hello?' I said questioningly into the receiver.

'Hello,' he replied, muffled intercom voice smiling just a little.

My fingers trembled as I buzzed him in, and I stood waiting at my flat door.

When his lean dark figure rounded the stairs, my stomach contracted with desire. He approached me, smiling – more to himself than in greeting.

He had a beautiful, bony, Slavic face. Just seeing that face made my inner thighs quiver. I didn't stand aside and, as he reached the doorway, he placed a hand on my hip and moved close. Above the V-neck of his grey T-shirt, in the dip between his collar bones, there was a hint of black curling chest hair. I allowed myself to be shuffled blindly into my excuse for a hallway. He was at least a head taller than me.

With a gentle backward kick, Ilya shut the flat door. Then he was edging me further into the hall until I was pressed against the opposite wall. His engorged crotch bulged against my belly and he bent his knees a touch to briefly grind himself into my pubis.

His hand rubbed gently on my side and I could feel its broad strength as he stirred my skirt around the jut of my hip bone. For a long, delicious moment we exchanged a steady gaze, silently agreeing on the need to just look.

His eyes were to die for. They were a deep blue-green, rimmed with black – intense like spilt petrol on tarmac. They were quite definitely not of this country, and they were set deep under dark craggy brows. The skin beneath them had a mauvish tinge. His nose was big and strong, curving like a scimitar. His lips were full and maroon, bruised almost.

I was smitten.

Ilya bowed into my neck and I felt the soft press of those lips there. I tipped my head back. He kissed, ever so lightly. His mouth moved along the stretch of my neck, pulsing damp heat as he licked and sucked. He nuzzled behind one ear. His shorn hair was silky against my skin.

I didn't move. I just let him smear his lips across my neck and throat. He leant his body into mine and my breasts were squashed beneath his hard chest. A pulse hammered between my thighs. My wetness seeped.

Ilya stepped back a little and, quite calmly, put his fingers to the first little button of my top. He unbuttoned it.

'I called earlier,' he said. He unbuttoned the second. My cleavage was bared. It gleamed with a thin film of sweat.

'I was out,' I replied thickly. I could hardly speak. My tongue felt as it were moving in honey. My throat was in knots.

'I know.' He smiled, eyes down as he undid the third button, then the fourth.

He wasn't slow and tantalising. He was just unbuttoning me with confident efficiency. I marvelled at his cool. It thrilled me utterly and I played up to it, accepting the downward crawl of his fingers with docile passivity. When my top was half-open, he eased the blue crochet from my shoulders and neatly tucked the fabric either side my breasts. My black bra was bared and he scooped a hand into one cup. The feel of his warmth on my flesh made me moan faintly. He lifted one breast free, then the other.

My nipples were bullet-hard. My groin was aflame.

My exhibited tits, half-framed in blue laciness, jutted awkwardly above underwire and rucked-down bra cups. Ilya's eyes trawled lazily over them.

'It was hot today,' he breathed. He spanned thumbs

74

and first fingers below each half-globe and began massaging upward. The callused balls of his thumbs grazed over my nipples and flicked gently at their stiff resistance. Sensation fizzed there and plummeted to my sex, swamping it in humidity. His caress was exquisite, so tender yet so firm.

'Yes,' I whispered. 'It was hot. Very hot.'

'Did it make you feel horny?' he asked.

With the same workmanlike detachment he'd shown in unbuttoning me, Ilya reached for the wavy hem of my skirt, fluffed it up my leg and then, holding the material against my thigh with his forearm, slipped his fingers into the gusset of my knickers.

I moaned. 'Yes,' I said breathily.

'Ah, yes,' he said in a whispered acknowledgement.

His deft fingers split my labia and he drove two deep inside me. He held the position.

'You're very wet,' he said in that deep husky voice. 'Very ready for me.' He teased the forward wall of my vagina. 'That wasn't the plan, Beth. You weren't meant to be ready for me. You weren't meant to be all juicy and full of lust.'

His two fingers churned in my molten hole and he nuzzled into my neck. His lips brushed over my ear. 'You're a horny little bitch, aren't you?' he murmured, his closeness blurring his words. 'I bet you've been ready for ages, haven't you?'

'Mmm,' I said in feeble agreement. Greedily, I pushed my groin toward him, pressing my clit to the heel of his hand and rubbing. He pushed a third finger into me, stretching me apart, and began shunting in and out. His sliding hand pressed back on my bud. I groaned, my pleasure mounting

'You sweet little slut,' he said softly.

I groaned again to show I liked his dirty talk. If it'd been a man I knew saying such things I might have heard only play-acting and cringed at his attempt. But I didn't know him, not in a dull, what-do-you-want-for-breakfast sense, and his words sounded good, unforced. I liked being a horny bitch, a sweet little slut. I liked being cheapened.

I heard the clink of a belt being unbuckled.

'You need fucking,' he said gently. 'You really need fucking, don't you?'

'Yes,' I replied, my eyes closing in bliss.

I heard his trousers drop, felt him step out of his shoes and lower clothes. Swiftly, he dragged my knickers down to my ankles and hitched up my skirt. I opened my eyes, about to suggest the bedroom, but, before I got the chance, I felt his cock between my thighs. With barely a position-seeking nudge, his glans was at my entrance.

'No,' I mumbled. 'Condoms.'

'It's OK,' he cooed. 'It's OK.'

No it's not, I thought, and he penetrated me in one easy glide. His bone-hard length rushed upward, slipping open my wet flesh and filling it.

My cry of protest softened to a moan of delight and my thoughts of big diseases with little names evaporated in a fog of brain-numbing lust. I clamped my muscles to his thick girth, fluttering my pulpy heat around his shaft. He gave a low-throated noise of enjoyment and cupped my arse while I struggled to get rid of my ankle-shackling knickers. Ilya lifted me, pressing me up against the wall.

My sandals clattered to the floor.

I gripped his hips with my inner thighs and then he was fucking into me, slamming up a series of ruthless, measured strokes. Every thrust jolted me, made my tits judder, my feet bounce in the air.

'Jesus,' I gasped, and he crushed his lips to mine, coaxing my mouth wide with a hot, probing tongue. I placed my hands either side of his face then stroked over his head. His close-cropped hair bristled on the up-stroke;

on the down-stroke, oh, it was velvet-smooth, so warm and sleek.

'Tell me a fantasy,' he said, breaking the kiss. He wasn't even breathless.

'Oh Christ,' I said, half-complaint, half-excitement. I couldn't stop caressing the roundness of his skull and I pulled his head close, running my hand up and down, from nape to crown.

Between my dangling spread legs, he pumped steadily. My back bumped and shuffled against the wall. My clit throbbed.

'Go on,' he urged. 'You hot little bitch. Tell me. Imagine we're somewhere else. Where is it? Tell me.'

I struggled to think. Ilya paused, his body held still on the withdrawal, his biceps curving as he balanced my weight. I panted and stuttered incomprehensibly, clutching his wide shoulders.

'Fucking tell me,' he snarled. Then he rammed his cock into me. One. Two. Three.

Three punishingly strong jerks that made my womb quiver, my senses spin. 'Tell me,' he repeated. 'Stop being so fucking coy.'

'Yes, yes,' I gasped.

And as he powered into me, I spluttered out words.

'I like nasty things . . . cheap things. Sleazy. Sordid.'

'Yes,' he hissed. 'More. More.'

He fucked me faster, harder. I felt the tension gathering in my thighs and lapping within.

'I'm going to come,' I wailed.

'No you're not,' he snapped, and he held still, clasping my upper body to his T-shirted chest. Hugging me tight, our groins locked beneath the fuss of my black skirt, he butted open the living-room door.

'The windows,' I protested, as he carried me past them.

'But I'm not at home,' he replied smoothly, somehow knowing where my bedroom was and making for it.

There, carefully, he set me down on the bed edge,

leaning with me so his prick stayed hilted. The room was shadowy because the curtains were drawn.

Ilya drew back a touch, one foot on the floor near my own, the other on the bed, his thigh supporting my hooked-up leg. I was half lifted from the duvet and I raised my hips further, seeking his thrusts. He smiled down at me and, one-handed, reached back to drag his T-shirt over his head.

A cloud of dark hair covered the scoop of his pecs, fading to sparseness on his hard, flat abdomen. His twinkling eyes meandered over my body, over my wrinkled clothes crushed this way and that.

His nudity contrasted sharply with my thrust-aside garments. He was magnificent and comfortable, while I was strategically exposed, hectic and lewd.

With unwavering control, Ilya ground into me. His thrusts were angled from a low point. He was avoiding my clit, the swine.

'Tell me,' he said kindly. He gave a quick strum of my clitoris with his thumb just to demonstrate that he was the one running the show. Intensity whirled in my groin.

'Well?' he said, his pelvis swinging in long, lazy lunges. 'How sleazy? Do people watch you in your fantasies?'

'Yes,' I murmured. 'Sometimes. Often.'

'Where? What's the setting?' Teasingly, he brushed the nub of my clit once more.

'Oh God,' I wailed, frustrated by the fleeting upsurge of pleasure. I screwed my eyes shut. 'Different places. Please. I . . . strip joints. Squalid, dingy rooms. Tacky pink neon. Me stripping, the centre of attention. Lecherous men. They all want me.'

'I love it,' he growled, his cock plunging, his tempo building. 'What do they do?' He reached a hand out and kneaded one breast. I could sense him restraining his urgency.

'Yes, oh fuck. Different things,' I cried, urged on by his

quickening rhythm. 'Sometimes they beckon me over. Or I sit on the stage, spread my legs. They crowd around me. Stuff notes in my knickers. Someone cheats, stuffs his fingers in my cunt. I groan. I like it. They laugh because I'm so wet. They ... They say coarse things. They egg him on.'

'Go on, give it to her,' he suggested, his voice rich and husky. 'She loves it, the randy little whore, the dirty little slut.'

'Yes,' I gasped. 'Yes.'

'Give her all your fingers. Someone hold her legs still. Let's see that greedy wet pussy taking all his fingers. Go on, harder. Make her beg for mercy. Make her beg for cock.'

'Yes, yes, yes,' I said in a near-scream.

He rewarded me. Wild and eager, he hammered his prick into my depths, a finger near the root of him rubbing my clit. Ecstasy raced through me, shivering and urgent. It bunched around my core, tighter and tighter, and I howled and cried as my release exploded in one giant, delirious, starbursting orgasm.

Oh fuck.

Ilya thundered on, grunting and pumping. His lips were stretched in a rictus of torment, his head thrown back, his neck corded and taut. On a prolonged groan, he came. I felt the tension in his body and the deep shudder of his thrust, and, to my utmost relief, I didn't feel the gush of him ejaculating.

When he withdrew, I saw the rubber wrinkling on his prick, its teat drooping with liquid. I just hadn't felt it. I guess my vagina wasn't concentrating. Thank God one of us is in control, I thought. He was obviously the type of guy who can distract you with one hand and slip a sheath on with the other. Expertise. I like that in a man.

Ilya snapped off his rubber, then flopped down beside me.

'Words fail me,' he said, harking back to our phone call.

'Mm-mmm,' I replied.

We lay there, silent except for our short, fast breath. No small-talk, no big-talk. Just a meaningless fuck. That was the deal, wasn't it?

After a while, Ilya said, 'I liked your fantasy. Have you got many more like that up your sleeve? Maybe I can help fulfil them.'

Satisfaction had sobered me up and I struggled with a niggling embarrassment.

I wasn't too keen on baring my innermost fantasies. They weren't exactly clean and sweet. Besides, I didn't know if I wanted them fulfilled. I might like the image of being fucked in some graffiti-scrawled toilet, but that didn't mean I actually wanted it to happen. In reality, it would probably be piss-stinking and grim as hell.

So I liked seedy, sleazy low-life, but I liked it where it was: in my head. Ilya obviously didn't. He wanted me to open up so he could make it happen, make my bad dreams come true.

If I'd realised how well suited he was to do that – to drag my dangerous, dirty fantasy down to his dangerous, dirty reality – I might have kept my big mouth shut. But I didn't. Bit by bit, I told him everything.

'Variations on the theme,' I mumbled.

'You mean the sleazy theme?'

I shrugged. 'Suppose so, yeah. I'm not really a Seychelles beach type of girl.'

'I can tell.' He grinned. He rolled on to his side and rumpled my top over my breast, squeezing my flesh through the blue crochet web.

'So what is it about sleaze?'

'Dunno,' I replied. 'Haven't really analysed it. I just like it.'

'But what is it that you like? Have you got a thing about neon or something?'

'No, I just like picturing things where I'm being used, objectified, degraded, that kind of stuff. It's liberating.

I'm in someone else's hands. I'm not being me. I'm made cheap. I'm just a thing for sex, a body, an orifice. And fantasy, I guess, is all about –'

'I thought you hadn't analysed it.'

'I haven't. But I'm trying to now.'

'Don't bother,' said Ilya, wearily dismissive. He flopped on to his back and gazed at the ceiling. 'I prefer the visuals. What about rape fantasy? Do you go in for that?'

My pulses gave a shocked little leap. It didn't seem right that a man should speak those words in such a free-and-easy tone, especially after having just cut short my attempts at self-analysis. Well, I knew more about this subject and I wasn't going to let him have his kicks for free.

'Yes,' I said boldly. 'And I don't have a problem with it. Well, not much. I'm not proud of it or anything, but I know it's common. Maybe I've got some deep, primeval guilt about sex. I dunno. I don't think I have, but . . . Yeah, I get off on the idea of, of being forced, of not being responsible. But it doesn't mean I want to be raped. It's just fantasy. I imagine it, so I'm the one in control. My . . . my rapist, he's just a puppet. He does whatever I make him do. It's –'

'Any accompanying visuals?' asked Ilya.

'No,' I said tetchily. I shrugged my top further on my shoulders.

Ilya leant into me again, propped himself on one elbow and regarded me with direct curiosity. 'One day,' he said, 'I'll rape you.'

My heart flipped over. He hadn't listened to a word I'd said. Oh God, what was I doing? Who was this guy? Why was I trusting him with things like this?

Then Ilya smiled, and added, 'If you'll let me.'

My fear sank away and I breathed a sigh of relief.

If I let him, then it wouldn't be rape, would it? It would be me pretending not to want him, pretending to resist, pretending it was violation. It was nothing major. Just a role-play. He was OK. He understood.

'Well, you'd have to ask very nicely,' I replied, trying to lighten the mood.

'Hmm,' he mused, easing back from me a touch and then gazing beyond into nothing. He pushed his hand under the buttoned half of my top and began circling it over my stomach. His touch was absent-minded – as intimate as a familiar lover's or as distant as an executive's playing with desk toys. I didn't know which. Maybe they were one and the same thing.

'What about whoring?' he asked, returning his eyes to mine. 'That's cheap and sleazy. Do you fantasise about that?'

'What?' I laughed. 'About me shivering my tits off on a street corner?'

'With a punter.' He smiled. 'Down an alley. Back of a car. Hotel room. Whatever takes your fancy.'

'Just the one punter?' I said with a sly grin.

He grinned back. 'A lorryload.'

'Yeah,' I drawled. 'I could get into that.'

Ilya crinkled down my bra cups, exposing me again, then trailed his tongue in wet rotations around a nipple.

Shit, I thought. I could seriously fall for this guy.

'So what about a fantasy with one punter?' he murmured.

'Maybe,' I replied. 'If I make him good at using and abusing me. But only when I've finished with the lorryload.'

'Oh, but of course,' said Ilya, smiling up at me.

'What about you?' I asked. 'What are your fantasies?'

He grated his teeth over my crinkling nipple then, holding the tip in a gentle bite, he drew my breast high until I felt an edge of pain. He released me.

'Fucking you up the arse,' he said.

I drew a quiet breath. 'You told me that one on the phone.'

'And?'

'And?' I repeated. 'And tell me another.'

82

Ilya took my nipple between his teeth again and slowly plucked upwards before letting my flesh drop back.

'OK,' he said, pushing my skirt higher and placing a hand on the swell of my mons. 'It's having a whore come round to my flat.' He thumbed strokes across my clitoris. 'She looks just like you. She wears a miniskirt, heels and stockings. Her tits are nearly falling out of her top. Lots of make-up. Tarty porn-style underwear. I make her do whatever I want her to do. I use and abuse her, tell her she's a cheap little slut.'

He looked at me fixedly, those jewel-bright eyes boring into mine. 'Next Friday, if you're free.' He didn't smile, he just kept on thumbing me, a smooth tease that made my clit flesh out.

I gave a little whimper. 'No, I don't know,' I said softly. 'I'm not sure. I might feel daft. It's fantasy stuff. And I'm not wearing –'

'Act it out,' he said. 'Reality's the ultimate fantasy.'

Then a finger slid through the wet valley of my sex to press on the indent of my anus.

I moaned as he massaged me there, spreading my juices over the little muscled ring. And I gasped as he gently eased his finger into my narrow hole.

'Anyone done this to you before?' he asked, driving slowly back and forth, his eyelids droopy with lust.

'No,' I whispered. It was a lie. I'm not that inexperienced but I didn't want to encourage his anal sex fantasy. I wanted to know him better before I even considered agreeing to it.

'Do you like it?' he breathed.

'Mmm,' I murmured.

'What about this?' he asked, and he brought his other hand to my pussy, his fingers swooping into the wet pout of my folds. He gazed down at my face, his buried digits moving in both orifices.

'Ah God, yes,' I groaned, squirming into his thrusts.

83

And with his thumb, he began rocking my clit, stimulating it until it was a knot of jangling nerves.

'Say you'll be my whore,' he said in a commanding tone.

I eyed his surging cock, traced with thick veins and flaring violently at the crown.

'Fuck me and I might,' I challenged. 'Fuck me hard.'

'Ah, you greedy little slut,' he enthused, disengaging his fingers. Then he began tugging at my clothes, yanking my top up, my skirt down, my bra off. His strength and roughness excited me desperately. In the chaos I lunged to grab a condom from my bedside stash. When I was stripped naked, Ilya flipped me on to all fours.

'Be my whore,' he said, circling my waist with his arm and clasping me tight. 'Or you don't get fucked.' His swollen prick pressed into the split of my buttocks.

'You swine,' I hissed. 'Yes, yes, I will.'

I heard him bite at the foil-packaged sheath. Then his rubbered-up cock nudged and, in one fierce, fluid movement, penetrated me. Again and again he penetrated. He was roused to a frenzy and he just plunged and plunged as if he wanted to fuck me to destruction.

'Hard enough?' he barked.

I gasped yes, no, and clutched the foot of the bed, locking my elbows rigid as he hammered into my depths, sending vibrations to my head. He dropped a finger to my clit and frigged it hard. It didn't take much and, in seconds, I'd hit my peak and I was crying out for him to hurry, to climax, because my body couldn't take much more. It was approaching stupor. With relentless vigour, Ilya ploughed on.

'Come,' I wailed. 'Please, oh God. Come.'

And he did – in his own good time.

We rested. Ilya was a smoker. I listened to him move soft-footed through the living room then rifle through his trousers, discarded in the hall. He shouted for an ashtray. I directed him to the very back of the cupboard under the sink in the kitchen, but he returned instead with an empty Coke can.

It was growing dark. A street lamp shone hazily through the muslin curtains.

As Ilya lay there, contentedly inhaling, I felt serious nicotine cravings for the first time in seven and a half months. Dangerous, I thought; he could make me weaken.

'We need to use a word,' he said. 'If this is going to work, we need a codeword for stop. So if you don't like anything I do to you – not just Friday, at any time – then say . . . say "cuttlefish".'

'Why?' I asked with a slight laugh.

'Because it's a nice word,' he replied. (Oh, how I adored him for that.) 'And cuttlefish are interesting. And I reckon they suit what we're doing. They change colour. They signal to each other.'

'And then they get eaten by budgies?'

'Yeah.' He smiled. 'But I was thinking of the creatures, not their bones.'

He drew on his cigarette.

'Anyway,' I said. 'I meant, Why a codeword? Sounds a bit Special Branch to me. Why can't I just say "no" or "stop"?'

'Slips out too easily,' he said. 'And "no" and "stop" are good words to use when you don't mean them. Cuttlefish is deadly serious.'

'Oh, right,' I said. 'But isn't that what people do who are into S/M and bondage? Safeword, I think they call it. Not my scene, I'm afraid. Too many Goths, too much equipment. And besides –'

'In fact . . .' cut in Ilya. He took a final thoughtful drag on his cigarette then dropped the butt in the Coke can. It landed with a plink and a fizz. 'In fact, let's make cuttlefish truly serious,' he said, exhaling a stream of smoke. 'This isn't a romance or a relationship. It's going to be a sex thing like we agreed.'

I said nothing. He sounded so certain of it.

'So,' he continued, 'let's make it into a bit of a game. What if "cuttlefish" means not just "stop" but "the end, finito"? No discussions. No analysis and future plans. Just "cuttlefish". The end.'

I pondered the implications of this. In theory, it sounded good: an affair that was pure lust with no messy break-up. Wasn't that what I wanted?

'So if I want rid of you,' I said, feigning a cool, cruel heart, 'then I do something you don't like and make you say "cuttlefish"?'

'Yeah,' he said, glancing at his watch. 'Or maybe you just say "cuttlefish". I have to accept. No arguments.' He swung himself from the bed, walked out of the door then returned, fastening up his trousers. 'And vice versa,' he said. 'If I think it's time to move on or whatever, then you have to accept me saying "cuttlefish".'

Seeing all his 'I'm about to leave' moves, I shrugged on my top and did up a couple of buttons.

'I think it's flawed,' I said. 'Supposing you want to ... or you're doing something I don't like. But I don't want things to end. Then what?'

'Ah,' he said, stooping for his T-shirt. 'Then you have to decide how much you don't like it.'

'But ...' I faltered. 'I don't know what you have in mind, but my pain threshold's not that high.'

Ilya flexed his chest into his T-shirt. 'Then I have to suss out that threshold, weigh up how much pain you can take,' he said evenly. 'Or how much humiliation or whatever it is. I don't want you to say "cuttlefish".' He smiled. 'Not yet, anyway.'

'Gee, thanks,' I replied.

'Friday, then?' he asked, arching his dark brows. 'Say, ten-ish?'

I nodded. 'Yeah, OK,' I said. 'Friday.'

'Great,' he said, and stroked a quick finger across my cheek. 'Make it good, Beth. I'll see myself out.'

Chapter Five

*I*had three days to shop for some whore clothes; and three days to try to work out just who – or what – I was getting involved with.

It concerned me that I was embarking on some weird sex-game relationship with a guy I hardly knew, who was inventing rules and safewords, and who was very keen on probing my dark, dirty fantasies. Was this hugely irresponsible of me? Was it dangerous?

Maybe it was, I thought. And while the idea of being reckless and abandoned gave me a delicious thrill, I wondered if I ought to tell someone about it – just like you're meant to tell someone when you arrange a date with a handsome, 6' 2", g.s.o.h. from the classifieds.

The sensible thing, I reckoned, would be to let Jenny and Clare know what I was up to. Then, if they hadn't heard from me for a while, they could go and get the police to check out this Ilya guy and look under his floorboards for my body.

But I didn't want to. I wanted whoring for Ilya to be my secret.

But I wanted that secret to be less of a mystery to me. I was hungry to know more about my partner-in-sleaze, mainly because I was nosy, but also because I was worried.

The nosy part of me wanted more stuff to go in that mental shoebox labelled ILYA. So far, it contained his handwriting, a near-nude photo, memories of our phone-call sex and memories of our 'no small talk' sex. Now I wanted to top that lot up with ordinary information – his job, his age, social life, blah, blah.

And that ordinary information, I thought, might make me less nervy. It would give Ilya some grounding in reality.

But I'm no supersleuth and I didn't have a clue how to go about it. I looked his name up in the phone book; he wasn't listed. I kept an eye on his window; his hours were irregular.

Did that make him less of a sex-crazed psycho-killer or more? Neither, I decided, because even madmen can have their number in the book and hold down nine-to-fives.

I was stumped. But accidents will happen, and my shopping trip for whore clothes turned out to be more eventful than I imagined. And it left me fairly spooked.

Ready for a spending spree, I left my house, knowing more what I didn't want to look like than what I did.

The trouble was, I didn't know how to translate my sleazy, seedy fantasies into actual clothing. And the more I thought about sleaze, the less I understood it. Wasn't sleaze just a word people used for sex they disapproved of? For sex that was furtive, guilty, hollow and quite often paid for?

The only thing I felt guilty about was liking guilty sex. And Ilya had really pushed those buttons when he'd called me slut and whore. I liked being told I was a bad girl for wanting cock.

But what did a bad girl wear?

Should I go for New York hooker in hot pants?

Or maybe the downmarket dregs of British police dramas with people saying stuff like 'Tart's in reception, Guv, wants a word,' and there's a woman there with pale bruised legs, being snotty and chewing gum?

Christ, should I chew gum?

No, Beth. Don't go overboard. And don't even think about the legs.

It was a bright, warm afternoon. Surrey Street was clogged with one-way traffic and, across the road, the pub's plastic tables were set out on the pavement. A group of people were sitting there, drinking lager and breathing in petrol.

I walked past small houses, past a couple of gutted shops and past the sex shop – wondering, as everyone must do, what happens in there and how they make their money, because hardly anyone seems to go in or out.

It's a horribly discreet-looking place, with a grubby cream facade, a cream sign and cream blinds permanently blanking out the window. There's nothing celebratory about it; no garish signs saying ADULT VIDEOS the way there are in London. It's just cream. Creepy cream. The whole frontage seems to say, 'And please wash your hands afterwards.'

Was that sleazy? I wondered. Or was it just rotten?

The shop reminded me of Ilya suggesting I dress in porno-undies. The very thought made me cringe. I don't do heels, frills and stockings. It's not me. While I got off on the idea of acting like a porn-slut, I didn't fancy looking like one, not in the way Ilya meant.

Back then, my porn-film virginity was still intact, although my porn-mag virginity wasn't. A few years before, I'd persuaded Rich – the then love of my life – to go out and buy something to satisfy my curiosity and – ahem – broaden my cultural knowledge and allow me to make an informed judgement as to the merits or otherwise of wank-mags.

I mean, I don't have any brothers so I never got any

sneaky peeks of their teenage kicks and I couldn't join in those conversations when people said, 'Yeah, but the real problem with porn is that it's just so bad.' I needed knowledge.

Rich had returned with a couple of skin-mags, muttering how, nowadays, it was less embarrassing for a woman to buy this gear than it was for a man – his argument being that a woman does it and she's sexually assured, she's hot, breaking out after years of male oppression; a guy does it and he's just a sad little wanker.

The magazines were seriously offensive – full of pricks and pussies, not much in the way of taxing reading matter. They didn't offend me on that level, not a cat in hell's chance. But aesthetically, they were rotten: airbrushed women with farcical pouts wearing fussy nylon lingerie and looking at least a decade out of date. There were black dots here and there, covering up the point of penetration and those great fountains of jism. It looked as if the men were ejaculating strings of jet beads – the devil's semen.

But once I got past the taste barrier and laughter factor, I found the stuff pretty horny. The brazen vulgarity turned me on, but, most of all, I liked the way the sex was so depersonalised and anonymous, so blatantly devoid of heart and soul.

I had an idea that sex with Ilya could be something like that. But the trouble was, I had heart and I had soul. And I also had taste.

Before hitting the shops, I stopped off near the train station to make a phone call to nobody. As I'd hoped, the booth was plastered with cards advertising things like 'busty blonde, just turned eighteen'. I stood there, nodding into the whining receiver while checking out the display.

I had half a mind to give Ilya a ring, not to speak to him – I had nothing to say – but just to hear his voice, answerphone or otherwise. I could find out if he was at

90

home. He wouldn't know it was me. I could just hang up. But I resisted. I thought it was too loopy.

Instead I just loitered and drank in the sight of all those whores touting for business, some with professionally printed cards; others with just handwritten squares of paper. One had a felt-tip drawing of a sun next to the phone number, its caption SEASIDE SEX.

It didn't help much in terms of what I ought to buy, but it gave me a buzz of sleazy energy. And sleaze, I decided, didn't have to be soiled with solemnity like the cream-coloured sex shop. Sleaze could be brash and bold, trashy and twinkly.

My sleaze-buzz got tarnished with squalor when I made my way under the bridge of Trafalgar Street, recalling Ilya's fantasy of fucking me in the doorway. As usual, someone was slouched there, lethargically begging for change. It was just too grotty.

Putting it from my mind, I headed for the North Laine, Brighton's pulsing rainbow heart. It's a grid of terraced streets, dotted with pubs, and the seam that runs through it is a heaven of quirky shops and cafés.

I was slightly jittery about bumping into someone, because the North Laine is big bumping-into-someone territory. It's the place you go to get your ethnic tat, your retro clothes, your alternative cred or your second-hand books. If you want your clit pierced, a pair of seventies platforms, an obscure remix on vinyl or some exotic Chinese spices, then you go to the North Laine. Even if you don't want anything, you still go to the North Laine, and preferably with your mates.

I wanted to look like a whore, and I did not want to meet anyone with time to kill who might fancy tagging along.

I browsed my way along Sydney Street, checking out shops selling fetish wear, kinky boots and glitz. But it was either too dominatrix or too damn good. I wanted to look tawdry and cheap, although not too tawdry and cheap – not like something the cat had dragged in.

I moved on to Snoopers Paradise: a jumble of second-hand stalls under one big roof. After getting distracted by some angle-poise lamps, circa 1950, I anchored myself in the clothes bit.

I browsed at leisure, rifling through decades of fashion: the good, the bad and the downright ugly. When I saw it, I knew I had to have it, not just for me-as-whore but for me-as-Beth. It was a plastic leopard-print mac – twice as fake as the real thing.

In a flurry of excitement, I held it to my body. It was mid-thigh length and just my size.

Buoyed up by my purchase, and churning with images of myself, I stepped out into the sunlight. My plan was to go in search of a bad-girl dress and some slut-undies.

But I never made it. Because when I merged into the slow-flowing crowds outside, I spotted Ilya. Or, rather, the back of Ilya's head.

My heart jumped. Of all the people I'd feared bumping into, he was not on the list. Seeing him in public felt weird; he didn't seem to belong there.

I had a moment's panic: I didn't want to exchange chit-chat with him in the middle of everyday bustle; I didn't want to meet him when I was clutching item one of my whore wardrobe.

But he was several people ahead of me. He didn't know I was behind him. He wouldn't know if stayed behind him, perhaps followed him for a while – just to see which sort of shops he went into, just to get a bit of detail for that mental shoebox of mine.

I dropped back a few paces, screening myself with people while keeping a sharp eye on his shorn head. Where was he going? To the Cheese Shop for some fancy cheese? To the Kensington for a drink? No, he passed them by. Moments later, so did I, keeping my head low as I skirted past the pub, fearing there might be someone sitting at the outdoor trestle tables who would call my name and ruin everything.

Ahead of me, Ilya took a left turn. Damn, I'd been hoping he would go straight on to Sydney Street. A left turn meant not many shops, and rapidly thinning crowds. Should I take a left? At the end of the street, I stood amidst a bottleneck of people and dithered.

I watched Ilya take a second left – going back the way we'd just come but along a quieter street. What excuse could I give if I followed him and he saw me? Upper Gardner Street: that meant boxy terraced houses and a few antique garages, some tatty, some posh. I could always say I was furniture-hunting. And of course I'd seen him ahead. Hadn't he heard me calling his name?

I did a left and a left, dawdling along so Ilya was about half a street ahead of me. Where was he going? And why had he more or less doubled back on himself? Was he a bit lost? Maybe he hadn't lived in Brighton long and he was simply exploring. Oh, there were so many things I wanted to know about him.

Ilya walked the full length of the street and took a right turn, disappearing from my view. I rushed to catch up, scared I might lose him. North Road next. I could always say I was en route to the Post Office.

Then it was another right into Queens Gardens. This was some zig-zag journey he was taking.

Queens Gardens: that meant a row of pale cottages. I could always say . . . what? That I was heading for Trafalgar Street and I was taking the scenic route?

My potential excuses were becoming more and more implausible. Maybe I should quit.

Yes, I'd just take a quick look down Queens Gardens then get back to shopping. I'd forget all about playing detective. It was a stupid idea anyway.

I turned the corner.

Ilya was there. I almost ran into him. He was just standing still, next to the picture-framing shop. He was facing my direction, waiting for me. He looked pretty pissed off.

'Oh hi,' I said brightly, willing myself not to blush. 'I . . . er . . . I saw you just back there. And I was wondering if, maybe . . . if you fancied a coffee or something. Do you? Do you fancy going for a coffee?'

'What are you doing?' he replied sternly. 'Why are you following me?'

'Following you?' I exclaimed with a laugh so artificially flabbergasted that my cheeks ached. 'I'm not following –'

'You've been following me since Kensington fucking Gardens,' he said, his blue-green eyes narrowing viciously. 'What's going on here? Have I landed myself with some kind of weirdo obsessive? Are you going to turn into a fucking stalker?'

'Christ,' I said, trying to hide my shock with another feigned laugh. 'Of course I'm not. Get a grip.'

The thought that he had similar fears to me was reassuring and yet deeply disturbing. Was I a weirdo obsessive? Maybe I was. Hadn't I recently considered phoning him in order to hang up? Hadn't I just been trailing him halfway around town? Was that normal?

Was my perspective warped? Or was his perspective warped? Maybe we were both crazy.

'Look,' I said, attempting to calm the situation. 'It's nothing. Stop overreacting. I was just trying to catch up with you. I was simply wondering if –'

'Well, don't,' he said in a tight-mouthed snarl. 'Don't ever try and catch up with me. OK?' I saw the hands at his side clenching and unclenching.

'Jesus,' I said, no longer bothering to conceal my amazement. 'Whatever you say.' An instinct for self-protection made me clutch my carrier bag to my chest. 'It was only coffee.'

There was silence, then Ilya's expression softened and he nodded at my bag. 'Been shopping?' he enquired, putting on a gentle smile.

'Yeah,' I said, wrapping the bag tighter.

'Anything special?'

I shrugged, my eyes downcast. I knew I looked sulky but I didn't give a damn. However wrong it'd been of me to follow him, I didn't think I deserved such aggression.

'Are we still on for Friday?' he asked. He reached his fingertips to my chin, tilting my face so I was forced to meet his gaze. His smile broadened and his eyes sparkled roguishly under their heavy lids.

He was trying to make amends. He knew he'd been out of order.

And his raw, rough beauty was so devilishly sexy that I couldn't help but crumble.

'Sure,' I said, attempting an easy smile. 'So long as I'm richly rewarded, you bastard.'

Ilya grinned and bent to press a kiss to my cheek. 'I'll do my very best,' he said. 'Which direction are you going in now?'

I didn't know if he was suggesting he might come along with me or suggesting I fuck off.

So I said, 'The opposite direction to you.'

'Fine,' he replied. And we said our goodbyes.

My shopping spirit had vanished. I went home.

Friday night, and the small strip bulb above my bathroom mirror made my features seem shadowy and gaunt. I gazed at my painted face, at those darkly shaded eyes and those glossy, fat red lips – BJ lips one of my exes used to call them, as in blow-job lips because they're very full and fleshy.

I hadn't planned on wearing gloss, hadn't even thought about the stuff. But when I'd first applied Tulip Red – not my usual colour – I looked too much like me out on the town, albeit me with brighter lips and trashier eye make-up.

I wondered if I should remove my nose stud but I liked the edge it gave me so it stayed.

Seeking inspiration, I clattered in the long-forgotten dregs of my make-up bag, and I found it – a real blast from the past: my lipgloss, once a much loved friend and now somewhat forlorn and cloudy in colour.

Nonetheless, I reckoned it might just be the finishing touch. I was glad I wasn't an organised kind of girl who did make-up-bag spring cleaning. I unscrewed the top, loaded the sponge-tipped wand with goo and slicked it over my lips. They glistened deliciously, almost to the point of dripping. Perfect. Nice and sleazy does it.

I dug a few pins in my hair and teased it this way and that so it looked temptingly tousled. The roots were dark against the tawny dye. I was pleased about that.

In fifteen minutes' time, I would cross the road to Ilya's and, for one night, I would be his common little whore, flaunting my easy ways, giving him what he wanted. I was eager and nervous, my stomach full of butterflies; and I was excited and horny, my sex full of juices.

But my face in the mirror looked scared and drawn.

I poured myself a vodka, wanting to replace my anxiety with the buzz of frivolity. In my mind, I kept going over our little confrontation in the North Laine. The more I thought about it, the more over the top Ilya's reaction had seemed. His flare of aggression unsettled me deeply. Could he turn nasty? Was he a paranoid soul? Or did he truly have something to hide?

Perhaps he'd been trying to shake me off because he was meeting another woman. Or perhaps it was something far worse than that, although I didn't know what. Again, I wondered if he might be dangerous.

Oh Jesus, lighten up, Beth. It's just a game. He's OK. He's even bothered to think of an opt-out clause: cuttlefish.

I sat on a stiff-backed chair, legs crossed. My lipstick left a cheap kiss on the rim of the glass and I imagined it would smear sluttishly when Ilya kissed me. But then, I thought, will he kiss me? I'm playing the whore, and I don't think they go in for kissing. Maybe I should say something when I go over there: 'I don't kiss, I don't do anal and I don't do anything without rubbers. Take it or leave it.'

I hoped I could do it without feeling self-conscious. The nearest I'd been to role-playing before was a few mild sessions of silk-scarf bondage. I'd feigned resistance, but there had been a playful, giggly edge to things. And that doesn't really do much for my arousal. I know sex can be funny, but that doesn't mean funny is sexy, not when you're really getting down to it.

That's why I like to keep my fantasies private: I don't have to make them acceptable by sugaring them with humour; and when they're safe in my head, there's only one person who might find them comical and that's me. And I don't. I find them hot, especially when they're crude and degrading. But Ilya seemed to be on my wavelength. He wasn't laughing.

I smiled to myself, starting to feel sassy and brassy once again. I liked the idea of our sex being a transaction – no intimacy, no seduction – just up front and down to it, clinical and sleazy. And, instead of cash, my payment was pleasure – not the kind of pleasure I might receive from a caring lover, but the pleasure I would take from being debased and used, from being Ilya's plaything – a worthless bit of trash he could abandon on a whim.

I looked down at my shoes, eyeing them with satisfaction. I'd borrowed them from Clare, much to her amusement. I didn't tell her the reason I wanted them. I made up some nonsense about fancying a little practice at fuck-me shoes. Don't think she believed me.

I'd bought an arse-skimmingly short, bright-red slip dress. It was deliciously tarty. The best thing of all was the zip that didn't lie flat and the bit of thread hanging from the hem. I'd splashed out on a plethora of stockings and sussies too, but they made me feel like I was in drag. So I opted for bare legs instead.

The dress was filthy-tight. It made me curve and splurge in all the right places and gave me a drop-dead cleavage, no bra required. My nipples poked through the shiny thin fabric.

Underneath I wore crotchless knickers – red gauze edged in black lace. They were scratchy, horrible things but I enjoyed the mild discomfort: it was a constant reminder that my undies were cheap and vulgar and, tonight, so was I.

Yes, I looked the part. I was sleazy and easy, a whore for Ilya's taking.

I drained the last of my vodka, shuddered, then went to my windowless bathroom for a final mirror-check. Looking good, I thought, as I touched up my gloss-slathered lips.

Then I planted one high heel on the edge of the bath and gently dabbed a tissue into the gaping split of my knickers. All the anticipation had made me horny as hell. My vulva was booming with thick heat and I was far too wet to be leaving the house in an itsy-bitsy slapper dress and knickers that were hardly there. I didn't want to drip my way across the road.

I was about to leave but a twinge of nervousness made me write down details of where I was, who I was with and our arrangement to act out a whore fantasy. Just in case. Then I slipped on my squeaky leopard-print mac, took a deep breath and left. It had just turned ten-fifteen.

Outside, the lamp-lit streets were quiet and the sky was sprinkled with stars.

I glanced up at Ilya's flat window. The bamboo blind was down and the light shining behind it was red. I smiled to myself. He'd put a brothel-red bulb in, whether as a joke or not I didn't know and I didn't care. I liked to see it, different from all the other windows. It was something for everyone to see, and yet only he and I understood it.

My excitement fluttered as I mused on how Ilya might treat me. I was hungry for more of his insulting, dirty talk; hungry to be his slut and whore.

Leggy and awkward on my borrowed heels, I teetered across the road. The night air was a cool breath, stealing under my skirt and whispering over my exposed juicy sex.

The front gate was open, and I made my way up the wide steps to Ilya's building, clutching on to the pale wall like a gin-soaked lush. In the gloom of the arched portico, I eyed the cluster of bells and laid a finger to his. I pressed long and hard. My short fingernails were red, and I'd chipped at the polish to enhance my slut image.

'It's Beth,' I said confidently when Ilya's voice crackled through the circle of tiny holes. Then, with a buzz and a click, the huge, paint-flaky door was mine to heave against and enter.

The lofty hall was in darkness for a moment then, with another click, it was flooded with stark light. Like my place, I thought, with switches here and there to give you rationed electricity. And, like at my place, there were a couple of bicycles propped in the hallway, making the place smell faintly of rubber. But it didn't look as good as my building. It was shabbier and the carpet was a hideously patterned brown monstrosity.

I wobbled up the communal staircase to the landing, my calves already aching from the shoes. At the end was a slightly open door, and I approached, seeing the brass number plate there. His flat. A touch of chivalry wouldn't have gone amiss, I thought, piqued that he wasn't holding the door for me.

I pushed in and the landing light clicked off behind me.

'It's Beth,' I said again, half expecting a stranger's voice to reply, 'Who?'

'I know,' came Ilya's voice, and I turned left to its source, seeing a door ajar with fuzzy red light bleeding from it into the unlit hall. Shoulders back, breasts thrusting, I stalked into the room, noticing the window that, had the blinds been up, would have looked across to my window. It felt a little strange.

Ilya was lying full-length on a sofa, ankles crossed, watching my grand entrance. In the crimson flush of the table-lamp, he was shadowy and indistinct, his close-cropped hair tinged with a ruby sheen. He didn't bother with a smile. He just looked me up and down, hooded eyes flicking in a quick check rather than lingering in a leer. His dark angular face – half-chiselled, half-crooked – was austere, unmoved.

For a moment he became the inscrutable bogeyman of my imagination again, but then I remembered we were playing roles. He was being my detached, arrogant punter and I had to be his whore. Inspired, I strode forward, taking a quick recce of my surroundings as I did so.

First impressions: not good. And it would have been a hell of a lot worse if it hadn't been for that red light blurring the room's harshness. There was a very temporary feel to the place, as if it had been let on a part-furnished basis and Ilya was keeping it that way. And there was nothing high on the walls the way there is in most people's houses. There were no pictures, no tall bookshelves. It was all very low-level, which really isn't good when you've got a high ceiling.

And his fireplace – a sturdy marble affair – was chip-boarded over, with nothing personal or nice on the mantelpiece – just dull-looking junk: a couple of batteries, packet of fags, scruffy stack of paper, that kind of thing.

I was slightly disappointed – not because I'd been expecting Ikea-catalogue swank, but more because I'd hoped to gain a few clues about him: his tastes, his lifestyle, et cetera.

But, apart from that, I didn't dwell on the spartan, shabby nature of his flat. I simply thought, Oh well, he's a bloke. They're not that good at interior design. Anyway, you wanted down-market, Beth. You've got it.

Ilya didn't move from his sofa-sprawl, so I slipped off my mac, cast it on to a sagging armchair, and turned to face him. I stood, legs apart, and struck a hand-on-hip pose. Giving a defiant toss of my curls, I stared boldly at him.

Here I am, I thought. Go on, check out the goods. Objectify me to your heart's content. Help me shake off the last vestiges of Beth and make me meat, merchandise, cunt for sale – a cunt so greedy that I'll do it for free.

As Ilya raked me with his eyes, his lips twisted in a vague sneer and he nodded to himself. The beats of my heart shot up.

I could tell he approved. I looked deliciously cheap, so easy and vulgar. How he could he resist such a hot little piece?

'Well?' I asked, giving the word an aggressive note. 'Do you like what you see?'

Ilya stood in a bored kind of way, as if he were forcing himself to go and make a cup of tea.

'You'll do,' he said, and then it was time up on me looking the whore. I had to start playing the whore and I was ready and willing. I was going to slum it beautifully.

'So, mister?' I ventured. 'What do you have in mind?'

Ilya gave a playful half-grin, came to stand in front of me and reached under the hem of my dress. It wasn't far from there to my knickers, and he gave a murmur of appreciation when his fingers alighted, not on a gusset, but on my moist, brazen sex. He did a cursory exploration, his thumb rubbing over my pubis to find the wisps of gauze and lace that were my underwear.

'Whore,' he whispered, and as he spoke he eased a couple of fingers into my vagina.

Lust tumbled to my groin and I gave a faint moan,

tottering slightly on my heels. Deftly, Ilya moved side-on to me, reaching round to cup my waist and hold me steady. We were standing almost at right angles, one of my hips pressing near to his hip, one of my feet placed between his. The heel of his hand rested against my mons, and the fingers within me were motionless, as if he were stopping up a dam.

He stayed that way while he lowered his eyes in blatant survey of my plunging cleavage.

'Nice tits,' he said, and he waggled the fingers in my hole. 'But you're very wet for a whore. I'd rather you were dry then I could fuck you, maybe with a bit of lube, and I'd imagine you were hating it. Imagine you were sick of cock because you'd had so many stuck up you.'

He moved his lips close to my ear. His breath tickled there.

'Yes,' he continued. 'You'd visit me with a sore slack cunt because, all night, you'd been taking dick after dick. And the men all want you. Not because you're anything special but because you're cheap. Cheap and dirty, and your standards are low. Yeah, you'll let anyone stick it in you. As long as it's hard, you don't care. You're just a slut. And sooner or later you'll be taking it up the arse because your cunt's too fucked to be of use.'

Then he slipped his fingers out of me and walked away, leaving me standing and stunned.

Vulgarity tripped so easily from his tongue and that little speech had been particularly foul. And the shock was that it inflamed me with a hunger I couldn't help but be ashamed of.

I watched Ilya head for the kitchenette, sectioned off from the room by a half-wall. As he passed his sofa, he dashed his fingers across the back, wiping off my juices. He was feigning contempt; I hoped he was feigning.

I stood there, unsure of what to do. I was desperately aroused and I was embarrassed by that. I wished I were proud of my taste for filth and debasement, but I wasn't.

Confessing to Ilya had been a first for me; acting it out was another.

It scared me a little that my vaguely expressed fantasies seemed as good as an open book to him and that he could say things to me and do things to me that struck a frightening chord within the barely explored recesses of my dank, dirty mind.

In the narrow kitchenette, Ilya reached a whisky bottle from a cupboard, poured himself a glass, then returned. The slut that was me was obviously not significant enough to be offered a drink. I challenged that.

'Don't I get a whisky, then?' I asked.

Ilya took a gulp.

'No,' he said. 'Your mouth's going to be full enough.'

He set down his glass on a table and, with his foot, eased a wooden chair from under it, turning it to face me. He unbuckled his belt.

'I want oral first,' he said, unzipping quickly and revealing snug grey trunks, their button-flies bulging. 'And I want it firm and good.'

He kicked off the bottom half of his clothing then perched himself on the chair. His prick jutted powerfully upright. The sight made my pussy swoon, and I was reassured, grateful to my body for getting heated up by something clean and wholesome rather than coarse and crude.

In the bloodshot, bleary room, Ilya sat there, legs wide and waiting for me.

'I don't swallow,' I said, asserting my whore-self.

'Oh, yeah?' he challenged. He linked his fingers behind his head and flexed his spine, stretching in readiness for the good time about to roll.

Oh God, I thought, I really don't swallow. Please respect that. And it suddenly struck me that I didn't know where one game ended and the other began.

I was playing a game within a game. In the small game, I was acting the whore and a whore can set ground rules: 'No this, no that.' But that was part of a bigger game, one where there was just one rule: saying 'cuttlefish' if things got seriously out of order, and knowing that 'cuttlefish' was also the big full stop, end of relationship.

I was hardly going to cry 'cuttlefish' because of a bit of come in my mouth, was I? Would Ilya exploit that and make me swallow? While I hoped he wouldn't, it gave me a thrill to think I didn't quite know what the limits were and that my saying 'no' meant absolutely nothing.

So, with a provocative half-smile, I sashayed over to him. Laying my hands inside his knees, I knelt between his open thighs, pressing his legs wider as I lowered myself down. I ogled his erect prick with eagerness and greed. He was unfurled and, in the red-stained room, his glans had a cherry-dark flush to it.

I love cocks. I love looking at them. I love sucking them. It turns me on hugely. I know some women say, 'Yeah, giving a blow job, it's OK, but you only really do it in part-exchange, don't you?' But I disagree. I genuinely love it.

So I dallied and teased, both for Ilya's pleasure and for mine, spinning out the moment before I took him deep in my throat. I rubbed my hands along his thighs, cupped and caressed his balls, feeling the taut spheres shifting within their sac. He murmured hunger and edged his arse further forward, seeking my luscious red-gloss lips.

I trailed my tongue along the underseam of his shaft. And, when that clear bead of pre-come seeped from the eyelet of his glans, I gave a couple of tiny, flicking licks there.

'Just do it,' growled Ilya, his hips lifting impatiently. So I did, my lipsticked pout sliding down his stiffness.

'Ahh,' said Ilya. 'Yess.' His voice was laced with bliss and my desire flared up at the sound.

Edging my shins back, I clasped the chair so I was near as damn it on all fours – submissively worshipping the cock in my mouth just like, I reckoned, a good whore ought to. Again and again, I sucked up and slipped down, working him with firm fleshy lips and a hot dancing tongue. I tasted the slight sweetness of my lipgloss as it smeared along his meaty length.

Ilya made soft approving groans. I felt him lean forward and then his hands were on my dress and he was reeling in the tight red fabric, shuffling it up and over my hips until it was all ruched about my waist.

So, I thought, while I'm busy fellating him, he gets to feast his eyes on my arse, half-concealed by those trashy red knickers. Lucky man.

My head bobbing steadily, I spread my knees wider, relishing the sensation of my labia peeling apart. I dipped my spine and thrust my buttocks high, offering him the best view I could.

I wondered if he would approve of me masturbating. My sex was in desperate need of attention and Ilya was in no position help out. I restrained myself for a moment, thinking that whores service their clients not themselves, and I imagined having another client, fucking me from behind. Foolish idea, because after that I had to touch myself. My clit was thudding and my pussy was so open, so achingly hot.

I reached between my thighs, my fingers diving straight past my split knickers and into my tunnel of slick heat. I groaned around Ilya's cock.

'Hey,' he warned, and he clutched a fistful of my hair. His pelvis reared sharply and he held my head firm as he started fucking into my mouth. His wiry pubes tickled my nostrils, my cheeks bulged and his domed glans butted ceaselessly against my throat. I fought against my gagging reflex, trying to draw back.

'Stop it, Beth,' he commanded. 'Stop wanking.'

Insolent and lustful, I ignored him. My fingers felt too good. I plunged and frigged, rushing my actions because I feared he was about to stop me. And, sure enough, he did. A hand clawed just above my elbow, and he tugged against my resistance until he'd manage to wrench my fingers from my sex.

'All in good time,' he said smoothly, gripping my wrist and raising my arm high. 'Right now, I want your undivided attention.'

He took my juice-coated fingers into his mouth and sucked up and down, mirroring the slide of my lips on his prick. The fist holding my hair loosened, leaving me free to give him head at my own pace.

Keeping my lips in a shaft-hugging O, I brought into play all the specialities I knew: I lashed with my tongue, teasing the circlet of his foreskin and his smooth sturdy crest; I grated my teeth along his length, oh so gently, suckling on his tip then going down deep. As I sensed him getting greedier, I kept my rhythm slow and steady, my mouth nice and firm.

'That's good,' he kept saying. 'Yeah, that's fucking good.'

He groaned even more when I reached between his thighs. His balls were packed solid, tucked up close to the base of his cock. I hammocked and caressed them, stroking a finger back along the ridge to his anus.

'Oh yes,' he said again, and then we were closing in on that moment, on that spit-or-swallow moment.

I felt his prick thicken and tense to its absolute limit. Under that stretched satin skin, he was hard as bone. Oh, please be a gentleman, I thought. Don't flood my throat.

I fought the urge to pull away, fearing I might be premature. I didn't want to see him tugging on his tool for those frantic extra seconds. I wanted to satisfy him, but not quite to the bitter end.

His thighs went still and taut. So did I. Briskly, Ilya pushed at my shoulders, snatching himself from my lips. He shoved his hips toward my body, angling his cock at my cleavage, and I heaved my chest up to meet him. On a long groan, his semen jetted on to me in descending arcs. The white liquor dribbled down the upthrust of my breasts and spread dark stains on to my cheap red dress. I was glad it was cheap.

'Thank you,' I said, trying to sound ironic even though I was genuinely grateful.

'Purely selfish,' replied Ilya. 'I want to watch you rubbing my come into your tits.'

'Any time,' I purred, kneeling back on to my heels.

The dress stayed more or less bunched round my waist and I opened my knees, wanting to give my punter the benefit of those crotchless knickers. I imagined my vulva, a slit of red shiny flesh framed by a slit of cheap black lace. Exquisite.

With the flat of my hand I spread Ilya's silky fluid over my cleavage, before sliding into my dress to cover my tits in a sticky caress. I watched him watching me, his eyes locked on the crawl of my fingers as they moved under the fabric. I nudged the spaghetti straps from my shoulders and pushed down the stretchy material so my tits could pop out, wanton and rosy-tipped.

When I'd palmed the cooling juice into my skin, I continued for my own delight, fondling the weight of my flesh, thumbing my sharp, hard nipples.

One hand on my breasts, the other on my thigh, I made a show of arousing myself. I rubbed along my leg and into my knickers, fingers skimming my poor, neglected snatch.

'Take them off,' said Ilya, standing up. 'Sit on this chair and open your legs. Show me your cunt and wank for me.'

At last. Satisfaction ahead. I got up and shimmied my half-knickers down. The dress uncrinkled a fraction and I scrunched it back. The shoulder straps hung sluttishly down my arms. From my shoes up to my waist, I was naked. Round my middle was a wrinkled band of red and my breasts poked above.

I sat on the chair and planted my heels wide. Ilya

107

stepped back to view the mouth-watering spread of my pussy, pouting lewd and rude from a neat clutch of brown-gold hair.

Much as I wanted to bring myself off with some nifty fingerwork, I resisted and instead decided to play up to him as if we were making movies.

I splayed my tingling labia for him, sawing along my milky crease with one slim finger. Dramatically, I sucked on that salt-sweet finger before inserting it deep into my juicy little well. I didn't dare touch my clitoris for fear my hunger would soar and drive me from performance to pursuit. I closed my eyes, rolled my head back and ran a salacious tongue over my lips.

Ilya, for some reason still in his T-shirt, watched from a distance, arms folded, as I squelched my finger in and out. His cock began twitching into its second life, then he walked away. Kitchenette again.

He returned, a sly grin on his lips, a bunch of bananas in one hand.

He couldn't be serious. He snapped off a banana. He could.

'Stop trying to be so fucking sexy,' he said. 'Use this on yourself.'

He held out his hand. A large green-tinged banana curved on his palm.

I gave a nervous, embarrassed laugh and did not take it.

'Use it,' he repeated, gripping the fruit and touching it lightly between my spread thighs.

I took it, feeling the heat colour my cheeks. Ilya moved away and lay on the couch, settling back, smirking.

Apart from their taste, bananas have no redeeming features. They are a comedy fruit; they are monkey food; they are a cheap fellatio gag; they are a slapstick staple when their skins are on the ground. Even the shape of them is a dumb smile.

I supposed that was why I was offered one rather than,

say, a good crisp length of cucumber. It was to humble and humiliate me by making me ridiculous, robbing me of all dignity because I had to fuck myself with stupid fruit.

Damn Ilya, but isn't that what I wanted? To be cheapened and demeaned?

Yes, I did, but I still wanted to be desirable at the same time. Could I possibly be desirable with a banana sticking out of my cunt?

It seemed I had little choice but to try. After all, I was eager to climax, and if it was a banana or nothing then I was going for the banana.

I poised the blunt end at my entrance and slowly curved it in to me. Despite my reservations, it was heavenly to be filled, and I couldn't stifle a moan of pleasure. Edging my arse forward on my seat, I opened my legs wider and began drawing the fruit in and out. My sex clicked wetly with my gentle thrusts and I was gaining in confidence.

I shut my eyes, wanting to blot out the situation, to forget about Ilya and the obscene picture I was offering him. Instead, I concentrated on sensation. With my free hand I circled the hard bump of my clitoris. My urgency rose and I fretted quicker, plunged the banana faster.

'Yes,' said Ilya. 'Go on. Fuck yourself harder.'

I snapped open my eyes, saw him lying there, his strong thighs lolling, his fist around his engorged cock, nudging ever so slightly. I closed my eyes again and the after-image burnt into my mind: Ilya watching me, his hand moving on his prick in a luxurious half-wank. Thank God. He found it arousing.

It spurred me to new heights and I fucked myself harder. I was frantically close to coming but my banana wasn't bearing up. It was beginning to lose its firmness, its shape. I could feel it softening inside me, growing pulpy, as if my pussy was a super-fast ripening machine.

In a panic, I thrust it faster and deeper but that only made things worse.

Ilya was chanting a steady mantra: 'You dirty little whore, Beth, you dirty little whore.' And I fretted my clit wildly until my orgasm gripped, and I was left as a panting, gasping wreck.

My inner thighs were smeared with warm slush and clammy greying threads. I unplugged the melting banana. It was in a sorry state, its skin split and blackening already, pale-yellow purée oozing from its wounds. Revulsion gripped my stomach.

I stood, holding the thing away from me in my upturned palm.

'Where's your bin?' I asked sharply.

'You don't fancy eating it then?' Ilya said, smiling, still rubbing steadily on his erection.

'Jesus Christ,' I said, giving him a contemptuous glare, and I stalked into his cramped kitchenette and splatted it in the sink. His mess.

As I rinsed my sticky hands under the tap, Ilya came to join me in the red-tinged gloom. I turned to see him whipping off his T-shirt, uncovering that burnished-bronze chest scattered with dark hair. His cock poked upright from his thick black thatch, full of vigour and fleshy lust. He was ready for action. I shook the drips from my hand. My groin, humming with the afterglow of my climax, roared up like a flame.

'You're a hot little bit of cunt, aren't you?' he murmured. 'I'm so glad we met.'

He moved close, his bare feet making a slight suck noise on the linoleum, and grated his teeth on my neck. There was barely enough space for us to stand side by side. His kitchenette was more like a corridor lined with an L-shape of unfitted fittings. He guided me deeper into the room, condom and T-shirt in one hand.

'I'm all bananaed,' I said, making a feeble attempt to

110

hitch a shoulder strap into place. 'I feel tacky and horrible.'

He bit the condom package and spat out the edge. 'You look tacky and horrible,' he replied without nastiness. 'Like a good slut should.'

He slid his balled-up T-shirt across the Formica work surface at the furthest end of the room. There was a fridge beneath and my thigh rested against it.

'Lean over,' he said, nodding at the work surface and beginning to unroll the sheath down his rigid prick.

I did as told, nudging aside a box of tea bags, an empty juice carton and a bulb of garlic before laying half my upper body on the Formica. My nipples pressed into the cool surface. I flattened my hands to the tiled wall and spread my heels wide, glad of the extra height they gave me. I was as wide as the kitchen, one foot touching the half-wall, the other touching a cupboard. I could probably have gone wider if space had allowed because I was so fiercely ready for the entry of his cock.

I felt Ilya's hands, first on the crease behind my knees then running firmly up my thighs to caress my arse. He kneaded and pummelled and I thrust my buttocks out in welcome.

'Such a good arse,' he said.

And then from nowhere his hand cracked down on my cheek. And it cracked down hard. His hands are broad and work-hardened, and that hand hurt.

I gasped in shock, hardly having chance to register the sting before another hefty slap landed on top of it. Then it happened over and over, faster and faster, a blitz attack on the right side of my arse. He tried a couple of left-handed thwacks but couldn't get enough force and there was no room to manoeuvre; so he returned to my right buttock, slapping it up to a flaming, raw pitch, spitting his abuse at me – whore, slut, bitch – as his frenzy intensified and his breath grew shallow.

I gasped, yelped, protested; I begged him to stop, not

knowing if I meant it. The blows merged together, making me jump and jerk, shriek and squeal.

The fridge whirred away, oblivious. The air was suffocatingly thick with the sickly scent of banana, the tang of Ilya's sweat and the pungency of my sex. Still he continued, and my arse grew so sore it felt as if he were flaying the skin from it.

'Please,' I wailed, my voice rising to a near-scream. 'Please stop.'

'Shut up,' he hissed. 'Fucking shut up or we'll have the neighbours at my door.' And he grabbed his T-shirt from the side and crumpled it into my face.

I nuzzled into the cloth and bit down on a mouthful of cotton, smothering my cries to keep the tenants at bay. I wondered if this was it, if this was the point at which he was going to flip into psycho-mode.

My legs began to quiver. My knees were on the brink of buckling. I wanted to heave for breath but I didn't dare in case breathing turned to screaming. Maybe I should scream. Maybe I should shout 'cuttlefish' before he was too crazed to recognise it.

'Whore,' he kept saying, snatching words between gasps as his hand cracked away. 'Cheap – little – fucking – whore.'

Then on a vicious slap my right leg gave way and the boniest bit of my kneecap went whack, hard into the fridge door. A bolt of pain shot through me. I reared my head and sucked in a wheezing stream of air. The agony was so acute I couldn't even scream.

As suddenly as the slaps had started, they stopped.

'Shit,' said Ilya, panting softly. 'You OK, Beth? Christ, I felt that.' He rubbed the nape of my neck and tangled his fingers in my hair. 'You OK, babe?'

His tenderness shocked me more than the assault on my arse had done. We were friends, thank God. He was human again. I pressed my cheek to the Formica surface and moaned for more sympathy.

'You bastard,' I whispered. 'I think I've smashed my fucking patella.'

I cocked my leg backward and my knee made a weird popping sound and I felt something twang. 'Ow,' I said quietly, setting my foot back down. The pain mutated to a dull throb.

'You OK?' he asked again.

'Yeah,' I said. 'Just.'

'Good,' he replied. I heard the smile in his word then felt his prick at the mouth of my cunt, where my hot flowing juices were busy sluicing out banana-goo.

He dug his fingers into my thighs and then, slam, his cock was up and in me, sudden and stern. I gasped, the vast pleasure of his penetration overtaking all my aches and pains.

Pressing my hands against the tiled wall, I braced myself as he began gliding into my depths, his big solid shaft filling me with slow steady strokes. I felt the gentle roll of his pelvis as he ground his cock, holding deep when he was embedded, lingering long on each withdrawal. Ah, such sublime control.

He traced a soothing hand over the burning globe of my arse, balm to my singing nerve ends. The glowing heat of my cheek sank deeper into my body and fused with the fire being stoked in my groin.

Ilya's thumb drifted over to the base of my spine and he rubbed there, sliding up and down in the cleft of my buttocks.

'Ah, yes,' I cooed, and his thumb edged further down to my anus. He stirred tiny circles there, a languorous rhythm to match his languorous fuck.

Excitement shivered through me as, oh so gradually, he increased the pressure on my rear entrance. I felt my little hoop of muscle relax, dilating to his massage.

'Good,' he murmured. 'Very good.'

Then he withdrew his thumb and made an exaggerated sucking noise. I knew what was coming next and I was hot for it. When his thumb returned to my arsehole it was very wet, slippery with spittle. I groaned impatiently as he moistened me, and I rocked back on to his shunting cock, hungry to have that intrusive little digit in my arse.

'Hey, I'm the boss here,' he said, and he teased a while longer before giving me what I craved. 'There you go,' he breathed, as he pushed his thumb to the knuckle and plugged my orifice tight. 'Satisfied?'

I uttered a rumble of throaty pleasure. 'Nearly,' I replied.

Ilya gave a quick laugh, reaching his other hand around me and finding my clit. He vibrated fast and light on the sweet swollen bud. 'Better?' he demanded.

I gasped in answer, and he started corkscrewing his thumb in and out of my rectum. As my orgasm rushed in, Ilya threw all his energy into fucking me hard. I sobbed freely, banging my fist on the worktop as I came.

'Ah yes,' he growled, powering into my vaginal quivers. 'Oh, what a hot little whore I've found.'

He gave a few more hard ramming thrusts then, on a roar of ecstasy, he held still, his body shuddering against my buttocks, his prick twitching in my clenching sex.

He stayed there until his size began to dwindle, both of us dragging in fast uneven breaths. When he slipped out of me, I remained slumped over the work surface, unable to move. I was utterly done in. And when I felt his hands on the hem of my dress, which was up round my waist, I still couldn't move. I needed to bask a while longer in my orgasm-induced weakness.

Ilya wrinkled the dress into decency, tugging rather than smoothing it down.

He did it silently, abruptly, and it felt horrible – as sexy as tissues. He left the kitchenette and I was reluctantly tucking my breasts in my dress when he returned.

'Knickers,' he announced, and I looked over my shoulder to see the scrap of red and black hanging from one finger. 'For what they're worth,' he added. 'Bend over again.'

I sighed and leant across the Formica, allowing him to guide my feet into the leg holes.

'Thanks,' I said. 'You're a real gent.'

I swore softly when I felt my heel catch and heard the fabric rip. Ilya pulled the knickers up to my thighs then left me to finish the task. Depleted of strength and wanting nothing more than to sink into a comfy arm-chair, I followed him into the living room.

He was already picking up my leopard-print mac.

I stood there, sticky with banana and sex, my arse sore, knickers torn, dress stained, hair and make-up no doubt wrecked, and with a knee that was on its way to a great big bruise.

I felt dirt-cheap and thoroughly debased.

'You can see yourself out, can't you?' said Ilya, grinning faintly as he handed me my coat.

I was a whore to the very end, it seemed. I wasn't even allowed to breathe in the fumes of his post-coital cigarette.

'Sure,' I said, putting on a brave smile.

Just as I was about to leave, Ilya said, 'So did I take you anywhere close to saying cuttlefish?'

I stood in the flat doorway and shrugged, unsure of the wisest answer. 'I didn't like it much when you laid into my arse,' I replied. 'You were too aggressive. I told you before, I'm not into pain. And my knee –'

'Fine,' said Ilya breezily. 'I'll remember that: she doesn't want more pain; she wants more humiliation, more degradation. Is that right?'

'Suppose so,' I mumbled, unnerved by his cold assess-ment of my coy desires.

Ilya gave a quick laugh. 'Ah, Beth,' he said, tipping my chin up. 'Sooner or later, you're gonna wish you *were* into pain. Now go on. Get out. You look disgusting.'

115

Chapter Six

'*B*eth Bradshaw, you look like shit.'

'Thanks, Clare. I feel like shit.'

'No, I mean really shit. I know you've got a hangover but –' Clare touched a hand to my cheek and angled my face to a dusty shaft of sunlight. I winced and jerked away.

Clare grinned, smug as fuck.

'Well, well, well,' she said. 'I do believe that's a beard rash. What did I miss last night? Who've you been snogging? Jenny never said anything. Who –'

'It's nothing,' I said, going behind the bar. I pulled down the door of the glass-washer and a great cloud of wet steam hit my face. I almost keeled over. 'Just exfoliated too much this morning,' I added, rattling out a tray of gleaming pint glasses.

Clare's got a dark, boyish crop and trendy, not-much-of-a-handful tits, and, even when she's wearing, as she was then, just flared jeans and a skinny-fit vest, I always feel slightly chaotic and dishevelled in comparison. That morning, I felt like a positive tramp.

'Bollocks,' replied Clare, helping me stack upturned glasses on the shelf above. 'Who is he? You've been weird lately. You hardly come to the pub any more. You borrow my shoes. You –'

'Christ, Clare,' I snapped. 'Will you be a bit quieter with those fucking glasses? My head's killing me. I just haven't been to the pub for a while 'cos it's at your end of town and sometimes I like staying in. OK? I like having my own place. I like being in it. It's no big deal.'

'And you're a grouchy cow,' she said brightly. 'What do you want me to do next?'

'Get that banner down from the stage,' I replied. 'Please. Sweetheart. And then could you do the posters as well? Just bin 'em. Cheers, Clare.'

Clare wandered off.

My venue for Body Language is a small room above a pub. I don't pay for it. The management makes its money on the beer; I make my money on the door. At night, when I've got a gig on, I do my best to create a cosy lounge-cum-bar atmosphere: couple of sofas, dinky little tables with candles, a low stage, decorations dangling here and there. It looks good in a subterranean sort of way.

But the place just doesn't suit daylight. It looks stark and harsh. You can see the cracks, the peeling burgundy paint, the rough floor where varnish has worn away, the tops of buildings across the street.

That morning, I didn't suit daylight.

Owen came over to the bar and set down a stack of emptied ashtrays. 'Shall I make a start on the PA?' he asked. 'Or are you still waiting for Denny?'

Instinctively, I checked my wrist, cursing when I remembered my watch wasn't there. I'd already hunted around for it in the club, but to no avail. Which meant I'd left it at Ilya's, along with the feather boa. I'd have to call in on the way back, maybe apologise again for being a drunken lush.

'We'll give him a few more minutes,' I said. 'If he hasn't turned up by then, make a start and I'll give you

117

a hand. Just need to reload the washer first. Oh, and thanks, Owen. Above and beyond the call. You're an angel.'

He grinned. 'Good night last night, wasn't it?'

I could see Clare casting suspicious glances our way. 'No,' I wanted to shout. 'I am not shagging Owen.'

'Yeah, it was,' I said. 'Bit blurry in parts, though.'

'Likewise,' said Owen, and he ambled off to put chairs on the cleared tables in readiness for the arrival of the cleaner.

Very blurry in parts. Oh, the demon drink.

The previous night we'd done the final Body Language gig of the season – a poetry slam that ended up being pretty wild and boisterous. I usually shut up shop for several weeks in summer because people have got better things to do with those long, warm evenings. And so have I. It starts kicking in again in October when the students return, though I might do some low-key events in the run-up. But, basically, last night was the start of me being a bit less hectic – not exactly on holiday, just less hectic.

And that plus the fact that one of the bar staff was leaving – an Aussie guy called Paul who was truly lovely – had called for some serious after-hours drinking. It was a kind of celebration combined with my way of saying thanks to all those people who had mucked in over recent months.

So we'd ended up getting completely blasted and stayed up far too late for a Tuesday – apart from Clare, who'd had a cosy night in with Tom, which was why she was so annoyingly out of synch with the rest of us. Still, deep down I appreciated her being there, stepping in for Jenny who – 'Course I'll help out tomorrow, promise I will, Beth, I love clearing up' – couldn't quite make it out of duvet-heaven.

I didn't have the luxury of staying in bed – partly because I was the boss and partly because, for the very first time, I'd woken up in Ilya's bed and he'd kicked me out at the brutal crack of dawn.

Well, it had seemed like the brutal crack of dawn, but, in truth, dawn was probably cracking as I was staggering my way home, grinning inanely and thinking, Wouldn't it be great to call in on my lovely, sexy Ilya and say, 'Hi there, you gorgeous hunk of a man. Fancy a fuck?'

So that's what I did, more or less.

'Speth,' I slurred into his intercom.

'What?' came a sleepy voice.

'Beth,' I pronounced carefully. 'It's Beth. The luvverly Beth.'

'Christ,' came a fuzzy whisper.

Then buzz, push and I was stumbling up the dark stairs to his flat. I had Jenny's purple feather boa round my neck, which can't have looked too great with my trainers, pencil-skirt and body-warmer; but it was purple and it matched my fingernails so I'd insisted on the right to wear it and take it home for the night because it was so, soooh soft.

At the door of his flat, there was Ilya, tying the cord of a navy bathrobe and looking none too pleased.

'Don't do that,' I'd protested, crashing past him and clawing at his robe. 'I'm here now. Don't get dressed.'

Ilya unpeeled my clutching fingers and made me sit on his sofa. I heard him turn on the tap in his kitchenette.

'Drink this,' he said, returning with a full pint glass. 'It's water.'

'But I don't wanna drink water,' I complained, slinging the boa over one shoulder. 'Water's really boring. Water's the most boring drink in the world. Hasn't got any colour. Hasn't got any taste. An' it's free. 'Sgotta be shit if it's free. I like coloured, expensive –'

'Drink it,' he said firmly. 'Or I'll turf you out.'

'I'm drunk,' I declared, proud and belligerent. 'Aren't you gonna take advantage of me? Fuck me up the arse or something, like you keep on promis–'

119

'Drink it, Beth,' said Ilya, putting the glass in my hand.

So I did. Then Ilya led me into his bedroom and set about undressing me with patient efficiency while I stumbled, swayed and smooched at him. Then he put me in his bed, got in beside me, switched off the lamp, and said, 'Shut up, Beth, and go to sleep.'

I was out like a light.

Next thing I remember was the sound of phone, trilling into the thick, black fuzz of my mind.

'Yeah, right,' Ilya was saying. 'Got that, yep. Uh-huh. OK. Got that. Yep.'

I rolled over, squinting into a room full of cruel, filtered sunlight. Ilya, mobile phone crooked into his shoulder, was scribbling something down on a bit of paper.

Oh God. It was morning. What the hell was I doing here, in Ilya's bed? We never slept together, not literally. Far too intimate.

I pieced the night back together in rapid jigsaw fashion: tequila slammers; Ilya fastening a blue bathrobe; Jenny tripping over a cable when she went up on stage; Paul introducing me to the delights of curaçao and beer depth-charges; Ilya in a blue bathrobe trying to undress me; being loudly drunk with Helen in the bright, white, 24-hour shop; Ilya making me drink water; me buzzing his flat.

Oh God.

Had we had sex? No, impossible.

Ilya pressed off his phone and turned to me with a smile. 'How's your head?' he asked, his jade and blue eyes veiled with sleepiness.

I groaned. 'Oh God, I'm so, so sorry.' My voice was croaky. I had to cough to clear my throat. 'I was well out of order. What time did I call? Was it really late?'

'Three fifty-two,' he replied.

'Oh shit. Sorry. What time is it now?'

'Nearly eight.'

'Ohhh. I need three times as much sleep and I've got to go and clear up soon. Have you got any pills?'

'What sort of pills?'

'Anything. Just pills. Pills to make me feel better. Pills to put me to sleep. Pills to wake me up. I love pills. Anything.'

Ilya went away with a jaunty morning erection and returned carrying a glass of water, some stuff for colds and flu, and some stuff for headaches. I was quite touched. He cares, I thought.

'Cheers,' I said, and swigged back a couple of pills. 'Was I bad? Did I say anything embarrassing? I didn't release my inner child or tell you I loved you, did I?'

'Nah,' he said, rolling into me and sweeping a hand over my contours. 'But you did mention something about wanting a good hard fuck when you woke up.'

He thrust his hand between my legs and crushed it into my sex. I gave a loud groan of rejection.

'Liar,' I growled, and then suddenly he was tender, his lips touching mine in little fleeting kisses, his hand stroking lazily on my thigh and smoothing caresses over my buttocks.

'Liar,' I murmured.

He began edging down my body, sowing kisses from my neck to my breasts. I curved my hand to his shorn silky head as he licked my nipples into peaks, his unshaven jaw scouring lightly against my skin.

Sympathetic to my hangover, Ilya demanded nothing of me. I just lay there, sprawled on the pillows, moaning quietly while he teased me to sweet arousal and indulged me in sensation. We exchanged long, humid kisses, hence the stubble rash that Clare got so excited about later on; he sucked my fingers, my toes; he kissed the creases of my elbows and knees; he went down on me and lapped between my thighs and I climaxed, feeling as if I were in some underwater dreamscape.

And we fucked missionary-style, which, as far as I'm

121

concerned, is the only way to do it when you're hung-over. Too much moving about and your head's in danger of exploding. Ilya, supporting his weight on his arms, drove his prick deep – nice and slow building up to good and hard. I came for a second time and he quickly followed.

My headache didn't feel half so bad after that. Don't know if it was the pills or the orgasms. Didn't really care.

I lay there, feeling perfectly blissed out until the phone rang again. The shrill noise seemed to hit a nerve in my brain and my headache began pulsing into life once more.

'Yep,' said Ilya. 'On my way. Just waiting for the taxi.'

It was all a bit weird. I didn't know anyone who had a mobile phone. They just weren't part of my world. They were things other people had, busy people, family people, sad people trying to appear popular. And not only did Ilya have a mobile: he had it by his bed and took important-sounding phone calls first thing in the morning. Definitely not part of my world.

'Come on, Beth,' said Ilya. 'Shift your arse. I've got things to do, places to be.' Then he bounded out of bed, whipping the duvet from me as he did so. I cursed him and reluctantly slouched over to my clothes, which were draped over a chair back.

'Where're you off to, then?' I asked, trying to make the question sound conversational. 'Have you got a high-powered job or something? Are you secretly rich? Because, if you are, I think you should take me to a big, posh restaurant.' He was buttoning up a shirt, virtually dressed, and I'd just about managed to get my knickers on.

'Long story,' he replied, picking up the mobile. He punched in a number and ordered a taxi. He didn't say where he was going. He half left the room then returned to grab the bit of paper he'd written on.

Damn, I should have sneaked a look at it. It was getting

to annoy me, all this being kept in the dark. He knew what I did for a living. Why wasn't I allowed in on the secret of what he did?

It was fun, at first, being mysterious with each other and holding off on background details. But, ultimately, it was impractical. You've got to put in a hell of a lot of effort to stop your tongue from slipping out something humdrum about yesterday or tomorrow or once upon a time or one day soon. But Ilya was putting in that effort and somehow making it seem effortless.

Since my debut as his whore, over a fortnight ago, we'd got into a thing of just phoning each other up or calling round if we were in the mood for some steamy action.

We hadn't done anything seriously wild. It'd been more about fucking and exploring, with Ilya throwing in lots of dirty talk to make me feel cheap and horny.

On a couple of occasions when I'd phoned him, he'd said sorry, he was a bit busy at the moment. But, whenever I heard his voice, my pussy would tingle and I'd invariably drop everything unless I was booked in to do a voice-over. Sod feminine wiles and dignity: I was infatuated; I was horny; I wasn't going to pass up any chance to be with him.

My cunt was turning Pavlovian. The phone would ring or the door would buzz and, pow, there'd be a flash flood in my groin.

I thought about him constantly; I wanted him all the time.

And I was still desperately curious about him. But that curiosity was difficult to satisfy because, quite often, we simply didn't bother with conversations. Ilya might phone, tell me he'd got a hard-on and an hour to spare, or fifteen minutes, and then we'd spend that time in bed, on the floor, over a table, wherever.

If we did talk, it was usually about sex – experiences, fantasies, the power of desire. More recently I'd started to talk about me and my life, hoping Ilya would do the same.

No such luck. And when I tried to probe he'd just deflect all my questions or laugh and say things like 'Ah, now that's classified.' I'd asked him where he was from and he'd said, 'Mars.' It wasn't fair. I know we had this thing about not getting emotionally involved. But I was only asking everyday stuff like 'Where are you from? What do you do?' It didn't mean I wanted his babies.

So why was he so cagey?

Ilya came back into the bedroom, whirring an electric razor across his jaw. I was dressed. My clothes stank of stale tobacco.

'Can't do you a coffee,' he said. 'Sorry. I'm in a bit of a rush.'

'No problem,' I said, peering into a little mirror and rubbing the grime of make-up from under my eyes. 'I'm off now anyway.'

We swapped a peck on the lips and said our goodbyes.

I popped home for a quick freshen-up and change of clothes, and it was then I realised I was without my watch. It had to be either at the club or at Ilya's.

I hate being without a watch.

Once we'd sorted out the aftermath of the gig, Clare and I went for breakfast in a nearby trendy café, lamenting the death of our usual greasy spoon.

I fobbed her off about the stubble rash with some cock-and-bull story about a drunken snog with Paul. Well, he was jetting back to Sydney soon. He was a good enough alibi.

I didn't want to spill the beans about Ilya because it was all too strange.

Clare would only start asking questions like 'So when do we get to meet lover boy, then?' And I'd have to say, 'No, it's not like that: we don't socialise. We just have this thing going, sort of a sex thing, and sometimes it's just fucking and sometimes it's to do with fantasies and that's why I wanted to borrow your shoes because I got into the idea of playing the whore because deep down I have these fantasies about sleazy, slutty, sordid sex.' And Clare would look at me open-mouthed and the hip young waiter would set down my second cup of tea and smirk.

Or she'd want to know what he did and I'd have to say, 'I've no idea. I just know he's got a mobile phone and his hours aren't nine till five. But that's no big deal, is it? How many people do you know who've got a proper job? Not many.'

'Yeah, OK,' Clare would say, 'but how come you don't actually know what he does?'

And I'd have to say, 'Well, he doesn't really open up much about that kind of thing.'

'Well, what's he into?' she would say. 'What makes him tick?'

'Sex,' I'd have to say. 'Good, dirty sex.'

'But there's got to be something else.'

'Well, there isn't. Not that I know of.'

So I told Clare nothing. I paid for breakfast and we trundled off in separate directions.

I decided to drop by at Ilya's before going home to recover in a darkened room. I wasn't sure if he'd be in but his flat wasn't exactly out of my way. May as well try.

I didn't think much about it. I wasn't about to put demands on his time or his body. I just wanted to collect my watch and Jenny's boa, then go.

And when I reached the big stone steps, and another tenant was just leaving the house, I simply said 'Cheers' when he held the communal door open for me.

Would've been polite to buzz and announce myself, I thought, as I made my way up the brown-carpeted staircase. But what the hell: he was probably going to be out anyway. I could leave a note.

At Ilya's flat I heard movement – just footsteps passing in the hall behind his door. Good, I thought, he's in.

I knocked. There was no answer. I knocked again, louder.

'Ilya,' I called. 'It's Beth.'

There was complete silence.

'I've just come to collect my things,' I said through the wood. 'I'm not stopping. And I know you're in.'

After a lengthy pause, Ilya opened the door a wary fraction, his foot wedged behind it. He looked slightly flustered. I caught a glimpse of his fingers: they were covered in white powder. There was some white powder on his jeans, too.

'I left my watch here,' I began.

'You can't come in,' said Ilya. 'Sorry. I'm busy.'

'I don't need to come in,' I said. 'I just want –'

'Beth,' he replied, obviously trying to be patient. 'You've called at a bad time. Now go on. Beat it. Go and sleep off your hangover or something. You look like you need to.'

And he just closed the door, giving me another glimpse of those white-powdered fingers.

I couldn't sleep. My mind was in a whirl.

White powder, I thought. Therefore drugs. But I knew enough about smack and coke to be pretty certain that you didn't go coating your fingers in the stuff and spilling it down your jeans: expensive mistake.

So maybe he was cutting something pure with crushed paracetamol or baking soda or whatever. Baking soda, I thought. Now isn't that how you make crack cocaine? You play around with powders, potions and microwaves, then hey presto – you've got yourself a pretty nasty drug. Was Ilya running a little pharmaceuticals industry?

Oh God, maybe I was having a weird fling with a seriously hard drugs dealer. He looked East European, though he seemed as British as the next person. So maybe

126

he had connections abroad – bad connections with bad people who sold bad drugs.

But it didn't fit; there'd have to be more dubious characters hanging around him.

Maybe I was still a bit drunk and once again my imagination was working overtime. Yeah, probably that. Just a dormant shot of tequila waking up to say hello.

'Hello?'

'Hi, Beth. What's my favourite whore up to right now?'

'I'm on holiday. I'm flat on my back on the living-room floor, lying in a sunbeam, listening to Galaxie 500 and talking to you on the phone. In fact, if you stand by your window and I lift my leg up, you might be able to see my foot. Can you?'

''Fraid not,' said Ilya. 'No, nothing. Ah, saw something move then. Anyway, you don't sound busy, so I've got something for you.'

'My watch,' I replied. 'Have you found it?'

'Yes, but I've got something else.'

'A purple feather boa.'

'Better than that.'

'Hmm. Let me see,' I teased. 'Couldn't possibly be a raging hard-on, could it?'

'Got it in three.'

'Well, well. What a surprise.'

'Do you fancy popping over to collect? I've got something in mind I think you're really gonna love.'

'Oh yeah?' I said. 'Will it hurt?'

'Maybe. But only a bit.'

'OK then. I'll be there in two ticks.'

'Strip to your underwear,' said Ilya, as I sauntered into his living room.

He was rolling down the last window blind. Splintered sunlight gleamed through the bamboo shafts. I glanced

127

around, searching for something to explain the white-powder weirdness, but saw nothing.

Should I ask him about it? I wondered. But there didn't seem much point: Ilya never gave me straight answers.

So I undressed, piling my outer clothes on to the sunken armchair, my pussy already juicing. I'd ask him later. I reckoned he owed me some kind of explanation.

Ilya surveyed my near-naked body without a flicker of interest. My underwear was good – black high-leg knickers with a hint of lace, and bra to match. Too good, I thought, deciding there and then to invest in something more appropriate to my slut-self.

'Lovely,' said Ilya blandly. 'Now get down on your hands and knees.'

As instructed I dropped on to all fours, a couple of feet in front of the sofa.

I twisted my head round, trying to catch sight of him as he moved around the shabby, sun-warmed room.

'Now remember the rule, Beth,' he said. 'Anything you don't like, just give me the codeword and I'll stop. OK?'

I nodded, feeling a pang of sweet apprehension. I took Ilya's reminder as a sign that I was in for some major torment. But whatever it was, I imagined I could handle it.

'I'm going to blindfold you,' announced Ilya, approaching with a tartan winter scarf.

I gave a tiny giggle of eagerness and tilted my head high, allowing him to fix the band in place. The wool was very warm on my skin and Ilya took his time to secure it, adjusting it so my nostrils were free, tightening the knot at the back of my head and questioning me all the time: 'Can you see anything? Is that better? Can you breathe OK? Is that too tight?'

When I was shrouded in darkness, nothing happened. Ilya fell silent. His hands were no longer touching me. I wasn't sure where he was standing. I felt giddy with expectancy, and my sex bubbled with little dancing pulses. I adored it when Ilya took control.

The scarf was wrapped either side of my head, muffling the sounds about me. It pressed in on my eyes and squashed the tip of my nose. When I cast my eyes down, there was a tiny hole of light. Depending on how I turned, I could see the flecked beige carpet or parts of my hands with purple-polished nails and the big violet ring on my right middle finger.

I raised my head and twisted it, trying to look up with a lowered gaze, but the angle made the hole of light vanish. And anyway, all that straining to gain a glimpse made my eyeballs ache. So I just accepted my blindness.

Nervously, I waited for Ilya's touch. My ears, sharpened by my lack of sight, yet dulled by the covering scarf, were greedy for every sound.

At irregular intervals, the noise of passing cars rose up from the streets below and in through the open windows. There was a hammer chiselling away at stone: someone was having repairs done to the front of their house. A rooftop seagull called out and its feathered friends took up the sound like a football chant. They all squawked away to a jangling pitch before falling suddenly silent.

Inside the room, when there were no cars on the road, I could just make out the ticking of a clock and the fridge humming in the adjoining kitchenette. Still no sound of Ilya.

I felt strangely disembodied. It was as if my limbs had all disappeared because I couldn't see them. I was nothing but the inside of my head. I was losing physicality.

A car door slammed outside and there was a brief exchange of male laughter and voices although I couldn't hear what was said.

The clock ticked away. Come on, Ilya. Touch me.

I half feared he'd left the room. Perhaps he was on his bed, reading a book or something, and amusing himself with thoughts of how long I'd stay there before daring to protest.

A bus went by along the bottom road – the number seven, the only bus to pass this way – and it made that little 'poof' noise that buses do as they change gear or whatever.

Then – ah – a touch, the softest of touches drifting across my back, making goosebumps prickle. I inhaled sharply and held the air in my lungs, recognising the velvet lightness as it swept over my skin: Jenny's feather boa.

My body, which had all but slipped away from me, sprang to sensation under its whispering caress. I felt the existence of my back more acutely than any other part of me. Then I felt my left wrist and hand as the feathered length tickled a path across me there. I released my breath in a murmur of delight.

I could feel the weight changing on the floor as Ilya moved. The boa trailed over my calves. I had legs now. In fact, I had my whole body back again, because it was singing in anticipation of the next touch. The nerves beneath my skin were set on red alert, ready to react immediately to the merest hint of contact.

For a while I felt nothing but dust motes. Then my feet exploded to a silken breath. Wispy feathers moved across my arched insteps and brushed the bottoms of my toes.

Then nothing again.

And then the back of my neck, a line of velvet fronds floating over my skin under and across my collarbone, then shivering away via the downy pit of my arm.

Not once did Ilya's flesh touch mine. Everything was feathers: across my lips, on my thighs inner and outer, snaking up around my arm, sliding under my belly and waist. I drew quick breaths as the feathers fell, always unexpectedly, and sighed pleasure as they dragged gossamer tracks over my skin, and left desire tingling in their wake.

Waiting for those touches to begin and end was like a torture designed by angels.

And the whole thing made me wary because Ilya wasn't into soft sex and gentle titillation. I reckoned he was up to something. Maybe he was trying to lull me into a false sense of security before subjecting me to some dirty degradation. The thought made my sex bloom open like some flower on time-lapse photography.

Then the boa came to a halt. Released from Ilya's guiding hands, it lay draped across my back. After all that teasing, the motionless feathers gained a weight completely out of proportion to what they were.

I felt Ilya's touch on my buttocks, then on my knickers, front and back. In one swift movement, he scrunched the fabric into a narrow band and gave a sharp upward tug.

I yelped as the stretched material split the flesh of my vulva and sliced into the gap of my arse. He jerked again, ramming the crinkled gusset hard into me. Then he began sawing back and forth, running the fabric along my moist groove and abrading my clit.

'What's with all this nice underwear?' he asked. 'I thought you wanted to play the slut, Beth. Why don't you wear whorish knickers like before? Cheap, gaudy bits of nothing. They suit you better, don't you think?'

'Ow,' I said as once more he slammed the crumpled knickers high. 'Yes. I was going to get some soon anyway. I swear.'

Ilya released his hold on my knickers.

'I don't want to see these again,' he said, hooking a thumb either side of the waistband. 'OK?'

'Yes,' I breathed.

And then he jerked the fabric down, leaving the black shiny cotton creased in the crook of my knees. I heard him move further away.

'Mmm,' said Ilya, and my sense of him surveying my sex was so strong that it seemed almost tangible.

In the darkness of my blindfold, that unseen gaze had

a magnifying power. My cunt swelled to a huge hungry pout: it swelled between my legs as blood pumped into my groin and puffed the lips apart; and it swelled in my mind until I could think of nothing but my cunt, hanging glossy and open below the line of my arse.

Everything else about me disappeared; my body ebbed away again. I was all cunt, inside and out. I was slick, scarlet flesh quivering with need.

Somewhere in the distance a car started up with a long whinnying sound. When the car drove away, I strained to hear the clock ticking, barely audible through the ear-covering scarf.

Ilya touched me. I groaned.

'Greedy bitch,' he murmured approvingly.

His fingers skimmed my outer labia, stirring the fringe of silky hair, making my arousal shoot. Then they dipped deeper to glide along my plump-sided inner crevice where I was so deliciously gorged with moisture. He rimmed circles just within the opening of my vagina, teasing out more wetness and warmth.

'Ah, Beth,' he said in a low voice. 'You're always so wet for it. Your pussy's always so ripe.' With his finger-tips, he smoothed my juices backward, up and through the furrow of my buttocks to the pursed mouth of my arse. 'It's getting predictable,' he continued, sliding up more cream.

My excitement sizzled as Ilya stirred damply around my rosebud hole. Then he drove in the length of his finger, making me moan soft and deep.

'So you know what I'm going to do to you . . .' he breathed, cramming a second finger alongside the first. 'Don't you?'

He moved his two buried digits in a few quick twists, and then they were skewering in and out of me, scissoring open and shut with an intensity so rapid and wild that a massive pleasure surge streaked through my body and I could only answer with a howl.

'Ah, you're so hot for it, aren't you?' he said, working away at my arsehole.

I uttered a stream of garbled pleasure, feeling him kneel between my calves. Then he doubled that pleasure by inserting two more fingers into the liquid centre of my pussy. I groaned and gasped as, with both hands, Ilya plunged into me back and front.

He matched his rhythm, shoving in both sets of fingers at the same time: Then he started to alternate, shunting in, out, back, front, back, front.

'So where shall I stick my cock today?' he rasped. 'Arse or cunt? Arse or cunt?'

'Oh God,' I said softly. I knew the choice wasn't mine.

Anal sex had been on the agenda right from our first phone call. And though I was keen to experiment, and though his fingers felt good inside me, now that the dirty deed was imminent, doubts started to crowd into my mind. It was going to hurt. His prick would not slot into my arse the way it slotted into my cunt. It was going to hurt. I'm not into pain. I'd already told him that.

Ilya pulled all of his fingers out of me.

I felt him stand and heard him undress. My body was burning up with eagerness and fear. Part of me wanted him to delay, to put off the inevitable for as long as possible; and part of me wanted him to get on with it then it would be over and done with, and I'd know the truth of how good or bad it was.

'I need better access than this,' said Ilya, tugging at the knickers round my knees.

I shifted position so he could remove them, then he pushed my bra up so the cups and underwire were bunched above my tits. I was getting to realise he preferred me with a bit of clothing on rather than completely naked. Nudity was obviously too pure, too much like lovers. A scrap of rucked-up underwear or a raised skirt made me look cheaper, tartier, greedier.

My breasts hung free and Ilya tweaked gently on my

nipples, pulling them floorward and stretching my flesh to points. I moaned, lustful and anxious.

Then I felt his hands on my scarf blindfold and he pulled the knot a little tighter, making it press on the tip of my nose again.

A floorboard creaked on the far side of the room. I froze.

'Who's there?' I asked. 'There's someone here, isn't there?' In a panic, I reached for my blindfold.

Ilya grabbed my hand to stop me. 'Don't be silly, Beth,' he soothed. 'It's just me and you. All alone.' He guided my hand back on to the carpet.

I listened and I could hear nothing. Ilya wafted the boa from my back. There was no one there. It was just the house groaning, the way houses sometimes do.

'Spread your knees wider,' said Ilya, and I did. 'Now don't move. I'm going to put some music on.'

'Oh Christ,' I complained as he moved away. I didn't need an accompanying soundtrack, especially when – judging from his scanty CD collection – it was probably going to be classical or heavy rock. Maybe anal sex was going to hurt so much that he wanted to drown out my screams with a guitar solo.

The music started, churchy and dramatic. I recognised it from the film *Rollerball* – Bach's *Toccata*, I think. Scary film. Scary music.

I sensed Ilya return. Seconds later, his fingers pressed into the crack of my buttocks and they were full of cool silky moisture.

He was using lube on me.

This was it: crunch time. My heart raced and I feared my bottle might desert me. But the lubricant calmed me; it felt so good.

With slippery fingertips, Ilya smeared the stuff generously up and down, lingering over my anus, rubbing steadily.

Then, with delicious ease, he slithered in a couple of fingers.

'Ahhh,' I said in a long sigh of pleasure. Then 'Ahhh' again as his two digits squirmed and pushed, greasing me richly within. I could feel myself loosening to his internal massage – and then a wider stretch on my tunnel made me gasp and squeal.

'What are you doing?' I implored as the doleful organ music boomed. 'Tell me. Please. Oh, tell me.'

'Three fingers,' he replied in a husky murmur.

'Oh God,' I cried, and he twisted those compacted fingers in and out of my tightness, adding a tinge of pain to the delicious invasion.

'Do you like it?' he enquired.

'Yes,' I wailed, and I had to drop forward to lean on my forearms because my body was crumbling from all the worried delight. I pressed my forehead to the ground, tilting my arse high for him and moaning constantly.

A sudden harder stretch on my walls made me cry out.

'Four fingers,' announced Ilya. 'Two from my right hand; two from my left. And feel that? Now I'm really opening you up, Beth. Pushing you wide, right and left, making a gap between my fingers.'

Christ, did I feel it. I mewled and gulped for air, and he kept on working his fingers, bringing them together then apart, like miniature bellows fixed high in my arse. His knuckles bounced at my tender entrance, forcing my muscles to a fierce expansion.

I thought about elastic bands, imagined them being tested for tension, and I half feared he might break me, snap me, because the stretch was so huge. I cried out wildly, overcome with terror, begging him to stop, begging him to continue.

'Tell me what you want, Beth,' hissed Ilya. 'Tell me, you –'

'Do it,' I barked urgently. 'Fuck my arse, now. Please, now, now, now.'

And God, did I mean it. The craving was violent and furious. I felt so wide open for him.

'Dirtier,' he urged. 'Talk dirtier.'

'Oh Jesus,' I complained, but this was no time for modesty. 'I want your cock in my arse,' I gasped. 'Rammed. Your cock rammed in my arse.'

'Say "dick",' he ordered, plunging his fingers over and over.

'Oh please, Ilya,' I implored. 'Dick! Dick!' And I fell in love with the word right there and then because it sounded so male, so deliciously coarse, dirty and obscene. 'I want your dick in my –'

'Up!' he snapped. 'Not in. Up.'

I spluttered and protested. Christ, would I ever get it right?

'I want your dick up my arse,' I panted, pronouncing the words as best I could. 'I want your fucking dick . . . up my fucking –'

'You foul-mouthed slut,' said Ilya, snatching his fingers from me.

I heard him fiddling with a rubber as he shuffled up close. Then I felt his warm muscular thighs on my buttocks and the head of his cock pressing at my anus, so stout and powerful.

With a slow push, he entered me. His glans prised apart the swollen hoop of my arsehole and then, in a sudden sweet rush, the rest of him just slipped into me until he was sunk to the hilt, lodged solid and groaning deeply.

I let out a banshee wail of delirium. It was the most savagely beautiful penetration I had ever taken in my whole life.

At the root of his cock, my sphincter was as tight as a noose.

During one of Bach's lulls, I thought I heard a noise

136

close by – very quiet, like the scuff of shoe on carpet. Again I had a fear we were not alone. A car roared by below the window. Again I reassured myself it was just imagination; the blindfold was making my hearing too acute.

Ilya began easing back, and the glide of his withdrawing shaft just set my opening on fire. I begged him not to move.

'Wait,' I pleaded. 'Stay deep. Let me . . . let me get used to it.'

And he obliged. He held still while I gasped away, trying to accustom myself to the sensation of being so completely stuffed, of having such a dense meaty mass pulsing in my snug little passage.

I had to open my eyes and peer down at the aperture of light between my nose and scarf, just to bring myself back to earth. With my forehead to the floor, I could see only a strip of carpet, Ilya's knees, Ilya's dark hairy thighs, and, when I twisted right and left, I could see my feet. They seemed miles away.

Steadied and ready for some thrusting, I moaned and rocked forward. Ilya took the cue and grasped me just below my hips, splitting my cheeks wide with the heels of his hands. Smoothly, he drew back before sinking into me once more, deep and then deeper.

What bliss, what wicked, brutal bliss, as again and again he plunged all that rock-solid flesh into my arse.

'Oh, yes,' he rasped, picking up speed. 'You lovely, dirty bitch.'

Each searing thrust took me closer to my peak.

'Can you take it harder?' he demanded thickly, not waiting for a reply.

'Yes,' I sobbed, as he rammed in shorter, faster strokes. 'Yes.'

My whole body was glutted with near-orgasm. It was stashed in every cell, screaming out for me to press the go button. I reached back for my clit and a couple of nudges were enough to hoist me heavenward. And, as I came, I shoved a bunch of fingers into my soaked pussy, giving my muscles something to shudder on.

With a shock, I registered the feel of his prick there, bulging into my wet vaginal walls and sliding against my fingers. It gave me a massive thrill. I could actually feel him inside me, feel his cock with my fingers rather than feel his cock with an orifice. We were touching each other inside my body. *My* body, I thought, and the intimacy of it all nearly lifted the top of my head off.

'Ah yes,' urged Ilya, his hips slapping at my buttocks. 'Fuck yourself, babe.'

So I did, crying openly as I came down from one crisis and hurtled towards another. Ilya was pounding furiously and so was I. Finger-fucking and arse-fucking made me a whirlpool of ecstasy. My bones turned to jelly. I felt like I was dissolving, losing substance. Blinded by the scarf, it was as if I only existed because of the beat hammering in my groin and the violence in my arse. I was pure sensation.

When I climaxed, the explosion was nuclear. For a moment, I swear I almost believed in God.

Ilya had been pacing himself and, as my second burst tore through me, he began thrusting without restraint, grunting until he came with one deliciously sexy, pleasure-soaked groan. I felt the swell and judder of his cock with my fingers.

He stayed inside me, easing himself to and fro, making little murmurs of contentment as I rubbed his slackening erection through the walls of my vagina. Semi-hard, he slid out of me. My arse felt tender and scorched.

'Mmm,' said Ilya, and his lips printed a kiss on one buttock. 'Good?'

'Ouch,' I said in answer. 'Can I take the blindfold off yet?'

'Er,' replied Ilya. 'I'm not sure. Maybe I like you like that.'

'Please,' I said, reaching back for the scarf.

Ilya gently clasped my wrist. 'Hey, I haven't given you permission yet.'

'Please,' I laughed. 'It's hot and itchy.'

'Go on then,' he said, and I pushed the blindfold up and off, then slumped on to my side, curling my body in a half-foetal position.

'Ouch,' I said again.

Ilya lay opposite me, bringing his knees up to match mine. Our faces were close and we stayed that way, our bodies like inverted commas.

'Is "ouch" good?' he enquired, brushing the tip of my nose with his.

'I think so,' I replied, jerking my head back from his Eskimo kiss because I reckoned it was just too heart-warming. 'I'll let you know for definite the next time.'

Ilya grinned. 'Did it make you feel degraded and humiliated and sluttish?'

'Afraid not.' I smiled. 'Not even with all your dirty talk. I'm getting used to it.'

'Thought you might be,' he replied. He reached for my hand and gently sucked on the tips of my fingers.

'You must be losing your touch,' I said.

Ilya released my fingers and laughed loudly before placing a kiss on my nose.

'Oh, sometimes you're just too damn sweet,' he said, rolling on to his back. 'Makes me feel like a complete and utter bastard. You've no idea what I've just set in motion, Beth. No idea.'

He was right. I didn't have a clue what he was on about.

Chapter Seven

*I*lya obviously had some wicked plan in mind; something nasty and debasing, I reckoned, to challenge my limits and stretch the tension of our game.

I found that pretty daunting because I wasn't sure what my limits were and I didn't think Ilya knew either.

We were playing a kind of sexual brinkmanship and the stakes were high.

Words like 'no' or 'ouch, too painful' or more likely 'ugh, too demeaning' counted for nothing in our deal. There was only one word to signal 'stop that' and it came with a heavy penalty because in the same breath it also meant 'stop' as in the end, finito, game over, goodbye.

If Ilya pushed too far, then he'd lose everything. So every push was a risk; a careful balancing of nudging the limits against the threat of collapse.

But I was smitten. I was ripe for exploitation. I could see how this game of ours might get seriously unbalanced.

I tried to think up a challenge Ilya would enjoy in order to put things on a more even keel. But I couldn't. When a man likes the idea of something, he just goes for it. Women have a much tougher time, even modern, clued-up women like me. I like cheap and sleazy. I like humiliation and abuse. I like fantasies of forced sex and being made powerless. But I don't like admitting to it.

I could think of plenty of challenges Ilya would hate. I could play the bitch: make him squirm and beg for mercy; drip candle wax on him; flog him with a belt. Or I could take his anal virginity with my vibrator.

But I'd hate it as well. I wanted Ilya to be my real man through and through. I wanted him to keep on dominating me, making me sluttish and getting me to do things I'd never done before.

Besides, I didn't want to take the risk of him calling cuttlefish. My fear was that, if the going got tough, he'd be prepared to say it. I wasn't.

Ilya didn't realise it, but he had the power to make me do anything. Cuttlefish was buried deep in my body. I wasn't going to say the word that would finish us.

I was so glad he didn't realise it, because that's where my power lay – in Ilya's constant awareness that, if he went over the top, I just might crack and cry out the dreaded C-word.

The implications of what we were doing preyed on my mind, as did Ilya's secretiveness.

I'd quizzed him about his powdery fingers and his refusal to allow me into his flat. He'd just said he'd been doing a spot of DIY when I called – real DIY, not wanking – and that his flat had been a tip and he'd just had an accident with some Polyfilla. I didn't believe him.

But I didn't feel in a position to demand a better explanation. While his strangeness still disturbed me, I was gradually accepting the fact that Ilya preferred to keep himself to himself and that I simply had to go along with that.

But then my life hit warp-factor eight, as it's prone to do, and my Ilya worries had to take a back seat.

* * *

It was mid-afternoon and I was at the desk in my poky, cluttered office, half listening to my answerphone messages.

There weren't many – or not many that mattered. I jotted down a couple of numbers I needed to get back to and shuffled at some paperwork.

There wasn't much to do. When Body Language is in full swing then I usually pop into the office daily to check my messages and I need to spend a fair few afternoons there per week, organising gigs, publicity, doing the accounts and stuff. But in summer, there's no need.

I didn't want to hang around and probably wouldn't have done except that the barmaid had said Shaun – big boss manager of the pub – wanted to see me.

My body ached from too much fucking. Ilya had called on me earlier that day, announcing that he had to go away for a while. He'd said he wanted to get in credit, dirty-sex-wise, to keep him going until he returned.

He was always so bloody flippant. And he was always doing disappearing acts.

Sometimes he'd let me know beforehand. Other times he'd just vanish, and it would only dawn on me that he'd gone because his flat was still and dark.

I really missed him when he was away. I couldn't imagine him giving me a second thought.

And wherever he went and whatever he got up to was clearly none of my business.

'Been away?' I'd ask, trying to be casual.

'Visiting friends,' he'd reply.

'Anywhere nice?' I'd say.

And then he'd say 'London' or 'not really' or 'yeah, it was OK'.

End of conversation.

He was, however, starting to reveal other snippets about himself: that he was British born and bred, father Bulgarian, mother Italian. So that helped explain his raw, dark beauty. The family had anglicised the name. Fair enough. He also said he was a builder by trade, that he'd come to Brighton looking for work but to no avail.

I didn't believe that one. Like a lot of things he told me, it just didn't ring true.

And on top of all the practical information I was lacking, there was also something about him as a person I couldn't reach. There seemed to be a kind of wall around him, as if he would never allow anyone to get too close.

At first, I'd thought, Well maybe that's a good thing: it fits with the game-plan of us being purely physical, free from heartfelt attachments. But on my part it was starting to feel strained, like a one-night stand on a tape loop. It was unnatural.

Ilya could still be tender and affectionate, but it was only surface tenderness, little more than a moment of his thinking I was cute or something. He was good at being emotionally remote. I wasn't, although I was doing my best to make it seem as if I were.

I wasn't going to reveal that this strange thing we'd got going meant far more to me than it did to him.

I was hooked. I was hooked on him and hooked on the game. Ilya occupied my every thought. It was obsessive, but not in the way falling in love is obsessive. It wasn't heady and floaty and euphoric. Oh, it was exciting, thrilling and all-consuming, but it wasn't celebratory like new love.

Our game was undercut with a bleak, intuitive knowledge: we weren't heading for blissful happiness and fireworks popping in the sky, but more towards a dark, dangerous implosion.

I told myself I preferred it that way.

I emailed some people to confirm gigs I'd got lined up for October, added a few more addresses to my mailing-list database, then abused the privilege of having a phone that the pub pays for – bills, rental, the lot. They do it because I'm good for business and they like to keep me sweet. I don't exploit it too much, but an occasional free natter doesn't hurt.

So I phoned Paul in Sydney for a quick hello. He said it was a cold winter's night and he wished he were still in Brighton. Then I phoned Jen, who had some advice to dole out about Martin, which made me feel irritated and horribly guilty. We chatted away until the expected rat-tat-tat sounded on my office door.

'Well, thanks for your help,' I said in my efficient phone voice just as Shaun poked his head round the door. 'I'll get back to you nearer the time. Goodbye.'

'Cheapskate,' came Jenny's voice as I hung up.

'Not interrupting, am I?' asked Shaun, entering.

'No, no problem,' I replied, swivelling to face him. 'I'm all yours.'

Shaun, dressed in his usual shirtsleeves and waistcoat, went to perch his arse on the small window sill. He's only a bit of a kid – barely out of pimples – but he manages the pub and likes to think he's a man of the world.

'I've got a proposition for you,' he said after we'd got through some small talk. He crossed his ankles and thrust his fists deep in his trouser pockets. 'How do you fancy doing a few more club nights? Maybe something a little different from the usual? You see, I've been doing a bit of thinking and –'

'Ooo, dangerous,' I teased.

He smiled uncertainly. 'I'm keen to push it,' he went on. 'Broaden the market, pull in more punters. And I know you can do it, Beth. You're just the person. You've got the contacts, the enthusiasm. You're a smart girl. And we're already halfway there with Body Language. It's getting a good reputation. But, like I say, that's only halfway there.'

I frowned at him. 'I'm not sure I follow,' I said. 'What've you got in mind?'

144

'To be basic,' he said, standing up and loosening his collar. 'More body.'

'Can you be *more* basic?' I said. 'Are you saying you want me to increase the amount of performance-art stuff? Because I won't. I'm cutting down on that side of things. Doesn't work. I've struggled enough trying to find decent artists. My idea was to make next year more language, more spoken word. People –'

'Yeah, but that's all smart-arse student stuff, isn't it?' said Shaun, propping an elbow high on the filing cabinet. 'Just . . . literary wank.'

I gave a small incredulous laugh. 'Shaun, you haven't got a clue,' I said. 'Have you actually noticed what goes on at my gigs? It's not full of precious, po-faced twats going, "Hail the great author and wasn't that deep." Jesus, get up to speed. People come along. They listen to some interesting stuff. They have a laugh. They drink beer.'

'Exactly!' said Shaun, slicing his hand at the air. 'But not in summer! You see, the way I look at it, you've got your audience – a young crowd, open-minded – but when term finishes they're thin on the ground. So you expand your catchment area. You spice things up. You bring 'em in and you grab 'em by the balls.'

I sighed heavily, hardly listening as Shaun burbled on about new ventures, chasing the market, competitive edge and loads of other bollocks.

I didn't really know what he was getting at, except that it sounded like he wanted me to work harder. He'd never stuck his nose into my club before. He just ran the pub and left me to it.

'So what've you got in mind for these extra nights?' I asked. 'If you give me something a bit more concrete then maybe I can think about it.'

'Sex,' said Shaun, walking over to the window. 'To be basic, sex.'

I had to bite my tongue to stop myself asking if he'd ever had it.

'Sex sells,' he continued, perching his arse on the sill again. 'If you do some sexy gigs, and I mean really sexy, then we can maybe keep the bar takings steady. Probably increase them. And it'll be great publicity for –'

'What?' I scoffed. 'You want me to put on lap-dancing shows or something? Like that place in Hove? Do you seriously think –'

'No, no, not that kind of sexy,' said Shaun. 'Something more, you know, younger, trendier. Something . . .' He trailed off.

'What?' I said impatiently. 'Something what?'

'I don't know exactly.' He frowned. 'But nothing too sleazy. Something women'll go for as well as blokes. But you know, still hot.'

I laughed to myself, wondering if I should mention that I'm a woman and I go for sleazy and, yeah, it's still hot. 'How hot?' I asked. 'Don't you need a special licence for hot?'

Shaun shrugged. 'Depends on what you have in mind.'

'Me? I've got nothing in mind. This is your idea, Shaun.'

He nodded thoughtfully, then drew a deep breath to make his chest big and important.

'OK then,' he said. 'To be practical, I'd say live sex acts are off the menu. But other than that, it's up to you. Within reason, of course.'

I was too stunned to answer. He was obviously pretty serious about this. I couldn't see the point.

Brighton's got more than its fair share of sexy goings-on. Apart from the massive gay scene with its bars, discos, strippers and cabaret, there's a whole host of other stuff. Club nights spring up all over the place – for fetish-fiends or cross-dressers or lipstick-dykes, or just for people who want to party in a spiced-up atmosphere.

Which is fine, but it's not what I do. I run a quirky little arts club.

Shaun carried on.

'Look at it this way,' he said. 'It'll consolidate the image of your club. You don't exactly do mainstream things, do you? So we build on that. We establish Body Language as something more underground. Risky. People around here'll get off on that. They like to think they're part of a scene which pushes things.'

'I already push things,' I argued. 'Christ, I don't get writers in who tell nice stories about . . . about breakfast in Tuscany, do I?'

'See?' said Shaun triumphantly. 'There you go again. Writers. It's just people reading on stage. You need to broaden your base. The club's got to get bigger. Bigger and better.'

I shook my head despairingly. In my book, bigger doesn't always mean better, and I wasn't in the mood for investing lots of time and energy in some new angle – especially when it centred on sex and risks. There was enough of that going on in my private life. Besides, I was happy with my own ideas for the club's future, and going at my own pace. My ambition isn't of the driving variety. It comes and it goes.

'Only otherwise,' said Shaun, 'we might need to rethink the arrangement we've got. You know, you having this office and everything.'

I narrowed my eyes at him. 'Are we heading into blackmail territory now?'

'Course not.' Shaun smiled, standing up. He began making his way to the door. 'Have a think, Beth. See what you can come up with and let me know. OK? I'd like to get it up and running pretty soon.'

'Yeah, I'll try,' I said despondently, spinning my chair round to the desk.

'Oh, and, Beth,' said Shaun, poking his head back in the room, 'phone bill was a bit steep last time. Keep an eye on your calls, will you?'

* * *

For a short while, I flirted with the idea of trying to find another venue for Body Language.

But I knew I'd never get a setup as good as The Hog. It cost me nothing; it was central; I was established there; and everyone knew how to find it. I didn't want another venue.

And, anyway, maybe Shaun had a point; maybe it would be good if I broadened my base. But it was a pain in the arse, especially since the pressure was on for me to get it all going quickly. I usually have gigs lined up months in advance, not weeks.

Reluctantly, I started to bounce some ideas around in my head.

It was tricky at first. I couldn't get past thinking about the gay and fetish scenes, and I started to get jealous of both. Wouldn't it be great, I thought, if there was a straight scene? Not straight-straight. Kinky-straight. Something for people who wanted a good sexy time, but weren't necessarily into playing at dungeons or whatever people did in fetish clubs.

And while I know the whole world is basically one great big straight scene, there still isn't enough for women. And I don't mean muscle-men with bad haircuts and toothpaste smiles, prancing around in bow ties and jockstraps. I mean sexy, sleazy, dirty, good – with just a zing of furtiveness to add to the thrill.

But the guys have colonised all that stuff.

I began to imagine a sort of slut scene, where you could be proud of your taste for filth. Perhaps with specialist cafés and bookshops where you could hang out, buy some smut, and nobody'd bat an eyelid. And there'd be clubs, bars and saunas, and you could go there in search of cheap easy sex. You wouldn't have to be single. You could go with the love of your life and pick up a third person, a fourth, an orgiastic truckload. Whatever. It wouldn't be a problem. Purely recreational. And everyone'd be friends afterwards.

148

Bi people would be part of it too. And I wouldn't be against queers, dykes, trannies and fetish-heads joining in either. But they've got their own parties and it might get confusing.

Dream on, Beth.

You've a gig to sort out, not your ideal world.

I reckoned a cabaret-style mish-mash of dancers, strippers, maybe someone doing some readings, would be good. Nothing too heavy or debauched. Just something slightly risqué and fun. Something to test the waters.

Maybe I'd add a glam-kitsch element to it. And maybe I could get one of Brighton's fetish shops to man a stall in the foyer.

The more I thought about it, the more enthusiastic I became.

And I always know someone who knows someone. So a few days and several phone calls later, it was starting to shape up.

Then Ilya returned.

He phoned me one afternoon when I'd just got in from meeting a couple of performers. I was buzzing about the gig and so I told him about it.

'Sounds great,' he said. 'I didn't realise your work was quite so interesting. What are you doing tonight? Are you free? Because I've got plans to use and abuse you.'

Now the thing was, I'd arranged to meet Jenny and Clare that evening. They were going to help me out. We were going to have a brainstorming session over a few beers to see if we could add to my ideas.

But Ilya was back. I hadn't seen him for days. He wanted to use and abuse me.

So I said, 'Yeah, free as a bird.' I wasn't proud of myself, but how could I resist?

'Great,' replied Ilya. 'Have you ever watched a porn film?'

'No,' I laughed. 'Never.'

'Well, you're going to see a scorcher tonight,' he said. 'A real scorcher.'

'Oh yeah?' I said. 'I thought you were going to use and abuse me.'

'Oh, I am, babe,' he said smoothly. 'Trust me. And when you wake up tomorrow, the word "humiliation" will have a whole new meaning for you.'

I climbed the stairs to Ilya's flat, full of trepidation and nervous lust.

I had no idea what was in store for me, but I was keen to pop my porn-film cherry.

Maybe we were going to act out some scene from it. Maybe it was to make me so horny that I would succumb to whatever badness Ilya had planned. But then I didn't need a video to do that.

Ilya, grinning mischievously, ushered me into his flat. I wanted to embrace him, squeeze his juicy little arse and kiss him long and hard. It seemed like an age since we'd last been together, presumably because I'd been so caught up in work. Or maybe it was a case of absence makes the heart grow fonder – and the cunt grow warmer.

He'd rejigged the living room a bit so the TV was at an angle in one corner with the sofa and armchair forming an L-shape several feet away. Plenty of carpet space for us to play in, I thought.

'Show me,' said Ilya, nodding at my leopard-print mac, which I was hugging to my body.

I smiled, opening up my coat to reveal the latest addition to my slut-underwear collection: fuchsia-pink PVC bra and knickers worn with black sturdy-soled boots. The bra was a peephole thing, with slits to expose my nipples. Ilya looked me up and down, smiling faintly.

His gaze was like a touch, and a flush of sexiness spread over my skin as I let him drink his fill. My nipples tingled excitedly and began crunching up until they were hard cones, spiking from the lurid pink apertures.

'And . . .' I said, slipping off the mac, 'I reckon the back view's pretty good too.'

I slung my coat on to the sofa. From the front, the knickers looked ordinary enough – a high triangle of bright-pink gloss. But when I turned, they were something else: they left my arse completely bare. A strap lay across the top of my buttocks and two more ran either side of my cheeks, forming a half-gusset between my legs. So instead of more fabric, Ilya got to see my naked rear.

I'd quickly learnt that Ilya was an arse man, rather than a tit man or a leg man, which I always find slightly unnerving because I prefer my tits to my arse. I mean, my arse is fine, but I think my tits are great. Ilya thought my tits were great and my arse was fucking lovely. So the knickers were chosen with him in mind.

Like my peephole bra, they were deliciously obscene. I'd bought them mail order – sex-catalogue stuff. I'd bought lots of things mail order. I was turning into a sleazy mail-order junkie.

'Ve-ery nice,' drawled Ilya, picking up the remote control. 'But get the boots off, Beth. You look like some whiplash wannabe.'

I had to silently concede that I'd been worried about that aspect too. So I unzipped and stood barefoot.

'Now come here,' he said, 'and get on your hands and knees.'

He gestured to the floor space near the end of the sofa. I always seemed to be going down on all fours for him. But I didn't mind. The very instruction was enough to make lust ripple up my thighs and spiral heat around my groin.

'Facing the TV,' he said as I knelt. 'That's better. Good.'

'What are you going to do to me?' I asked.

'Wait and see,' replied Ilya, aiming the remote control at the video.

Slinky, synthesized music started up and, on screen, the title appeared in bold blue letters: *Sleaze*.

'Oh God,' I murmured.

Ilya turned off all the lights, making the TV colours our only source of illumination.

'Have I got to stay like this?' I frowned as Ilya moved around in the gloom. 'I'm not exactly comfortable.'

'You'll be wanting popcorn next,' he said, returning with a glass of whisky. He perched himself close to me on the sofa edge. On TV a blonde was strolling along a deserted beach, being soulful. 'Get your back nice and flat, Beth,' said Ilya, pausing the video with the remote. 'Your spine's dipping. Tuck your arse in more.'

I obeyed and, though it felt as if I was arching my spine upward, Ilya seemed satisfied. He ran his hand over the level plane of my back. My skin leapt to his warm touch and arousal melted into my sex. 'Perfect,' he said. 'Now don't move.'

From the corner of my eye, I saw him reach an ashtray from the floor. Then he placed it on my back. I giggled to feel the cool disc of weight resting on my heated skin.

'Keep still,' he cautioned, then he stood his glass of whisky near the ashtray.

It was cooler than the ashtray and it didn't feel as secure. That glass made me nervous: it was fragile and full of liquid. The need to be absolutely motionless dominated my thoughts. I felt giddy and silly, and I suddenly seemed to have a hundred and one itches that wanted scratching. Imaginary ants tiptoed over the soles of my feet and things with wings fluttered around my midriff.

'What are you doing?' I asked, trying my best not to disturb Ilya's balancing act with laughter. If only I could have taken one deep breath, I would've felt steadier and calmer.

'You're a table,' answered Ilya, and he swung his legs

up on to the sofa. In my peripheral vision I saw him lie back, propping his elbow on the sofa arm close to my arse.

'What?' I said, confusion tempering my giddiness.

'You're a table,' he repeated. 'That's how I'm using you. So shut up. Tables don't speak.'

I fought the urge to turn round. It seemed so important not to spill the whisky. 'But –'

'Shut up,' he said, and his words were mumbled as if there were something between his lips.

Every muscle in my body was tense with playing at statues. I heard the rasping click of a lighter then caught a glimpse of Ilya pointing the remote. As the video started playing, I heard him drawing on a cigarette.

Disappointment swamped me. I wanted to be teased and pleased. I wanted to be used and abused – as a slut, not as a table. I didn't want to be ignored.

But it didn't look as if I had much choice. Damn Ilya, the smart-arse.

The pale marble fireplace took on an orange hue as a sunbed-tanned rear filled the screen. Then a blonde with too much make-up began pulling faces while rising up and down, presumably impaled on some guy's dick. Her balloon-round tits didn't move once.

'Silicone,' I complained.

'Shut up,' said Ilya again, and I felt him tap his cigarette into the ashtray on my back.

I repressed a sigh, hoping that maybe later he would use me in the manner I was accustomed to. After all, we were watching porn. Surely he'd want to get his rocks off at some point.

I tried to concentrate on the video. The blonde was doing a dreamy, thinking-aloud scene, but I couldn't understand a word. The sound quality was rotten. It didn't look very sleazy either. Then I got confused because suddenly there were two silicone blondes doing some slurpy stuff on a kitchen table and I couldn't tell which was which.

Ilya lifted the glass from my back, drank and replaced it, pressing a different cool patch on to my skin.

I wondered if he found the video arousing. Surely not.

When the blondes had finished messing around with each other, a scene popped up of three guys in an office. From what I could make out, they were planning a storyline for a film, arguing about what was too corny and deciding they had to make it sexy.

'Oh, I see,' I said, unable to curb my sarcasm. 'It's postmodern. How clever.'

'Shut up and watch,' said Ilya.

'I can't,' I protested as yet another load of characters was introduced. 'I can't follow the plot and it's crap. I haven't even seen a cock yet or a –'

'You want something harder?' he demanded, getting up from the sofa.

'Yes,' I replied as Ilya ejected the cassette. The room was plunged into momentary darkness, then the screen lit up with a fast-forward frenzy of credits and flesh.

Ilya settled back on to the sofa, while images of a fully dressed, ordinary-looking woman doing a piece to camera shuddered on high-speed.

'What's she saying?' I asked

'Just some bollocks about how she's never done this before,' said Ilya, lighting another cigarette. 'Now will you shut up or I'll gag you?'

So I kept quiet, doing my best table impression, as the fast-forward woman was joined by a fast-forward black man, who twiddled with her curly perm and stroked at her clothes. While Ilya tapped his cigarette into the ashtray and took an occasional slug of whisky, the porn stars, jerky, smiley and comically fast, shed their clothes and rolled around on a big white bed.

The black guy had a enormous, slightly curved dick. And there were lots of close-ups of it, along with close-ups of tits, mouths and pussy. It looked seriously dirty and I ached to see it on normal speed.

When the guy went down on the woman, Ilya relented. My sex began to throb as I gazed at the blown-up image of a wet, dark-haired vulva, its flushed lips being sucked and gently stretched by the guy's mouth.

The woman was groaning – proper horny-sounding groans, not like the pseudo-ecstasy of the earlier video. And when we got to see her contorted face, it was sweat-glistening and make-up smudged. She looked like she was having one helluva good time, oblivious to the off-screen voices encouraging and complimenting her. The thought of this woman, giving vent to her pleasure, while surrounded by a lewd eager film crew, made my juices really flow.

'Mmm, she's hot,' said Ilya, and I imagined his cock imprisoned in his trousers and pulsing with vigour.

I wanted him so badly. I caught a breath when I felt his hand brush my arse. His fingers nudged into my barely-there gusset and I struggled to remain motionless and silent as they trawled through the wet cleft of my labia.

'Just checking,' said Ilya, withdrawing the touch.

I trapped a squeaky protest in my throat, barely able to watch the TV as that lucky woman splayed her legs and squirmed, ready for that huge black prick. When the guy penetrated her, we saw the lot: his shiny length disappearing into the gaping flesh-lips of her pussy.

'Oh God,' she was crying. 'It's so big. So big.'

I was creaming with lust, my cunt drumming inces-santly. I needed Ilya more than anything I'd ever needed. Seeing that guy's arse, humping and flexing between the woman's open thighs, was sheer agony.

Then a sudden loud noise in our room made me jump almost clean out of my skin. In my shock, I registered the thud of glass and ashtray tumbling from my back before I registered the first noise: buzzz.

It was the entryphone. There was someone at the street door, someone buzzing Ilya's flat. And we were watching a dirty video, with me half-naked and churned up with arousal.

'Shit,' I said, twisting round to share my alarm with Ilya. Instinctively, I grabbed a cushion from the sofa and clutched it to my pink, peephole bra.

But Ilya wasn't panicking. Light from the video danced on his smug, calm face. He looked at me, his lips curling in a sly little smile.

'What's going on?' I asked warily.

Ilya pushed himself up from the sofa.

'Well, well, well,' he said, snatching away my cushion. 'Looks like we've got company, Beth. Must be your lucky night.'

Chapter Eight

'*A*ll right mate,' came a male voice from the landing. I could not move. I remained kneeling up, gazing at the door as the two men sauntered into the flickering half-light of the room. The porn stars were groaning and gasping in the background, and gravity had made all my juices gush and spill.

He was fortyish, sandy-haired, tall, and – oh horror – he was wearing navy tracksuit bottoms with elasticated ankles and a leather blouson jacket.

He scanned his surroundings quickly, taking me in like I was part of the furniture. In one hand he held a video cassette, in the other a half-smoked cigarette. Sticking the cigarette between his lips, he strolled further into the room, ogling first the TV screen, then me.

He wasn't bad-looking in a lived-in kind of way, but his eyebrows were far too pale. He surveyed me from head to knees, his cigarette tip flaring amber as his eyes roved.

'All right, sweetheart?' He grinned. He tossed his video on to the sofa, followed by his jacket, and released a slow-drifting plume of smoke.

Ilya was just standing in the shadows, arms folded, smirking.

The stranger squatted on his haunches in front of me, his cigarette dangling loosely from his mouth. His face was slightly pock-marked and he had a half-growth of beard – an attempt, I reckoned, to conceal some of that scarring.

With a faint smile, the guy just reached for my tits, pushing a callused thumb into each peephole of my sleek pink bra.

I was too stunned even to protest.

His thumbs scuffed over my nipples. They hardened rapidly. I couldn't help it because, despite the shock, I was still painfully horny – and Ilya had barely touched me all evening. My inner thighs were damp and hot and I could smell the trickling hunger of my sex.

'Mmm-mmm,' said the man, his low-angled cigarette bouncing upward. His tanned arms were muscle-corded and covered in sun-bleached hair.

He moved one hand from my breast to his cigarette, and left the other hand where it was, massaging his thumb into my nipple with heavy pressure.

The video was still moaning and wailing, and I moaned too, although I was much quieter.

'Ilya was right,' he said, turning to blow smoke away from my face. 'You are a hot little bitch, aren't you?'

My heart was going ten to the dozen.

The man reached for the fallen ashtray, righted it and rested his cigarette in the groove.

'What's her name again?' he called over his shoulder, his thumb still pressing my nipple in and out.

'Beth,' replied Ilya.

'Oh yeah,' said the man, looking at me. 'Beth. I'm Pete. Nice to meet you, Beth.'

He dropped one knee to the floor, steadying himself, and fixed me with bright-blue eyes set in laughter-line creases.

'I won't bother shaking hands.' He smiled, bringing

his lightly pitted face close to mine. 'I reckon you'll like this better.'

His head twitched a fraction as he winked at me. Then his free hand swooped down into the front of my slut-knickers and the PVC gave a muted creak of protest.

'God, she's wet,' he chuckled. 'What've you been doing to her, Illie?'

I whimpered pathetically, as Pete drove his short, broad fingers straight up into my dissolving cunt. My pulse-swollen sex flushed in gratitude and my jaw went limp. I knew I was gaping at him, panting for more. But I didn't care.

Whoever this Pete was, if he wanted me, he could have me. So what if he was a bit of a Neanderthal? I was prepared to lower my standards. Pete just grinned back, fingers of one hand playing radio-dials with my nipple, fingers of the other stroking my slick vaginal walls.

'I haven't been doing anything to her,' said Ilya blandly. 'She was supposed to be my table but she's not very good at it. Think I'll have to rename her.'

Ilya came towards us, the light of the TV glowing on his strong bony features. He stooped to put the spilt butts in the ashtray, picked up the fallen glass and rubbed the scattered ash into the carpet with his foot. Then he went to lift my coat from the chair and began rummaging in the pockets.

'Did the video get you hot, sweetheart?' said Pete, regarding the TV with casual interest. The porn stars had changed position but they were still going at it hammer and tongues.

'I want to come,' I protested, liberated by the unasha-med appetites on screen. 'Please make me come. Touch my clit. Oh, somebody . . . just fuck me. Please.'

The two men laughed, sharing conspiratorial glances.

'But I've brought us another video to watch,' said Pete, nodding to the cassette on the sofa. He took his hand from my nipple and bent awkwardly to retrieve his cigarette. His thick, rough fingers rose and fell in my depths while he drew on his cigarette then stubbed it out.

I pitched Ilya a tormented look, appealing for mercy. He was holding my whore-lipstick and he approached, twisting up the red shaft.

'I need to rename you,' he said, kneeling behind me in the gap of my calves.

'Then will somebody fuck me?' I moaned. 'Please. I don't want to watch another stupid video. I want –'

'Shhh, darling,' said Pete, still steadily fingering me.

He dropped his other knee so all three of us were kneeling upright, me sandwiched in the middle. With his free hand, the stranger edged my squeaky knickers down until they were around my knees. I think there was some anal action taking place on screen. I wasn't sure. I had other things to concentrate on, but, whatever it was, it was noisy.

'Shhh,' said Pete again, pursing his lips like he was cooing to a baby. 'Shhh.' And he pushed his fingers up me in a high leisurely thrust.

I couldn't sshh. I groaned excitement and Pete's sky-blue eyes twinkled with lecherous delight.

'Get her titties out while you're round there, Illie,' he said.

I whined in complaint, mentally telling him they were tits, not titties. But whatever they were, I hoped he would touch them nicely.

'Just about to,' replied Ilya, and he unhooked my bra and slipped the straps from my shoulders. I let the garment fall.

'Put your hands behind your head, darling,' said Pete.

I did as instructed, linking my fingers and praying that my bared jutting flesh would whip him up to a frenzy; that he would shove his trousers down and fuck me – in any position he wanted, so long as it was fierce and fast.

'Nice pair,' he said lightly, and he clamped a hand to one breast, rolling his palm in big strong circles. 'Mmm.'

I rocked back and forth, moaning pleasure and leaning into his heavy caress. I was so needy I imagined flopping into his body, forcing my lips on to his smirking mouth, ripping off his clothes and straddling him.

And this was a guy who, if we'd passed in the street, I would not have looked at twice. But that moment, all I cared about was the fact that he had a cock – a cock that was lifting and making a tent of his groin. He might be vulgar and boorish. He might be treating me like I was just some bit of trash. But wasn't that the kind of thing I got off on?

Yeah, it was. And that was obviously why Ilya had invited him over. He was bringing my fantasies to life again.

I just wished he'd warned me. I wanted to know what they'd said about me. I wanted to know what they were going to do to me. And I wanted to know *when* they were going to do it, because if they planned on tormenting me for hours then I needed to start thinking about dull things.

Pete withdrew his hand from my breast – much too soon – and pressed it to the flat of my chest, telling me to keep still. It was difficult. Passion made my thighs tremble and my head swim.

Then I felt the cool tackiness of Ilya pressing the lipstick to my back.

'What letter's this, Beth?' he asked as the lipstick snaked a winding path from a few inches below one shoulderblade and down almost to waist level.

'S,' I whispered.

'Good girl,' breathed Ilya. 'And this?'

As he stroked a lipstick line down my back, the other guy gave my clit a series of tiny circular rubs, the pad of his thumb hard and abrasive.

161

'Oh God,' I cried, my body swaying with delirium. 'I can't take it. Please –'

'Keep still, Beth,' urged Ilya. 'What letter was that?'

'L,' I gasped. 'L.'

Pete carried on leering, giving my clitoris the odd teasing flick or two. Ilya continued drawing on my back.

'And that one?' said Ilya, quietly demanding.

'U,' I said, a hint of weary resignation in my voice.

'Well done, Beth,' said Ilya. 'S-L-U – What's the next letter?'

I could feel all my juices flooding from my pussy on to Pete's hand. My arousal was more humiliating than being humiliated.

'Teeee,' I wailed, screwing my eyes shut as Pete twisted his fingers up and down in my sex.

'Perfect,' said Ilya, and he traced the final letter on my back. 'Now bend over and show Pete exactly what you are.'

Pete plucked his wet fingers from my groin and got to his feet, stepping back to smile down at me.

'Go on, Beth,' said Ilya, standing and pushing gently at the back of my neck.

Making a weak protest, I dropped forward on to my hands. My head hanging low, I imagined how I must look, crouched at Pete's feet, knickers round my knees, those big red letters branding me as their slut. I felt thoroughly debased and desperately cheap. But, somewhere deep inside, I revelled in the filthy attention.

I watched Pete's dirty-grey trainers as he moved to join Ilya behind me. Bet he can't read upside down, I thought bitterly.

'That's good,' said Pete. 'I like sluts. Take your knickers off properly, sweetheart.'

I crawled forward, reaching back to get rid of the last scrap of PVC, then I held still for my men again, aching with need.

162

'Spread your legs, Beth,' said Ilya, and I shuffled my knees wide apart.

'What are we gonna do first, Ill?' came Pete's voice. 'Her or the video?'

'Meee,' I said in a shameless whine. 'Do me.'

I heard Pete's laugh and saw one of his feet lifting from the ground.

'God, she's a dirty little cow,' he said, and I felt the rubbery toe of his trainer between my thighs. I groaned, appalled at my coarse lust, as Pete's foot rubbed up and down over my folds. 'Aren't you, sweetheart?' he breathed. 'Why don't you bring yourself off on my shoe?'

I probably would have done if he'd given me chance. But he didn't. He set his foot down and once again I was wretched with hunger, pressing my arse back and pleading for more. They ignored me.

'We'll do the video,' said Ilya. 'I haven't seen it yet.'

'No,' I argued. 'I'm sick of videos.'

'You'll like this one,' declared Pete. 'It's a beauty.' He reached the cassette from the sofa. 'Shot it myself,' he continued, bending to show me the hand-written side-label.

It read: ANAL VIRGIN. Pete turned the cassette to show me the bigger square label. It read: ANAL VIRGIN: SHE BEGS FOR HIS DICK.

I huffed and turned aside. Why were they so interested in celluloid sluts when I was here: a real flesh woman who was wet and willing, her legs wide open for some hard male meat?

Pete squatted by the video and ejected the cassette. As he slotted his home-made porn into the machine, I covertly scrutinised his body. The seat of his rotten jogging pants was smooth over his arse and his thighs bulged with muscularity. Bit beefy for my taste, I thought, as I caught my tongue darting over my lips.

'I'm not interested in videos,' I bleated, casting a reluctant eye at the TV. 'I just want sex. Oh, Ilya, please.'

The screen was snowy for a few seconds, before a confusion of feet and walls flashed here and there. Then a sunny room came into view – a horribly familiar room with a shabby sofa, low-level furnishings and a boarded-up marble fireplace.

Dismay and disbelief crept through my body as the jerky camera angle came to rest on a near-naked woman. She was on her hands and knees, breasts hanging beneath a dislodged bra. The guy behind her was fully naked. He was working his fingers within the cheeks of her arse. She was gasping and groaning like a cheap porno slut. And she was blindfolded with a woolly tartan scarf: she didn't know she was being filmed.

Oh Christ.

It was me. I was the cheap porno slut.

Memories of that afternoon flooded into my mind, all those little floorboard creaks; Ilya's reassurances that it was just the two of us; my own reassurances that it was just my imagination.

White-hot fury ripped through my body. Half on my knees, I swung round and made a lunge for Ilya's legs.

'You bastard!' I raged as the muffled boom of Bach's *Toccata* played.

Ilya stumbled a little but he was quick to grab my wrists. He held them high while I squirmed and thrashed in his grip, cursing and swearing at him, trying to kick his ankles with my knees. I wanted to lay into him with my fists. I wanted to beat the shit out of him. I wanted him to be writhing around in agony and begging my forgiveness.

'You bastard,' I shouted. 'You cheating, fucking bastard.'

And in the background, Pete was chuckling to himself and my own stupid voice was going, 'Oh God, yes, yes, ahhh yes.'

Acid tears burnt my eyes and I had a tearing impulse

to scream 'cuttlefish', to call the whole thing off and storm right out of Ilya's flat and right out of his life.

But rationality squeezed the passion down, telling me to bite my tongue. It was just a reckless urge for vengeance and I would regret it bitterly. Because, no matter how outraged I was, my desire for Ilya ran deeper.

'Whoa, Beth,' said Ilya. 'Whoa. C'mon there. It's only a video. Cool it. Cool it.'

'But you didn't tell me,' I sobbed, my face close to the lump of his groin. 'You didn't tell me about it. You broke the rules, you bastard. I never agreed to it. I didn't get the chance to say no. You broke the rules, you . . . you . . .'

I slumped back on to my heels, defeated. Ilya released his hold on me.

'I just didn't want you to be self-conscious,' he said gently. 'That's all. I thought you'd see the sense in it – in me being a bit . . . sly. You do see the sense, don't you, babe?'

'Yeah,' I sniffed meekly. 'Suppose so.'

I threw a glance in Pete's direction. Standing in the pool of light from the TV, he was watching the screen me. I was crying in pleasure-pain as Ilya stretched my oiled arse open with sideways pushing fingers. The picture wasn't exactly grainy, but it had that camcorder quality: edges not quite sharp enough with something plasticky about the colours.

I was mortified to think some stranger had secretly filmed me.

'What about him?' I asked, my anger boiling up again. 'How does he fit in? And why did he have to come round and deliver the fucking film? Why didn't you –'

'We've got to pay the cameraman.' Ilya grinned. 'Now come on, Beth. Play the game. You'll love it. Two blokes treating you like a slut. Don't pretend you're not hot for it. Turn around. Get on all fours again and watch the video.'

Ilya sank into the armchair and, grudgingly, I dropped

back on to my hands and knees. He was right. Of course I was hot for it – so hot that I was close to combusting. Pete was hot, too. He stood there in the semi-gloom, gaze locked on the TV. His navy jogging pants held no secrets and his cock was sticking out like a flagpole.

On screen, Ilya was urging me to talk dirty. I cringed to hear my video alter ego crying out over the backtrack of Bach, crying out to have Ilya's cock rammed in my arse.

'Oh, baby, go,' said Pete in a low rumbling voice, and his hand drifted to his crotch.

As if he were standing alone, he began stroking himself up and down, cupping the fabric beneath his jutting stem while slowly rubbing the underside of his prick. His complete lack of inhibition made my pussy ache. I wanted a crude, rough fuck from him and I wanted him to growl, 'Oh, baby, go,' when he gave it to me.

'Oh yeah, what a dirty, dirty slut,' murmured Pete, seemingly in a world of his own.

My video self was propped on her forearms, offering up her backside and wailing for Ilya's dick: 'I want your dick up my arse,' I was saying. 'I want your fucking dick ... up my fucking –'

'You foul-mouthed slut,' came Ilya's muted video-voice. I watched his hands unroll a rubber down his stout, veiny length and I listened to myself wailing as his prick penetrated my anus in a slow, deep lunge.

The horniest thing was seeing Ilya's body: a muscled thigh, the hollowing of his buttocks, the strength in his arms. His face was out of view. The picture was of me, side-on to the lens, and of the important stuff happening to me. Ilya's expression was obviously not important.

'This bit's great,' murmured Pete, without taking his eyes from the TV.

The image wobbled a bit, zoomed in on my rear, went blurred, then came into sharp focus again. The cheeks of my arse, split open by the heels of Ilya's hands, dominated the screen. The wide shiny valley of my buttocks ran down the middle and we got a shot of a larger-than-life cock sliding out of a larger-than-life hole.

It could've been anyone but the knowledge that it was me – being buggered by Ilya for the very first time – made it a million times more obscene and thrilling. Heat thundered between my legs as I gazed, awestruck, at the image.

'Mmm, nice camera work, Pete,' came Ilya's husky drawl from the armchair behind me.

I whimpered in feeble objection, wanting someone to notice the flesh me instead of the video me. But the video me was making louder noises. I gazed at my on-screen anus, red-raw and glistening, making a pout round Ilya's girth as his shaft plunged in and out.

'Top shot, isn't it?' said Pete distractedly, his hand still moving beneath the thrust of his trapped hard-on.

I wondered how many times he'd watched this film. How many times had he wanked to it? And when he'd wanked, had he known that he was going to meet the star of the show?

'Oh, yeah,' said Pete softly, as the camera panned out again. 'The greedy little cow. Look at her go.'

And there I was, reaching back for my clit, my body bouncing, my tits swaying as Ilya's arse pumped faster and faster. I was howling. Ilya was grunting. My arm was nudging as I frigged myself. I climaxed. It sounded nothing like me. Surely my voice wasn't so throaty. Surely I didn't cry and gasp like that.

Oh God. I recalled the next bit: me finger-fucking myself to a second peak. I was torn in two: I wanted to watch myself and yet I couldn't bear it. If I hadn't had 'slut' scrawled across my back in red lipstick, I might have been a more comfortable viewer.

'Oh, greedy, greedy, greedy,' said Pete, his words growing louder. Then he swung around to Ilya.

'Oh fuck, Illie,' he breathed, his face energised with

lust. 'My dick's killing me. Let me give her one. Let me fuck her. Dirty little bitch, let me fuck her.'

He was already jerking at the drawstring of his baggy trousers.

Anticipation slammed into my groin. 'Yes,' I said in a barely audible whisper. 'Let him.'

'She's all yours,' said Ilya. 'But, if you can hang on a minute, I'd like to see her beg for it.' The armchair creaked as Ilya stood up.

'Oh, yeah,' enthused Pete, clutching his loosened jogging pants in one fist. 'Let's make her beg for it. Beg like a dog.'

'C'mon, Beth,' coaxed Ilya, moving around me. 'Be a good girl. Sit up and beg.'

He had to be joking. He nudged at one of my arms with his foot. He wasn't joking.

Oh, how low would I have to sink before I got what I craved? As low as it goes, I thought, because, right at that moment, I wasn't going to let self-respect stand in the way of hunger.

I sat back on my heels, lifting my limp-wristed hands high, and glowered at Ilya. He smiled down at me, his face all shadows and light.

The sound of our video fuck filled the room, mocking me with its unchecked passion. I heard myself reach clamorous orgasm and I was jealous to the point of bitchiness, inwardly cursing that slut on tape who could take her pleasure a thousand times over and take it hassle-free.

'Put a bit of effort into it, Beth,' taunted Ilya. 'Look like you mean it.'

I straightened my spine and half-heartedly flapped my hands.

'Oh, sweetheart,' mocked Pete, moving a couple of feet in front of me. 'That's so disappointing.'

From the TV speaker came the deliciously deep groan of Ilya's climax, followed by some quieter moans that soon snapped off into fizz. I glanced at the screen. It was snowy and I was thankful, although I couldn't work out if my audience had just halved or doubled.

Ilya switched on a table lamp, filling the room with low-watt yellow and smudgy gloom.

'You wanna see what you're missing, mmm?' boasted Pete, circling his pelvis. 'You wanna see if it's worth begging for, do you?'

He released his hold on his trousers, stretched two waistbands over the hump of his erection, then dropped his clothes to his ankles. His cock sprang free, ramrod stiff and capped with crimson.

My liquid sex fuzzed like electricity as Pete kicked off trainers and trousers.

'Go on,' he growled, pushing his hips forward and stripping off his T-shirt. 'Beg for it, you little tart. Beg for my dick.'

'I'm begging, I'm begging,' I cried brokenly.

'Like a dog,' insisted Ilya. 'Stick your tongue out and pant for it.'

I winced inwardly, casting him a look of distaste. For a split-second I was stubborn, but then I thought, what the hell, it's only dignity. You get it back – I think.

And so I sat bolt upright, thrust out my tongue and made lots of quick huffy noises as my perky-puppy hands waggled away.

Ilya laughed. 'Oh, lovely,' he said. 'Very nice.'

Then all of a sudden Ilya was behind me, wrapping an arm beneath my breasts.

'Go on, Pete,' he urged, arcing me backward as if making an offering of my flesh. 'Put the girl out of her misery. But use a rubber. You don't know where she's been.'

Relief made my heart light and my cunt, choked with pulses, blazed up like an inferno.

I scrambled with Ilya as he dragged me towards the sofa then plonked himself at an angle on the edge.

Roughly, he hitched me upward, stretching my upper body across one of his thighs. My knees hovered inches above the ground and Ilya, arm locked tight round my ribcage, kept me that way.

Pete muttered about condoms and I pleaded with him to hurry as I bucked into thin air. Ilya mauled one breast with the hand that held me, lowering his mouth to my ear.

'You beautiful whore,' he said in a rasping whisper.

The nearness of those words made my consciousness go hiccup. I had a sudden sense of intimacy – of Pete, rather than me, being the outsider who didn't quite know the score.

Ilya's free hand delved past my pubes to my raised clit. Taking the blistering bud between thumb and forefinger, he pinched lightly and rubbed.

'Yes,' I howled. 'Oh yes. Please, Ilya.'

'Oh, man,' breathed Pete, positioning himself between my wide, welcoming thighs.

His cock butted at my slippery vulva then he drove in fast, packing my overwrought pussy with stone-solid flesh.

I wailed reckless delight, struggling for balance as Pete launched headlong into a strong, frantic fuck. The urgency of his high-speed pounding dislodged Ilya's fingers, but in an instant they were back on target.

'Greedy, greedy,' murmured Ilya, vibrating my clit as Pete hammered and gasped.

'Oh, yes, yes, yes,' Pete was chanting. 'Oh, she's so fucking wet. Oh yes, baby, yes. Take my dick. Take my dick.'

But I drowned him out with my own noises, feeling my orgasm rush and squeeze the very core of me to wring out every droplet of pleasure.

'Oh yes,' gushed Pete. 'Oh, man, her snatch.' And he was jabbing into my spasms, shunting me higher, and for a moment I thought I was falling somewhere.

But we were all leaning – me and Ilya backward; Pete forward, striving to keep rhythm and depth.

I was near enough sprawled across Ilya's chest, and his hands were free to roam. Pete swung a foot on to the cushions, clasped the sofa-back and, in a half-squat, continued fucking me, his hips lunging in sharp little jerks.

Ilya mashed my breasts hard, squashing them together and pressing them up for Pete's rapt gaze.

'Oh yes,' said Pete, eyes glued to my tits. 'Oh fuck, baby, yes.'

With his spare hand, Pete shoved into Ilya's caress, fighting for a grope of my flesh. He grabbed at the cleavage Ilya had made. 'I'm gonna shoot,' he gasped, his rough fingers pummelling and clawing. 'I'm gonna shoot. I'm gonna –'

And, with a groan that became a roar, he shot. His whole body tensed as his rooted prick quivered to fulfilment.

Then he held himself over us, his gleaming chest swelling in and out as he chased his breaths.

'You horny cow,' he said, and he pushed himself from the sofa, leaving my cunt bereft.

'No,' I murmured. 'More. Ilya.'

'Get up, Beth,' said Ilya, and I slipped to the floor as he stood. 'I need to piss first. So lie back.'

He unzipped his flies. Pete laughed knowingly.

'Lie back,' repeated Ilya, and he stood there, legs astride, aiming his semi-hard cock in my direction, clearly intent on pissing on me.

'No way,' I said, scrambling out of range. 'You're not using me as your fucking urinal.'

'Oh, but I am,' said Ilya, smiling. 'Grab her Pete. Keep her still.'

Pete pounced and I wrestled uselessly against his strength, shouting, 'No, no, let me go.' I'd had enough of degradation. I wanted sex and nice orgasms, not stinking piss and mockery.

But Pete gripped my forearms and I was on my back, writhing and protesting. Ilya was laughing mirthlessly, obviously not desperate to piss, just waiting for my frenzy to abate.

'Open your mouth, Beth,' said Ilya. 'I won't get hard until I'm emptied.'

'No,' I shouted, kicking at nothing and trying to wrench myself from Pete's grasp. 'You're a couple of fucking bullies. Let me go.'

I felt Pete relax ever so slightly. 'Hey, Illie,' he said in a mildly concerned voice, 'maybe you should give it a rest. Maybe she's just not into it.'

'She's into it,' replied Ilya coldly. 'When Beth says no, she doesn't really mean no. And if she doesn't fucking keep still and open her mouth wide, then I've got one word to say to her – and she knows what it is – and then she's out of here and she won't be coming back. Ever. She's got five seconds to decide. One. Two. Three.'

I held myself rigid.

'Four,' said Ilya.

I went limp and opened my mouth.

Ilya gave a little snigger.

'Nice one,' said Pete admiringly as he released me.

Leaning back on my elbows, mouth gaping, I waited for the watery insult.

As Ilya's piss curved towards me in a shimmering parabola, I screwed my eyes shut.

I felt the point of impact, shockingly warm and powerful, splash on my breasts. Then it snaked up to my neck, as if he were drawing on my flesh in urine. Bathwater heat coursed over my flesh, dribbling everywhere.

When his liquid hit my chin, I quelled the instinct to clamp my lips together. It gushed into my mouth and I locked my throat, swallowing nothing but tasting all the vile sharpness as it bathed my tongue. Overflowing piss spilt from my lips, trickling down my neck, my ears, and soaking my hair.

'Mmm, that's better,' said Ilya, as his stream tailed off and went drip, drip, drip down my body.

I coughed and spluttered, wiping the back of my hand across my tainted face.

'I'm ready to fuck now,' said Ilya, his drained cock thickening.

'You gonna stick it up her arse again?' asked Pete.

'Might do,' replied Ilya. 'Or I might let you do the honours.'

'Suits me fine,' answered Pete, his hands reaching for me from behind.

'No way,' I snapped, pushing myself up. 'You're not –'

'Yeah, but you don't really mean that, do you?' laughed Pete. 'You'll have to teach me that five-second trick, Illie. Works a treat. We can do what we want with her, can't we?'

They subjected me to all manner of indignities.

They made me crawl and catch semen on my out-stretched tongue.

I had to stand behind the sofa, bent over the back, wrists tethered, while Pete fucked my arse, while Ilya fingered me, while the blood rushed to my head and I climaxed wildly.

They made me colour my vulva with lipstick then lie starfish-style on the floor. They prodded and poked me, jotting down a punishment tally for my every moan and squirm. Then they spanked my buttocks, counting out the score.

Throughout they avoided all male-genital collisions. I pleaded with them to take me at the same time – one front, one back. But they wouldn't. 'Homophobes,' I cursed.

They phoned for pizza and I had to collect from the

front door, wearing my dress-to-please-him undies. I think the pizza boy was more embarrassed than I was.

The two men ate, with me as coffee table, and I didn't get a morsel.

The abuse continued until, finally, Pete and Ilya decided they were shagged out. They had no use for me any more.

Pete rang for a taxi.

I was sent home, my body aching, my mind reeling.

I don't know why, but it just hadn't occurred to me that Ilya could threaten me with cuttlefish if I refused to submit.

I'd thought that cuttlefish was my power; that Ilya wouldn't dare do anything too nasty in case he pushed me too far and forced me to call time. And yet suddenly it seemed to have changed.

I had no idea if Ilya was serious or bluffing. But I wasn't going to risk finding out by disobeying him.

Had he seen through me? Had he realised that only under pain of death would I scream out that final word?

If so, then Ilya had a lot more power in this game than I was comfortable with. And, in turn, I really didn't have much.

Things were starting to look pretty damn scary.

Chapter Nine

*H*ot Sex.

That was to be the name of my new-style gigs.

In a powwow at the pub with Jen and Clare, we invented lots of acronyms using Body Language: Blush, Blue and Blister. But we couldn't think of any decent phrases to fit the letters. We had silly names, like Blowjob, with silly words to match – Body Language orders women to jump on boys; and better names, like Bliss, still with silly words – Body Language is Shaun's shite.

In the end, we all plumped for Hot Sex.

Jenny was full of ideas to make the room look good, and I was happy to let her deal with it. 'Bordello chic,' she'd said. 'Trashy, glam and sumptuous.'

She was going to make some great big love hearts to dangle from the ceiling – cut from polystyrene and covered in red fur – because, Jenny said, you've got to have love. The biggest and best heart was going to have the words 'Hot Sex' sewn on glittery fabric and it was going to hang in the landing outside the room, over the desk where you pay your money.

Or maybe that would be a waste and we'd use it as part of the stage backdrop. Or maybe, if there was time,

Jenny would make two great big furry hearts with Hot Sex lettering.

There wouldn't be time. It was a serious rush-job because Shaun was eager to get the nights up and running – so eager that I'd persuaded him to invest three hundred quid in my new venture.

And I'd been so busy that I'd actually had to say to Ilya 'Sorry, no can do' when he'd phoned once or twice to fix a dirty date. Maybe that was a good thing.

Jenny and I merged into the leisurely bustle of Bond Street, Jenny swinging a carrier bag of glitzy bits.

It was hot and sticky and the streets were milling with all the bright young things being sexy for summer. They strolled along in the middle of the road, drifting blithely to one side whenever a car tried nosing its way through.

'Martin was round at ours again yesterday,' said Jen, hooking her plump arm in mine.

'Oh God,' I murmured, my heart sinking. 'Has he got over me yet?'

'I think he might be getting there,' replied Jenny. 'He still thinks you're a bitch, though, only he doesn't say it with as much venom these days. I think you've been a bitch as well, just cutting him out of your life like that. But you know my position.'

'Yeah, yeah,' I said wearily.

'Oh, come on, Beth,' said Jenny. 'You used to be bosom buddies. It's not right to throw it all away because of a stupid affair you had together. You've got to put some effort into getting it fixed. You can't just brush it under the carpet and –'

'I've been busy,' I said. 'I've had a lot on my mind. Look, I'll get in touch with him soon. I know I've been rotten but ... I've been busy, that's all. Anyway, it was Martin who suggested we didn't see each other for a while, not me.'

We let the dawdling North Laine crowds dictate our pace while I wallowed in some silent guilt – a double load of it: guilt because I'd neglected Martin who was once so important to me; and guilt because I still hadn't told anyone about Ilya. I was always lying, making excuses, pretending I was in such-and-such a place when I was actually with Ilya.

Maybe I'd tell Jenny soon. Not in detail, just that I'm seeing some guy but I'm not ready for you to meet him yet.

At the end of Gardner Street, we merged with a jumble of people, some waiting for the traffic lights to change, others trying to squeeze past. There was a great gaggle of language students there, all with their little yellow rucksacks.

A bunch of them jostled and screeched and a couple of kids lunged heavily into Jenny. 'For fuck's sake,' she cursed quietly.

Two pairs of big brown eyes gazed up blankly at us. '*Pardon*?' pronounced one kid.

Jenny gave him an enormous smile. 'You daft tosser,' she said politely.

And then the kid was off, giggling and shoving at the ones who'd just shoved him.

'C'mon. Let's detour,' said Jen, as the cars collected and the man went green. 'I'm not getting stuck behind that lot.'

The kids crocodiled across the road like a yellow-humped monster, and we snuck up between the cars to escape the rabble.

Upper Gardner Street was, as usual, quieter. The shops along there aren't really shops. They're more like open-fronted garages – small warehouses, I suppose – and they're stuffed full of antiques and junk.

I had a memory pang of the time I'd trailed Ilya down the very same street. It seemed so long ago and it was strange to remember him as a man I hardly knew; strange to think of him rounding on me when he realised I'd been following him. Given the chance, I thought, would I do the same thing again?

I reckoned I probably would, even though the mysteries of Ilya's life didn't concern me as much as they once had done. I was more concerned about the way our game was developing and whether it might start getting too nasty because Ilya had the driving reins in a pretty tight grip.

Jen and I strolled along in a lazy, summer's day fashion. Jenny was telling me some story about a friend of a friend that I'd heard before. Jenny's good at repeats so I was only half listening.

My eyes were drifting over the motley assortment of furniture on the pavements in front of the garages. I was fantasising about spotting a neon sign for sale that said HOT SEX or maybe a lush chaise-longue for a tenner.

Then, all of a sudden, my attention was grabbed because there, just inside one of the garage entrances, was Ilya.

I carried on walking, fed Jenny with a little laugh. In my head, a confusion of thoughts whirled, but there was only one image, clear and sharp: Ilya, leaning against a clunking great wardrobe, a mug of something in one hand, talking to someone deeper in the room, laughing. He'd looked very at home. He wasn't shopping.

What was he doing there? Had I stumbled on the reason for his secrecy? Was he some kind of dodgy antiques dealer?

Oh, please, I thought, don't let that be true. Don't let him be a wide-boy in sex god's clothing. I'd rather have him as an unemployed builder. Or a powdery-fingered drug baron with foreign connections

Maybe it wasn't him at all. Maybe my eyes were just playing tricks. Perhaps I ought to go back and take a second look, just to put my mind at rest.

We reached the end of the street and turned down towards the shops again.

'Ahh,' said Jenny, drawing me over to some little chess-board-top table. 'Tom and Clare've been after one of these. I told them to come down here.'

Please linger, I thought. Give me a chance to decide what to do. I recalled Ilya's anger the time I'd followed him. He'd accused me of being a weirdo obsessive. I didn't want any of that shit again.

Jenny stroked the table. 'It's not in very good nick though, is it?' she said.

'Jen,' I said. 'I'm just gonna bob back to one of those places we passed. Won't be long. Will you be hanging round here?'

'I'll come with you in a sec,' she said, bending low to inspect the table legs.

'No,' I said. 'It's OK. Don't. I just . . . I saw something.' I struggled for a reason to deter her in case I had to do something odd like a sudden about-turn. Inspiration hit me.

'It's a certain somebody's birthday soon,' I said, putting on a mystery voice. 'And I spotted something she might like. So you can just stay right where you are.'

Jenny beamed. 'Well, if that's the case, you take all the time you need. Still got some of that money left from Shaun, have you?'

I made a mocking retort then retraced my steps. Was I doing the right thing?

As I neared the warehouse, I decided my best bet would be to play it lightly. I wouldn't risk trying to be sneaky in case he spotted me and thought I was spying on him. I'd be open about seeing him and I'd just make it seem like a little tease, a jokey dig at him for always being so cagey.

Hopefully, he wouldn't fly off the handle like the first time. But I didn't think he would; we knew each other better now.

Ilya was no longer standing in the big square doorway.

Had he seen me and disappeared inside? No one seemed to be around, so, tentatively, I walked in.

The floor was cobbled stone and, either side of me, furniture was stacked on top of furniture, making the room feel more like a corridor. There was a fair amount of junk: a floral armchair with foam spilling out, a broken bookcase, some lumpy shapes covered in green canvas, an enormous mirror dulled with dust.

The corridor opened out into a broader space, which was heaped with wooden furniture, and bright with sunlight because the roof was corrugated plastic. A pair of stone lions stared impassively at me.

High on the far wall, near a fringe of brown, withered ivy, was a sign saying: SORRY – STRICTLY TRADE AND EXPORT.

I felt uneasy. Did that mean Joe Public browsers weren't welcome in here? Maybe 'strictly trade and export' was a code for 'strictly small-time crooks'. Or was I getting carried away with the mythology of the antiques trade as being full of wheeler-dealers, stolen goods and fakes?

But no. The more I gazed around, the more lifelike that myth became. A lot of the furniture was quality stuff: sturdy, well-polished, delicately carved – the kind of thing you'd expect to find in a posh antiques shop. That didn't sit too well with the child-size billiard table or the West Ham fixtures list taped to the wall.

The place just smacked of people who wanted to make grubby money, rather than people who cared about antiques. They wouldn't say, 'Fine example of Neoclassical design'; they'd say, 'Yeah, nice bit of wood that, darlin'.'

I ran my finger over a marble-topped table. Somewhere down the line, I thought, if you could trace it back, there are some seriously miffed toffs who used to own all this stuff.

Was Ilya really part of this scene?

I wandered through to an adjoining room. The roof there was made of rafters, pointing upward like a barn, and it smelt musty and damp. In the midst of the tall furniture were several rows of stripy chairs, all facing the same way – like a congregation of ghosts. Fluorescent striplights buzzed quietly above.

Where was he?

And, more to the point, what was he? Honourable rogue? Vicious criminal? A friend just passing who'd stopped for a coffee?

I feigned interest in a glass chandelier until a noise in the far corner caught my ear. A door opened and three men emerged, laughing and chatting. One of them was Ilya.

Now what?

He glanced my way. When he saw me, his smile faded a touch before he forced it back. He walked a few paces with the two men, slapped one on the shoulder, then turned towards me. I wove my way through the clutter to meet him.

'Well? he demanded, his tone hushed. 'Aren't you even going to fake surprise and pretend you're looking for furniture?'

We were standing between a tall chest of drawers and a round table with a travelling trunk on top. Once again, Ilya was not pleased to have me on his tail.

I smiled, attempting lightness. 'No,' I said. 'I was looking for you. Do you have contacts here? Because, if you do, I quite fancy a cheapish pine –'

Ilya seized my wrist.

'Come into the office,' he hissed, giving my arm a sharp tug.

He strode away and I followed. Maybe we were getting somewhere at last.

Ilya led me along another junk-lined corridor with another garage-style doorway at the end. It looked out on to the street and for a moment I thought he was showing me the exit. But instead he opened a side door, urging me inside with a brisk nod.

The office was pretty small, with a huge, leather-topped desk dominating one half. There was hardly anything on the desk except some pens in a pot, a phone and a notepad. Its sole function was obviously to make whoever sat behind it feel important.

'What the fuck's going on?' said Ilya as he rattled the door shut.

'I might ask you the same question,' I replied coolly, folding my arms.

'No,' he snapped. 'I've had enough of your fucking questions so why don't you just give it a rest because I'm fast getting sick of it? It's none of your fucking business where I go, what I do, blah, blah, blah. It doesn't affect you. It doesn't fucking –'

I was about to protest that all I'd ever been was mildly curious and that he was exaggerating wildly, but Ilya just moved closer and carried on with his rant, jabbing a finger at the air. He had that mad, angry glint in his eyes again and it made me wonder what he was capable of.

'Christ,' he said through set teeth. 'Can't you just keep your distance? Wasn't that the deal we had? A game. A stupid, meaningless fucking little game. And we – you, *you* – you thought you could handle it and you can't. You're always crowding me. You think I owe you something and I don't. I fucking don't. Just like you don't owe me. It's –'

'But at least I give something,' I argued, nervously backing away. 'I don't put up some great big barrier. I tell you stuff about me, about what I do . . . what I think of –'

'Well maybe you shouldn't,' he snarled, fury etching a groove between his dark brows. 'Because maybe I don't want to know. Maybe I'm not that interested. Can you get your head round that? That I'm not interested in you – in who you are deep down inside and what goes on in that pretty little head. I'm interested in your cunt. Nothing else. It's a game. It's about fucking each other. That's all we are. That's all we amount to – just a few cheap fucks. Got that?'

'Jesus,' I murmured in shock. 'You are one vicious bastard.'

Ilya stood still, glowering at me. I struggled to stay calm under the fire of his stare but inside I was a riot of emotions: fear, anger, but more than anything a hurt so sore it made my eyes brim with tears. Surely I meant more to him than that? Surely he could not think that what we had together was so callously hollow and worthless?

Ilya swept a hand back over his shorn head then, in a poisonous little whisper, he said: 'You stupid bitch.'

Hot resentment bristled up inside me, overtaking all my pain.

'Oh, fuck you,' I spat, and I made a move to leave.

Ilya took a step to block the door. I drew up short.

We stood several feet apart, motionless, like two angry cats trying to psych each other out.

Then with a quick jerk of his elbow, Ilya began unfastening his belt.

I made a noise of incredulity as the leather hissed through the loops. Was he going to try and thrash me?

But no. Ilya slung the belt to the floor.

'Get your jeans down, Beth,' he said steadily. He turned to unroll a blind over the half-windowed door, unbuttoning his flies at the same time.

'No fucking way,' I replied.

'Do it, Beth,' he barked, turning back to me.

His jeans were open and his fingers were curled round his semi-erect cock. He moved towards me, pulling gently on his length to make himself harder. Of course he wasn't going to thrash me: not his style. He wanted to fuck. That was ten times as disturbing, especially since he was having to get the blood flow going to do it.

'C'mon,' he urged.

'No way,' I repeated, inching backward, my hands groping in search of the desk behind.

Ilya scared me. I didn't like his sour cruelty or his simmering rage; I didn't like the scornful spark in his eyes. I wanted out.

'What's the problem?' he taunted, his fist still sliding on his now-swollen cock. 'It's not like you to turn your nose up when a guy's got his dick out. Look at me, Beth. I'm rock hard. Isn't your cunt dripping at the sight? Aren't your knickers getting hot and wet?'

'No,' I said, my voice all quivery. I fumbled for the desk-edge, needing support. Ilya came closer, a malicious little sneer turning up one corner of his mouth.

'Get your jeans down and lean over that desk,' he ordered.

I drew a tremulous breath. 'Or else?' I said quietly.

'Or else I'll fucking well force you,' he said, flashing a triumphant smile.

I shook my head, my heart beating crazily. 'I'm serious, Ilya,' I said. 'I want to leave now. I'm not faking. I'm not playing –'

'But we're always playing,' he smirked. 'That's all we'll ever do, right until the end, the final curtain. Play, play, play.'

'No,' I said. 'Not now. This isn't playing. You're for real because you're sick. You're a cold, twisted bastard and you're scaring me. And I'm for real because I'm scared. I want to leave.'

He carried on pumping his cock. 'Are you saying no?' he asked. 'Are you saying, no, you don't want me to fuck you?'

'Yes,' I breathed. 'I am.'

'And are you saying no, you don't want me to force you?'

I nodded.

'And how do you spell this no of yours?' he gibed.

184

'Does it begin with the letter C? Followed by U and a couple of Ts and so on?'

I gazed at him in silent horror. All I was saying was no because emotions were running high and anyone could walk in on us. Surely he could appreciate that. But maybe he couldn't. Maybe he was too far gone with his strange, mad fury.

'Well then,' he said, when I didn't reply. 'This is all shaping up to be a pretty decent rape fantasy, isn't it?'

My blood ran cold.

He was truly warped.

My hands, working of their own volition, crawled blindly over the desk, searching for a weapon. I wasn't going to allow Ilya to pervert my refusal. He was damn well going to accept it. In the movies there would have been a great big ashtray on the desk, or a knife for slitting envelopes that could also slit throats. My right hand found the pot of pens.

'Back off, will you?' I said, aiming a bunch of biros and pencils at him.

'What are you going to do?' jeered Ilya. 'Draw on me?'

'No. I'm going to poke your fucking eyes out,' I bit back.

Ilya laughed – a cruel, mocking laugh. I suddenly didn't know if he was playing nasty or feeling nasty. But either way it didn't matter because I had no taste for it.

Ilya didn't come closer. It felt as if he were waiting for me to make a move, then he could pounce and over-power me. I wished I had the muscles that he had.

I struggled for a way out of the situation, wondering if the best thing would be to just drop my jeans and let him get on with it.

Plenty of people had done that before – obliging their lover when they're not in the mood. I wouldn't struggle; I wouldn't show my genuine resistance because that would make it seem like some rape-fantasy scenario. I'd feign indifference, maybe pleasure, and invalidate it.

But no. I had a point to make. And the point was: it takes two to play out fantasies and right now I'm not playing, so that makes this one too damn real.

But then reality didn't count for much in our cuttlefish game. The word no didn't count. I couldn't make my point – except maybe by quitting. And isn't that what they call cutting off your nose to spite your face?

And supposing he threatened me with cuttlefish if I refused to drop my jeans, to struggle or whatever?

Oh God. My brain was scrambled. Maybe I should just knee him in the balls and run for it?

Ilya started to move in on me. I tensed, rigid with indecision and a fair amount of fear.

Then he grinned, suddenly throwing me into confusion by bobbing left and right, feinting like a boxer, until he pounced and hurled his full weight at me.

My pens clacked and tumbled and I screamed, staggering backward under the force of his launch. Ilya clamped a hand to my mouth.

'Shut up,' he hissed. 'Shut up, shut up, shut up.'

The wall slammed up behind me and my head hit with a bump. I wriggled and flailed, protesting into his hot, damp hand, air huffing in and out of my nostrils, my nose stud hurting.

Ilya just crushed me hard against the wall, leaning into me with the whole of his body. I could feel his bared erect prick pressing a ridge near my belly. His fingers were yanking open my button-flies.

The most terrifying thing was the hand over my mouth, half covering my nostrils. I felt panicky because I couldn't breathe properly. I wanted to suck in lungfuls of air. I wanted to breathe like a sprinter would breathe at the end of a race. I wanted to breathe like a drowning men splashing at the surface. I couldn't get enough air.

I just wanted to breathe. And the more I battled against him, the more desperate I was for that air.

The overwhelming need threatened to turn me stupid.

I couldn't think straight, but there was some part of my brain screaming for me to pay attention to it. 'This isn't fair,' it kept saying. 'Listen to me, Beth. This isn't fair.'

Ilya was pulling wildly at my jeans, battling to get them down with one hand. He was struggling to do it because I was writhing against his body, clawing at his arm, frantic to prise that hand from my mouth.

'Come on, Beth,' he growled, panting slightly. 'Dirty bitch. You know you want it.'

I felt his scrabbling fingers above my knickers, trying to push their way down.

My neck ached. My head couldn't move except to swivel a bit against the wall behind. My muffled cries made the hand covering my mouth hotter and wetter.

Then it hit me: that smothering hand prevented me from speaking. Supposing I'd wanted to him to stop – so badly that I was prepared to say cuttlefish? Impossible. He was robbing me of my only means of escape. I was powerless – not because he was stronger, but because he wouldn't let me speak.

The cheating bastard had taken me out of the game.

So I did what was only fair: I bit him. I managed to latch my teeth on to a finger and I clamped down, so hard and so strong that I felt his skin puncture and I tasted blood.

I heard him roar in pain; I felt him trying to wrench the flesh and boniness of his finger from my vicelike jaw. But I held on and, only when he stepped back, stopped crushing me with his weight, did I release him and spit out the blood.

He looked at me in amazement. 'You fucking bitch,' he rasped, clutching his injured hand in his good one. 'You fucking ... ah, shit ...' He waggled his hand. 'You vicious little tiger.'

He made a move to retaliate but I was quick to dodge him. Gasping and heaving, I rushed for the door, but before I could reach it, someone burst into the room.

'What the fuck is . . .'

A guy stood in the doorway. It was Pete – crude, boorish, lecherous Pete.

'Well, well, well,' He grinned. 'If it isn't the star of *Anal Virgin*. We meet again, eh, Beth?'

I fumbled to button up my flies, but my hands were shaking and all I could do was hold the flaps of denim together and stretch my T-shirt down.

'Get out of my way,' I said, heading for the door.

Pete moved to block my exit. 'You don't fancy staying?' he mocked, nodding at my groin. 'If Illie's out of juice, I wouldn't mind giving you another –'

I was about to lunge at him, fists flying, but Ilya's voice – as cold and clear as ice water – slapped my rage into numbness.

'Let her go, Pete,' he said. 'This is between me and Beth. She wants to leave, so let her.'

With a smile and a shrug, Pete stepped aside, and I bowled past him, rearranging my dishevelled clothes as I strode towards the big sunlit exit.

Jenny was leaning against the blue building at the end of the street and smoking in a pissed-off kind of way.

In the afternoon brightness, I felt slightly woozy and very hot. But it was a strange hot – not a sunshine hot; more a hot that felt as if my insides were melting and trying to ooze through my skin in their new liquid form.

'Sorry, Jen,' I said, trying to smile. 'I got a bit side-tracked.'

Jenny huffed a sigh of acceptance, her scowl fading, then she looked at me quizzically.

'You OK?' she asked.

'Yeah, I'm fine,' I lied.

'You sure?' she said, tapping her cigarette. 'You look a bit hectic, that's all. And you're the wrong colour. Kind of greeny white. Doesn't suit you.'

I felt the wrong colour. I felt as if vampires were at my

feet and my blood was being sucked downward. Something was catching up with me – fear, outrage, shock? – I wasn't sure. Maybe it was all those things.

I leant against the wall.

'You're not OK, are you?' said Jenny, gazing at me with a face full of concern and compassion and many years of friendship.

It made me want to cry.

I shook my head. 'No,' I said quietly. 'I'm not OK. Do you fancy a drink or something? I really need to sit down.'

I'd peeled and shredded my way through two beermats and I was toying with a third.

The Heart in Hand was green, woody and tranquil. On the jukebox Aretha Franklin was saying a little prayer for me.

'Then give him an ultimatum,' said Jenny, lining up a cigarette paper with tobacco. 'If you're so against dumping him then get the biggest apology you've ever had in your life and tell him he's got to come clean. Or you'll say cuttlefish. Can you do that? Can you say cuttlefish to each other? I mean, when you want to talk about it in conversation and stuff ? Or do you have to go, "the C-word"?'

'No,' I replied. 'We can say cuttlefish.'

'So do that then,' said Jenny, licking the edge of her Rizla.

'But there's no point.' I shrugged, running a finger round the rim of my pint glass. 'He might just tell me another pack of lies. Or he might tell me the truth and I might not know it's the truth. Or he might say tough shit, none of your business, cuttlefish and goodbye.'

Jenny shook her head and took a long, irritated drag on her roll-up.

'Besides, I'm not that bothered any more,' I continued, lowering my voice even though there was no one sitting near us. 'So what if he's got some dodgy scam going connected with knock-off antiques. I don't care. Good luck to him. The point is he scares me sometimes. Like back then. I thought we understood we were playing out fantasies. But . . . I'm just not sure if he knows when to draw the line. The rape fantasy thing. I mean, if we're going to do it, I've got to be up for it. And I wasn't then. It wasn't right. It was horrible. Like he wanted to, to punish me by fucking me and . . .'

I broke off, blinking back angry tears, and tapped the beermat hard on the table.

'And he wouldn't let me speak,' I said in a choked voice. 'The bastard wouldn't let me speak.'

'Hey,' said Jenny in a soft, consoling tone. 'Don't get upset.' She rubbed at my hand, giving my fingers a gentle squeeze 'He's not worth the salt in that tear. He's a heartless shit with a nasty temper. And he's got some pretty unhealthy ideas about relationships and how to treat people. You need to take a step back and reassess. Get your head straight, Beth. Or, like I said, finish it now.'

I dashed my hand across my cheek and turned aside, staring at a stained-glass window and trying not to cry.

'But I can't,' I said, when the threat of tears had gone. 'You don't understand, Jen. I can't walk away and just forget it all. It's . . . I know that's not good, but I can't help it. I know he said some rotten things today, but I can't believe he meant it. He was angry, wound up. And, yeah, maybe he overreacted to me going in there, but maybe I shouldn't have been so nosy. I dunno. It was just a weird one-off. And everything else . . . it's, it's good. I'm not ready to finish things. I'm so immersed in what we've got going. I can't help that and I wish I could.'

Jenny tried to conceal a weary sigh. I could tell she was tiring of all my buts. A silence fell between us, starchy with friction, and for a while we just drank our beers. Jenny fixed herself another roll-up.

Then Jenny said, 'Look, maybe the way to get him out of your system is to end it. OK, so it might be painful. But in the long run, it's got to be for the best. Sooner or later it's got to end. So do it now before this guy really oversteps the mark.'

'But I can't,' I protested. 'It's too compelling. The sex, the game, the not knowing what'll happen next. It's not just him I'm gripped by. It's the game as well. I know you think it's weird – me being a closet sleaze-bag –'

'Each to their own,' Jenny shrugged. 'I'm not going to judge, am I? I just think there must be a better way of exploring these fantasies of yours. And I don't understand why you didn't do it before – when you were with someone you cared about. Someone you trusted and loved.'

'Too late now,' I said.

'Then wait,' she urged. 'Wait until some guy comes along who makes your heart sing. Save it all up, and wham. You'll have a great time. Mr Right won't believe his luck.'

'I don't think it'd work,' I said disconsolately. 'It's . . . I just see it as separate from love. That's part of the buzz.' I dropped my voice as a glass-collecting barmaid passed our table. 'We don't do ordinary stuff or open up about our feelings or, or make love. That was the deal. Keep it simple and pure – sex without complications. And I get off on that idea, of sex that's detached, whorish. Or I did. It's . . . I mean, we're just playing a game together. That's all. We're not emotionally entangled and –'

'But you are, Beth,' insisted Jenny. 'You are emotionally entangled. Maybe he isn't, but you are and that's not a good combination. It's not a good basis for this, this *game*, as you call it. He could really exploit that. He'll treat you like shit and you'll keep going back for more. It's crazy, completely crazy. I mean, like this afternoon, if

191

he thinks he's got away with behaving the way he did then maybe next time it'll be worse. Much worse. Get out of it, Beth. End it. Dump him.'

I didn't answer.

'Oh God, Beth,' murmured Jenny, looking at me with worry and suspicion. 'You want it worse, don't you?'

I shrugged and began splitting the corner of my beermat.

Jenny released a long breath and slumped back in her seat, shaking her head reprovingly.

'You're asking for trouble, Beth,' she said. 'You really are.'

Chapter Ten

*I*lya sent me some white flowers – a great big bunch of furled lilies, sprigged with tightly budded carnations and some spiky flowers I couldn't identify. They were delivered in a box by a flower delivery-man carrying a clipboard.

In my flat, I read the accompanying little card: 'My finger's really sore. Guess I got off lightly.'

It was written in big round letters and there was no name there. I mentally added 'from Ilya'; but 'from Karen, the seventeen-year-old whose job it is to write these cards' seemed more appropriate.

I was livid.

If the flowers hadn't been so infuriatingly beautiful, I would've chucked them in the bin. But I didn't have the heart; they hadn't done anything wrong. And they hadn't even lived yet. They were still in bud, swollen with promise.

I wasn't too bothered that there was nothing like 'sorry' or 'forgive me' in the card – although it might have been nice. But 'sorry and forgive me' are only words and the whole package was basically saying the same thing; it was just spelt differently.

And I hated the way it was spelt. It was dull, thought-less, bland, anonymous and insulting.

What was I supposed to think? Oh, how wonderful, he's gone to the effort of sending me flowers, so deep inside he must have a warm and tender heart?

Well, I didn't. I just thought, He's gone to the effort of getting his credit card out. Big fucking deal.

I didn't contact him. I didn't phone to say thanks or 'Hey, let's talk' or 'You nasty, vicious, cheating bastard, what the hell were you playing at?'

And he didn't contact me either. Fine, I thought. We'll have a practice run at cuttlefish, see how I get on without you.

I might've been asking for trouble, as Jenny had said, but I certainly wasn't prepared to go and beg for it.

Besides, I was busy. I had some hot sex to sell.

The bars and clubs on the seafront are under the arches where, in the olden days, fishermen used to hang out, mending nets and puffing on pipes.

The arches are still there but the fishermen are a bit thin on the ground.

In some of the bars, the vaulted stone ceilings are a feature; other clubs do their best to hide them. The club we were in had a warehousey feel to it and the dance-floor crowd shimmered and pulsed under a kaleidoscope of lights.

'Hot sex. Two quid,' I shouted over the pumping music as some guy with turquoise-blonde hair approached the group I was with. I thrust a flyer into his hand. He took it, raised his eyebrows in a show of mild interest, said 'Cheers', then I resumed my loud conversation and he started one with someone else.

That's the trouble with Brighton and flyers. You could hand out slips of paper saying 'Baboons Fuck Live' and people would just nod and put them in their pockets or chuck them to the ground, depending on how polite they were. And they wouldn't think much about it. And, if they did, they'd just think 'Baboons Fuck Live' was some local band or a new club night. Or they'd think it was the real thing, but so what? It's Brighton. Anything goes.

Word of mouth was the best publicity machine. So I'd started the ball rolling by telling lots of people about the gritty reality of Hot Sex. I seemed to have whetted quite a few appetites, but at that stage in the evening I was wearying of it. So I was easing up on the sales pitch and starting to enjoy myself.

I shouldered my way through the crush, back to base, where Jen, Fiona, Ellie and a bunch of others were clustered around a tall, chrome table, all shouting in different directions.

'Vodka for the pimp,' yelled Jenny drunkenly, holding up a glass for me.

I took it and drank, making loud chit-chat with some guy I vaguely knew who thought he was a poet.

Then a voice close to my ear barged in with: 'All right. Beth, isn't it?'

I turned to face this young and beautiful, peroxide-blond guy who had a sleeper in one eyebrow. He was jerking his head in time to the music, doing his best to appear cool and casual while awaiting my response.

He was familiar but I couldn't place him. But then lots of people say 'hi' to me – because of the club – and I can't place them. So I just returned a bland smile.

'Luke,' he hollered, and he began drumming away on the table-edge, his whole body bobbing to the beat. 'We were at the beach together. A while back. Just chillin'.'

For a moment, I thought he meant The Beach as in the club. Then it clicked. Ah, he means the pebbly thing with the sea at the bottom.

I caught Jenny watching us. She gave me a wicked little grin because one of her many solutions to the Ilya saga was for me to find another lover, take my mind off things.

So I gave Luke a wide, welcoming smile.

'Hot sex?' I said, raising my voice and offering him a flyer. 'Two quid?'

He grinned, took the flyer in one hand and combed his other hand through his softly spiked hair. 'That's cheap,' he said, briefly leaning closer because of the music.

I leant forward, and in a loud voice, said, 'Well, that's the kind of girl I am.'

'So how old are you?' asked Luke, as we crunched quickly over the pebbled beach, away from the lantern-lit esplanade with its big arty sculptures and cluster of bars.

'Thirty-six,' I lied, my ears still ringing from the noise of the club.

'Wow,' he said. 'You don't look it. I've never been with someone so old before.' He took a couple of sideways skips, grinning in the moon's half-light as he made a mock inspection of my face. 'Straight up? Are you really thirty-six?'

'No,' I said, my feet sinking into the shingle as I hurried to catch up with him. I gave his waist a playful nip, relishing the feel of hard, youthful muscle. 'I'm thirty. Still in my prime.'

'Yeah?' he exclaimed. 'Well, thirty's pretty cool. Makes you my oldest woman by four years. So who's the oldest guy you've ever been with?'

'Er, there was one bloke called Methuselah,' I replied. 'He was pretty old.'

'Yeah?' said Luke. 'Weird name. How old was he then?'

'Oh God,' I said, and I pulled him to me. 'You are fucking lovely.'

And he was: good-looking, empty-headed, complete slag.

If I was going to kick the Ilya habit then what nicer way was there of doing it? I figured Luke could be my methadone substitute while I weaned myself off the hard stuff. But there was no way I would get addicted to him. He would be just sex, in the way me and Ilya were meant to be just sex.

Standing on the open beach, we exchanged a greedy, tongue-probing kiss. It was a warmish, cloud-streaky night, with a pretty decent-sized moon, and there were a few people dotted around: little ragged crowds, laughing and screeching; couples lying side by side, snogging and groping.

But it didn't matter: they were either drugged up or drunk. I was pretty out of it, too – not enough to have regrets in the morning, but enough not to care if someone saw us.

I let my hands roam greedily over Luke's body. I caressed the sweat-damp flesh under his big, droopy T-shirt, then pushed down past the waistband of his low-slung combats. I'd already worked out that there was no underwear beneath so, straight away, I got Luke's naked, upright prick. Desire tore through me, urgent and demanding, and, as I curled my fingers round that warm, rigid shaft, Luke moaned into our kiss.

Back at the club, I'd been covertly massaging his groin under the table. The crotch of his trousers was baggy enough for me to mould the fabric to his prick, and I'd felt every twitch and stretch of his growing erection.

My ferocious flirting had unsettled him at first. As I'd chatted away, he kept on trying to adopt a vacant, disinterested look. He would scan the room, his head nodding with the music, as if my small talk was just too dull for him and that being felt up in a nightclub was a run-of-the-mill event.

But eventually he'd relaxed and got into the swing of things. He'd started rubbing my skirt along my thigh, telling me how much he fancied me, how my lips were really gorgeous, and lots of standard chat-up rubbish like that. But at least that rubbish had been better to listen to than his earlier rubbish – an enthusiastic monologue on skateboarding and how he'd once gashed his knee really badly because pads are, like, so uncool.

He'd got slightly flustered when I suggested he go to the gents to buy a pack of three. 'I can't,' he'd hissed, with a downward glance. 'I can't buy condoms when my dick's like this.'

Sympathetic to his plight, I'd done the dirty deed myself.

'Come on,' I urged, breaking the embrace and grasping his hand. 'Bit further along.'

We hurried and stumbled, searching for somewhere less exposed, away from people and the CCTV cameras on tall spiky poles.

My sex was pulsing with wet heat and Luke had a boner to die for. I was frantic to get those two things matched up. Our encounter had the inevitability and sweet simplicity of a primary-school sum. I had only a couple of niggling worries: one was that he might come too quickly, in legendary young-bloke style; the second was that he might, deep down, be a truly sensitive soul who was tiring of casual sex and hoping to strike up a more meaningful relationship.

I needn't have worried on either score.

We hurried back up to the soft yellow lights of the walkway because one of the stone groynes that divide up the beach was about to halt our progress. Ahead, close to the paving, there was a kind of boat park – a long, rectangular patch of boats stacked this way and that, their masts angling high.

'What about there?' said Luke. 'We could hide between some boats or, like, get in one.'

'Nah, too close to civilisation,' I countered.

To the right, above the arches and beyond the wide road, was the floodlit Grand Hotel, its white elegance and wrought-iron balconies gleaming in the night. It looked like a glossy cardboard cut-out of a splendid wedding cake. Next door was the red-brick Metropole, stern, foreboding and shadowy. It looked like a Victorian prison.

The road stretched along the coast, a row of orange-dot street lamps that got tangled up and confused with the bulbs of the broken West Pier.

To the left was unadulterated night – well, almost unadulterated. The piers, one behind us, one in front, twinkled out, casting faint silver patches on to the water.

But apart from that, it was sea and sky – vast and exhilarating in a scary kind of way. The sea was inky and the cloudy moonlit sky was all marbled in blacks, greys and blueberry jams. You could see the line of the horizon. France was out there somewhere. There was a strange compulsion to all that darkness, a force of gravity that sucked you towards it like a black hole.

So we turned and headed seaward. The shingle shelved steeply at one point and the pale groyne rose up like a wall to our left, cutting off the nightlife we'd left behind and offering us something in the way of privacy.

'Here,' I said, sinking to the ground.

Further down the slope, frothy waves somersaulted on to the beach, crashing in and making gentle slushy noises as they dragged back their haul of tiny stones.

But we weren't talking *From Here to Eternity*. The air was sharp with the tang of mulchy seaweed, and there was a cool, damp feel to the spot I'd chosen. The pebbles were huge – more like rocks – and they scraped harshly against each other as we banked down. It was damned uncomfortable.

'Is it OK?' said Luke, cautiously running his fingers over the ground and scanning our gloomy patch. 'No dead fish or dog shit and stuff?'

'Ah, the spirit of romance,' I said, drawing his body to mine.

'Sorry,' he said. 'It's just that –'

'Shut up,' I cut in, and I silenced him with a kiss. Luke was much better when he was silent.

His hands moved over me with a surprising lack of urgency – not because he was hesitant or intimidated by me-the-older-woman but because he was mindful of giving me pleasure.

My skirt was ankle length and he caressed my thighs and arse without greedily shoving up material and hunting for bare pussy. When he began roaming under my T-shirt, he paid attention to my midriff before sliding up to fondle my breasts with tender explorations. His kisses were hot and sweet, and sometimes, while his lips throbbed on mine, he just held my face or tangled his fingers in my hair. I wanted, at the very least, those fingers in my knickers.

There was a certain 'I have studied' element to Luke's way of handling me. It was as if he'd learnt that women like lots of foreplay – and fore-foreplay – and that going straight for the jugular of fucking was a fault made only by young, inexperienced men. So he was determined never, ever to do that. He didn't yet have the sophistication to appreciate that sometimes a jugular fuck is perfectly appropriate.

So once I'd allowed him the luxury of proving that he wasn't an archetypal, hot young blood, I took the lead.

'Feel how wet I am,' I whispered, hitching my skirt up at the front. I guided Luke's hand into my knickers.

'Oh, yeah,' he murmured, and his eager-to-please fingers danced in my folds, coming to an abrupt halt when they located their treasure: the hard bump of my clitoris.

'You like that?' he asked, stirring slowly around my bud and making its pulses spread deeper.

'Yes,' I moaned, seeking out his zip fly. I undid his trousers and clasped the sturdy thrust of his cock.

Though Luke's fingers were delightful, I badly wanted his prick inside me. I get so greedy at the prospect of fresh meat, and my cunt was achingly hollow. So, doing a quick check to make sure we were still alone, I hurried out of my knickers and knelt astride his thighs, my back to France. While Luke encouraged me with mumbled excitement, I dealt with the condom stuff, then impaled myself on his granite-hard length.

I groaned as I sank down. His thickness filled and stretched me and I held the position, drawing deep sighs and fluffing at my skirt to conceal our union.

When I was ready to roll, I rummaged under my skirt, rested my hand on Luke's pubis and knuckled my thumb into my clit. Perfect. I resisted the upthrust of his pelvis the best I could, pressing down on him so I could anchor my needy bud to my thumb-joint.

Leaning half over him, I moved on his shaft in deep-rooted thrusts, rocking my hips to and fro and telling Luke how good he felt. The slight shunting of my knees pushed awkward, angular dents into the pebbled ground and the stones bashed viciously into my bones.

'Oh, baby, more,' Luke kept saying, and he reached to grip me beneath my skirt. He clutched my arse, holding my cheeks apart as he strove to make me lift higher on his stiffness. The night air tingled deliciously in the cleft of my buttocks and I continued grinding myself to the root of him until my clit was scorched with intensity and my orgasm was a dead cert.

'Oh, yeah,' drawled Luke as I began to really fuck, rising and falling, bouncing eagerly on his dick.

My tits jiggled under my T-shirt and our groins mashed together, increasingly hectic. We kept our gasps and groans furtively quiet, but even so – with the muffled thud of the clubs in the distance and the irregular surge of the water's edge – we sounded noisy and out of place. The big pebbles clacked beneath us as we pounded ceaselessly.

When my climax clenched and scattered, it was truly sublime. Maybe it was because of all the enormous night surrounding us; or maybe it was because I'd seduced someone a decade younger than me; or maybe I had a flash of feeling liberated from Ilya – I don't know. I just know that my first orgasm with Luke was one I'd remember for a long time, and I gave vent to a wail of pleasure that was far too loud.

And when I crashed the waves didn't. My noisiness came in a lull of one wave retreating, another about to hit.

'Oh, baby,' cried Luke in a voice hoarse with delight. He slammed me down to meet his driving cock until my quick-gripping cunt milked his juices and he came – like me – with a wail that was far too loud. And, like me, it was not simultaneous with the sea.

We froze, our bodies tensed, hardly daring to breathe as we locked gazes and waited. We were like thieves in the night who'd just dropped the telly.

Then Luke broke our silence with an experimental laugh.

'Wow,' he said, and normality returned.

'Wow,' I said back to him, and we both relaxed, laughing gently at our noisiness and that silly moment of fear.

I eased myself from him.

'So do you do this a lot?' enquired Luke, packing his condom under a hefty stone.

'Do what?' I said, scrambling for my knickers. 'Pick up toy-boys and lure them down the beach?'

'Yeah,' he said. 'But like, you know, casual sex? One-night stands?'

'Who said anything about one night?' I replied, wriggling into my underwear. I tried not to smile as a shadow of concern crossed over his face. 'I might not have finished with you yet.'

'Er, you mean like you want us to be on together?' He frowned as he did up his trousers.

'Meet each other's friends?' I suggested. 'Go for walks

in the park? Have dinner? Yeah, sounds great. You could teach me how to skate, maybe.'

He looked at me steadily. Then he said, 'That's a joke, isn't it?'

'You're learning fast.' I grinned, and he visibly sighed with relief.

'I mean, you're really nice and everything . . .' he began.

'Oi,' I said in a mock-warning tone. 'Save all the soft-soap for the girls who want it. I'm not looking for anything more than this. OK?'

'Oh yeah, sure,' he said. 'So are you saying that's it? It was OK, wasn't it? You came, didn't you? I mean, like, properly. You weren't . . .'

'Faking?' I laughed. 'I'm out of practice on that score. Grew out of the habit years ago.'

'Cool,' said Luke, brightening. 'So, like, do you think we'll get it together again?'

I shrugged. 'Dunno. Maybe we could come to some sort of sexual arrangement.'

Luke gave me a broad grin. 'Cool,' he said. 'Yeah, cool.'

My lilies trumpeted into big beautiful blooms. I had them in a glass vase on a shelf near my desk – away from the window and so out of Ilya's sight.

There was something obscene about the lilies, especially set next to the demure laciness of half-open carnations. Their pale pointy petals curled back at the tip, inviting you to look deep into the funnels of their streaked, yellow-green throats. They were proudly vulval – the beaver shot of the flower world. And they were also pretty phallic, with bulbous-tipped stamens that started to ooze fluid: a clear liquid, like pre-come shimmering on a glans.

Lilies, I decided, were deliciously pornographic. And

the box they'd been delivered in had a warning to say their pollen could stain. That made them even lewder.

Maybe I was just missing Ilya. He hadn't contacted me. I hadn't contacted him.

It was stalemate. Who would crack first?

My first Hot Sex gig went down pretty well. It was more warm sex really, but it was damn good fun.

Clare and Vee were my door whores, kitted out in wet-look leotards, flaunting fishnet-clad arses and Betty Boop cheeks. They took people's money, offered them heart-shaped biscuits and novelty-shop love potions. (The free-bies were Jenny's idea. She really got into her love theme; I think she was trying to make a point.)

On stage we had a fashion show, a mix of fetish and glitter. We had strippers, male and female; some dirty dancers; a local amateur poet who does a witty monologue called 'Homage to Self Abuse'; a porno Punch and Judy show; and a whole host of other frolics.

Steve and Joe – multimedia wizards – set up projections as a backdrop: a shifting montage of pervy pictures and dirty words. We had a raffle with a vibrator kit as top prize, some furry handcuffs as second, and a really tacky wank-mag as third.

People liked it. They wanted more. I started to plan my second gig.

Having Luke stay the night was not something I enjoyed. I would've preferred to send him packing after sex, the way me and Ilya sent each other packing.

But I was very keen to have him wandering around in my flat, with the curtains open, at a morning hour that would make him a lover rather than a friend. Ilya, of course, would see everything, fly into a jealous rage and call me.

The lilies were beginning to die.

'So have you read all the books in this flat?' enquired

Luke, returning to my bedroom with two mugs of tea. He was wearing boxer shorts – for the sake of decency – because I'd asked him to open the living room curtains so the sun could warm the place up. He'd fallen for it.

'Yep,' I said. 'Read the lot. Cover to cover.'

'Straight up?' he replied. 'How many are there?'

'Six hundred and seventy-two.'

He looked at me uncertainly and I returned a smile.

'Joke?' he asked.

'Yeah,' I said. 'Joke. I've no idea how many there are. A lot. And no, I haven't read them all. Nowhere near.'

Luke nodded then went to select a book at random from my bedroom shelves. He sprawled on top of the duvet, opening pages in chunks.

'I suppose I should read things,' he said quietly.

'I'll teach you,' I replied. 'We can start with the alphabet.'

He raised his head and gave me a cute-as-hell grin, which I knew I hadn't earned. I had a pang of guilt about continually taking the piss but then I reassured myself: he's got to learn not to make himself such an easy target.

Luke cast the book aside, making a comment about the front cover, then launched into some story about the time he and his mates did mushrooms and ended up on the Palace Pier and, like, he started having a really bad trip.

Luke had the attention span of a gnat. I was getting used to his non-sequitur mode of communication.

I sipped my tea, letting him burble on, and when the phone rang in the living-room I was half inclined to answer it, just to escape. But I decided not to bother. The only people I'm prepared to speak to before ten in the morning are people who would never call at that time.

'Aren't you going to get that?' asked Luke.

I shook my head. 'Answerphone'll get it.'

So Luke resumed his boring drugs story while I kept my ears tuned for whoever might leave a message. It was Ilya.

'Hush, hush!' I snapped, urgently flapping my hand at Luke. He fell silent.

'I know you're busy at the moment,' came Ilya's tired-sounding voice from the adjacent room. 'So I won't bother asking you to pick up the phone.'

A warm, smug glow spread through me.

'But I'd really like to see you,' he continued. 'In fact, I need to see you. Soon. I need to talk to you, Beth. About lots of things.'

My smug glow got even bigger, and I was positively on fire when Ilya asked, *please*, would I go over to his flat as soon as I had the chance.

'I could always come to yours,' his message went on. 'If you want me to, that is. But I'd really prefer it if you came here. Please, Beth.'

My heart danced in delight. He was grovelling. He couldn't bear us being apart. He was asking, oh so nicely, for me to go back to him. He was even prepared to talk.

'Who was that?' asked Luke, observing me curiously as the tape rewound.

I had a stupidly happy grin on my face. I knew I did. I couldn't help it.

'It's my other lover,' I replied, flexing my spine and stretching my arms wide.

Luke looked at me steadily. 'Joke?' he asked, smiling faintly.

'No, Luke,' I said. 'Not this time.'

'Jesus Christ!' I breathed, as I reached Ilya at his flat door. 'What the fuck happened to your face?'

There was a dark stormy bruise on one cheekbone; his left eye was half-closed and, under its sagging, swollen lid, it was horribly bloodshot; there was a cut on the eyebrow above; and, at the corner of his mouth, there was an ugly crimson scab.

My plan to be sternly aloof, slightly distant, then ultimately forgiving flew right out of the window.

Ilya made an attempt at a smile but it obviously hurt too much and turned into a grimace. His right hand was half-wrapped in a crudely fashioned bandage with bits of wadding sticking out. There was another wild bruise on his jawbone. He was unshaven and tired-looking.

'Spot of bother,' he said, walking into the sunny living room with a stiff, slow gait.

'Are you injured?' I asked, floundering and shuffling behind him. I wanted to touch him, to help him somehow, yet I didn't dare in case I pressed something that was tender. A sudden affection tore through me, so strong it was like aggression.

'Bruised ribs,' he said. 'Only hurts when I breathe.' He sat gingerly in the armchair, easing himself down like an arthritic pensioner.

'Well, what happened?' I blustered, staring at his misshapen, bashed-up face. 'And when? Have you got some . . . some ointment or painkillers? Do you want me to do anything?'

'Like what?' he replied, with the best suggestive smile he could muster.

I shrugged, feeling utterly useless and desperate to help. 'Plump up the cushions. Make a cup of tea. I don't know. Sorry, but I'm a shit nurse. I . . . Are you OK?'

'I'm fine,' he said, regarding me with his lopsided gaze. 'Really. Looks worse than it is.'

'And what?' I pleaded, starting to feel frustrated. 'You had an argument with a bus? Or . . . or I should've seen the other guy?'

'Yeah,' he said gently. 'Sit down, will you? And stop doing that thing with your hands. You're making me nervous.'

I perched myself on the sofa, my hands clamped together, waiting for a story to unfold.

His eye was truly hideous: the lid was bloated, its skin stretched to a lilac-tinged sheen. And the eye trying to peep from under that fattened flesh made my stomach turn over: to one side of his iris his eye was white and clear; to the other side it was clotted with tiny blood vessels, all spiderwebbing out from a violent red dot.

Ilya gazed at me, opened his mouth to speak, stopped, then started again.

'Look, Beth,' he said. 'I owe a lot of money.'

'Jesus,' I murmured. Most people I know owe a lot of money, but I suspected Ilya's definition of 'a lot' was pretty different from mine. This clearly wasn't a case of being slap-happy with the plastic.

'And I came to Brighton to buy myself some time,' he went on, picking at a fingernail. 'And to set something up so I could pay off what I owe. Because I need to. But my time's running out and . . .' His woolly explanation tapered off into a gloomy silence.

'Are you saying you got beaten up by, by your creditors?' I prompted.

'Yeah, indirectly,' he said.

'Well, who are they?' I asked. 'How much do they want? Why?'

Ilya started a deep breath then touched a hand to his ribs, his shoulders sinking again. 'I know I've been less than honest with you,' he said. 'And I know that's pissed you off. But it'll have to stay that way for now. I'm sorry. But it's the safest thing, Beth. You're better off out of it.'

'But what's "it"?' I persisted. 'Is it antiques and stuff?'

Ilya shook his head and smiled, sort of. 'No. Pete . . . well, his business – it's just a way around something. I'm sorry. I can't say anything more until –'

'So is it drugs?' I asked. 'Is that what you do? Are you a dealer?'

He shook his head again, eyes downcast.

'So, you know that time I called on you once?' I began. 'When I came to get my boa and my watch and you wouldn't let me in? And your fingers were all white and powdery . . .'

Ilya looked puzzled.

'You told me you'd spilt Polyfilla,' I continued. 'Or some bollocks like that. Well what was that all about? 'Cos I kept thinking it was something druggy. You can tell me if it was. I'm a woman of the world, you know.'

Ilya laughed and ouched. 'I'd forgotten that one,' he said, his good eye glittering. 'No, it wasn't . . . Look, I suppose it's pretty obvious that I'm not Mr Clean. So here goes: I got offered some fake twenties and . . .' He paused, as if he was uncertain whether to continue.

'Money?' I said. 'As in counterfeit notes?'

'Yeah,' he said with a sketchy smile. 'And, well, to make them look older you rub talcum powder on them. I was doing a big batch.' He grinned foolishly. 'Good tip if you ever need it.'

I tutted in mock reproof. So what if he knows about forged money? I thought. Wouldn't mind some fake twenties myself.

'I think you and I move in different circles,' I said.

'Yeah,' he replied. 'We do.'

Then, looking sober and miserable, Ilya said: 'Look, Beth, I . . . I've got to go away for a couple of weeks.'

Disappointment sank into my stomach and stayed there like Christmas cake. Then a horrible thought came into my mind, so horrible that my heart fisted up and I felt the blood drain from my face.

'You . . . you are coming back, aren't you?' I breathed, and the fear that he might not be – that he was telling me yet more lies or that something bad might happen to him – made my eyes sting with unshed tears.

He gave me a wan smile. 'Yeah, course I am,' he said softly. 'Come over here.'

I went to kneel between his feet and took hold of his undamaged hand. I kept my head low, making a show of nibbling his fingertips while secretly smearing a tear or two on to his trousers and blinking back the next lot. I wouldn't let him see me cry.

'I've missed you so badly,' he said, twisting a strand of my hair.

'Serves you right,' I mumbled.

'Yeah, I know,' he said in a quiet, guilty voice. 'And I'm sorry. But . . . the antiques thing, in the office . . . you got me on a bad day. I was stressed out, and I know that doesn't excuse what I did, and I didn't mean the stuff I said, and I should never have –'

'Shut up,' I said gently. 'It's over.'

We let a comfortable silence wrap itself around us and I just nuzzled against his knee.

Then Ilya said, 'Wish I didn't have to go away.'

'Mmm,' I agreed. 'Are you going to tell me where, or is it another secret?'

'Prague,' he replied. 'And honestly, it shouldn't take more than a fortnight.'

Oh, that was too many miles away. But I didn't ask him why, or what he was going to do there. For once, I just accepted it: Prague. A fortnight.

'Will you do me a favour?' he said, and he took my hand and placed it over his crotch.

I raised my head, gently massaging his groin and feeling him swell rapidly beneath my palm. 'I haven't got any money,' I said.

Ilya's face contorted into one of its wincing smiles. 'No, nothing like that,' he replied. 'Just suck me off, Beth.' He gave me a little grin and lifted his bandaged right hand. 'I can't even wank properly at the moment. It's been hell.'

I smiled back. 'I suppose a fuck's out of the question.'

"Fraid so,' he answered. 'Anyway, I probably wouldn't last long.'

And so I peeled the zip over his humped-up dick and let his cock spring free. His shaft was broad and hard, its blue veins up and pulsing. My cunt ached. It didn't seem right that such strength and virility could emerge from a virtual cripple.

'Don't mind if I join you?' I breathed, unfastening my Levi's.

'Be my guest,' he replied.

I shoved my jeans and knickers to my knees, then I opened my mouth wide above his prick. I went down, hardly touching him until my gaping lips were at his root. Then I clamped my mouth around him, smothering his erection in wet heat.

He groaned, long and low, and I reached between my thighs to finger my dampening pussy. Sunlight warmed my bare arse. Ilya kept on groaning as I sucked and slipped, fellating him slowly while I brought myself off.

He was right: he didn't last long, and nor did I.

With a muted cry, Ilya climaxed, and I drank his juices – that's how much I liked him – still frigging myself until I'd peaked too. I didn't even allow myself to gasp and groan freely, preferring instead to keep Ilya's cock in my mouth for as long as possible.

Lazily, I rolled my tongue around his retracting size, letting him slip from my lips when he'd shrunk back to normal. I rested my cheek against his thigh.

After a while, Ilya said, 'So who was the guy this morning?'

I struggled with my memory. The morning seemed a million miles away, and when I recalled Luke he seemed as big and important as a pin. I gazed up at Ilya. Was he jealous? Threatened? Of course he wasn't. Stupid notion.

'It's my new blond bimbo.' I smiled. 'My main squeeze dried up so I needed someone to fuck.'

Ilya controlled a grin. 'And?' he asked.

I shrugged, not sure what he meant, and rested my head on his leg again.

'Did the earth move?' said Ilya. 'Have I got competition?'

'Well, he can walk,' I said. 'So that's one up on you. And he doesn't look like a cyclops.'

211

Ilya stroked my cheek. 'Just wait till I get back,' he said. 'Your cunt won't know what's hit it.'

I toyed with his lolling prick, wondering when that would be.

'I might even try raping you again,' he said softly. 'If you play your cards right and promise not to bite.'

I gave his inner thigh a reprimanding little nip.

'So tell me about him,' said Ilya, his tone mildly curious but nothing more.

'There's not much to tell,' I said truthfully. 'Luke's just into marathon fucking sessions. And that's about it. He's got stamina, but not much imagination. I might work on him though. Let him settle in first, then pow.'

'Lucky guy,' murmured Ilya. 'Maybe the two of you could give me a floor show one day.'

'Don't think he's quite ready for that,' I said. 'Not yet.'

'Shame,' he replied. 'It'd be nice to sit here and watch the two of you going at it. I could fuck you by proxy.'

I pursed my lips, raising my eyes to meet his, trying to give him a 'shut up' expression. It seemed to work, and Ilya just smiled.

More than anything I wanted to hold him, to wrap my arms round him and soothe away his aches and pains and troubles. And my own. But that barrier which said 'do not touch me emotionally' seemed to have gone down, only to be replaced by one that said 'do not touch me physically'. He was too sore. I hate ironies when they're cruel.

'When are you leaving?' I asked, unable to keep the melancholy note from my voice.

'Tomorrow evening.'

'Oh, I see.'

We were quiet for a while. I half wanted tomorrow evening to come faster so that his fortnight would be over faster.

'Beth,' he said questioningly. 'What are you doing for the next twenty-four hours?'

I smiled up at him, lifting my brows.

'Only I've got this great idea for a role-play,' he began. 'It goes like this: I'm a fragile old man – who might manage a gentle fuck if he's on his back and very, very comfortable. And you're a dirty little slut who wants to sit on my cock, straddle my face, dance for me, wank for me, suck me off . . .' He raised his bound hand. 'Oh, and maybe rustle up some food as well.'

I stretched to kiss the tip of his cock. 'My diary's suddenly empty,' I said. 'And you're in luck because I'm a pretty good cook. But, when I'm naked, I am kitchen dynamite.'

Chapter Eleven

I was sitting at my computer, cranking out a book review for a local magazine.

Several feet to the left of me was the big bay window that looks across to Ilya's flat. A late-August rainshower dappled the glass and the telephone wires sloping down to my building carried droplets of water like tiny glass cable cars.

For five days, nothing had stirred. Ilya's blind remained half-up – a position unsuited to day or night; the lights didn't go on or off.

They wouldn't do. He was in Prague. For at least a fortnight.

But old habits die hard, and I couldn't stop myself from continually checking the view.

And forever in my mind were thoughts that ranged from 'maybe he'll come back early' to 'maybe I'll never see him again and I'll just keep gazing at his window until one day someone else will move in'.

So I was typing in bits of my review, ruffling through notes, staring at the screen, and every now and then casting a glance beyond the rain speckles to Ilya's flat.

His departure after the 24 hours we'd spent together –

24 hours of deliciously claustrophobic bliss, both domestic and debauched – had left a void inside me so vast that I couldn't imagine anything would ever fill it. Not even Ilya's safe return.

I didn't know how things would be between us when – if – we were together again. There was nowhere left for us to go. 'No emotional entanglements' – that was one of the early rules of our game. Well, we'd broken that one, big style. And it couldn't be fixed.

Ilya, apparently, tends not to stay in the same place for long: he gets bored, he moves on. That's his lifestyle. And it doesn't do to get too involved with people, he'd said. He prefers to keep his distance; that way no one gets hurt. But his feelings for me were becoming harder to control. That scared him and sometimes it made him angry – with himself or with me.

Hence the antique-shop aggression. He'd wanted to try to take things back a few paces, get us on track again; but he didn't know how, and all those confused, pent-up emotions got expressed via the wrong outlet.

So where to next? We'd been silent on that subject, both of us tacitly agreeing to delude ourselves by pretending it wasn't an issue.

And our options were pretty limited and unappealing. Would we try to rewind, box up our feelings and play at playing the game for a little while longer? I couldn't begin to see how that would work.

And becoming more involved, in terms of a relationship, was surely not on the cards. Ilya and I belonged to separate worlds. Besides, as much as I cared for him and desired him, I didn't think I could ever love or trust him.

I glanced across to his flat. I did a double-take, my heart going pitter-patter like the rain. Something – someone – had moved in the shadows.

I kept on staring. My computer hummed away. Everything was still over there. Was he back or had my eyes been playing tricks? Was it just the reflection of a tree in the breeze?

But no, there was movement again. Joy tamed by disbelief bubbled up inside me. He was home. My excitement mounted. The dark figure was moving closer to the window. Perhaps he was going to signal to me.

Then a slab of cold dread thumped into my guts, because Ilya does not wear caps with black-and-white bands. That's what policemen wear.

My eyes riveted to the dark figure, I eased back my chair and stood.

I padded over to my rain-streaked bay window and, though it's only a few feet away, that walk seemed to take for ever, as if I were wading through zero-gravity in huge, clumsy moon boots.

Below, parked outside Ilya's building, was a police car, its Day-Glo stripe gleaming in the shower-murky street.

He was dead.

For five days, he'd been lying in a pool of blood, slowly rotting, and nobody knew except the man who'd murdered him – shot him, stabbed him, beaten him to a pulpy corpse – because he owed too much money.

He wasn't in Prague. He was dead.

They would need someone to identify the body.

I slipped on my sandals.

'And so do you know where Mr Travis is?' asked the officer. 'Or how we might contact him?'

I was going to say Prague, but I stopped myself. I didn't know if I was allowed to give that information to the police. I shook my head. 'Just on holiday, I think. I'm not sure where.'

The relief was overwhelming. It was still sluicing through me, like rainfall in the gutters outside. He wasn't dead. He'd just been burgled, though nobody seemed to know quite when.

Ilya's landlord was poking at the splintered wood of the flat door.

'So you're not a close acquaintance of Mr Travis, then?' continued the officer.

'Not really, no,' I said. 'We're more, just a bit neighbourly really.'

'So you're not in a position to confirm that the television and video are missing?'

'No, suppose not.' I shrugged, but it was pretty bloody obvious that they were.

'Well, I'm afraid there isn't a great deal we can do,' he said, flicking shut his notebook.

And that was that, more or less. Mr Travis could contact them on his return if he wished to report anything missing.

I didn't bother asking if they were going to fingerprint the place. I knew what the answer would be: No point. Happens all the time. Mr Travis was simply unlucky.

Better that, I thought, than dead.

Luke has the face of a dazed angel.

His eyes are chestnut brown with lashes so long they ought to belong to a woman or a camel. His summer-bronzed complexion is flawless – he doesn't even seem to have pores – and his features are perfect, clean lines. If it weren't for the bleached hair with dark roots, and the ring piercing his brow, mothers might coo over his fresh boyish health.

And however much he wittered on about drugs and clubs, skate-punk and easy sex, he was, to my mind, disappointingly wholesome.

I yearned for Ilya's craggy masculinity – for that too-big nose, those hooded eyes and that swarthy skin. I ached for his wit, his intellect, his menacing charm and his big bad secrets. I didn't want to play the older woman to Luke's eager appetite. I wanted to play the insignificant slut to Ilya's sweet-sick demands. I wanted tender kisses from Ilya, too, but I tried not to dwell on that.

He'd promised to phone me. I heard nothing.

Prague, for a fortnight, came and went.

Luke was lying naked on my living-room floor, resting his cheek on folded arms.

This, for him, was an unusually serene posture, and his mood, too, was surprisingly mellow. More often than not, Luke couldn't stay still for any length of time and he treated all silences as uncomfortable ones. Maybe he was starting to feel more relaxed in my presence. Maybe he was just tired.

Late-morning sunlight, muted by the gauzy muslin curtains, glowed warmly on his back and shot glints into his rumpled blond hair. Against the honey gold of his body, his arse was deliciously creamy. I trailed a finger down the groove of his spine, then continued further into the cleft of his buttocks.

'Bisexual?' I said, trying not to smile. 'You kept that one quiet.'

'Yeah well,' he said, with a dismissive little shrug.

I didn't quite believe him. It was too much.

All I'd been trying to do was develop his fuck-centric sexuality a little. I'd been gently pushing him to open up about his fantasies, the perviest thing he'd ever done or seen, what he thought about when he wanked, that kind of stuff.

His answers had been pretty scanty, to say the least. He'd been more interested in batting the questions back to me.

I didn't think he was ready to hear the dark side of my desires, so I'd lied and said having anal sex was my wickedest deed to date.

This seemed to intrigue him and he'd started quizzing me – Was it better than vaginal sex? Did it hurt? Why did I like it? Do lots of couples do it? Straight couples, not just queers?

Then, after a little more probing from me, Luke had said, 'Well, I suppose I'm a bit bi.'

Now whether he was saying this because he wanted to rescue himself from naivety, or whether he thought it put him in a suitable position to bugger me, I didn't know. I just knew I didn't believe him. I thought it was another example of Luke wanting to be in everyone's gang.

Fighting to contain my amusement, I carried on rubbing my finger in the split of his arse.

'So what do you mean by "I suppose" and "a bit"?' I asked. 'Are you saying you've actually been with other blokes? Or you just want to?'

At length, he said, 'I've been with a couple of guys. A while ago. Not at the same time or anything.'

'Oh? And what did you do together?' I asked, pressing gently into the crinkled pit of his anus. 'How come you're so curious about my anal experiences? Didn't you fuck?'

'No,' he said, propping himself up on one elbow and looking at me with those big doe eyes. 'It was more, like, messing about. Just touching. You know, wanking. Sucking.'

I pictured his lips, stretched and taut round some other guy's cock, and the image charged my cunt with a sudden erotic shock.

'Tell me more,' I coaxed. 'Who with? When? Why only twice?'

He shrugged and poked at the carpet as if he were uneasy discussing the subject.

Luke was incapable of feigning emotion and discomfort. Maybe he wasn't making it up after all. I really hoped he wasn't.

'It just happened,' he replied. 'And my mates don't know about it. So . . . I mean, they'd really rip the piss if they found out. You'd better not tell anyone. I'll kill you if you do.'

'Course I won't,' I said kindly. 'Anyway, who would I tell? I don't really know these mates of yours. But if you ask me, they don't sound that great.'

'They're OK,' he said defensively. 'They're cool. Cool people.'

I massaged his buttocks, kneading into the muscle under the layer of softness. 'Fancy any of them?' I teased.

Luke gave me a filthy look.

'Sorry,' I said sheepishly.

Then the phone started to ring. Luke sighed heavily.

A few days before, my heart would have leapt excitedly because, in the run-up to Ilya's expected return, it had done so for every phone call. Then his fortnight in Prague had become fifteen days, sixteen, seventeen. We were now into the twenties and my heart was tired of leaping. I let the phone ring.

'You should unplug it more,' said Luke. 'It's always interrupting.'

'Could be important,' I mumbled. I nibbled gently on his shoulder, trying to crush a rising hope as my answerphone message played then beeped.

'Beth. Ilya.'

There was a silence as if he were waiting for me to pick up the phone. I scrambled for the receiver and the answerphone whined with feedback, recording my echoey greeting as I fumbled to turn it off.

With another sigh, Luke got up, walked into my bedroom and quietly closed the door. He could still hear me from there, but it was a nice gesture.

'Where are you?' I demanded breathily.

'Back in Brighton,' replied Ilya in a chirpy tone. 'Have you missed me? Hope you've been keeping your cunt warm and supple for my homecoming?'

'Where in Brighton?' I spluttered. 'At home? Have you seen your landlord? How did –'

'No, I'm in a bed and breakfast,' he said.

'You've been burgled,' I went on. 'Someone broke in. Do you know? Christ, you didn't need to go to a B and B. You should have just come here if you couldn't get in. Is everything OK? Did you get stuff sorted out? Business or whatever? Are your ribs better? And your face? Someone's nicked your telly and your video. The police –'

'Yeah, yeah, I know all that,' he said. 'It's OK.'

'Well, when did you get back?'

'Couple of days ago,' he said breezily.

There was an ugly little silence.

'Been seeing the sights?' I asked in a tight, brittle voice.

Ilya gave a short harsh laugh.

I couldn't understand it. Why was he being so offhand and remote? Was this his way of erasing the intimacy we'd shared?

'So what are you doing tonight?' he enquired. 'Any plans?'

I allowed silence to spin out as I willed a carapace to form around my heart. 'Not sure yet,' I said crisply. 'Might be going into town.'

'How do you fancy being my whore again?' he asked, barging past my aloof tone. 'Get your slut gear on and pay me a visit? You'll like it down here. It's squalid and seedy. Just your thing.'

'Is that it?' I asked, struggling to curb my anger. 'We just step back into playing our game? Pretend nothing's happened?'

'Yeah,' he said. 'Why not? I could do with a good dose of madness and sex. Couldn't you?'

I drew a deep shivering breath. My bottled-up emotions pulsed like a migraine that filled the whole of my body. In any other relationship, with any other person, I would've torn into him. I would have lambasted him for trying to duck reality, for refusing to confront the truth of our situation.

But this wasn't any other relationship with any other

person. It was a game I'd embarked upon with Ilya – a game that had veered wildly off the rails at some point.

Perhaps he was trying to get us back on track again.

Or perhaps we hadn't even been close in the first place. I'd simply played nursemaid and slut when he was bruised and battered. I'd misread things. He hadn't been warm and compassionate, or emotionally open, or heart-meltingly fragile and needy. He'd just been a bit off colour.

Whatever. If he could be hard and cool, then so could I.

'What's the address, then?' I asked tersely.

I jotted down details, fixed a time, hung up, then I just sat for a while, thinking.

Luke didn't emerge from the bedroom. Music came from behind the closed door – some faceless thump, thump stuff that meant he'd tuned my radio to a different station.

I was annoyed with myself for succumbing to Ilya. I wished I'd had the strength to say: 'Fuck you, you can't treat me like this. I won't stand for it.'

But I was slave to my corrosive lust. It gnawed too deeply for pride to get a look in.

I wondered if I should go to him without playing the whore. Going to grotty B-and-B land, dressed as a slut, to take shit from a man with a heart of ice was tanta-mount to having my nose rubbed in my abasement. I'd sunk low enough. I ought to haul myself up. I ought to show him that I wouldn't kowtow to his every demand.

Would wearing jeans and trainers be a big enough gesture? Hardly.

My mind ticked over, searching for a way to achieve a minor victory. My emotions became increasingly venge-ful, but my ideas failed to satisfy them.

Then it clicked: delicious and wicked.

As I walked into my bedroom, I barely gave a second thought to how cruelly exploitative it was, nor what

Ilya's reaction might be. Would he cuttlefish me? Did that word still count?

Well, if it did and he said it, then it would just go to prove how little I meant to him. And if that was the score, then it was high time we went our separate ways.

I met Luke in the Great Eastern, a narrow, book-lined pub midway between our houses. I wore my black shift dress and geisha-girl sandals; no tart's clothes for me – apart from a pair of flimsy scarlet knickers. We downed a couple of Dutch-courage whiskies, then headed out into the September night.

I was nervous and eager and so was Luke – but for very different reasons.

Luke thought I was helping him to explore his bisexuality; he thought we were going to meet a friend who might be interested in doing some stuff with him. We'll play it by ear, I'd told him, because I'm not sure how my friend, Ilya, will react. He said it was OK, but sometimes, when it comes to the crunch, he can get a little edgy, uptight. So maybe I'll join in, I said. We could have a sexy threesome to make it all go smoothly. Trust me, Luke. It'll be great.

Oh, I was a prize bitch.

But I wanted the upper hand for a change, and Luke, poor Luke, just happened to be in the wrong place at the wrong time.

The two of us walked down Grand Parade, which is no longer grand and you wouldn't want to parade there. The faded beauty of yesteryear's houses overlooks a confusion of traffic lanes leading down to the sea: buses go this way, cars go that, cyclists go the other, and pedestrians negotiate.

Under the darkening sky, the place was full of lights: headlights, brake lights, traffic lights and street lights. Buses with hardly any passengers purred and puffed down to the shelters at Old Steine, their brightly lit interiors stark and clinical.

I hoped Ilya wouldn't fly off the handle. I hoped he would agree.

I imagined the three of us entangled on some strange guesthouse bed: my soft curves between those beautiful hard bodies – one nut brown, one gold brown. I pictured the two of them touching – perhaps tentatively for a while – then Luke taking Ilya's cock in his mouth, or maybe in his arse, depending on how far I could push things.

I couldn't imagine Ilya returning the compliment. He wouldn't take Luke's prick into any part of his body: it would compromise his big butch masculinity. But he might be prepared to use Luke's orifices the way he would use a woman's.

And if he said no, I'd say, 'Well, how do you spell that? Does it begin with a C followed by a U?' and so on.

That, at least, had been the original plan. But I was starting to have doubts.

In silence, Luke and I mooched along, past tall crumbling terraces with chessboard-chequered steps rising from pavement to door. They were all narrow and bow-fronted, as if someone had concertinaed the street together and the facades had buckled under pressure. Fops in breeches used to party in those houses; now they're all flats, bedsits, offices and guesthouses – where the guests are homeless people who stay for months on end, watching satellite TV.

Street lamps cast silver shards on lumpy black binbags. My mood got bleaker and bleaker.

I hoped Ilya's B and B wouldn't be too scummy.

'You swear this is nothing weird?' piped up Luke as we skirted past some scaffolding. 'I mean, this guy, you know him pretty well? And it's not a setup? It's not, like, one of your jokes, is it?'

'No,' I said guiltily. 'It's not a joke.'

We paused at the corner of Edward Street, waiting for the traffic lights to change.

'You don't have to do this,' I went on, still not sure if I wanted him to back out or stick with it. 'If you're worried, or just not into it any more, we can easily forget about it. It's not a problem. I'll understand. Me and you could go for a drink. We'll be in gay central. I could be a fag hag. And I'll chose a nice man for you.'

'I'm not gay,' said Luke snappishly.

'Hey,' I said, giving his hand a quick squeeze. 'I know. And even if you were –'

'But I'm not,' he said. 'I'm into girls mainly. Blokes are just . . . different. Harder. I don't mean . . . I mean, like, grittier. Anyway, I might not like it the third time. Might have changed my mind.'

'OK, OK,' I said, and I let the conversation drop.

I didn't understand Luke. I'd always regarded bisexuality as just another playground for sexually adventurous people. I didn't think you could swing both ways and be slightly embarrassed about it as Luke was. Still, it was interesting.

Wordlessly, we crossed the road. On the opposite side was the floodlit Royal Pavilion – Brighton's very own Taj Mahal – its pale-gold turrets and onion domes stamped against the night sky.

For some reason, the fairy-castle foolishness of the place cheered me. And when I saw the Palace Pier's garish lights, winking and swooping at the bottom of the road, I felt a frisson of childish excitement.

I suddenly wanted to run to Ilya's place, throw my arms round him and tumble into a strange bed. I didn't want to liaise and persuade while Luke stood there like a lemon. I didn't want to rebel against Ilya's wrath or refusal.

I just wanted things to be good between us. We could continue having lots of sex – dirty, brash, sluttish sex – but underlying our games there'd be something new: a mutual trust and understanding, a shared sense of what we were doing and where we were going. We'd stop trying to outdo each other and, instead, we'd be equals who were equally committed, equally honest.

But the cheery indifference of Ilya's phone call suggested he wanted to go backward rather than forward. Well, I thought, maybe I could give it a go.

As we turned into St James Street, brighter and busier, my resolve strengthened. I started to feel the aura of sleaze, both brazen and stealthy. The zing of the gay scene infected me. Not so much the vibrancy of its clubs and bars: more thoughts of easy pick-ups, tatty saunas and all the cottaging rumoured to go on in the seafront toilets.

I started to anticipate my first experience of some hot boy-on-boy action in a seamy bed and breakfast. If Ilya wanted to rewind, then fine. But I was calling the shots tonight. He could take it or leave it.

'This is going to be fun,' I said, squeezing Luke round the waist. 'You'll like Ilya, once you get used to him. Promise.'

I burbled on in a similar fashion, feeding Luke with encouragement, lies and a little bit of smutty talk to get him in the mood.

We passed dingy sidestreets full of cheap hotels with shallow ironwork balconies; and I thought of how, years ago, when sex was difficult, people would book into those places as Mr and Mrs Smith. The night just seemed full of lust: clandestine and forbidden, anonymous and raw – as if it had all layered up over the decades.

'Somewhere down here,' I said, spotting our side street.

'Ugh,' said Luke, adding a little nervous laugh.

And he was right: ugh.

The narrow road was shadowy and grim, lined with squashed seaside houses in greys and grimy pastels. Street lamps spaced too far apart gave off a feeble white haze, and illuminated guesthouse signs jutted out at random.

I eyed an unlit bay window, grubby net curtains stretched behind it. Handwritten signs taped to the glass advertised the price of rooms. Please, Ilya, let it be one of the better ones.

I fumbled with my slip of paper, looking around at names and door numbers, then, relieved, we moved on.

Ilya's B and B didn't look too bad: it was bigger, squarer and slightly sprucer-looking than most – but then that wasn't too difficult.

The door wasn't open, though, and we had to press a bell. A man in a beige jumper with face and hair to match answered.

'We've come to see someone in room nine,' I said.

The beige man just sighed and nodded us into a small lobby, which, for all its tawdry splendour of gilt-framed mirrors, two delicate little tables and an overbearing chandelier, was pretty low-watt and gloomy.

Luke and I, following the man's directions, made our way up a narrow stairway, its red carpet threadbare where too many feet had trudged. The air was metallic with the tang of polish – chemical pine needles – but nothing really shone; it was more as if someone had sprayed the stuff around like air-freshener.

The unfamiliarity of the place excited me, as did the prospect of seeing Ilya. And when we reached door number nine, I was buzzing with nerves and horniness.

'It's Beth,' I announced, knocking.

'Yeah, it's OK,' came Ilya's steady voice. 'Come on in.'

Hearing him made my emotions dance, but I was determined to play it cool.

I opened the door, took a step into the room, then froze. My heart slammed to a halt. My vision went muzzy.

'Oh, fuck,' I breathed, as my stalled heartbeats tumbled.

'Oh fuck,' came Luke's quiet voice at my shoulder. Then he added softly: 'You bitch.'

I reached back to clutch at his wrist, scared he might run. It was the only movement I could make. In petrified disbelief, I surveyed the cigarette-hazy room as it swam back into focus.

The walls were papered in mock-Regency stripes and I felt as if I were standing at the entrance to a cage – a cage full of beasts. There were six men in all, but, in the small space, it seemed more like twenty. It didn't take a genius to work out that they weren't the most savoury of characters.

They were scattered here and there, drinking and smoking: three were on wooden-framed armchairs, sitting around a low circular table which was strewn with playing cards; one was on the bed, reclining against the teak, wall-set headboard, his legs sprawling comfortably; another, bull-necked and thuggish like a nightclub bouncer, sat incongruously on a white and gilt dressing table; and there was Ilya, leaning near the floor-to-ceiling curtains of the big bay window, his arms crossed, his face stony and grim.

My skin broke out in sudden heat, then sweat started to prickle.

All eyes were on us. It was patently obvious we were expected – or, more likely, I was. Ilya had really excelled himself this time.

Nervously, I looked at the bed again. The guy lounging there was holding the biggest, blackest dildo I have ever seen. It was surely a joke sex toy. He was bouncing the thing, tick-tock fashion, from palm to palm. He returned my gaze, a malevolent leer on his cruel, sharp face, then he pointed the dildo at Luke.

'Who's the pretty one?' he asked.

I could have kneed him in the balls for that, except my legs wouldn't have carried me.

228

I swallowed, trying to lubricate my dry throat, and addressed Ilya.

'What's going on?' I croaked.

Ilya walked towards me and, despite my fear, the sight of his dark, rough-hewn beauty made me melt – heart and sex. We'd been apart far too long.

'Get rid of him, Beth,' he said gently.

I shook my head, tightening my grip on Luke's wrist as he tried to withdraw.

'What's going on?' I repeated.

Ilya stood close. I could smell him; I could feel the heat from his body; I could see the faintest yellow tinge on his cheekbone, the last vestige of a bruise.

He gazed down at me, his blue-jade eyes softly pleading.

'I need you,' he said in a tormented whisper. 'Please, Beth. Help me out.'

His fingertips brushed fleetingly against my own.

'I'm so sorry,' he murmured. Then, nodding at Luke, he said, 'I'm afraid your journey's been wasted, mate. You're surplus to requirements.'

In a daze, I released my hold on Luke's wrist.

'Beth,' hissed Luke, as if he were trying to recall me to my senses.

'Nice try though, Beth,' added Ilya, giving me a lame smile.

In the room behind Ilya, conversations were rolling, jocular and animated, like they were all down the pub.

'Tell me what's going on,' I said, quiet and numb. 'Who are they?'

'Lose the friend,' insisted Ilya.

I paused, moistening my lips. My heart was hammering so wildly I half fancied it might break out of my ribcage.

'Go, Luke,' I said, without turning to him. 'Just go.'

'But, Beth,' he protested. 'You might –'

'Please,' I said sternly. 'I'll call you tomorrow. I can handle it. I'm OK. Just leave.'

After several silent seconds, floorboards creaked behind me and Luke retreated.

Ilya closed the door. The chatter died down.

'Pretend it's fantasy,' murmured Ilya, ushering me deeper into the dull-lit, stripy room.

If I hadn't been so frightened, I might have laughed at that.

'Okaaay,' said the bed-man in decisive, sing-song drawl. 'Let's have a look at her, Travis.' Briskly, he swung his feet to the ground and stood.

He looked like an elongated pixie: tall and sinewy, with a smidgen of a sandy beard and wavy hair caught back in a ponytail. His lips were thin and cold.

He jerked his head towards the bed. 'Get her on there,' he said to Ilya. 'And spread her open so I can take a gander.'

'You can go fuck yourself,' I said. The words came out louder than I'd intended. I'd just wanted to breathe them to myself – a small act of defiance while I waited for guidance from Ilya.

'Oooo,' jeered pixie-face, as gruff laughter crackled and wheezed. 'Bolshy little bitch, isn't she? Well, Travis? Are you going to fill her in or am I?'

The laughter spluttered up again. 'I'm second,' said a youngish guy with slicked-back hair and a silver hoop in one ear.

'No, you're not, you dirty bastard,' guffawed the bouncer-thug. 'I'm not touching anything you've had your dick in.'

'An orderly queue if you please,' mocked another voice.

My rage simmered up as the moronic banter continued, interspersed with bawdy laughter. Ilya, standing a little way behind me, said nothing.

'Nice company you keep,' I said tartly, turning my head a fraction.

'I didn't fucking choose them,' came Ilya's clenched-teeth reply.

Pixie-face approached me, rangy and snake-hipped. There was an air of louche threat and incipient violence about him.

'You see, Beth,' he began jauntily. 'It goes like this: your friend Ilya needs to buy himself some more time. He's not coming up with the goods and I'm not happy. So I thought to myself, Well, Tony, what could Ilya do to keep you sweet for a while? And I thought, Well, maybe I'll have a go at his girlfriend. She looks all right to me.'

He grinned, that slash of a mouth stretching narrow and white. Then, flopping his hand at the wrist and putting on a high-pitched, girly voice, he said, 'I want your dick up my arse! Oh Ilya! Yes! Yes! I want your dick up my arse. I want your fucking dick up my fucking arse! Oh! Oh! Give it to me, big boy.'

Laughter erupted, deep, lewd and prolonged. Despair spread through me like an ink stain. In a better frame of mind, I might have spat at him.

'The video,' said Ilya in a dull, defeated tone. 'Sorry. The tape was in the machine.'

My head spun, trying to sort out too much information and too many emotions. They'd seen me. They'd watched me. I wasn't even embarrassed. Then I felt contempt rise – for them and for Ilya.

'What?' I said incredulously. 'Are you saying ... are these just a bunch of fucking burglars? Some blokes who nicked your telly? Christ, I assumed –'

'Oh, no, no, no,' cut in Tony, giving me a sardonic smile. 'We didn't mean to rob the stuff, darling. It just – ooops – slipped into our hands. We were only popping round to say, "Well, hello Ilya. We've got your number." And look what we ended up with: you! A porn star! So do as you're told, eh?' He chucked me under the chin. I recoiled from his bony fingers. 'You'll make us all very happy.'

My voice trembled when I spoke. 'And if I don't?'

Tony shrugged and, with airy arrogance, said, 'Then I'll just have to blow your boyfriend's kneecaps off, won't I?'

Icy horror squeezed me.

Tony watched, smug and delighted, waiting for me to react to his vile information.

I had no idea if his threat was hollow or deadly serious, but the sentiment was sufficient to start a wave of sickness sweeping from my guts to my throat. My own knees felt bloated with squeamish sensitivity and my dizzying consciousness reeled with the roundness of knees, with the floatiness of patellas, with splintered bone and blood-splashed pavements, and cartilage, and that fluid that stops the ball and socket joints grinding to dust.

'I need to sit down,' I whispered.

'That's more like it,' drawled Tony. He gestured grandly to the bed where the freakishly huge dildo rested on the insipid blue bedspread.

I couldn't move. My knees would dislocate. I just stood, trancelike, wishing I knew what I was caught up in.

Tony sighed theatrically, shaking his head. 'Warm her up, Trav,' he said. 'I don't think she likes me.' Then he sauntered off to light a cigarette.

I stared after him until, from behind, I felt Ilya's strong arms gently encircle my waist. His nuzzled close to my ear and his teeth pulled softly on the lobe.

'Hey,' he whispered, his voice tender and reassuring. 'It's OK, babe. He's bullshitting. It's not that serious. I swear. If you want to leave, just say the word.'

He nibbled at my ear and kissed my neck, his broad hands rubbing beneath my breasts, moving slow circles over my dress, as if I had stomachache rather than heartache.

232

The echo of his voice played a refrain in my head: Just say the word. Just say the word.

Was he speaking figuratively? Or did he mean *the* word: cuttlefish?

For one blinding moment of madness, I wondered if this was all some elaborate setup, a variation on one of Ilya's surprise role-plays that had started somewhere in the past – with the burglary? The bruised face? I didn't know.

But surely not. While Ilya was damn good at acting – as my arrogant punter or bad-mouthing debaser – I couldn't imagine he had five friends capable of doing the same.

I rested my head back on his chest. 'What word?' I asked hesitantly.

He got my drift at once.

'No, no,' he said with an edge of urgency. 'I didn't mean that. I just meant tell me if you want to leave. It won't be a major problem. I swear. You can go. Or . . . or if you want to say the word, the big one, then . . . sure, I'll understand.' His breath was warm against my ear and, when he spoke again, his low blurred voice had a smile to it: 'But I'd hate to fucking cry in front of these guys.'

Oh God, how I ached for him. He continued caressing me, his hand moving in bigger circles, moving down to stroke over my belly. His groin, pressing against my buttocks, grew larger and, for a while, it was as if we were alone.

Tony and his cronies paid scant attention to us. They just lumbered on with their crass conversations, presumably waiting for the action to hot up.

'But I thought you'd like it,' murmured Ilya. 'Deep down inside, once the shock had worn off. You don't need to be scared. It'll be good.'

I wondered if Ilya was acting now. Was he being smoochy and schmaltzy in a bid to win me over? Trying

233

to save his own skin by telling me these men were OK when really they were vicious hoods?

Questions I didn't much care about wafted lazily around my brain. I allowed Ilya to carry on, relishing the feel of his firm hands and the warmth of his nearness.

'Indulge in your fantasy,' he breathed, dreamily seductive. 'Maybe you'll never have another chance as good as this. Think of it: you, the centre of attention. Lecherous men. They all want you, Beth. They're so hot for you because you are so fucking beautiful and so fucking easy.'

His teeth scraped lightly on my neck and a hand stroked up to palm one breast. I could feel myself weakening, moistening.

'It's just like your fantasies,' he continued huskily, 'but bigger and better. It's so liberating. You're in someone else's hands. They laugh. They say coarse things because you're just a cheap little slut. And everybody wants a piece of you and, God, you adore it. All those hands, all those cocks, all that appetite. Just for you, babe – so dirty, so horny, so wet.'

He clasped me steadily, a thumb brushing to and fro on one nipple, his other hand massaging my pubis through my dress. His swollen crotch dug into the softness of my arse and he ground his hips, ever so slightly. My nipple puckered beneath his touch and my pussy tingled with desire for him, my wetness quickly gathering.

'Did you know?' I whispered. 'When you phoned me earlier, did you know they'd be here?'

'Yes,' he said, tender yet confident. 'But I knew, if I told you, you wouldn't come.'

'I might have done,' I replied quietly, knowing it was a lie.

'Mmmm,' he said, murmuring idle pleasure as he fondled and caressed. 'You turn me on so much, Beth. Ah God, I want to see you naked on that bed, gasping

234

and groaning, hands all over your body. I want to hear you panting and wailing while someone screws you, making you come, again and again and again.'

A moan escaped my lips. Pretend it's fantasy, I thought. You'll never see them again. Different social circles. I could just wipe them from my brain, like men of imagination. After tonight, they'd cease to exist.

And Ilya was here to keep me safe. We were a team. It was all OK. It would be hot – so good, so dirty, so cheap. My vulva swelled as my sense of reality become delirious and deliciously veiled. I felt a little drugged, even though I wasn't, unless Luke was part of the game and he'd slipped something into my whisky. But no, this wasn't the game. Remember. It was bigger than that. Better than that.

I had a misty awareness of Ilya whispering in my ear, shepherding me towards the bed. We sat together on the edge and his caresses continued. Then the two of us were leaning backward and Ilya's hands were sliding on my bared thighs, nudging under my little black dress.

'Show us all what you've got,' he breathed, and he wriggled my dress higher.

I whimpered pleasure and widened my legs as Ilya pushed the fabric up over my hips. He stroked my filmy red knickers and my sex quivered and pouted, warm milkiness seeping into the gusset. Then he slipped my knickers down and off.

Someone in the room gave a low appreciative whistle. I tensed slightly, fighting to stave off shards of fear and disdain which would puncture my lustful haze. Then I relaxed, gazing up at the cracked ceiling rose, allowing Ilya's hands to press on my inner thighs and open me up.

When he drew away from me, I kept my feet where he'd placed them, spaced far apart on the floor. The plump creases of my cunt were split and wet, advertising my easy availability.

'Hallelujah,' came Tony's monotone voice.

In my peripheral vision, shadows moved on the stripy wall. Briefly, I craned my neck. I had a greedy, smirking audience: a couple of the guys had shifted their chairs for a better view; another with short curly hair was leaning against a wardrobe, chewing gum in that rapid, cocksure manner; Tony was approaching me.

Though I loathed myself for it, I couldn't help but respond to all that attention. They were the enemy, dull-witted and crude; and they wanted to use me as their cheap little whore because Ilya owed them money. I was just a pawn in someone else's game, played by someone else's rules.

It was degrading and scary. I loved it and I hated it. Arousal pumped its hot blood into my groin and my sex-lips fattened with sordid hunger.

Tony knelt on the ground between my spread feet. I dropped my head back on to the mattress, eager to take whatever he had to give, yet reluctant to show it. His fingertips pinched lightly on my inner labia and he parted my lips. I sensed him peering.

'Ooo, dark up there,' he said. Then he added, 'Whoops-a-daisy,' and slid two fingers deep into my hole.

It felt good, but I released only the lightest of groans as, high in my vagina, he twisted left and right.

'She's fucking soaking,' he announced with a gleeful titter.

'She always is,' replied Ilya blankly. 'She's a dirty little bitch. Told you she was.'

His words bewildered me. Did that mean we were no longer a team? That it wasn't me and him in the hands of bad men, suffering for some greater good? That it was just me?

The mattress dipped and Tony's pointy face, smirking and shifty, loomed up to confront my own. He held himself above me, one hand on the bed, the other plunging fingers into my sex, and grinned.

236

In the yellowish half-light, I squinted up at his silver-grey eyes, and decided that Ilya hadn't abandoned me. He wouldn't do that. He was merely pretending to side with the enemy in order to make my part easier: it was still me versus the bad men, but they couldn't really be that bad because Ilya was one of them. He was helping me. Of course he was.

So I surrendered to the luxury of groaning and squirming, embracing my sluttish hunger, and bucking my hips to meet Tony's finger-thrusts.

'You're ready for a good shafting, aren't you?' he leered, his fingers picking up speed.

'Yeah, go on, Tone,' said the bouncer thug. 'Give her one, but be quick about it. My dick's itching to get in there.'

I really disliked the bouncer thug.

Tony strummed my clit.

'You ready for a good shafting?' he repeated.

A groan rolled in my throat as a flurry of pulses flooded my sex. 'Yes,' I growled. 'Yes, I'm fucking ready.'

'Well, isn't that a shame?' Tony smiled. 'Because I'm ready for a good blow job, see? So you'd better get on your knees and do it, hadn't you, darling?'

I moaned a complaint, yet scrambled from the bed to oblige, smoothing my dress down in the process. The sooner I did requests, the sooner I'd get a taste of the action.

As I knelt on the carpet, Tony unzipped, freeing his bulky erection from the constraints of his underclothes. His flaring prick jutted lewdly from his flies, obscenely fat when compared to the rest of his body. My lips parted as I reached to take him into my mouth. But he took a large step back, thwarting me.

'C'mon, darling,' he teased. 'Crawl for it.'

'Yeah,' came someone's voice. 'You're into play-acting, aren't you, girl? So you be the donkey and that's your carrot.'

The loutish men laughed as I shuffled to catch up with Tony. I wondered what Ilya had told them about us. It hurt too much to linger over the thought, so I pushed it away.

There wasn't much space and Tony just moved in backward circles, clasping his big, hard cock and aiming it at my mouth. Willingly, I gaped to take him, but he teased and dodged, urging me to suck him, offering himself, then denying me the chance. His domed glans kept skimming my open lips like I was bobbing for apples.

But it was just a little entertainment to amuse our spectators and Tony soon tired of it.

'There you go,' he breathed, as if he were doing me a big favour, and he drove his length into my mouth.

I engulfed him, wrapping my lips round his turgid shaft, then gliding up and down.

My awareness of those ogling men, with their keen eyes and bulging groins, fired me with the glory of filthy lust. Beneath my dress, my inner thighs were sticky with sliding juices. I massaged Tony's slender buttocks, my hands roaming eagerly on his jeans.

'Mmm, yes,' he said, his pelvis rocking lightly. 'Go on. Suck it, bitch. Suck it good.'

And I did, with the dawning realisation that this man might last for ever. Then a mobile phone started ringing, shrill and close, and I faltered, feeling Tony fumble to retrieve it.

'You just keep at it,' he urged as the ringing stopped. 'Yep?' he answered. 'All right, Mick. What can I do for you? ... Yeah, spoke to him yesterday. No worries. Should be ready before the month's out.'

Tony continued with his conversation and a streak of resentment made me reach into his clothes to fondle his tensed-up balls. I drew extra hard on his cock, lashing my tongue and sloshing saliva.

He uttered a rumble of pleasure, then followed it up with a hasty laugh.

'Nah,' he said into his phone. 'Just got a whore on my dick, that's all ... Yeah, she's not bad. Bit eager for a whore. Sucks like a dream though.'

Anger made me want to clamp my teeth on him. But I resisted, determined instead to just suck like a dream. I wanted to make him come, mid-phone-call. That might ruffle his feathers.

'Anyway,' Tony said. 'Kline Leisure are sorting the paperwork ... Yeah, the miserable old bastard, but what can you do? Told him we'd get someone else in next time.'

We carried on that way: Tony talking; me fellating. My cunt throbbed heavily, revelling in my apparent worthlessness. I was just some two-bit whore, sucking on a stranger's dick, so insignificant that I hardly deserved a mention, never mind attention or – God forbid – respect.

The pleasure my body found in that made me feel diseased, because all the men around me saw my whorishness as the truth. This wasn't how things were with Ilya, when afterwards we might say, 'Hey, that was fun.' As far as my audience was concerned, I was a slut through and through. Nothing else; no one else.

In my mouth, I felt Tony's cock flicker with a surge of tautness. He was as inflexible as iron. He had to be close. Victory was in my sights.

Tony, his thighs straining, made a strangled noise into his mobile. 'Call you back, mate,' he croaked, then he beeped off his phone and tossed it over to the bed.

'Ah, yess,' he hissed, clutching a fistful of my hair, keeping me steady as he thrust and thrust.

Then he snatched himself from my lips, jerking my head back. With a rumbling sigh, he climaxed, directing his cock so that his spurting liquor splashed on to my upturned face.

I tasted his bitterness on my lips and pressed them together, not wanting any more.

Dragging my forearm across my chin, I heard a growl of cheers and guffaws that sounded dutiful rather than enthusiastic, the way applause sometimes is.

Tony tidied his prick away and I smeared the last of his juice from my face, drying my hands on my dress.

Then the bouncer thug swung himself purposefully from his dressing-table perch and strode over.

'Next!' he hollered cheerfully, as if we were in a doctor's waiting room.

My heart sank but my treacherous sex rejoiced. He had huge rugby thighs, and his movements were graceless and stiff because of all that bulk and muscle. I really didn't like him, but his crotch was packed to bursting. I wanted someone to fuck me and I was in no position to pick and choose.

So I made no complaint and, when he hooked his hands under my armpits and lifted me effortlessly to my feet, my groin began to pound frantically.

'So you're not after a blow job,' I said bravely.

'Nope,' he said, undoing the back zip of my dress in one fluid swoop.

Then, just as swiftly, he pulled the dress up and over my head, flung it to the ground and fumbled with my bra. The guy with the ring in his ear put his fingers in his mouth and wolf-whistled.

When I was naked, the bouncer thug, his arms like tree trunks, steered me quickly to the bed, ordering me to stand at the foot, to bend over, to grab hold of that rail ''cos you're gonna need to, girl'.

I clutched the low, brass-coloured footrail and fearlessly, wantonly, I spread my feet for him. I heard his trousers drop, felt him shuffle up close and don a rubber, which surprised me, but I guessed it was just the way it had been with Pete: motivated by a selfish 'you don't know where she's been' rather than out of any concern for me.

Then – oh bliss – the bouncer thug drove his prick into me, packing me with flesh.

Buried in my eager wetness, his cock felt like his body – stocky and thick, stretching my pussy walls wide. I cried out, overwhelmed by pleasure, and he went straight into top gear, gripping my hips with his big stubby hands, pounding fast and furious.

He emitted a series of sharp snorts, rutting like a beast, and I gasped and panted as my cunt turned to liquid fire.

'Trav,' said Tony calmly. 'Suck her clitty or something. I like watching whores come.'

'Yes,' I wailed. 'Yes.'

With indecent haste, Ilya ducked down beneath me.

'Fifty quid she comes in a minute and a half,' came a voice from the table.

There was laughter. 'Make it a minute and you're on,' said another.

'Done,' came the reply.

My bouncer thug, his breath increasingly snuffly, was slamming my body back to meet his frenzied thrusts. Ilya's fingers struggled to hit their moving target and, before they could, the bouncer thug climaxed with an oafish roar of triumph.

I howled in disappointment, which mutated into delight as Ilya's knowing fingers found my clit. But I wanted both.

'More,' I wailed as the bouncer thug withdrew. 'Someone else. Oh, more. Someone fuck me.'

I needn't have asked.

The guy who chewed gum was already whipping his belt undone and swaggering across the foggy room, his face immobile apart from that fast-rolling jaw. I felt Ilya's warm wet lips mould to my pulsing clit and my orgasm soared to closeness as his tongue-tip danced.

241

But when the gum-chewer got into position, Ilya quickly replaced mouth with fingers.

'You fucking dirty slag,' said the gum-chewer stickily, and he penetrated me with a fierce jab.

'Come on, girl,' yelled a voice. 'Come on. Twelve seconds. Ten . . . Nine . . .'

Somewhere in the countdown and the horse-racing cheers, I climaxed, much to the delight of Tony and whoever had won the bet.

And as the gum-chewer fucked and cursed, my second crisis started shivering up. And when someone clambered eagerly on to the bed, I barely registered who it was. I just saw that a guy was kneeling before me and his cock was bared and erect and he wanted me to suck. So I did.

With a cock hammering into my cunt, another into my throat and Ilya below, skilfully frigging, I climaxed again, my cries desperate and muffled.

'Oh, man,' drawled Tony. 'That's some wild little bitch you've got there. Oh, fuck yes.'

His voice exploded in my blissed-out mind because its tone was so alarmingly different from before. That snide detachment had gone and, instead, he sounded genuinely enthused, fired up with passion and wonderment.

From the corner of my eye, I saw him tugging his shirt over his head. He was pale, and muscular in a skinny kind of way. On his upper arm there was an ugly tattoo – a dagger wreathed in swirls.

'Get off her,' he barked, stripping urgently. 'I've got to fuck her arse, see? Jesus, let me fuck that whoring little arse. Someone get me some lube. Now!'

The men around me fell away, spitting curses and muttering under their breaths. I felt terrifyingly isolated, and when Ilya traced a gentle stroke along my thigh, the feeling intensified.

'Get on the bed, on your back,' snapped Tony as he shed the last of his clothes.

Long strands of his hair had come free of their band and his pixie-like face was slightly reddened. His eyes were narrowed and bright and I simply did what everyone else had done: obeyed him at once. The prospect of his losing control scared me stupid. I imagined him flipping, flying headlong into maniac mode and becoming a man no one could reason with.

As Tony bounced on to the mattress, Ilya grudgingly chucked several packaged condoms and a tube of K-Y beside us. So he was the medicine man, was he?

I shot him a look, wondering if he was also responsible for the grotesquely large dildo. He just answered with a covert wink, but he did not smile.

Tony positioned himself in the gap of my parted thighs, sat back on his heels and roughly grabbed one of my ankles.

'Ow,' I protested, as he hooked my leg high on to his shoulder.

'Take it easy, Tone,' said Ilya, but his warning carried no threat. It wasn't going to have any impact.

Tony squeezed a generous amount of lube on to his fingers then slapped his hand into the split of my buttocks. Grinning with energised fanaticism, he rubbed and rubbed, mumbling obscenities before driving a bundle of fingers hard into my anus.

'Oh, God,' I wailed as my pinched muscles were suddenly forced to yield. 'Oh God.'

'Yes,' hissed Tony, plunging rapidly. 'Nice and slippy. Still tight, though.'

He snatched his fingers from me.

'Fucking lovely,' he snarled, rubbering up with lightning speed and slathering lube on to his shaft.

Horniness tore around my veins as Tony's knees nudged under my arse-cheeks. He hitched me up the slope of his thighs and I couldn't stop myself from moaning and writhing. I was so greedy for the power of buggery.

'Oh yes,' he rasped, and he manoeuvred my other leg so both were resting on his shoulders. 'You are fucking hot.'

His bulbous cock-tip pushed briefly at my anus. Then, with a heave and a lunge, he surged past my closure and his stiff, solid flesh slithered into me.

I cried out, my arse crammed to capacity.

'Oh, angel,' he said hoarsely. 'Yes.'

Reaching his hands forward, Tony clawed at my tits, then he clasped my hips and started fucking into my narrow hole. A halo of pain burnt around the pleasure as he shoved his thrusts deep. Strings of his hair stuck to his sweat-damp face, and his quick breaths grew spittly as his tempo increased. He powered remorselessly, his face lit up with craziness, and I sobbed in delight.

'Oh fucking yes,' he said. 'Oh, baby, how much cock can you take?'

Then suddenly he stopped, shifted us a fraction and lunged for the dildo. One of my legs slipped from his shoulder and I let the other fall, too, arching my back in a bid to keep him deep.

'Shall we see, eh?' he said, grasping the huge black tool and flashing me his deranged grin.

'No,' I squeaked as my cunt fluttered hungrily. 'It's too big.'

But already he was rubbing the vast rounded tip along the wet seam of my folds.

'Tone,' came Ilya's voice, now threaded through with threat. 'You'd better take it easy.'

'Nah,' piped up someone else. 'She'll fucking love it. Gagging for it, she is.'

'Yeah,' growled Tony, leaning back.

He levelled the cool dildo head at my vagina and, with a gentle twisting motion, he edged an inch or so of the beast into the mouth of my slippery orifice. The opening of my cunt strained round its girth, hugging violently, more stretched than it had ever been.

I released a long, shrill wail, managing somehow to cry out words.

'Yes, yes, yes,' I was saying. And I carried on wailing as, with exquisite slowness, Tony fed the unyielding phallus into me, easing in its big black length until it would go no further.

I gasped frantically, my head rocking on the bedspread as I tried to accustom myself to its gloriously brutal size.

Tony held the position, my legs splayed round his waist, my back slanting down the angle of his thighs. His prick was lodged deep in my arse and several thick inches of the dildo were sticking out from my pussy-lips.

'Take a look at that,' he said proudly, tilting his torso back.

I cried without restraint because my lower half was so dense with sensation. It scarcely seemed to belong to me. I felt as if a section of my body, from my belly down to my thighs, was levitating away. My stuffed-solid orifices melded into one massive intensity. I could not distinguish my arse from my cunt. I was just a thing congested with other things. It was heaven.

'See, Travis,' said someone. 'Told you she'd fucking love it.'

'Yeah, Mr Boyfriend,' gibed Tony, starting to thrust into my anus again. 'Come and join the party. Why don't you spunk over her? Load her tits up. Yeah.'

Tony grasped the dildo end, half thrusting it, half rotating it, as his cock pumped in and out of my arse. I was crying, sobbing, groaning, but I caught Ilya's flat answer.

'No,' he said above the noise.

'Well, I fucking will,' said a voice, and the bed dipped as someone scrambled on to it. Then again, another person.

I was hitting orgasm – loudly – my muscles clenching on the great ebony shaft. The two guys on the bed bared their cocks and started wanking furiously. They squeezed and mauled my breasts as Tony, eyes bulging wildly, rammed into me with dick and dildo.

And then there was banging at the head of the bed. Someone in the room next door was hammering on the thin wall and shouting, telling us to fucking well shut up.

But what did I care? What did anyone care?

I was coming again and so was someone else. Their fluid splashed warmly on to my tits, and Tony, his hair plastered in chaotic directions, his neck taut and sinewy, fixed his insane eyes on my semen-splattered flesh. His mean, scraggy face was crimson; blue veins snaked on his temples.

'Yes, yes, yes,' he was spitting. 'You're mine, see? You slut, you slut. You're fucking mine.'

His lunacy chilled me. Moments later he threw his head back, climaxing with a blood-curdling howl.

Hardly pausing for breath, he started urgently fretting my clit, glaring wide-eyed at my face, beaming his broad, psychopathic smile.

'Come on, come on,' he panted, his hand shaking away. 'Come for Uncle Tony. Come on, queenie. Fucking come. Fucking come.'

His rapid friction pushed me towards the brink. I gulped and sobbed, terrified and abandoned, as he began waggling the dildo in my depths, levering it up and down, pushing it in and out.

My orgasm crashed, wave upon wave, my cunt contracting on the slipping hardness, my whole body shaking. I screwed my eyes tight, wanting to shut out the image of Tony's wild, exultant face.

'Oh, yes, yes, yes,' he raved. 'That's my girl. A big fucking comer, see? That's my girl. Oh, yes. She is for me. She is mine.'

My orgasm shuddered to its close and I heaved for breath as the dying pulses sapped my energy. For a long, long time, I kept my eyes closed. I didn't even look up

246

when more semen splashed on to my neck. I just lay there, inert, trying to block the sound of Tony's mad mantra.

I wished I were a million miles away. I wished I knew what the score was. Was Tony a man who you just had to get used to? Or was he frighteningly demented and you wouldn't want to bother? And who were his friends? And when could I go home?

I felt someone get off the bed. Gradually, Tony calmed. He withdrew from me and pulled the dildo from my aching sex.

Reluctantly, I opened my eyes just as Tony threw the glistening phallus in Ilya's direction.

'Catch!' he barked, and, deftly, Ilya caught.

Under his olive-dark skin, Ilya was ashen. He said nothing. He just gazed at Tony.

'That's for you,' Tony said to him. 'Leftovers. Suck on it if you want.'

A couple of the men sniggered.

Ilya shook his head in astonishment rather than refusal.

'I want to get dressed now,' I murmured, pushing myself from the bed.

Tony flung himself alongside me, drawing me back down. He brought his face close to mine, our noses almost touching, and brushed a bedraggled length of hair from my face. Then, smiling faintly, he stroked a gentle line along my jaw. It was truly scary.

'But, sweetie,' he cooed. 'Tony doesn't want you to get dressed. Tony likes you undressed. And what Tony says goes. See, baby?' He drifted his finger down my neck. 'Now why don't you trot across the room, pour me a whisky and fetch my cigarettes? Mmm?'

I nodded dumbly.

'That's my girl,' he breathed.

I moved slowly – the way police do when they're trying to persuade a madman to hand over his weapons. Except I was moving away from one.

The room was very quiet.

I padded over to the coffee table, where the near-empty bottle of whisky stood, found a glass on the floor and collected them both. I looked around at the scattered cigarette packets, trying to recall which brand was his. I didn't want to upset him.

I glanced across to the dressing table and that's when I saw it. My heart twisted in shock. A gun. It was just lying there, small, black and angular.

I'd never seen a gun before, not in real life. It was casually pointing into the centre of the room, its tip a dark shadowy O. Bullets come out of there, I thought. Then they whizz into someone's body. Kill them.

'Oh fuck,' I said, staring at it, half fearing it would go 'bang' any second.

These people were serious trouble, far worse than I'd imagined.

'What is it, queenie?' gasped Tony, sitting bolt upright.

'It's a fucking gun,' I breathed, turning to him accusingly. 'You . . . Get it out of here. Get it away from me. I swear, I'll do anything you want. You don't need . . . Just . . . Oh God.'

My words melted to silence.

Tony uttered a stream of mad cackling laughter, raising his hands in a show of innocence. 'Not mine, sweetie. Not that one. That one belongs to Mr Boyfriend.'

My eyes darted to Ilya.

He gave me a jittery smile. 'It's OK,' he said. 'It's not loaded.'

I stared at him, speechless.

'What's all the fuss?' taunted Tony. 'I thought you two were close. Doesn't he let you play with his weapons, then?' He flopped back on the bed, chuckling to himself and rubbing his pale chest. 'Ho-hum,' he said. 'Naughty Ilya. Keeping secrets.' Then he sat up again and grinned at me. 'So you don't like guns?'

I shook my head. 'I'm not overkeen, no.'

'Then you'd be better off with me,' he said brightly, angling his head. 'Now I'm not saying my cupboards are empty of the things. Oh no. But if I were you, queenie, and I really didn't like them, then I wouldn't stay with a man who deals in thousands of them. It might make you unhappy, see? Thousands and thousands. Day in. Day out.'

Then he threw himself back on the bed again, laughing manically and gazing at the ceiling.

I looked at Ilya.

He held my gaze and raised his brows, putting on a guilty little smile.

'Sorry,' he mouthed, shrugging his shoulders.

'Thousands and thousands,' sang Tony. 'Thousands and thousands.'

Chapter Twelve

Tony was exaggerating. Of course he was. Ilya wasn't equipping a goddamn army.

I sat with him in one of the seafront cafés, dunking my teabag into a cup of milky water.

Ilya had refused to come to my flat because there were too many eyes watching him. I'd refused to go to his B and B. Full stop.

Local radio was playing in the café and there weren't many people around. Nevertheless, we spoke in low voices, hunching towards each other across the plastic-topped table.

'So what sort of guns?' I asked morosely.

Ilya shrugged. 'A lot of Russian stuff: AK-47s, Tokarevs, Makarovs. Czech gear's good too, popular, especially Skorpions. Then there's –'

'Whoa,' I said quietly. 'Will you say that in English, please? You know, do they go bang-you're-dead or ack-ack-ack?'

Ilya grinned. 'Sorry,' he murmured. 'Not much call for bang-you're-dead. Automatics. You know, assault rifles, sub-machine guns, handguns.'

'Christ,' I breathed, searching my mind for more questions.

Ilya, for once, had promised me absolute honesty. I had the freedom to probe, and that freedom was tyrannical. It made me feel obliged to ask, ask, ask, and yet I wasn't sure if I wanted answers.

'So how does it all work?' I frowned, toying with a sugar sachet. 'I mean, where do you get them from? Who do you sell them to? How do you . . . What if . . .'

My questions dried up.

'Look,' said Ilya in a hushed tone. 'There are loads of firearms floating around Eastern Europe. And really good stuff – fucking top-notch, quality war guns. They –' He broke off and glanced over at a table where an elderly couple sat munching.

'Stocks aren't controlled,' he resumed, his voice even lower. 'Certificates get faked. Stuff's crossing borders left, right and centre. And the amount of weaponry the Russian army just, just loses, it's . . . Then there are factories churning out gear that the military can't afford. Someone's got to take up the slack. Ends up on the black market. And, like I said, I don't work alone. We're part of a chain. We sell to someone who sells to someone else. My role's more setting things up in Prague, Sofia, Budapest, then making sure it's all smooth at this end.'

'But then where do they go?' I demanded. 'Are they for armed robbers? Or . . . or terrorists? Or what? Where?'

Ilya sipped his black tea and grimaced. 'Everyone wants to be tooled up these days,' he replied. 'Best not to ask too many questions.'

I didn't know if he meant best for me or best for him. Or both.

'Jesus, don't you have any scruples?' I asked, accidentally ripping the sachet and scattering white sugar granules everywhere.

Ilya smiled. 'Not one of my strong points, no.'

I didn't return the smile. We fell silent and I just stared

out of the window, beyond the quiet shingle beach to the washed-out sky. It looked like it had been coated with those paints you can buy: white with a hint of apple or peach. The sky that day was white with a hint of misery.

The summer season's coming to a close, I thought. The tourists have gone home; the kids are back at school; the Victorian merry-go-round is all wrapped up in green canvas, showing only its stripy top. A lot of the seafront souvenir shops and ice-cream bars have closed, and so have a fair amount of cafés. Along the arches there are more metal shutters than open doors. Some café owners keep on determinedly putting tables and chairs outside, but there's no one sitting there.

Brighton at this time of year has a very melancholy feel; it's like a clown with no friends.

I dropped my teabag into the ashtray and turned back to Ilya. 'So how do you get the . . . the things into Britain? I asked. 'Are they hidden inside other stuff?'

Ilya lit a cigarette. 'Kind of,' he murmured. 'You can stash crates in with legit freight.'

'Well, what sort of legit freight?'

He dashed a knuckle across the bridge of his nose. 'Anything, really. Depends who I'm working with, how we're organising it. Perishables are good, you know, fruit, flowers. It gets taped up, has to travel fast, so customs don't poke around too much. Or it might be timber or . . . like the next run, it's a big consignment and we're shipping it in with machine parts.'

'Christ,' I said softly. 'I just, I can't get my head round it all. It's . . . There's suddenly so much metal in my life. And my life isn't like that. My life is, is softer. And this is Brighton. I know the town's not all candyfloss and doughnuts but . . .'

My words petered out.

'I didn't want my life to be like this,' said Ilya testily. 'It's not easy, you know, always having to look over your shoulder, trusting no one except yourself, wondering if today's going to be the day your luck runs out. It's a fucking pain. But it's not something you can just walk away from. And the pickings are good. I make a lot of money. Trouble is it's all tied up in property and deals at the moment. I haven't got thirty grand to spare.'

A troubled silence thickened between us.

Ilya drew heavily on his cigarette, then said, 'Look, Beth, I know I said I'd be straight with you, but it's probably best if you don't know too many details. For your safety and for mine.'

'I'm just curious,' I said sullenly. 'And since I'm caught up in this mess, I reckon I deserve something of an insight. I mean, what you're asking me to do is pretty heavy-going.'

'Yeah, fair enough,' conceded Ilya. 'Sorry.'

'So are you going to move back into your flat?' I asked, trying to steer away from the subject. 'Now Tony's tracked you down, there's not much point staying in some B and B, is there?'

'Yeah, but I reckon I'm safer there,' he replied. 'It's more public. Anyway, my flat's too close to yours. I'd hate Tony to burst in with one of his little reminders when you're with me.'

'Well, I wouldn't visit your flat. You could come to mine.'

Ilya shrugged. 'Tony'd find out. He always does.'

'Well, are you going to move back in when this is all finished? I asked. 'And what about your stuff? Are you paying rent? You could store it at my –'

'Beth, please,' said Ilya, with a hint of exasperation. 'I'm not thinking more than a few days ahead at the moment. Anyway, there's hardly anything worth having in my flat. I took what I needed when I left for Prague.' He smiled. 'The TV and video were the best things there. Oh, and the *Anal Virgin* cassette, of course.'

'Where is it?' I asked wearily. 'Has Tony got it?'

'Yeah,' said Ilya. 'But don't worry. When I'm in a

better position, I'll get it back. Or I'll get someone else to get it back.'

At length, after mentally toying with the worst question of all, I whispered: 'So have you ever shot anyone? Killed anyone?'

'Nah, too much hassle,' he replied in a cloud of smoke. 'I'm better off low profile. I mean, if I wanted someone dead, I could hire a guy to do it. But not me personally. I wouldn't do it. And before you ask, no, I don't want Tony dead. It wouldn't solve a thing.'

'Jesus,' I said, and we lapsed into silence once again.

I'd always known Ilya and I belonged to very different worlds, but I'd never imagined anything on this scale. The enormity of the gap between us was overwhelming. He could talk quite calmly about getting people to kill people. I kill spiders. Hardly comparable.

'So this next thing, this run,' I began, 'when that's all cleared, then Tony'll be off your back?'

'Yeah, no problem,' he said lightly. 'But, like I said before, Tony's nobody. He's just some fucking nutter who collects debts for other people. And right now, I can't pay. So he's making the most of it, turning the heat up because that's how he gets his kicks. And I've just got to see it through until the money comes in.' He ended with a resigned shrug.

'*We've* got to see it through,' I corrected.

'Yeah, sorry,' he breathed, his black lashes sweeping down.

'And supposing it goes wrong?' I said. 'What if it's discovered? Are you going to end up in jail?'

Ilya shook his head. 'I've got friends in high places.' He smiled. 'I'll get a tip-off. That's why I left Teesside. Intelligence were sniffing around. We needed a fresh base. I had contacts down here – Brighton, London, Southampton. It wasn't really to escape the debts. I was planning to level it eventually. You leave people smiling in this game. But all the shit up north made it tricky.'

'But if it goes wrong,' I protested, 'then Tony'll still be on your back.'

'So I just move somewhere else,' he said indifferently. 'Keep on running till I don't need to. But this time I won't tell a soul. There'll be no one to blab.'

That, I thought, included me. He would simply go and I'd never hear from him again. I couldn't bear it.

'And if I refuse to do this thing for Tony, then what?'

'Maybe I'd dodge him,' replied Ilya. 'Get out of town. Or stay and take the beatings. Check out the food in the local infirmary.' He smiled weakly. 'I really appreciate this,' he continued. 'Are you sure about it?'

'No,' I said firmly. 'You know I'm not. It's fucking embarrassing – putting on a show that could seriously offend, getting on stage in front of a crowd I know. And I'm probably going to have to pay my performers double. And I'll never be able to walk down a street in Brighton without blushing to the roots of my hair. The whole thing stinks and I loathe and detest Tony for actually –'

'Hey,' cut in Ilya. 'You don't have to do it.'

It was true; I didn't have to do it. But the alternatives – Ilya taking shit from Tony and his boys or just disappearing – were much worse. In the scheme of things, what was being asked of me was pretty small. And to keep Ilya that little bit longer, I was prepared to make sacrifices.

Ilya clasped my fingertips across the table. He looked levelly into my eyes as if he were about to propose marriage or declare his undying love.

'But you make a great little slut.' He grinned. 'The gig'll be fantastic.'

I tried a smile. 'I'm still sore,' I complained. 'I could hardly walk yesterday.'

'Yeah,' said Ilya gently. 'But you were great. And you loved every minute of it, didn't you?'

'What?' I said flatly. 'Being gang-banged by a load of

255

hoods? Yeah, fantastic, thanks. The most fun I've had in ages.'

'Oh, come on,' countered Ilya. 'Don't pretend –'

'Tony's too scary,' I replied. 'And that bouncer thug is rotten. And I hated that guy who chewed gum and kept calling me slag and cow and –'

'Hey, he's harmless,' said Ilya. 'Just doesn't know how to handle it, that's all.'

'Yeah, well I'm not sure I do either,' I murmured. 'Not when it's on someone else's terms. I'd rather be a great little slut on my terms.'

Ilya smiled sympathetically. 'So what did lover boy say about it all?'

'Luke?' I said with a small laugh. 'I told him it was a surprise get-together. Some people I hadn't seen in a while. Don't think he was convinced. But he says I'm odd anyway. Secretive.'

Ilya squeezed my fingertips.

'So after this gig,' I said, 'then you promise that'll be it? Tony'll leave you alone until this, this deal is sorted?'

'Yeah,' said Ilya. 'No problem.'

I knew he was lying but I didn't care. I'd started to prefer his lies.

The room was small, hot and crowded. Coloured lights from the mirror-ball glided over the punters, and I leant against the bar, swigging from my bottle of Becks, searching for Ilya.

I couldn't see him anywhere. Maybe he's just gone for a piss, I thought. Or maybe everything's been sorted and he's gone back to his B and B. Perhaps Tony can't make it, and I don't have to go through with this after all.

Tears stung my eyes but I turned to the low stage and I didn't let them spill.

A woman with chemical-red hair, dressed in purple latex, was sitting spread-legged on a chair. She was plunging the haft of a multi-tailed whip into her vagina. Leather thongs spewed from her open thighs like entrails.

Some of the audience seemed to like this. They were clapping and cheering. Others were visibly .shocked. Nobody had warned them that, tonight, Hot Sex had got to be seriously hot.

And all for Ilya because, if I didn't do this, Tony would get nasty and Ilya would then suffer or run.

It was blackmail, clear and simple. And it came about because Tony liked me. Because Tony wanted me. Because Tony got a kick from the power he had over Ilya and consequently over me. Because I, stupidly, still cared for Ilya.

It's the way Tony works, Ilya had said. That's why he does what he does. He could never be a hit man who takes someone out with a single shot because he revels in tormenting people. He likes to make them squirm, sometimes physically, sometimes mentally. He's a cruel sadist. A moral blank. And the state of his mental health is up for debate.

The thought made me shudder with fear.

I couldn't speak to Ilya during the gig. He knew that. I'd told him to keep away because, whatever his behaviour, he was bound to make me lose it. If he acted sympathetic and reassuring, I might crumble into a heap of tears; if he was jokey and encouraging I'd probably want to thump him.

Better, I'd said, if you just blend in with the audience. Be anonymous to me. I want to feel detached from this mess, to concentrate on being a pro.

I wondered if it had disturbed him when I so obviously left the room with Luke in order to go and fuck in my office. Doubtful. He'd never been jealous yet. He'd probably thought, Ah, Beth's gone to grab a cheap loveless fuck from her toy-boy in order to get into character and dilute the intensity of 'us'.

And he'd be right. I'd also felt horny. Would he have appreciated the simplicity of that?

Maybe I shouldn't have agreed to do it. Maybe it puts me at the top of a slippery slope and Tony's going to push it and push it until Ilya coughs up the money.

On stage, the woman – who performs under the name of Mistress Zed, but who I know as Debbie – was making one of the black guys suck on her pussy-wet whip handle. It was all quite feisty stuff, but then that's what my female dancers do. They'll strip, they'll strut, they'll flaunt; but invariably they'll up the dominatrix tempo, and their male dancers will have to grovel at their feet or feel the sting of their whip.

The guys – Mikey, Leo and Skitz – will do anything for the money. They're complete whores, lucky them.

I didn't think Tony would be too keen on it – if he ever arrived. But then it was me he wanted to watch. Me he wanted to see squirm.

Well, I wasn't going to let him. I'd get on that stage, no matter how hellish I was feeling, and I'd make it seem as if I were loving it.

I wondered how many people would recognise me. I'd be wearing a gold half-mask to cover most of my face. My lips are pretty distinctive though, but then the lights were low and ever-changing. Maybe I'd get away with it.

If I didn't know anyone, it wouldn't be quite so bad. But I was on speaking terms with at least half my audience.

Martin was in the crowd. Would he suss it was me? Jenny knew – not quite everything but she knew it was serious. And she thought I was stupid – not because I was doing it but because I was doing it for Ilya, who, as far as she was concerned, was a complete shit and never in a million years would he do something similar for my sake. She's probably right.

I felt someone nudging, trying to get to the bar. I

moved slightly, then, from behind, a voice cooed in my ear, 'Queenie, I've missed you so much,' and a hand stole in to cup my groin through my jeans.

Tony's here. It's now. It's happening. The nightmare has begun.

An inward tremor quivers through me but I don't flinch. Instead I take a carefully judged step back as I turn, and the heel of my trainer presses squarely on the toe of his shoe. If only I wore stilettos.

Tony doesn't flinch either. He merely slips his foot from under mine.

'Watch your step, queenie,' he says in a menacingly soft tone, a hand touching my hip.

'So sorry,' I reply, giving him a steely smile.

He grins back, those horribly narrow lips pulling tight, then his glassy grey eyes drop to my tits. He steps back a few inches and his scrutinising gaze trawls down my body.

I crane round to see Ilya slipping back into his seat – at the only table in the place to have a reserved sign on it. The bouncer thug is with him. So is the ear-ring guy and someone I haven't met before.

'I think I prefer you in dresses,' says Tony, moving too close once again.

He smells of soap and it makes my skin crawl because I imagine that he's washed before coming out and that it's for my benefit. It scares me too, because the thought of Tony wanting to impress me is terrifying.

I drain my beer and set down the bottle. 'Well, Tony.' I smile. 'I'd love to stay and chat but duty calls. Afraid I need to get changed.'

'Want a hand?' he leers.

I put on a big, false smile. 'Want a knee in your groin?' I ask politely, and I walk away, Tony's mad Tommy gun laughter scattering endlessly in my head.

* * *

The closer it gets to show-time, I become, strangely, less nervous and less scared.

The kitchen behind the bar, half-covered in sheets, mirrors propped here and there, serves as our dressing room. It's not great, but it's the best I can do.

Polly, one of the dancers, offers me a line of coke, but I refuse, telling her I want to play this one straight.

I'm wearing turquoise PVC hot pants with criss-cross lacing up the front. Above, I have a red, gauze-thin top – long-sleeved, high-necked – and beneath, peeping through, is a purple sequinned bikini top. I've got my black knee-length boots on and a glittery gold half-mask. Jane has done something weird with my hair, involving lots of back-combing, coiling, goo and pins, and the end result is two cones either side of my head, like devilish little horns.

Tony had better bloody well recognise me.

I smile to myself. I'll make damn sure he does, the bastard.

Leo, his black body glistening with sweat and oil, bounds into the kitchen and grabs the nearest bottle of water. Outside, the volume of the music goes up a notch – time for people to mill around, buy drinks, talk about how shocked they are, maybe leave.

'Wowee,' beams Leo, dragging his arm across his lips. 'You look cute as hell, Beth.'

'No, she doesn't,' argues Polly, laughing. 'She looks gorgeous. Beth is not cute. Beth is hot sex personified, aren't you, honey?'

'Yeah,' I say. 'Got that, Leo?'

'In one, chief.' he grins, giving me a playful salute. 'So are we gonna run through this routine one more time?'

'Yeah, why not,' I reply, doing a little shimmy.

'Oh, I love this gig,' enthuses Leo. 'It's so fucking weird, man. I love it, love it, love it.'

* * *

The stage doesn't have curtains or wings. It's just a low wooden platform that gets packed away at the end of the night.

Our start-up music is Grace Jones and, as the slow, sultry beats of 'Nightclubbing' begin, the three of us – me, Leo and Mikey – slink and sway theatrically through the audience.

It's tricky because the room is so crowded, but people shuffle to make space. I linger wherever I can, moving sinuously as I run my hands along the contours of my body.

My heart's pounding with the fever of performance and my two black partners, supple and athletic, make a display of trying to paw me. Leo's in sparkly gold shorts; Mikey's in military gear – peaked cap, army trousers, braces over his bare chest and mock epaulettes on his shoulders.

I ham it up, wafting the ends of my purple feather boa at them, blowing vampish kisses as they fail to touch me, because tonight I am the Queen of Sleaze. That's how I was introduced. That's who I am.

When we reach the stage, we continue in a similar vein: me as the self-absorbed prick-tease, full of mock sensuality; the men as my admirers, lunging to touch, sometimes stroking down my legs then spiralling away.

As I sway, caress myself and pout, I survey the room before me through the eye-holes of my mask. Jenny's furry red lovehearts, flecked with moving spots of colour, hang from the ceiling. They look good. The glare of lights makes the furthest reaches of my audience a faceless, amorphous blob. But closer to the stage, where the little tables are clustered, I can clearly make out people – most of them smiling at our burlesque display. Good.

Ilya's group have, of course, some of the best seats in the house. Their table, laden with beer glasses and shorts glasses, is just off-centre, slightly to my right. Tony, his keen eyes fastened on me, leans to say something in Ilya's ear. Ilya, watching me intently, smiles and nods.

I wonder if Ilya recognises the purple boa from the time he blindfolded me, buggered me and turned me into a video star for his friends' consumption. I hope he does, because that's why I'm wearing it.

Our opening track ends, just as my eager men move in either side of me. They lower themselves up and down, trailing their hands over my body, rubbing their crotches against my thighs. I throw my head back, making an exaggerated show of abandoning myself to lust.

The music segues, almost neatly, into another Grace Jones number – 'Use Me' – and we flip into action as the tempo steps up.

Mikey grasps my wrists, lifting my arms high, and I feign confusion, my head turning left and right, as he takes a backward stride and steadies himself. My body arcs back a little, supported on his, and I'm held that way, on show for my spectators, as Leo kneels and traces his hands up my legs to my groin. From below, he rubs the crotch of my glossy hot pants and, as rehearsed, I press my hips forward, making it seem like I'm so greedy for it.

My pussy twangs with arousal. That didn't happen in rehearsal, but then rehearsals were briskly efficient, sometimes frustrating, sometimes funny. They weren't horny.

But now Leo is being more indulgent, caressing me firmly so I feel all the strength of his massaging fingers. And now I'm on stage in a darkened, colour-dancing room. The lights are on me, the music's pulsing and everyone's watching. That thrills me more than anything.

While Grace is chanting about how good it feels getting used, Leo leaps up, deftly finds the tiny cut in the neck of my gauze top and tears – one, two, three. The filmy garment rips down the middle, exposing my midriff and glitzy purple bikini. I feel a rush of exhilaration.

Then, acting delighted, Leo starts to write on my bare flesh in lipstick, darting from side to side, spinning away and back, so the audience can see the word as it forms, letter after letter: S – L – U – T.

I can't see Ilya's face because I have to keep my head tipped back, but I wish I could. Will he get this reference? Will he remember the time he wrote the same thing on my back? When he and Pete humiliated me for hours? Once again, I hope so, because that's what my performance is: it's a jumbled montage of stuff we've done together.

I'm not sure why yet. I don't know if I want to show him how good it was, how bad it was. I don't know if I'm wrapping things up or asking for more. I don't know if I'm trying to say, 'Look, you swine, I'm doing all this for you,' or, 'Hey, it's a public arena and only we know what these little things refer to and isn't that great?'

I'm just doing it because I needed some kind of structure, a theme to build my performance around, and this popped into my head and I thought, why not? It's as good as any.

When I make my fake getaway from Leo and Mikey, I cast my shredded top to the floor and stand proud before my audience, my pelvis rolling as I bend my knees, snaking my body, flaunting the 'slut' label on my midriff.

I let my hands drift sinuously. I trace an hourglass up and down my curves, rub flat-palm rotations over the swell of my hips, cup my sequin-clad breasts and squeeze them together.

The mask is good: it blocks a lot of my peripheral vision and I see things in a frame of black.

Ilya is trying to suppress a broad grin: I think he's got the allusion. Tony looks self-satisfied and greedily intense, no doubt thinking that this is all for him and that I'm putting on a great show, but that deep down I'm dying with shame and embarrassment. Well I'm not. I'm OK. Getting better all the time.

My two stage partners are at my feet, doing sort of undulating press-ups while gazing at me adoringly and lapping at thin air. They're perfectly synchronised; they've done this before. I'm a bit more freeform, trying my best to time things the way we'd planned.

With striptease drama, I start unlacing the criss-cross cords of my hot pants, eyelet by eyelet.

If this were one of my sleazy fantasies, my boorish male spectators would probably be gearing up to pull me down into the bear pit of their greedy lust. But it's not fantasy; and my spectators, while you wouldn't quite call them civilised, are not boorish, greedy men – Ilya's table excepted, of course. They're behaving pretty well, though, and they'd better stay that way.

Playful whistles and drunken shouts of encouragement compete with the music. I adore it. I feel like I'm pulling an audience into my power, and the buzz that gives me is strong and erotic.

When my hot pants are unlaced, I slide a hand into the front flaps, nudging my arm up and down. I roll my head back and pant as if I'm close to ecstasy. I slip my fingers into my purple G-string knickers, past my newly hairless mound, to caress my vulva. No one can see that I'm really doing this, but I am, and I'm so wet. I feel gloriously wicked.

Turning my back to the room, I remove my hot pants, bending straight-legged from the waist as I shimmy them down. That way, everyone gets a view of my arse jutting up and my buttocks swelling tautly. The hot pants aren't easy to remove with my boots on, but Leo and Mikey shield the messiness while helping me.

And anyway, so what if the performance isn't perfect and slick? I don't care. Rough edges are good. And people are cheering and hollering. It must be OK.

The music changes into some good old seventies disco

– no lyrical significance; I just like it. While my hands and the boys' are at my feet, Mikey covertly passes me my prop – a plastic banana. Leo looks up at me, gives me a cheeky little wink and waggles his tongue salaciously. I grin and waggle mine back.

People laugh and whoop as I turn to face them, rubbing the tip of my plastic banana from my groin to my neck.

My audience, I know, take this pretty much on an ironic level, which is fine. It's not exactly pastiche-free. But I look around and see swollen groins and I ask myself: Can you have an ironic hard-on? I think not.

I lick and fellate my plastic banana as Leo and Mikey roll around, feigning torment and desire – except Leo's not feigning the desire bit. His cock is a bulge in his spangly shorts and he doesn't give a damn. He rubs himself, his hips surging up and down, his six-pack abs shimmering.

Does Ilya get the banana reference, I wonder? Does he remember when I played the whore and he made me fuck myself with stupid fruit?

I'm about to glance over but I catch sight of Martin, propping up the bar, grinning inanely.

It's obvious that he's seen beyond my mask, and it's also obvious that it doesn't matter one scrap. His smile is big and generous, warm and familiar, and so full of easy love.

I feel a rush of awkwardness and guilt, but it sinks away when I read the forgiveness in his face. And, best of all, everything about him – his stance, his expression, his eyes – is free from lust and pain and anger. He looks like the Martin I knew before we started our stupid affair: Martin, my closest friend. And he's grinning simply because he's happy for me.

It's catching, and suddenly I feel lighter, happier, more free.

I wish I had a pole to writhe around. I wish I had showgirl tassels on my tits.

Hardly concentrating, I see that Mikey's on all fours for the next bit and I plant my boot on to his broad ebony back. Edging aside sequins and skimpy gusset, I ease the plastic banana into my sweet shaven slit and begin sliding it in and out. It feels so good, moving in my wetness; but the best feeling of all is that, yeah, I'm doing this for Ilya, but it doesn't have to be that way. I can add an extra layer to it and do it for me.

In a way, it was always for me. I wanted to appease Ilya's bully-boys not for his sake but for mine, because I couldn't bear the thought of him leaving town. But I don't like the baggage Ilya comes with and now this is for me because I'm enjoying it. Pure and simple.

I withdraw my banana, which is glistening with juices, and clasp it in both hands. I feel buoyed up with naughty delight as I point it at Ilya's table, brandishing it like a gun, and slowly, slinkily, I step down from the stage.

Tony thinks it's funny. He thinks he's part of an in-joke, but pretty soon I'm going to wipe that smile off his face. This part of the show was always planned, but the reasoning behind has suddenly changed. Now, I'm more concerned about seeing Ilya's reaction than I am about trying to spite Tony.

I make my way to the table, my bikini sequins sparkling, and make a charade of drifting caresses over the heads and shoulders of the men sitting there. Ilya, looking worried and mistrustful, watches me closely.

When I reach Tony, I linger, and he shifts his chair side-on to the table. I stand wide-legged before him, stirring my hips and lowering myself into half-squats.

Tony leers and gloats, lapping up his status as the man who's forced me to perform. His eyes are bright with eagerness and intrigue. He thinks I'm about to give him the star treatment, and I am – in my own special way.

Holding my banana gunlike, I wave it close to his thin

lips and then close to mine. I lap at the tip, tasting my musk, then offer him the same. He grins and his lizardy tongue flicks out. I allow him to taste me just enough, then I take the thing to my mouth and lick along its length.

Bit by bit, I offer Tony more. It's like there's just me and him there, playing a silly little banana game. Tony responds by trying to outdo my teasing, attempting to take more of the banana than I seem prepared to give.

Eventually, his mouth closes over half of it. His lust-sharp eyes are locked on mine, and he looks an utter fool.

Then, making it seem as if it's just a flourish gone wrong, I sweep a near-full pint of beer from the table.

The glass falls into Tony's lap, the liquid spills, and he jumps up in shock, spitting the plastic banana from his mouth.

People at a nearby table squeal and laugh.

My eyes dart to Ilya. Anger flares up in his face, not because he's wet – he isn't – but because he's furious with me. I've seen that anger before, the way it streaks through him and wrecks his composure.

When he catches me looking, Ilya does his best to conceal his rage and turns his attention to poor, soaked Tony.

But I saw him. I saw that brief betrayal of what's ticking in his mind. He knows I'm fucking up on purpose, and it makes him livid because all he wants right now is for me to be a good little slut who can placate his creditors.

The clarity of my situation is stark, vicious almost in its suddenness: Ilya's not concerned about me, not to the extent I want him to be. His priority is his own neck, and he's using me in a way I don't want to be used.

As Tony wipes at the damp patch on his trousers, and someone makes a fuss about getting a cloth from the bar, I swank away to another table.

There's no point slutting it up for the bully-boys. I've done enough of that.

And, at last, I've reached my decision.

Today was good and today was bad.

Last night, shortly after my little accident with the beer, Ilya and his gang left the gig. Ilya said nothing to me – not even 'Goodbye, never mind, thanks' or 'That was great' or 'You stupid bitch, what did you go and do that for?' He just smouldered for a while, face like thunder, then they all trooped out.

It worried me for a long time. I kept thinking that maybe Ilya would have to bear the brunt of Tony's wrath. Or maybe I would.

I couldn't sleep – not just because of that but because of a thousand other things running through my mind. And, as I lay in bed, I was forever expecting the phone to ring or the door to buzz and for me to be summoned to take some ill treatment from Tony.

And if I didn't agree, then Ilya would get his kneecaps blown off or cigarettes stubbed out on his face, or the tip of his tongue cut off with scissors. Or, more likely, my refusal would count for nothing and Tony would just get on with whatever he fancied doing to me.

I had lots of horrible, sick thoughts as I tried to imagine the worst kinds of sadistic torture Tony might be capable of. When your head is suddenly clogged up with violence, as mine was last night, it's a truly nasty experience. And it was so hard to escape from. However much I tried to focus on nice things, some part of my brain kept working of its own volition, chucking up foul images to better the ones I already had.

But nobody called and, when daylight brought rationality, I figured Tony wouldn't have reacted to what was, after all, just a bit of spilt beer. He didn't have Ilya's explosive rage. To be unhinged the way Tony is, you need a certain coolness, a psychopathic calm.

So I more or less reassured myself that Ilya would have seen the night through unharmed.

Around midday, I headed for his B and B.

I'd spent all morning wavering between decision and indecision – not about whether to do it but how to do it. Perhaps it would be easier if I just dropped him a line. If I say it to his face, maybe he'll try to persuade me to change my mind; maybe it'll get messy and emotional and I'll start to weaken.

But I didn't think that would happen. The one constant in all we'd been through was our respect for cuttlefish, the end. Even in the B and B, surrounded by thugs, Ilya had given me the option of saying the word, of walking away and leaving him to deal with Tony and his cold, gleeful violence.

There was something almost sacred about the clean death of cuttlefish.

So yes, I would say it to his face. Besides, I wanted to see his reaction. Would he look relieved? Hurt? Would he start frantically packing in a scramble to leave town now he'd lost his prize bargaining tool?

It was a warm, freakishly windy day. I walked along North Street and everyone's hair and clothes were being whipped this way and that. When I reached the Old Steine, the force of those winds, powering in from the beach, almost took my legs from under me. The waves were crashing in like I'd never seen them before and the sea was swollen and choppy. It was weird weather.

At Ilya's B and B, I pressed the bell. The beige man answered the door again, and again I told him I'd come to see someone in room nine.

He shook his head. 'Left this morning,' he said. 'Not here any more.'

It took a while for this to sink in. I just stood there, the wind tunnelling up the street, lashing my hair across my face.

'Are you sure?' I said, raising my voice because that wind wanted to whip my words away.

'Yep. Is your name . . .' The man frowned, and beckoned me into the gaudy red lobby.

'Are you sure?' I repeated, as I closed the front door and deadened the noise of the weather. 'Dark guy. Ilya Travis, his name was – is.'

'Yep,' said the landlord, and he disappeared into a room full of empty breakfast tables, spinsterish lampshades and net curtains. 'Something odd like that,' he called back. 'Room nine, he was.' He returned with an envelope, looked at it, then at me. 'What's your name?'

'Beth,' I breathed. 'Beth Bradshaw.'

He handed me the envelope and I took it with shaky fingers. This wasn't how it was meant to be.

I saw my name scrawled on the front and gave a silent breath of relief when I recognised the writing as Ilya's. I'd half feared it might be unknown to me and inside there would be some horrible message about Ilya's fate. Maybe there still was. Maybe it was a blood-splattered farewell, written by Ilya while he had a gun pressed to his head.

I didn't want to open it.

'Do you know where he's gone?' I asked. 'Was anyone with him?'

'Just paid up and left.' The landlord shrugged, resting his hand on the wooden banister as if he were about to go upstairs. 'Not likely to tell me where he's going, is he? It's a bed and breakfast. People come. People go. Quite early it was. Now, anything else I can do for you?'

'No,' I whispered, feeling slightly foolish. 'Thanks.' And I left.

Outside, I leant against the spiky black railings, my back to the sea in order to shield my envelope. I opened it with strong, sure fingers, terrified the contents would be snatched away from me, sucked up into the sky, and I'd never know what they were.

Inside was some Brighton picture postcard. I turned hastily to the reverse, my eyes scanning wildly for the whole sense, rather than reading in sentences.

'Cuttlefish' was the first word I registered. It leapt out at me – cold and brutal.

No, I kept thinking, that's my word. That's why I'm here. It's mine. I was ready. I was going to say it. It's been running through my head all morning. You've stolen it. It's not fair.

Then I read the message:

Sorry, Beth. It's been great. You've been great – more than I deserve. But I don't know how to play fair any more. Maybe I never did. Tony wants more of you – I suppose you knew that'd happen. And so do I. But the two things don't go together, and so I guess this is it, babe. You're worth far more than me. It's time I moved on. I'll never, ever forget this summer. Hope you won't either.

Love and cuttlefish, Ilya.

PS Your stage show blew my mind last night. I'm gonna have a hard-on for decades. Keep at it.

I went to the beach.

The shingle was all banked up near the promenade, littered with debris chucked up by the sea.

I didn't cry.

The waves were enormous, hurtling forward, caving in and spuming up as if they were hitting cliffs rather than beach. And, against the groynes, the water was even more violent, sending white foaminess splashing high into the air.

It was so noisy.

I found out afterwards that we'd got the tail-end of some hurricane from America, but I didn't know that then.

The wind buffeted me and, every now and again, my

steps went crooked and drunken because it was so ferociously strong. It was warm and arid too: my eyes didn't stream the way they would do in a chill wind. That rushing air had the opposite effect; it made my eyeballs feel strangely dry. Probably a good thing.

There were quite a few people about, just walking along and looking out to sea, gazing at its big angry beauty.

I felt numb for a long time. Then I began to feel bitter and resentful because *he'd* ended it and that was surely my right.

It was as if, once again, he'd turned the tables by landing a surprise on me and I just had to take it. From start to finish, it was always Ilya who had to have the upper hand, who had to compete to outdo me. And now he'd walked away. He would never know that I was ready to quit; that I'd seen enough of his violent, deceitful, twilight world; and that our game was over because it got swallowed up in a bigger game was far too dark and dirty for my taste.

I stood facing the sea – not too close because I didn't want to invite danger. I was through with that; and, anyway, I'd never meant to do it in the first place.

The gales were so fierce that I could actually lean forward and stay that way, supported by the constant push of air. It was difficult to breathe. The wind was too fast to inhale though my nostrils, so I had to open my mouth and my cheeks wobbled as the breath I wanted poured into my throat. It was delicious because it was so warm and sharp with brine.

It made me laugh. I felt giggly and exhilarated. A fine sea mist blew steadily into my face, making my skin damper and damper. And I had a sudden upsurge of delirious happiness and a feeling that I could conquer the world.

Negative ions, someone once told me. You get them from the seaside and they make you feel good. Maybe that's true. Or maybe it was the sight of all that furious water cresting in and exploding into whiteness like some advert for bad aftershave.

Or maybe I had every reason to be deliriously happy. Ilya was right: it was a summer not to be forgotten and, yes, it had been great. Most of it.

But in a way, I was glad that all the horrors of guns and bully-boys and whatever else Ilya's life was had crept in to destroy our game. At least we hadn't had to say cuttlefish because we were getting bored or because one of us – me, probably – wanted the other to give more. After all, it seemed pretty unlikely that either of us would quit because the sex was too debauched.

And isn't that what I'd asked for in the beginning: just a summertime fling?

I worried a bit about what would happen to Ilya. Would he be safe? Would he sort Tony out? Where the hell was Tony now? Would I be safe?

Time will tell, I thought. But I had a sense that it would be OK. I didn't think Ilya would leave me to face any danger. And I reckoned he knew how to handle himself. He seemed to have managed so far.

I crunched on a little further, the wind roaring into my left ear. The shingle was strewn with trails of slimy seaweed, broken shells, bits of rotting wood and the flotsam and jetsam of a modern-day beach: a dead biro, a crushed tin can, a lighter, another tin can.

I have Martin, I thought, and I'll probably love him for ever, because we're back where we used to be: just great mates. We'd spoken the night before, briefly, and he'd laughed delightedly at what I was doing, said I was a soppy old tart and that we ought to go out soon, drink some beer and bicker over the best flavour of crisps. He's sorted himself out, I can tell. He knows we're better at being friends than we are at being lovers.

So Martin and I are solid and platonic.

I still desire Ilya – in my groin more than anywhere

else – and I'll probably miss our sleazy sex games. But he's gone now.

And I'm fucking Luke who's kind of sweet but he doesn't make me swoon.

I imagined taking the best of all three situations, putting them in a blender, and bam – I'd have the lust and love of my life in one delicious package.

But then, I thought, I don't want that yet. I'm only thirty and, while some people are seriously settled, done and dusted at that age, I don't want to be like that.

I want to play around more. And anyway, when I do meet Mr Right, I'll probably want him to share me with his friends. Assuming they're nice friends, of course.

A shard of bone-whiteness on the ground caught my eye and I stooped to pick it up, smiling wryly.

On one side it was like a female giant's badly manicured fingernail, while the scooped underside was packed with something that was a bit like that oasis stuff you stick flower arrangements into, all pitted and scarred.

Oh, how bloody symbolic, I thought, turning the thing in my hand. I reckon that's a bit of a dead cuttlefish, the bone they give to parrots. Nice timing, God.

I stuffed the thing into the pocket of my fleece and walked on, mulling over last night's gig. People liked it. They said it was horny, funny, exciting, wild. The finale to my little performance was me whipping off my mask. That wasn't in rehearsal, but I'd got so fired up by the cheers and applause that it seemed the right thing to do. The roof nearly lifted off when people realised who I was.

Maybe I'll strip and strut again; I don't know. But one thing's for certain: I'm going to have many more nights of Hot Sex. It's a winner.

I toyed with the bone in my pocket, fingering its rough, frayed edges as a wicked idea began to blossom in my mind.

Luke, I thought. Now Luke and I are just sex. And never in a million years will the two of us become involved, because what we have is light and frothy and carefree. And Luke, poor Luke, has shyly confessed to being a teensy bit interested in other men, but he isn't sure because he hasn't really explored it properly. Not yet.

So maybe I should give him a helping hand. Maybe I should introduce him to a little game I've learnt. I'll be better at it than he is. I know the ropes. And also I know how to play fair.

The wind lashed my hair across a great big grin.

Yes, I thought, that's what I'll do. I'll play a game with Luke. He'll love it.

I think I'll call it Cuttlefish.

LOOK OUT FOR THE ALL-NEW BLACK LACE BOOKS – AVAILABLE NOW!

All books priced £7.99 in the UK. Please note publication dates apply to the UK only. For other territories, please contact your retailer.

DARK DESIGNS
Madelynne Ellis
ISBN 0 352 34075 4

Remy Davies is under pressure as the designer for an opulent gothic wedding. There's the over-stressed bride, a trinity of vampire-obsessed bridesmaids, a wayward groom, and then there's the best man . . . Silk looks like he's been drawn by a *manga* artist; beautiful, exotic, and with a predatory sexuality. Remy has to have him, in her bed and between the pages of her new catalogue. Remy is about to launch herself into the alternative fashion world, and Silk is going to sell it for her whether he knows it or not. But Silk is nobody's toy, and for all his androgyny, he's determinedly heterosexual. Pity, since Remy's biggest fantasy is to see him making out with her Japanese biker, sometime boyfriend, Takeshi.

Coming in December

THE SOCIETY OF SIN
Sian Lacey Taylder
ISBN 0 352 34080 0

Or, perhaps, 'Lust and Laura Ashley'. The Society of Sin is an erotic, gothic thriller set in rural Dorset in the late 19th Century, a period when educated women were beginning to question their sexuality.

The Society of Sin was conceived on a hot and sticky summer's evening inside a mansion house on a large country estate when, after an opium-fuelled night of passion, Lady P and her close friend Samantha Powerstock succumbed to desires they had both repressed for years. Now, a year later, they have invited a select few to join their exclusive association. But only genuine hedonists need apply; prospective members are interrogated over a sumptuous dinner then given an 'assignment' which they must fulfil. Failure to do so results in instant expulsion and the prospect of being 'named and shamed' in the exclusive circles they currently frequent. However, successful completion of the task opens for them a Pandora's box of pain and pleasure:

Summer sees the arrival of Miss Charlotte Crowsettle, who immediately falls under Lady P's spell.

CONTINUUM
Portia Da Costa
ISBN 0 352 33120 8

When Joanna Darrell agrees to take a break from an office job that has begun to bore her, she takes her first step into a new continuum of strange experiences. She is introduced to people whose way of life revolves around the giving and receiving of enjoyable punishment, and she becomes intrigued enough to experiment. Drawn in by a chain of coincidences, like Alice in a decadent wonderland, she enters a parallel world of perversity and unusual pleasure.

Coming in January 2007

BURNING BRIGHT
Janine Ashbless
ISBN 978 0 352 34085 6

Two lovers, brought together by a forbidden passion, are on the run from their pasts. Veraine was once a commander in the Imperial army: Myrna was the divine priestess he seduced and stole from her desert temple. But travelling through a jungle kingdom, they fall prey to slavers and are separated. Veraine is left for dead. Myrna is taken as a slave to the city of the Tiger Lords; inhuman tyrants with a taste for human flesh. There she must learn the tricks of survival in a cruel and exotic court where erotic desire is not the only animal passion.

Myrna still has faith that Veraine will find her. But Veraine, badly injured, has forgotten everything: his past, his lover, and even his own identity. As he undertakes a journey through a fevered landscape of lush promise and supernatural danger, he knows only one thing – that he must somehow find the unknown woman who holds the key to his soul.

STELLA DOES HOLLYWOOD
Stella Black
ISBN 978 0 352 33588 3

Stella Black has a 1969 Pontiac Firebird, a leopard-skin bra and a lot of attitude. Partying her way around Hollywood she is discovered by Leon Lubrisky, the billionaire mogul of Pleasure Dome Inc. He persuades her to work for him and she soon becomes one of the most famous adult stars in America. Invited on chat shows, dating pop stars and hanging out with the Beverley Hills A-list. But dark forces are gathering and a political party is outraged and determined to destroy Stella any which way they can. Soon she finds herself in dangerous – and highly sexually charged – situations, where no one can rescue her.

Black Lace Booklist

Information is correct at time of printing. To avoid disappointment, check availability before ordering. Go to www.blacklace-books.co.uk. All books are priced £6.99 unless another price is given.

BLACK LACE BOOKS WITH A CONTEMPORARY SETTING

☐ ON THE EDGE Laura Hamilton	ISBN O 352 33534 3	£5.99
☐ THE TRANSFORMATION Natasha Rostova	ISBN O 352 33311 1	
☐ SIN.NET Helena Ravenscroft	ISBN O 352 33598 X	
☐ TWO WEEKS IN TANGIER Annabel Lee	ISBN O 352 33599 8	
☐ SYMPHONY X Jasmine Stone	ISBN O 352 33629 3	
☐ A SECRET PLACE Ella Broussard	ISBN O 352 33307 3	
☐ GOING TOO FAR Laura Hamilton	ISBN O 352 33657 9	
☐ RELEASE ME Suki Cunningham	ISBN O 352 33671 4	
☐ SLAVE TO SUCCESS Kimberley Raines	ISBN O 352 33687 O	
☐ SHADOWPLAY Portia Da Costa	ISBN O 352 33313 8	
☐ ARIA APPASSIONATA Julie Hastings	ISBN O 352 33056 2	
☐ A MULTITUDE OF SINS Kit Mason	ISBN O 352 33737 O	
☐ COMING ROUND THE MOUNTAIN Tabitha Flyte	ISBN O 352 33873 3	
☐ FEMININE WILES Karina Moore	ISBN O 352 33235 2	
☐ MIXED SIGNALS Anna Clare	ISBN O 352 33889 X	
☐ BLACK LIPSTICK KISSES Monica Belle	ISBN O 352 33885 7	
☐ GOING DEEP Kimberly Dean	ISBN O 352 33876 8	
☐ PACKING HEAT Karina Moore	ISBN O 352 33356 1	
☐ MIXED DOUBLES Zoe le Verdier	ISBN O 352 33312 X	
☐ UP TO NO GOOD Karen S. Smith	ISBN O 352 33589 O	
☐ CLUB CRÈME Primula Bond	ISBN O 352 33907 1	
☐ BONDED Fleur Reynolds	ISBN O 352 33192 5	
☐ SWITCHING HANDS Alaine Hood	ISBN O 352 33896 2	
☐ EDEN'S FLESH Robyn Russell	ISBN O 352 33923 3	
☐ PEEP SHOW Mathilde Madden	ISBN O 352 33924 1	£7.99
☐ RISKY BUSINESS Lisette Allen	ISBN O 352 33280 8	£7.99
☐ CAMPAIGN HEAT Gabrielle Marcola	ISBN O 352 33941 1	£7.99
☐ MS BEHAVIOUR Mini Lee	ISBN O 352 33962 4	£7.99

BLACK LACE BOOKS WITH AN HISTORICAL SETTING

☐ THE HAND OF AMUN Juliet Hastings	ISBN 0 352 33144 5	
☐ THE SENSES BEJEWELLED Cleo Cordell	ISBN 0 352 32904 1	
☐ UNDRESSING THE DEVIL Angel Strand	ISBN 0 352 33938 1	£7.99
☐ FRENCH MANNERS Olivia Christie	ISBN 0 352 33214 X	£7.99
☐ DANCE OF OBSESSION Olivia Christie	ISBN 0 352 33101 1	£7.99
☐ LORD WRAXALL'S FANCY Anna Lieff Saxby	ISBN 0 352 33080 5	£7.99
☐ NICOLE'S REVENGE Lisette Allen	ISBN 0 352 32984 X	£7.99
☐ BARBARIAN PRIZE Deanna Ashford	ISBN 0 352 34017 7	£7.99
☐ THE BARBARIAN GEISHA Charlotte Royal	ISBN 0 352 33267 0	£7.99
☐ ELENA'S DESTINY Lisette Allen	ISBN 0 352 33218 2	£7.99
☐ THE MASTER OF SHILDEN Lucinda Carrington	ISBN 0 352 33140 2	£7.99
☐ DARKER THAN LOVE Kristina Lloyd	ISBN 0 352 33279 4	£7.99

BLACK LACE ANTHOLOGIES

☐ WICKED WORDS Various	ISBN 0 352 33363 4	
☐ MORE WICKED WORDS Various	ISBN 0 352 33487 8	
☐ WICKED WORDS 3 Various	ISBN 0 352 33522 X	
☐ WICKED WORDS 4 Various	ISBN 0 352 33603 X	
☐ WICKED WORDS 5 Various	ISBN 0 352 33642 0	
☐ WICKED WORDS 6 Various	ISBN 0 352 33690 0	
☐ WICKED WORDS 7 Various	ISBN 0 352 33743 5	
☐ WICKED WORDS 8 Various	ISBN 0 352 33787 7	
☐ WICKED WORDS 9 Various	ISBN 0 352 33860 1	
☐ WICKED WORDS 10 Various	ISBN 0 352 33893 8	
☐ THE BEST OF BLACK LACE 2 Various	ISBN 0 352 33718 4	
☐ WICKED WORDS: SEX IN THE OFFICE Various	ISBN 0 352 33944 6	£7.99
☐ WICKED WORDS: SEX AT THE SPORTS CLUB Various	ISBN 0 352 33991 8	£7.99
☐ WICKED WORDS: SEX ON HOLIDAY Various	ISBN 0 352 33961 6	£7.99
☐ WICKED WORDS: SEX IN UNIFORM Various	ISBN 0 352 34002 9	£7.99
☐ WICKED WORDS: SEX IN THE KITCHEN Various	ISBN 0 352 34018 5	£7.99
☐ WICKED WORDS: SEX ON THE MOVE Various	ISBN 0 352 34034 7	£7.99
☐ WICKED WORDS: SEX AND MUSIC Various	ISBN 0 352 34061 4	£7.99

BLACK LACE NON-FICTION

☐ THE BLACK LACE BOOK OF WOMEN'S SEXUAL   ISBN O 352 33793 1
   FANTASIES Ed. Kerri Sharp

☐ THE BLACK LACE SEXY QUIZ BOOK Maddie Saxon   ISBN O 352 33884 9

To find out the latest information about Black Lace titles, check out the
website: www.blacklace-books.co.uk or send for a booklist with
complete synopses by writing to:

    Black Lace Booklist, Virgin Books Ltd
    Thames Wharf Studios
    Rainville Road
    London W6 9HA

Please include an SAE of decent size. Please note only British stamps
are valid.

Our privacy policy
We will not disclose information you supply us to any other parties.
We will not disclose any information which identifies you personally to
any person without your express consent.

From time to time we may send out information about Black Lace
books and special offers. Please tick here if you do not wish to
receive Black Lace information.   ☐

Please send me the books I have ticked above.

Name ....

Address ....

....

....

....

Post Code ....

Send to: Virgin Books Cash Sales, Thames Wharf Studios, Rainville Road, London W6 9HA.

US customers: for prices and details of how to order books for delivery by mail, call 888-330-8477.

Please enclose a cheque or postal order, made payable to Virgin Books Ltd, to the value of the books you have ordered plus postage and packing costs as follows:

UK and BFPO – £1.00 for the first book, 50p for each subsequent book.

Overseas (including Republic of Ireland) – £2.00 for the first book, £1.00 for each subsequent book.

If you would prefer to pay by VISA, ACCESS/MASTERCARD, DINERS CLUB, AMEX or SWITCH, please write your card number and expiry date here:

....

Signature ....

Please allow up to 28 days for delivery.